THE LAST RITE

THE LAST RITE

Jasper Kent

BANTAM PRESS

LONDON · TORONTO · SYDNEY · AUCKLAND · JOHANNESBURG

TRANSWORLD PUBLISHERS
61–63 Uxbridge Road, London W5 5SA
A Random House Group Company
www.transworldbooks.co.uk

First published in Great Britain
in 2014 by Bantam Press
an imprint of Transworld Publishers

A CIP catalogue record for this book
is available from the British Library.

ISBN 9780593069554

Addresses for Random House Group Ltd companies outside the UK
can be found at: www.randomhouse.co.uk
The Random House Group Ltd Reg. No. 954009

The Random House Group Limited supports the Forest Stewardship
Council® (FSC®), the leading international forest-certification organisation.
Our books carrying the FSC label are printed on FSC®-certified paper. FSC is
the only forest-certification scheme supported by the leading environmental
organisations, including Greenpeace. Our paper procurement policy can be
found at www.randomhouse.co.uk/environment

Typeset in 11/14½pt Sabon and New Century Schoolbook by
Kestrel Data, Exeter, Devon.
Printed and bound by
CPI Group (UK) Ltd, Croydon, CR0 4YY.

2 4 6 8 10 9 7 5 3 1

For P.K.

AUTHOR'S NOTES

Measurements
Tsar Peter the Great based much of the Russian Imperial measurement system on the British system. Thus a *diuym* is exactly equal to an inch (the English word is used in the text) and a foot is both the same word and measurement in English and Russian. A *verst* is a unit of distance slightly greater than a kilometre.

Dates
During the first part of the twentieth century, Russians based their dates on the old Julian Calendar, which in the 1910s was thirteen days behind the Gregorian Calendar used in Western Europe. In the text, dates of events in Russia are given in the Russian form and so, for example, the abdication of Tsar Nicholas II is placed on 2 March 1917, where Western history books have it on 15 March. On 14 February 1918 Russia adopted the Gregorian Calendar and so from then on all dates in Russia and the West were the same.

With thanks to Mihai Adascalitei and Hildegard Wiesehoefer respectively for advice on the Romanian and German languages.

Selected Romanov and Danilov Family Tree

Reigning tsars and tsaritsas shown in **bold**.
Fictional characters shown in *italic*.
'#' indicates unmarried relationship.
Dates are *birth–[start of reign]–[end of reign]–death*

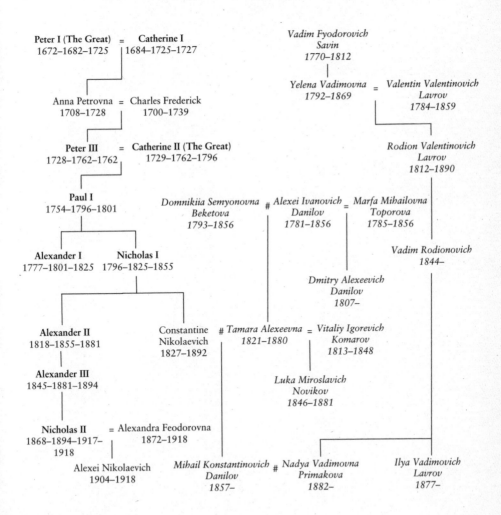

Cowards die many times before their deaths;
The valiant never taste of death but once.
Of all the wonders that I yet have heard,
It seems to me most strange that men should fear,
Seeing that death, a necessary end,
Will come when it will come.

Shakespeare, *Julius Caesar*, Act II, scene ii

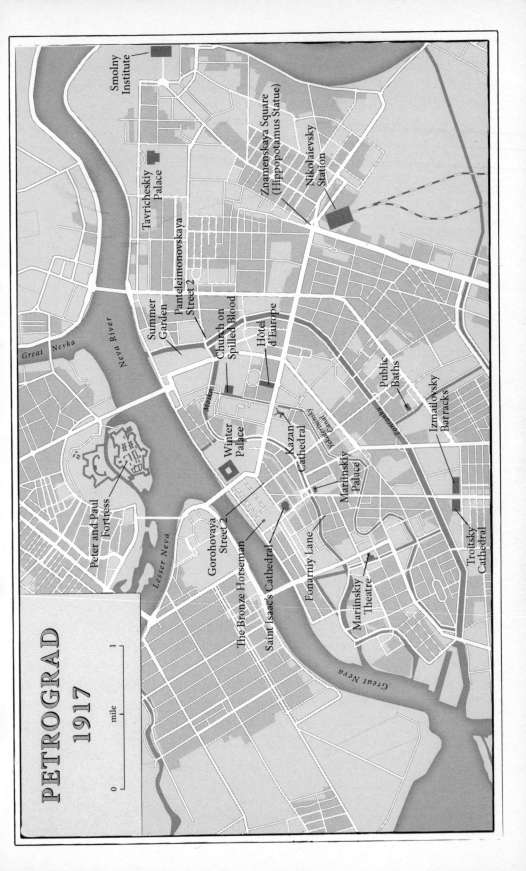

PETROGRAD
1917

0   mile   1

Smolny Institute

Tavricheskiy Palace

Znamenskaya Square (Hippopotamus Statue)

Nikolaievsky Station

Panteleimonovskaya Street 2

Summer Garden

Neva River

Great Nevka

Church on Spilled Blood

Hôtel d'Europe

Moika

Public Baths

Izmailovsky Barracks

Winter Palace

Kazan Cathedral

Mariinskiy Palace

Ekaterininsky Canal

Peter and Paul Fortress

Lesser Neva

Gorohovaya Street 2

The Bronze Horseman

Saint Isaac's Cathedral

Fonarniy Lane

Mariinskiy Theatre

Troitsky Cathedral

Great Neva

PROLOGUE

An Anatolian Folk Tale

On the twenty-third day of the month of Nisan, in the eighteenth year of the principate of the Emperors Diocletian and Maximian, in the city of Nicomedia, the gift of martyrdom was bestowed upon the Tribune George – son of Gerontius – his head severed from his body for his refusal to renounce his faith. For this sacrifice he was acclaimed a saint. The anniversary of his death, 23 April, came to be celebrated as the feast day of Saint George. But it is not for his death that he is famed.

Long before, as the Roman Empire swept across the world, the Tribune George had slain the monster which was to make him renowned throughout history. By command of his emperor he had been dispatched to the province of Libya and one day, journeying with his slave Pasicrates, he found himself near the city which some call Lasia and others Silene, by which they may mean Cyrene. There George encountered a hermit, who told him of the city's curse.

'Close to this place,' the hermit said, 'lies a great lake, as wide as the Earth and as deep as the sea, beneath whose waters a monster makes its lair: a dragon who demands a tribute of the people. Every day they must offer up two sheep from their flocks upon which the beast may feed. They offer no resistance. They do as they are told, for they know that if they refuse the monster will drag itself from the depths and descend upon the city, breathing destruction.

'But it is not fire that the monster breathes as many such

creatures do. It breathes poison – a noxious miasma far worse than flames, which may be extinguished. The dragon's breath brings all who scent it to die in agonizing torment, such that no man who has witnessed it can describe.'

'Two sheep each day seems a meagre price,' said George.

The old man shrugged. 'Greater than our king is prepared to surrender. He paid the tribute for many years, but then famine came, and the flocks dwindled, and even two became more than the people could afford. And so now they offer up a human sacrifice, a subject of the king, which the beast is more than happy to accept. All are equal before the serpent. Lots are drawn. Any might become the chosen one – young or old, male or female. But today the duty has fallen upon the king's daughter, the Princess Sabra. The king has tried to prevent it, but the people are adamant. They insist that the princess must obey the law which binds them all. And the princess herself is willing, knowing justice better than her father.'

The hermit looked up and pointed out across the plain towards the water. 'Behold! There they go now, the princess and her entourage, down to where the serpent waits. It will not take long.'

But George felt only anger at the story; at the greed of the dragon, at the ingratitude of the people to their king, and at the disobedience of his daughter. The tribune mounted his horse and rode swiftly towards the lake. He passed Sabra and her attendants and shouted that they should stop; that he alone would face the creature. They did as he told them, some believing that he would do what he had said, others reasoning that this stranger would make an ample sacrifice, if only for today.

As the saint approached the shore he slowed his horse and surveyed the water, gazing into its still depths, searching for the monster. And then the waters became turbid and began to boil, even though the day was cool. The surface rose and separated and the monster was revealed, half serpent, half dragon. Its head towered above George, its body's length five times greater than the saint's height, with more still submerged and invisible beneath the waves. George looked up into its eyes and knew that this was no animal; no part, however vile, of God's creation. This was a manifestation of Satan himself that had somehow burst up through the Earth from the flames below. Perhaps the monster he faced truly was the Beast of Saint John's Revelation.

George turned his horse and galloped away from the water's edge, seeming afraid. But the act was not born of fear. Soon he turned and saw what he had hoped to see, that the creature had followed him out of its watery domain and into the realm of men. George levelled his lance, holding it out in front of him, pointing its iron tip at the leviathan's heart. Then he spurred his horse and began to charge. The monster reared its head, inhaling deeply before expelling a vast cloud of its noxious, death-delivering breath. But George was not deterred. As he rode forward he spoke loudly, without a break between words so that he would never have a chance to breathe in, reciting the Lord's Prayer. Thus even if some of the deadly vapour did infiltrate him the holy words would protect him from the venom.

And so George arrived beneath the creature's shadow unharmed, and his lance was true, and although it was shattered into a thousand pieces by the armour of the monster's scales, its iron-clad tip penetrated through them and into the dragon's heart, killing it and sending its soul back down to Hell. But even as the dragon perished, its head thrashed and its teeth fell upon the saint, and bit into him, and drew his blood. It was the tiniest of wounds, and caused him little pain, and healed quickly. And yet he would always remember it, as would his children and their children too.

Afterwards George went into the city of Lasia and was honoured for what he had done. The king begged to know what reward he would accept, and in return George asked only that the people of Lasia should become Christians, a request to which the king happily agreed. That day twenty thousand were baptized, not counting the women and the children. The king had a church built in honour of Saint George and of the Virgin, and from its altar there still issues a natural spring whose waters cure all illnesses.

But this is not George's story. Neither is it the story of the monster he slew, nor of the princess he saved nor even of his slave Pasicrates, though it is through Pasicrates that we know all this to be true. This is the story of the lance that George used to slay the dragon, an artefact that would outlive all of them; that as yet did not even have a name.

As George was returning to Lasia to claim his laurels, it fell to Pasicrates to deal with the destruction he had wrought. Pasicrates surveyed the scene and felt proud of his master. The monster was dead. The lance was broken. But as Pasicrates looked he saw that the tip of the spear still protruded from the serpent's scales. He reached forward and grasped it, putting his foot on the creature's chest to brace himself. And after more than a little effort the shaft came free – like the sword Arthur pulled from the stone, although that story was yet to be written.

Pasicrates looked at his prize. There was little of it left – less than the length of his forearm, and he was not long-limbed. The iron tip remained embedded in the monster's heart, but the wood he held was still sharpened to a point – still stained with the blood it had drawn. It would make a fine relic, better certainly than the other shattered fragments of the lance that lay strewn beside the lake. Others might take them and sell them as sacred artefacts, but his was the shaft that had killed the beast. And he would not sell it. He would keep it for when the time came for him to write his story – which was to say the story of his master, the Tribune George.

Pasicrates travelled with his master until George's martyrdom in Nicomedia. But a slave cannot be held to account for his master's faith – and Pasicrates lived long enough to write an account of the life of Saint George. He left Nicomedia and travelled throughout Anatolia and into the Holy Land, settling finally in the town of Ashkelon on the Mediterranean coast, not far from Jerusalem. And there he died, bequeathing the lance and all his possessions to the Karaite elders of the city by way of thanks for the kindnesses they had shown him. For almost eight centuries the lance remained there.

And it was during that time the lance inevitably acquired its name – the name of the city in which it dwelt – 'Ashkelon', or 'Ascalon' as the Crusaders who captured both the city and the relic pronounced it.

It was in 1099 that Ashkelon fell to the Christian knights and that Ascalon was taken from it, along with the rest of their plunder. Many of the Crusaders had been looking for relics – for the Ark of the Covenant or for the Holy Grail – but none of them understood what they held in their hands. A few might have taken it for a fragment of the true cross, but there were plenty enough of those being sold in market places across Palestine – across the whole of Europe.

The Karaite elders of Ashkelon pleaded for the return of their treasures, and for the ransom of captives, offering money they had collected from every citizen. Whether they got all they wanted, no one knows, but it was not the Jews that the Crusaders regarded as their enemy, and so Ascalon was returned.

But the lance did not stay long in the city whose name it bore. The Karaites were a scattered community and they shared their possessions across the world, knowing that anywhere would be safer than the turbulent Holy Land. Ascalon was sent north, across the Dark Sea to a citadel high in the mountains, known as Chufut Kalye. The Karaites who lived there claimed they had settled in the cave dwellings at the time of the Babylonian Exile, but few believed it. They lived there by the sufferance of the Crimean Khanate, but Ascalon could not be kept hidden from the ruling Tartars and soon it disappeared once again.

And it is here, just as we might expect mists of history to begin to reveal their secrets, that the story becomes its most vague. Ascalon was next seen in Buda, a city on the river Hister, also known as the Danube. It was 370 years since the Crusaders had taken it from Ashkelon, 200 since it had arrived in Chufut Kalye. How it reached Buda remains shrouded in confusion, but it cannot be mere chance that Constantinople had so recently fallen to the Muslim hordes, and it would have been no great journey for the lance to be carried from Chufut Kalye to the ancient capital of the Roman Empire. Who it was that brought it from there to Buda is untold, but it is claimed by some that the man who then took it from Buda to Visegrád was Fyodor Kuritsyn, emissary of the Grand Prince of Muscovy. Others deny that Kuritsyn could ever have been in Hungary at the time, but none doubt the identity of the solitary prisoner in the castle at Visegrád.

Prince Vlad, later known as Ţepeş, once Voivode of Wallachia, had been betrayed by a man he thought his friend; it was neither the first nor the last time it would happen to him. He had come to Hungary seeking refuge and had instead been thrown into gaol, and left there friendless and alone. Is it any wonder that, when he was visited by the Russian Boyar and spoken to kindly by him, he began to place his trust in the man?

Kuritsyn – or whoever it may have been – showed Ascalon to the Wallachian prince, showed him the traces of the dragon's blood that still tainted it, and told of the power that it possessed. The Muscovite ambassador had reasons of his own for what he disclosed, but that did not mean that the magic he spoke of was not real. He spent many long hours talking to Vlad, but in the end he left him alone, left him with Ascalon, and with the knowledge of what it could do for him, if only he would dare allow it.

And so in the depth of his despair, after twelve years in gaol, with no hope of release – with no hope at all – Ţepeş took Ascalon, cradling it in his hand. And with only a moment's hesitation he performed with it the rite that Kuritsyn had described. And just as the Boyar had explained, Vlad entered immortality. And at the same moment, just as Kuritsyn had known he would, but had never told, Vlad descended into Hell.

FEBRUARY

CHAPTER I

'HIPPOPOTAMUS!'
The shout was accompanied by a sniggering laugh that didn't sit well with the sombre mood of the people in the square, but amply reflected their anxiety.

I turned and looked. Bodies were pressed tight around me. It hadn't been like that when we arrived, but two or three dozen police mounted on horseback had been slowly advancing, corralling the crowd of several hundred together. To one side waited a group of Cossacks, also mounted. If the police weren't strong enough to deal with us, they wouldn't have far to look for support.

At first I couldn't see who had spoken, but my eye caught that of a young factory worker who saw that I had heard his shout. I gave a brief smile of acknowledgement and hoped it would be enough not to appear rude. Much as I wanted to express my solidarity with these people – why else had I come here? – I was incapable of feeling at ease with them. Even in this era of modernity – in 1917 – we were separated by every fissure that existed in Russian society: by age, by wealth, by class. We were from two different nations. The joke about the hippopotamus had been amusing enough when I'd first heard it, but it soon wore thin – for me at any rate; not, it appeared, for everyone.

The man read me perfectly, and revealed that I had misread him.

'No,' he said, not shouting any more, but raising his voice above the murmur of the frightened crowd. 'I mean, it's written down.'

He pointed, indicating somewhere towards the base of the

statue. I pushed my way through and stood beside him. He grinned victoriously and nodded downwards. As soon as I saw it I knew that the tide had turned – victory was inevitable.

Гиппопотам
Gippopotam

It was scratched on to the plinth with heavy, deliberate strokes. I looked up at the statue. The epithet was entirely appropriate. It was supposed to be a monument to Tsar Aleksandr III, reflecting the power of his autocracy, but it simply looked like a small, stout nonentity astride a massive, exhausted horse, its head bowed and despondent. The idea that it was the Russian people who were represented by the horse was not hard to grasp, though it was the term 'hippopotamus' that had caught on to describe the squat, pathetic animal. When it was first erected a rhyme had done the rounds, describing the statue – plinth, horse and tsar:

> *Here stands a chest of drawers,*
> *On the chest a hippopotamus,*
> *And on the hippopotamus sits an idiot.*

The absurdity was obvious to anyone who looked at it, and yet Nikolai, Aleksandr's son, had been happy to have it put on display a decade and a half after his father's death. The idea of the statue was to remind the Russian people that the tsar was immovable, that the tsar's power was unchanging. But the people didn't need reminding of that. They knew it. They experienced it every day of their lives. Even those of us whose existence was tolerable knew that nothing would change. With each new tsar we hoped, but it always came to nothing. No one would ever have portrayed Tsar Nikolai II as having the brutish strength of his father. If Aleksandr believed himself immovable he might have been right. Nikolai most certainly believed it, and was quite mistaken.

I let out a brief snort. The factory worker, still close to me, would have taken it for a response to the graffito, but it wasn't that. I was laughing at myself and the fact that in my own mind I referred to them as Tsar Aleksandr and Tsar Nikolai. Was I trying to hide, even from myself, the simple fact that I was one of the family – that Aleksandr III was my cousin?

'This is your final warning. Hand it over.'

It was the sound of the police captain's voice. The 'it' in question was a red flag being held up in the crowd. Earlier it had been right at the front, but as the gendarmes had tried to get hold of it, it had made its way to the centre of our group. I couldn't see whether the people carrying it had moved or whether it had just been passed along from hand to hand, but now it was defended on all sides by a shield of human bodies. I doubted they would protect it for long against bullets and sabres. It wasn't even as if there was anything written on the banner, but the colour alone was enough. It went back to 1848, the Year of Revolutions, and perhaps longer. Both sides understood what it meant. Russia hadn't had a revolution in 1848, and now we were making up for lost time.

'Come and take it!' rang a shout from somewhere in the crowd. The captain hesitated. There was no doubt that that was precisely what he had been planning to do, but now it would seem as if he was taking his orders from the mob. The dilemma didn't trouble him for long. He turned his horse and trotted away from us, back towards his men who stood in mounted ranks in front of the railway terminus. I didn't hear him issue any instructions, or even make a gesture, but a moment later he turned again and as one they charged forwards, their right arms extended and their sabres horizontal. It would have better suited the battlefields of the Crimea than a square in Petersburg. But this wasn't Saint Petersburg. This was Petrograd and had been for the last three years. And Petrograd was turning out to be a very different place.

I was close to the back of the crowd and therefore safe for the time being. None of us around the statue moved. Some at the front – maybe half of them – tried to turn and run, but the ranks of protestors behind them remained still and there was nowhere for them to go. A few tried to escape by going forwards, slipping between the charging horses. I saw at least one – a woman – trampled. Perhaps others made it through.

Now the horses were among us. As the front line of protestors finally gave way, a wave of motion – like the blast running through an explosive – raced through the crowd and almost seemed to hit me. I stepped back from it, bumping into those behind me and perpetuating the wave through the mass of bodies. I could hear screams from the front and saw the police sabres rise and fall. I could not make out where the blows landed, but each time the blades were lifted high to strike again there was more blood on them. I'd heard that this was how the police were dealing with protests, but I'd not seen it for myself; not truly believed it. If I had done I doubted I would have come here. The same was true for most of those around me; we'd been brave enough to face the police if all they did was stand and watch, but now it was time to flee.

I turned and ran, but those around me were faster. An elbow barged me to the left. I turned, instinctively wanting to apologize, but I'd been pushed into someone else's path – a sailor, head and shoulders taller than me. He didn't even notice that he'd knocked me to the ground. I tried to get up, but a knee hit me in the back of my head, and then I felt a foot between my shoulder blades. I tried to crawl towards the statue, hoping it would give me some kind of shelter. I kept low, like I'd been taught in the army, as though to avoid enemy fire, trying to use my forearms to gain some purchase on the paving slabs.

It seemed an eternity, but it can only have been a matter of seconds before a pair of hands gripped me and lifted me up, leaning me against the plinth on which the hippopotamus stood. I was protected from the stampeding crowd, forced to pass it on one side or the other. I never saw who had saved me, and they didn't stay to receive my thanks.

I clutched at the leg of the bronze horse, desperate to stay on my feet. It was pointless for me to run. I could feel the air rasping in my chest as I breathed. My arms were weak. When the charging gendarmes got to me I'd no reason to suppose they'd see me any differently from how the crowd running past did, how I saw myself: a weak, pathetic old man, clinging to a statue because his own legs weren't strong enough to hold him up. They wouldn't regard me as a threat.

I looked back towards the railway terminus to take in the slaughter. I knew the sight would not sicken me as perhaps it should – I'd seen worse in battle. I didn't relish it either, but someone had to bear witness to it, to report it. The more brutally they treated us, the sooner it would end – as long as people heard what was happening.

But I didn't see what I'd expected. The mounted gendarmes were not amongst the crowd, hacking away at them. Most of the people in the square had managed to get away and some had even stopped and turned to look, like me, at what was happening. There was still a battle taking place, but it was not between police and protestors.

The Cossack troop which had been stationed to one side of the square, as if in reserve, had entered the fray. But they had not gone to the support of the police. Instead they had moved to protect the crowd. They outnumbered the gendarmes, and knew better how to use a sabre from the back of a horse, though some of them were more practical than that. I heard pistols firing. The police thought too late to use their own guns – a sword is a fine weapon for scattering a group of protestors, but it's not so much use against a Cossack.

Shouts and cheers began to rise up from the crowd, which was now reassembling. They were fickle, but in times like these it was madness to be anything else. A few minutes before they had been jeering at those same Cossacks they now hailed as their saviours. And why not? We were no longer in a world of certainties, of officer and *ryadovoy*, of noble and peasant. What mattered now was not what you were, but which side you were on. The Cossacks – this troop of them – had chosen. It was a choice I'd made only months before.

The battle was quickly over. The police weren't prepared for any kind of resistance. There were no orders given, but they soon disengaged – those that could. They headed north at the gallop, up Ligovskaya Street. The crowd had once more become emboldened, and a hail of stones and other projectiles followed the retreat, though to little effect. The damage had already been done. I could see four gendarmes lying there in the middle of Znamenskaya Square, alongside the bodies of those they'd cut down. Two riderless horses stood close, calmly awaiting some form of instruction. The others must have followed the herd.

One of the gendarmes managed to get to his feet. He eyed the Cossacks fearfully, but they'd now lost interest, or been gripped by the realization of what they'd done. The policeman roused one of his comrades, then another. I heard one of them shout 'Sir!' and shake the fourth prone body and it was then I realized it was their commanding officer, and that he was dead. The Cossacks were experienced enough in battle to know that the best strategy was decapitation – take out the opposing leader and those who remained would be powerless. The other gendarmes were lucky that the operation had been so clinical.

I turned and walked away. The crowd was thinning now and I had my breath back. Suddenly I didn't feel quite so old – quite so self-pitying. I'd be sixty in a few months. That wasn't so ancient. There were plenty of officers still active at the Front who were older than me. And I'd managed to achieve a riper age than that police captain, or those he'd killed in the crowd. There'd been a time, years before, when I'd thought the whole purpose of my ex- istence on Earth had been fulfilled. And so it had been, with the death of a single man – a single vampire. Since then I'd found new reasons to live.

'Mihail!'

I turned at the shout of my name, but there were still crowds around, and I couldn't make out who had uttered it.

'Mihail Konstantinovich!'

Someone was walking towards me. It took me a moment to rec- ognize her: Yelena Dmitrievna Stasova. I wouldn't have called her a friend, but our paths had crossed more than once. She was an extremist – a Bolshevik who'd only recently returned from exile in Siberia – but now wasn't the time to worry about our petty differ- ences. For the moment we were all on the same side.

We shook hands. 'Were you in that?' she asked, jerking her head towards Znamenskaya Square.

I nodded and we began walking side by side up Nevsky Prospekt.

'I thought it was going to be like '05 all over again,' she said.

I shuddered at the thought. 'Bloody Sunday' they'd called it, though you only had to say 'The Ninth of January' and people knew what you meant. I'd been seven thousand versts away, fighting the Japanese, but the news had still reached us. The official figure was around a hundred dead, shot and trampled, but I'd heard as many as four thousand. All they'd wanted to do was deliver a petition to the tsar asking for decent working conditions. Nikolai hadn't even been in the city, but the Imperial Guard had fired on them anyway. Half of the crowd had been singing 'God Save the Tsar'. They didn't want to get rid of him, they just wanted him to rule for his people. Times had changed.

'Back then it was the army against the people,' I said. 'It wasn't even a contest.'

'And now?'

'You saw whose side the Cossacks were on.'

'One platoon? What difference is that going to make?'

I smiled to myself. 'You weren't expecting it to be Cossacks, were you?'

'Their loyalty's to themselves,' she explained, 'but they're human – some of them.'

'Is that why you've never bothered putting your *agents provocateurs* in amongst them?'

'I don't know what you mean, *tovarishch*.'

I didn't press the point, and the Bolsheviks weren't the only ones trying to infiltrate the army. It wasn't that the men needed pushing into revolution – three years of war had done enough of that – but we all knew that the real battle would be for what came after the revolution, about who took the reins of power. It would be in that struggle that troops – certainly those stationed in Petrograd – could be decisive. The navy was completely infiltrated, but wasn't such a presence in the city, not with the waterways frozen all the way out to the Baltic. Only the Imperial Air Force – the service that in recent years I'd come to know best – was free of the infiltration, but I couldn't see how it would have much part to play in the events to come.

'Did you think it would happen so quickly?' I asked her.

She considered for a moment before answering. 'We all knew it would be this year. Like you, we had a timetable, but revolution has a life of its own.'

'Like us?'

'I was told it was planned for next month. Nikolai would be

deposed. The tsarevich would succeed, with his uncle as regent, and a few senior nobles would hold the real power.'

She was right. I wasn't a part of the plot, but I knew all about it. It would have been a very Russian way for power to change hands, like when Yekaterina had her husband, Pyotr III, imprisoned, or when a handful of senior officers murdered Pavel I and set his son on the throne as Aleksandr I. But I wasn't going to admit anything to her.

'I'm hardly a noble,' I said.

'Oh, come now, Colonel Danilov.' She'd switched to addressing me more formally simply to tease me. 'You're a member of the nobility by dint of your rank alone. And your family's reputation goes back to the Patriotic War. You should relish your status. In a few days it will mean nothing.'

I laughed briefly. She had no idea just how high-born I was – the bastard son of Grand Duke Konstantin Nikolayevich, Tsar Aleksandr II's brother. It was a quarter of a century since my father's death. I never saw him in his last years. He had a stroke and his wife took control of his affairs. She made sure his mistresses and his illegitimate children never got to visit him, though I don't think she ever knew about me, or my mother, Tamara Alekseevna. And Mama was already long dead by then.

'So a plot set for March would have beaten you then,' I said. 'I take it you were planning something for May Day.'

'Perhaps,' she replied, noncommittally. 'But then fate trumped us both – the hint of an early spring, and the streets are filled.'

I looked around. Only a Russian would see any signs of spring here, but the winter had been particularly harsh and so any slight thaw was a respite. We were just crossing the Fontanka. The ice on its surface was still thick. The streets were covered with snow and it was mostly sleds, not wheeled carriages, that travelled up and down Nevsky Prospekt. The automobiles couldn't replace their wheels with runners, but their tyres were wrapped in chains for grip. It was still below freezing, even in the middle of the day, but only by a few degrees. That meant people weren't afraid to come out on the streets. Nevsky Prospekt was crowded, even for a Saturday. Mind you, with so many strikes the factories were mostly empty, and where else were people to go? The warmer weather had started two days earlier on International Women's Day. Everyone knew there'd be demonstrations and the people had taken to the streets. They'd begun to sing the Marsiliuza – the Marseillaise, if they'd known how to pronounce it – recalling another revolution of over a century before. Nikolai had banned the song, just as Bonaparte did in his day. But it was a signal to all that Nikolai could no longer expect such pronouncements to be obeyed. If it hadn't happened now, it would have been on May Day, or some day before very long.

'I'll take my leave of you here,' she said.

We both stopped. She glanced ahead, meaningfully, and I looked to see another confrontation about to take place. Further up Nevsky a crowd of workers stood tightly together, their backs towards us. Beyond them I could just see the upper bodies of mounted troops, blocking their way. Yelena offered me her hand and I shook it.

'Keep in touch,' she said as her fingers squeezed mine, making sure I understood it was no simple platitude.

She turned and made her way along the embankment of the Yekaterininsky Canal. Ahead of her I could see the coloured onion domes of the Cathedral of the Resurrection of Christ, better known as the Church of the Saviour on Spilled Blood. The spilled blood in question had been that of Tsar Aleksandr II and the church had been built to mark the spot of his assassination, on 1 March 1881. It had been carried out by an organization known as *Narodnaya Volya* – the People's Will. I had been a reluctant member, though I'd not been there to witness my uncle's murder. I'd been close though; just a few blocks away in a tunnel beneath the street.

However tragic 1 March had been for Russia, for me it was a day of celebration. It was then that I'd finally destroyed the monster who had plagued my family for three generations, a vampire who called himself Iuda, or sometimes Cain, or a dozen other names. In 1812 he'd murdered three of my grandfather's closest friends. In 1825 he'd forced my grandfather, Aleksei Ivanovich Danilov, into exile for thirty years. In 1856 he'd finally killed Aleksei, and tricked my uncle, Dmitry, into becoming a vampire himself. But in 1881 I'd had revenge for all of them, and for my mother too, and killed Iuda. I'd lured him down into that cellar just a few blocks east of here and exposed him to a new form of electric light, one which had the quality, if not the intensity, of the sun itself. It was enough to incinerate the flesh of any vampire, and so he had died in deserved agony. I'd never encountered a *voordalak* since. But that didn't mean they weren't still out there, somewhere. I was always on my guard.

I carried on over the canal towards the crowd, as did almost everyone else on the street. A few, like Yelena, decided to turn away, but for the majority it was confrontations such as this that were the purpose of the day. We were just outside the Kazan Cathedral. The mounted troops were Cossacks again, but not the same ones I'd seen earlier. They were stretched across the street, three ranks deep, stopping anyone from going further. The Winter Palace, just a little way beyond, was the focus of attention for most of the protestors, even though its significance was purely symbolic – the tsar was seldom in residence, and certainly not today.

The crowd was pushing left, towards the Kazan, in some sort of outflanking manoeuvre that was never going to work. The cathedral's two curved wings attempted to embrace them like welcoming arms and I wondered if they might not do better to seek sanctuary within rather than face the soldiers in front of them. The Cossacks were tight up against the far wing, and there was no room to slip past. I looked at the faces of the men on horseback. They were hard to read. Cossacks had their own customs and their own culture, and even in wartime they didn't mix much with the regular army. They looked anxious, almost afraid, and that wasn't a good thing. A nervous finger could pull a trigger more easily than a steady one.

I wondered whether they'd heard what had happened at Znamenskaya Square, of how their fellow Cossacks had fought to defend a similar crowd. Yelena and I had walked slowly up Nevsky and word could have got ahead of us. Even if the news had reached them, that didn't mean they would imitate what their comrades had done.

Suddenly the air was filled with silence. The hubbub of the crowd and the catcalling towards the mounted troops vanished. Those who were still speaking noticed it, and themselves fell quiet. All heads were turned towards the cathedral.

I looked. A little girl, no older than twelve, had stepped out of the crowd. She was better dressed than most of those around her, wearing a fur hat and a cloak, but she wasn't wealthy. I guessed her father had a cleaner job and a higher wage than many here, but he would still be a worker. The girl walked forward purposefully towards the Cossack captain, looking at her own feet as she placed one in front of the other, as though she were practising a ballet step. Perhaps she didn't dare look up, in case it broke the spell that had been cast on the soldiers. If it had been a man, or even an adult woman, they might have opened fire. If it had been police, rather than Cossacks, they might still have fired, even on this girl. But no one so much as raised his rifle.

At last she stood in front of the captain, close enough that she might stretch up and pat the horse's nose. She smiled up at the officer and reached inside her heavy coat. I gasped silently as an awful vision entered my mind. Would the girl pull out her hand to reveal a grenade? There were fanatics around who were mad enough to send their own children to achieve what they could not, and what better way to blow up half a platoon of Cossacks than by using a girl whom no one would suspect.

But she wasn't carrying a bomb, nor a pistol, nor any weapon. It was a bouquet – a ring of bright red flowers. I guessed they were roses, though I couldn't see clearly from where I was. The girl held them upwards, offering them to the captain. As a symbol, the flowers had a double meaning: an offer of peace, certainly, but the colour was the colour of revolution. It was too clever for the girl to have thought up for herself. And it couldn't have been easy to get hold of roses in February. But there were still plenty of rich men in the city who had greenhouses for such things and wouldn't miss a few blooms.

It seemed to get quieter still as not a soul dared even to breathe. The Cossack captain glanced back over each shoulder, as if seeking advice from his men, or trying to judge their mood. Then he shifted himself in his saddle and leaned forward, reaching out with his hand and taking the flowers from the girl. He smiled broadly under his moustache.

A huge cheer erupted from the crowd, to which my own voice made its contribution. At the same moment, the invisible boundary between horsemen and protestors vanished and they began to mingle. Arms reached out to shake the hands of the Cossacks, or pat them on the leg, or to stroke their horses. The girl was lifted up to sit in front of the captain, hugging his horse's neck. The two of them paraded back and forth in front of the cathedral to further exultation from the masses.

I stayed for a while, chatting. A bottle was passed round which I drank from without asking what was inside. It turned out to be whisky. Vodka would have been more appropriate, but it had been banned since the start of the war, for fear it would lessen the troops' ability to fight and the workers' to make shells for them. But the British ran Scotch into Arkhangelsk during the summer, and some of it got through to Petrograd.

Generally the mood was that it was all over; the revolution was complete. With the Cossacks on the side of the people there was no one to stand between them and the tsar and he'd have to accede to their demands. But Cossacks weren't the only forces in the city. As Yelena had said, their loyalty was to themselves. By far the greater number of troops were still loyal to the tsar – or their officers were, and however much the war might have knocked the discipline out of them, the men were still too scared of their superiors to go against them. At least that's what I used to think. Now I wasn't sure. And if the officers themselves switched their loyalty then the whole game would change. I'd been an officer once – still was, in name. But I'd given up on Tsar Nikolai long ago.

It was getting on for seven o'clock when I left them. It was dark now, and turning cold. I headed down Malaya Konyushennaya Street and then cut through a courtyard that I knew would lead me back to the Yekaterininsky Canal. The wide thoroughfares that Peter the Great had designed for his city were impressive, but were not always the quickest way to get about the place, especially now when they were jammed with expectant crowds. But many of the buildings were constructed as four sides looking in on a courtyard, providing a convenient shortcut for those in the know.

It was darker here, with the walls high around me and only the light from a few windows seeping downwards. Ahead I could see the silhouette of the archway that led to the canal. I walked briskly towards it, realizing I might have made a mistake coming this way. Not everyone in the city had the same sense of euphoria as the crowd I'd just left. Some just saw the breakdown of authority as an opportunity – not for the betterment of the many, but for the enrichment of themselves. I was carrying very little that might be worth stealing, but as an old man, alone and in the dark, I wouldn't be putting up much of a fight.

I heard a noise, somewhere in the darkness to my left – a yelp of pain or fear. It might have come from an animal rather than a human. A wiser man would have walked by on the other side, but I went over to see what was going on. In each corner of the courtyard stood a doorway leading to stairs up to the higher floors. The sound had come from the one to the north. In the dim glow of the electric light I could see moving shadows. As I approached I heard a voice – a man's voice. I didn't think it was he who had screamed.

'I want more than that.'

I carried on towards the sound, deliberately trying to make my presence known, but my footsteps were muffled by the soft, settled snow. As I got closer I could see the back of an army greatcoat. The soldier was looking away from me. In his hand I saw the glint of a knife. Beyond him – beneath him – was a girl lying on some sacks of coal. I was reminded of that other girl outside the Kazan Cathedral and how brave she had been. This one could only have been a year or two older – fifteen at most. She had no hat and her long hair hung over her shoulders. It was probably blonde, but so dirty that I could only guess.

Her fingers scrabbled at the buttons of her clothes. Her coat was already undone, as was the top of her blouse, partially revealing her breasts. It was warmer here than out in the courtyard, but still cold, and her fingers were too numb to quickly do what she had evidently been commanded. The soldier ran the point of his blade across the pale, soft skin of her chest, not with enough pressure to draw blood, but hinting at what would happen if she did not give him what he desired. I'd been thinking only moments before how the breakdown of law and order was seen by some as a chance to take what they couldn't otherwise have. There were men who were not solely interested in money.

'Get off her,' I said, attempting to hide both my age and my fear. It didn't seem to impress.

'Fuck off!' The soldier turned his head only slightly as he spoke. He preferred to keep his eyes on his victim.

I put my hand on his shoulder and tried to pull him round, speaking as I did so. 'I said, get off her.' I had no idea how I was going to force him to comply, but I knew that discipline still ran deep in every man of the army. Just the presence of an officer telling him what to do might suffice.

This time he half-turned towards me, brushing my hand from his shoulder as he did. His tunic and shirt were already undone, revealing the sparse grey hairs of his chest. I took in the insignia on his uniform. This was no enlisted man; he was a lieutenant. 'And I said, fuck off,' he growled.

'Just do what he said, granddad!'

It was the girl who spoke this time. Apparently she didn't want rescuing. A repellent understanding gripped me. This was not rape, and certainly no act of love. It was a mere business transaction. Whether this new interpretation made the situation better or worse I couldn't say, but it meant I could no longer regard her as a victim. And who was I to object? My mother had made her living in much the same way, though she had done it for her country rather than merely for money. I was just lucky that her clientele included men like my father. I stopped myself. There had been more between them than that. And she'd had her reasons. I was sure this girl did too. Even from the few words I had heard I could tell she was well spoken, although she attempted to hide it. Probably came from a respectable family. There were plenty who had fallen on hard times thanks to the war.

I stood there, unsure of what to do, but the girl had no patience. 'Get rid of him,' she said.

There was a moment's pause and then the soldier turned swiftly, letting me see him clearly for the first time. The knife was still clutched in his hand and even though he didn't raise it to attack I suddenly understood just how much danger I was in. I fled. As I did I realized that his was a face I knew, though I saw no hint that he recognized me. It was no time to renew old acquaintances.

I only made it a few paces before tripping over something

hidden in the snow. I landed on my side. I felt a pain in my hip and hoped it wasn't broken. The lieutenant walked towards me slowly, still not raising the knife. I tried to stand, but my heels merely slid over the frozen ground. At last I managed to get my feet under me and was upright again. I turned and ran, this time keeping a better eye on where I was going. I heard his feet behind me and knew I wouldn't be fast enough to escape him. My only hope was to make it out of the courtyard and on to the canal, where I'd be back among people and be safe, but there was still ground to cover.

'Leave him. Come back here.' The tone of lascivious allure that the girl forced into her voice revolted me, but it was of no concern now. I had no idea whether he obeyed her – I just continued to run, desperate to escape. I erupted from the archway and on to the embankment like a bullet from a gun, only then realizing how little space I had to stop or turn. I tried to dig my heels into the pavement, but they cut through the snow to find solid ice beneath. Only the railing saved me from falling into the canal.

'Oi!'

I didn't look to see who'd shouted; I'd barged more than one person aside. The embankment was brightly lit and busy, but I continued to run. Only when I was level with the Church on Spilled Blood on the opposite side of the canal did I slow down, and then because my body forced me to. I looked behind me, but the lieutenant hadn't followed. He had better things to do. I paused for a moment, trying to catch my breath. I felt a familiar tightness in my chest, like a weight pressing down on it, even though I was standing up. My instinct was to rest and let the pain go away, but I knew that wasn't the right thing to do. I had to get home.

It didn't take me long, though my discomfort had in no way diminished by the time I got there. It was a four-storey building on Panteleimonovskaya Street, just a little way in from the Fontanka. It was a matter of pure chance that it was in the same block of buildings as the notorious Fontanka 16, headquarters of the Third Section and after that the Ohrana. The tsar's secret police liked to change its name on a regular basis. My mother had worked there for a time. She'd been as capable as any of the male officials who staffed the building, but her role had been one deemed more suited to her sex: seducing men who were thought to be enemies of the state and reporting back what secrets they whispered to her between the bed sheets. Iuda had worked there too – under the alias of Vasiliy Innokyentievich Yudin – though his path and Mama's had not crossed until later, in Moscow. Back then she hadn't the smallest inkling that Iuda was her father's darkest enemy – she hadn't even known who her father was.

But perhaps I should have held some affection for Fontanka 16. It was here too, in one of the cells on the top floor, that I'd first met my father, Grand Duke Konstantin. I'd been arrested for trying to assault him, but in truth my aim was only to pass him a letter revealing that I was his son. It had proved unnecessary; he had known who I was simply by looking into my face. He had come to the cell to speak to me, and to free me.

I shook the ancient memories from my mind. The Ohrana weren't based here any more – they'd moved to a much more central address on Gorohovaya Street. They must have been busy over the past few days, and they'd be busier still if the revolution failed – vengeance against those who opposed the tsar was meat and drink to them. I could only pray that it would not come to pass. I turned to my own front door.

We didn't use many of the rooms in our house any more. We only had one servant left, Syeva, and we rarely entertained. As I went inside I looked at the stairs that led up to where we lived on the top floor. They seemed forbidding, but they had to be climbed.

'Everything all right, colonel?'

I didn't see where Syeva had come from, but it was rare for him not to be at the door when I came in. I looked at him, trying to catch enough breath to be able to speak. He was only a couple of years older than the girl I'd seen in the courtyard. In a civilized nation both would still be at school, but I knew if we hadn't given him a job whatever else he found would be far worse.

'My pills,' I said. My voice was almost a whisper.

Without another word he was off up the stairs, faster than I could have managed it even if I'd been able to breathe properly. Even so, he couldn't climb them like the rest of us would. He'd put his right foot on one step, then lift his left on to the same one rather than on to the next. That was as high as he could raise it, but it didn't slow him down. He'd been like that since birth, so he told us. He coped with the deformity, but hated it because it kept him out of the army. I never told him what a blessing that was.

He was down again in seconds, handing me the silver box which held the little white discs that could keep me alive. I took one out and placed it under my tongue. The bitter flavour began to infuse into my saliva and wash across my taste buds. It was a pleasant sensation, not in itself, but in the anticipation of the relief it would bring. Already the tightness in my chest seemed to have lessened, although I doubted whether there had been time for any real effect.

And I enjoyed the taste too for the memories it brought back – distant memories of my youth. It was something to marvel at that one chemical compound could be put to two such different uses. When I was a soldier, I'd used nitroglycerin as a weapon – to undermine cities and to destroy armies. It had been inevitable that some would get on my hands and that I would taste it, but I knew it was best avoided; too much would make me nauseous. And now that same nitroglycerin acted as a cure for my angina – or as a palliative. It certainly wasn't a preventative, or I would long ago have been immune to the disease.

Syeva returned – I hadn't noticed him leave – with a glass of water. I took it from him with a half-whispered 'Thank you, sergeant.' He always – quite correctly – addressed me as 'colonel' and somewhere along the way I'd started calling him 'sergeant', almost to try to rebuff his formality. But I could see how much he enjoyed having the term applied to him – it was the closest he would ever get to the army – and so I stuck with it.

I let the tablet dissolve completely before drinking the water, swilling it around my mouth to take the taste away.

'Feeling better, colonel?'

I nodded, but didn't reply.

'Shall I get supper started?'

'Thank you.'

He disappeared. I remained seated on the steps. The pain in my chest had almost gone, but I knew if I stood I'd feel dizzy as a side-effect of the drug. I waited a few minutes, listening to the sound of Syeva preparing the meal in the kitchen. For over a year now food had been in short supply in the shops and markets, but he never failed to find something, and to make it palatable.

Eventually I stood and hung up my coat and hat before ascending the stairs to the top floor. The door of the living room was ajar. I stood at it for a few moments looking in. Nadya was sitting with her back to me, reading. Polkan lay faithfully beside her, a heap of white fur.

'Darling,' I said softly as I went in.

She looked up and I bent forward to kiss her lips. At the same time I reached out to stroke the dog's head. He rubbed his muzzle against my hand and then rested it on the floor between his paws, glancing from Nadya to me and back again. He was almost eight now, but didn't show his age. He was a large specimen of his breed – a Samoyed – the same breed that Amundsen had taken to the South Pole. Or was it the other way round?

I fell into an armchair. Nadya knew me well enough to tell that I'd had an attack, but she understood that there was no benefit to be drawn from talking about it.

'What's it like out there?' she asked.

I sighed, and then answered a different question – the one she'd really been asking. 'I'd give him days, weeks at most.' I didn't need to explain that I was talking about His Majesty.

'Good riddance to him.' Her voice was bitter. 'He should be hanged for what he's done to us. All of them should.'

I looked at her, hoping she didn't mean it. For a moment she seemed ugly to me, but it was only the anger in her face. I couldn't share it. I wanted change, but I saw no need for vengeance. Sometimes I tried to make her see, but she would tease me about how I pretended to be wise in my old age – and I hated it when she reminded me of the gap between us. And perhaps her youth was another reason we saw things differently. She was born in 1882, a year after Aleksandr II was murdered. He was the tsar I'd grown up with – a reformer, as much as a tsar could be, but for me he was the image of what a tsar should be, what a tsar might achieve. If his successors did not live up to that, it was down to their inadequacies; it did not deny the possibility of a good tsar.

But for Nadya a tsar could mean only one thing: an idiot – first a thickset, boorish idiot and then a weak, reactionary one. I'd kept hoping for something better, but now I realized it could never be. Still, though, I didn't hate them, not least because of the blood we shared.

'I just hope it happens quickly,' I said. 'The country can't be without a leader, not now, with the Germans knocking at the door. And the city's falling apart.'

'Is no one taking charge?'

I shook my head. 'The police are still loyal to Nikolai and so are some of the army. I've seen Cossacks switch to our side; I'm sure more will follow. But with the police trying to hold down the crowds, they're not doing their real jobs. There's looting and robbery all over the place – and worse. As I was coming home I saw a girl – God knows how young – selling herself in a doorway.'

'Didn't you stop her?'

'I tried, but what good would it do? If she doesn't get the money, she'll starve.' I didn't want to tell the story of my humiliation, but there was something else about the incident that I needed to discuss with Nadya, though I knew I had to be cautious. 'If the army can make up its mind, then the police can go back to doing what they're supposed to.'

'Will that happen?'

'I don't know.' I pretended to change the subject. 'I don't suppose you've heard from Ilya.'

She shook her head sadly. 'It's been too long. I've given up writing.'

I knew well enough that I was the cause of the rift between Nadya and her brother. Though in truth it wasn't a matter of 'I' but 'we'. The relationship between Nadya and me – the fact that we weren't married – meant that none of her family would speak to her. And yet she stayed with me.

'He's still at the Front, as far as I know,' she added.

There was a knock at the door. It could only be Syeva.

'Yes?' I said.

He came in. 'Supper's ready, colonel, ma'am.'

'Thank you, sergeant.'

We went through to the dining room, just next door. It was a pretence of orderliness, of propriety, to sit at a table and eat in a room set aside for the purpose, even though the meal today consisted only of black bread, cheese and pickled herring. We still had wine though. We sat opposite each other. I spoke the words of the grace quickly and softly. They seemed to mean more now than when food was plentiful.

'O Christ God, bless the food and drink of Thy servants, for holy art Thou, always, now and ever, and unto the ages of ages. Amen.'

I squeezed Nadya's hand. 'I'm sure he's safe,' I said.

She nodded and tried to smile, then began eating. The words did nothing to reassure her, but she didn't know what I did – that they were more than just words. I'd seen her brother, Ilya Vadimovich, seen him that very day; recognized his face from the briefest glimpse. But I wasn't going to tell Nadya that her brother was just streets away, hunched in a doorway, screwing a young girl for the price of a few kopeks.

CHAPTER II

I LAY AWAKE WITH NADYA IN MY ARMS. FROM TIME TO TIME I HEARD noise outside. The raucous drunken laughter and cheering was an irritation, but it didn't strike fear in me as much as the occasional isolated, determined shout and the patter of running feet, followed by silence. Beside the bed I had a shotgun and a sword, and under the pillow a revolver. Polkan was asleep next to Nadya's side of the bed. The windows were shuttered and the door locked and bolted. Petrograd was no longer a safe place to live. There hadn't been any burglaries in this part of town – not yet – but I wasn't taking chances.

We'd lived here since 1910, though I'd known Nadya and her brother Ilya much longer than that; longer than she could remember. After 1881 – after I'd killed Iuda – I went away from the capital, still called Saint Petersburg back then, and spent some time in Saratov, the town where I'd grown up. The Lukins were the closest thing I had to a family and I stayed with them for a while, trying to find some purpose to my life now that my one goal – Iuda's death – had been achieved. It didn't take me long to realize that the only thing I understood was the army, so I rejoined my regiment. At the time they were stationed in Moscow and I decided to take the opportunity of looking up another family who had been just as kind to my mother as the Lukins, if not kinder.

Our connection with both families was through my grandfather, Aleksei Ivanovich. Back in 1812, two of his closest friends and comrades had been Vadim Fyodorovich Savin and Maksim Sergeivich Lukin. Neither survived the war. Maks had no children, but his family always remembered Aleksei and when his

43

daughter Tamara came to them, pregnant with me, they took her in as one of their own.

I never knew my grandfather, but my mother told me how, in the few hours they had together at the end of his life, he put his hand on her pregnant belly in the hope of feeling me kicking, though I was still too young for that. Most of what she knew of Aleksei she'd learned in that rushed conversation, every word of which she recited to me over and over as I grew up. It was from what Aleksei told her then that she learned of the Lukins.

But she already knew something of Aleksei's other friend, his commanding officer Vadim Fyodorovich. Vadim had a daughter, Yelena, whose married name was Lavrova, and when Aleksei went into exile it was with Yelena and her husband Valentin that he left his infant daughter Tamara, to raise as their own. And so, when I was in Moscow in 1883 I decided to visit the Lavrovs, and discover if anyone remembered my mother or even my grandfather.

Yelena and Valentin were both long since dead but their son, Rodion, still lived at the family home in the Arbatskaya region of Moscow. He was in his seventies by then, having retired from the navy with the rank of captain second rank – *kapdva* as he liked to be addressed. He lived there with his son, Vadim Rodionovich, named after the earlier Vadim. Vadim Rodionovich had been eleven when he had last seen Tamara, but still remembered her fondly. Vadim now had a wife and family of his own. Ilya Vadimovich was six when I first met him, and Nadya was just one year old.

Military service took me away from Moscow, but I kept in touch with the Lavrovs, mostly with Ilya, giving him advice and help with his career in the army. And then in 1890 I met Irina Davidovna and the following year we were wed. It wasn't a happy marriage. The fact that we failed to have children didn't help, but what made it worse was that I could accept that state of affairs, while Irina was distraught. After I returned from the war against Japan, in 1906, we didn't even bother to make the pretence of living together. I was becoming interested in politics and wanted to be in Petersburg where the Duma – Russia's first attempt at a parliament – was being formed. Irina lived in Moscow.

And it was because of my interest in politics that I met Nadya Vadimovna Primakova, who was the wife of a member of the Duma. We fell in love and began an *affaire*. It was after the third time we made love, as we held each other and talked softly, that she told me about her life and told me that her maiden name was Lavrova, and I realized that we had met before, when she was scarcely more than a babe in arms. Eventually, when her marriage was broken beyond repair, we decided that we had to tell her family about us. I didn't want to hide behind her, so I went to see Ilya, hoping he'd be able to see things from our point of view.

He punched me on the jaw. He didn't even tell me to leave his sister alone. It was too late for that – the damage had been done. Then he went and told his father, Vadim. Vadim had never seen his daughter face to face since then, but he still wrote. Ilya didn't even do that. Now I knew he was in Petrograd. I didn't think he'd recognized me during our encounter, but then his mind had been on other things. I'd no idea what I would say to him. I couldn't see much prospect of a reconciliation, but I knew how much Nadya would love to receive just the occasional letter from him. I'd seek him out.

Once I'd made that decision, I finally managed to get some sleep.

The following day was Sunday, so no one was up very early. I left the house soon after ten o'clock. Ilya was in the Izmailovsky Regiment and their barracks, when they were in Petrograd, was on the other side of the city, but as close to the Fontanka as we were. I took Polkan with me and he trotted happily at my heel, his white fur indistinguishable from the snow, at least where it was clean and fresh. The river ran south and then curved to the right. On every bridge there was a picket of either police or troops. I didn't see any Cossacks. It might have been pure chance, or the authorities might have come to realize just who they could and couldn't trust. Their job was to stop strikers and protestors – anyone really – from getting into the centre of town. In a city like Petrograd, cut through by so many waterways, it wasn't an impossible task. If they could hold the line here at the Fontanka and to the north at the Neva then it might be achieved. There were only four bridges to guard on the Neva and about a dozen on the Fontanka, and several of them could be raised.

But it only really made sense in the warm. Bridges in the frozen Petrograd winter were less of an irrelevance than they had once been, now that motor vehicles were getting ever heavier, but on foot the easiest way to traverse any waterway in the city was simply to walk across the ice. On the Fontanka it was harder to climb down to the water level, and with the bridges so closely spaced most of it was within range of the soldiers' rifles. But on the Neva it was as simple as walking across an open field. They even laid tramlines on it in the winter months.

Fortunately I could make my whole journey without crossing the river, though if I'd needed to my papers probably still carried enough authority for me to be allowed through without too much trouble. As yet, there weren't that many people trying to get across. Even during a revolution, Sunday remained a day of rest. Some observers might have taken solace in the fact that so many of the people chose to spend the morning in church, but it wasn't true. The population of the city had doubled in the last two decades as the prospect of factory work brought ever more peasants in from the countryside. As badly as the city adapted to such an influx – failing to provide adequate transport or education – the church did worse. We'd discussed it in the Duma once. There were churches in some areas that would have needed to hold thirty thousand if everyone in the parish had bothered to attend. It was worse in Moscow. And so the church lost them, and they spent Saturday night drinking, and Sunday morning sleeping it off. Or some did. Others talked all through Saturday night and into Sunday morning, planning revolution.

Polkan stopped to mark one of the railing posts alongside the river and I peered down on to the ice below. I grimaced. There were bodies there, piled together. I was just down from the Anichkov Bridge, where Nevsky Prospekt crossed the waterway. I shouted to the guard there.

'Hey!'

He turned towards me and leaned against the pedestal of one of the *Tamers* – a series of statues of a man taming a wild horse that stood at either end of the bridge.

'What?' he shouted back.

'What happened here?' I asked, gesturing towards the bodies.

'Was yesterday. I wasn't here. Some strikers tried to force their way through. Two or three of them got shot.'

'Shot?' I shouted back.

'Shot, stabbed, trampled. Who gives a shit?'

He went back to his comrades. His indifference repelled me. There were four bodies, not the two or three he'd so vaguely acknowledged, and although I couldn't see the wounds on all of them, the one on the top of the pile most certainly hadn't been shot. There was a bloody wound straight across his throat, just what you might expect from a sabre in the hand of a horseman slashing at an enemy on foot. It was a method of killing that had long fallen out of favour in battle, thanks to the far greater efficacy of the bullet, but it still seemed popular when controlling a crowd. The corpse was deathly pale – in part from the cold, in part from loss of blood. It didn't look much like a striker to me – that was to say, like a factory worker. He was too well dressed. But anyone who opposed the tsar, whatever their status, got tarred with the same brush.

I walked on, past more bridges patrolled by more pickets. This wasn't a route with which I was particularly familiar. For me, like many, journeys in the city tended to follow a radial path, along the great prospekts such as Nevsky and Voznesensky, travelling either to or from the centre. To skirt the city as I did now was more unusual for a man of my position. It would be common for the workers who traipsed each day from the overcrowded slums where they lived to the overcrowded factories where they earned a living.

But I could recall one precise occasion when I'd walked along this stretch of the Fontanka before, within only a few weeks of my setting foot in the city for the first time. It was to visit the wife – the widow, strictly speaking – of my uncle Dmitry. The apartment where they'd both lived wasn't far beyond the Izmailovsky barracks. It probably wasn't a coincidence – that had been Dmitry's regiment, though they wouldn't remember him now. He'd fought in the Crimea, died soon after, and risen again as a vampire. As far as I knew he was still alive – still undead. We'd met, but somehow we'd never become enemies. Perhaps that

47

was down to the blood we shared, or perhaps we each simply had our own more pressing concerns at the time. He'd told me he was going abroad, to the New World, but I never found out if he did, or if he'd even meant what he said.

At last I turned away from the river and soon I was at the barracks. It was a wide, low building – only two storeys high. The main gate was a little too grand for the scale of the rest of it. A triangular pediment stood on four pairs of white columns, which seemed purely for show since in the gaps between them stood perfectly solid walls. The entrance itself, between the inner two columns, had its own more diminutive columns, supporting their own rectangular pediment.

The sentry eyed Polkan suspiciously as he sniffed around, but beyond that seemed uninterested in my presence. There was no reason for him to know that I was a colonel, but not so many years before a soldier such as him would have stood to attention for someone like me, simply taking a judgement on the way I was dressed. The war had changed all that. I couldn't fathom why. Every other war I'd known – or heard of – had drawn the people of Russia together. We called 1812 the Patriotic War. Mama had told me how in 1855, when the British and French were blockading the city from the Baltic, Petersburg had been united. But this war was different. From what I heard it was the same across Europe. Germany was as ripe for revolution as we were. Britain was becoming demoralized by the death toll. And still there was no end in sight.

'I'm here to see Colonel Isayev,' I said. I could have asked for Ilya directly, but I'd no reason to suppose he'd want to speak to me. It was better to approach him through a senior officer – and Isayev was an old friend.

The sentry turned his attention away from Polkan. 'Who wants him?'

'I'm Colonel Danilov.'

On hearing my rank he straightened up a little, but then deliberately overcame his instincts and slouched against the gatepost again. He turned his head to look into the barracks and raised his hand, sticking two fingers in his mouth to produce a loud whistle. He repeated the sound and then turned back to me.

'He'll be here in a minute.'

It was less than a minute, but it wasn't Isáyev, merely a corporal. 'What?' he asked.

'I'm looking for Colonel Isayev.'

The corporal raised his hand to point down the street, uttering a single word. 'Troitsky.'

For a moment I thought he'd said 'Trotsky', but it would have made little sense. Lyev Trotsky was a hero to men like these. But at the moment he was thousands of versts away, in exile like all the revolutionary leaders; in America according to the most recent news.

The corporal's outstretched finger indicated what he'd really meant: the shining blue domes of the Troitsky Cathedral, just a little way down the road. The Cathedral of the Trinity was the regimental church of the Izmailovsky. It would be no surprise to find Isayev in there, especially at times like these.

I thanked them and called Polkan to heel. It was only a minute's walk to the cathedral. I tied Polkan to the railing and went inside, taking off my hat as I entered. There was no service going on, but there were several dozen people there – both soldiers and civilians – some praying, others sitting in quiet contemplation. Amongst the soldiers I didn't see a single enlisted man; there was no one below the rank of lieutenant. These days it seemed only the officers were bothered to pray – only the officers needed to.

The space inside was enormous – almost as big as Saint Isaac's. I skirted around the nave, looking at the faces of those who sat. I knew Isayev from Manchuria, when we'd been up against the Japanese. We fought together at the Battle of Sandepu, when we were both much more junior in rank than today. I soon recognized him. He was alone. I went and sat beside him, crossing myself as I looked at the iconostasis.

'Roman Pyetrovich,' I said quietly.

He turned and then smiled broadly. 'Mihail Konstantinovich. It's been a long time. You running the country yet?'

'I think that rather depends on you, doesn't it? What's the mood in the regiment?'

He grimaced. 'We're scarcely in control any more. It was bad enough at the Front. Now they're pulling battalions back into the city, and everyone knows why – to turn their guns on our own people.'

'Will they do it, if they're ordered to?'

He lowered his voice still further. 'I won't give the order, and I'm not the only one. But that's not to say there aren't plenty who will.'

'So even the officers are divided?' I asked.

'We always have been – even in your day. There are those of us who had to work to get where we are, and those who were born into it. But now it's got to the point that they'll recruit anybody. We're losing men by the barrel load, but we're losing officers too. And all they can do to replace either is draw people in from the country. I've got a lieutenant who's spent his entire life farming rye. He's got a better idea of how to harness a plough to an ox than a gun to a carriage.'

'Not surprising the Boche are pissing all over us.' I glanced around, realizing I shouldn't use such language in a church, but it was the way soldiers always spoke to one another.

'It's madness. Everyone's out for what they can get. Example: years ago – after Japan – it was obvious that you didn't need eight-gun batteries. The latest breech loaders can fire at twice the rate we used to manage, so you only need four in a battery, right? Wrong. We still have some eight-gun batteries, even today. Why? Because a four-gun battery can be commanded by a captain, whereas eight guns need a major. And no major wants to put himself out of a job.'

'You think it'll be better?' I asked. 'If he goes?' There was no need to explain who I meant by 'he'.

'It can't be worse. It's up to you lot to make it better.'

'If we get the chance.'

'It has to be the Duma that takes over – or something like it.'

I nodded, but I wasn't so sure. It was easy enough for all of us, of whatever party, to agree now. We had a common cause. But afterwards I could foresee only bickering. But Isayev was right; it couldn't be worse.

'Anyway,' I said, 'that's not what I'm here for. I'm looking for one of your men: Lieutenant Lavrov – Ilya Vadimovich.'

Isayev squeezed his bottom lip for a moment, then shook his head. 'Don't know the name. You sure he's one of mine?'

'He's in the regiment. I don't know who his commanding officer is.'

Isayev stood up. We walked out of the cathedral and down the steps on to the street. By the time I'd untied Polkan, Isayev was already across the road. We caught up with him just before he entered the barracks. At his arrival the sentry showed somewhat more respect than he had for me, but not much. We walked across the courtyard and then through a door and into an office. There was a desk, but no one in attendance. Isayev tutted and went over to the filing cabinets against the wall, looking at their labels until he found the drawer he wanted. He squatted down to pull it open and began to leaf through.

'Can I help you?'

I turned. A captain was standing at the door with an air of irritation. This was evidently his office. Isayev stood upright, with a file in his hand, and the captain snapped to attention. It was a refreshing show of discipline compared to what I'd seen from the sentry, but an army couldn't function solely on the obedience of its officers.

'Too late now, captain,' said Isayev. 'I've got what I needed.' He held up the file briefly, then sat in the captain's chair, putting his booted feet up on the desk. He began to inspect the papers, a frown appearing on his face.

'So what do you want to see him for, this Lavrov?' he asked after only a few moments' reading.

'He's an old friend – family friend. We lost touch but I thought I ought to look him up.'

'Close friend?'

I shrugged. Perhaps if I'd said he was then Isayev would have broken the news to me more gently.

'He's dead.'

I felt the colour run from my cheeks. I might even have staggered a little. Isayev was on his feet in a moment, guiding me to the chair with the help of the captain.

'Sorry to be so blunt,' he said.

'That's all right,' I replied. 'Just a bit of a surprise.' I didn't tell

51

him quite how much of a surprise, nor the fact that I'd seen Ilya only the previous evening, nor how that and the news of his death were quite compatible – to me anyway. 'He's definitely dead? Not missing?' I was clutching at straws.

'That's what it says here. Fifth of September 1916. Not sure where. There's a cross reference.' He handed the paper to the captain, pointing to what he had read. The captain busied himself at another filing cabinet.

It hardly mattered. For most people, the explanation would have been that one or other of us was wrong. Military reports are imperfect; Ilya might well have survived. And I was an old man, with poor eyesight, who saw someone briefly through the darkness and thought it was an acquaintance he'd not seen in over ten years. But I was in a position to know better. I knew something they didn't.

The captain soon found what he was looking for. 'It was at the Battle of Cobadin, sir. The first one.'

'Where's that?' I asked – not that it much mattered. Though when the answer came it made perfect sense.

'Near Constanţa, on the Black Sea coast – Romania.'

They must have thought it strange to see me chuckle when I heard that. It was as if that last fact had been thrown in deliberately, just in case I couldn't work it out for myself. But I could. I'd got by for thirty-six years without encountering one and somehow I'd begun to hope that I never would again. But that was not to be. They'd persecuted my grandfather, my mother and myself. And now they had come again.

It was the only explanation. Ilya Vadimovich Lavrov was a vampire.

CHAPTER III

I TOOK POLKAN HOME. AS WE APPROACHED THE ANICHKOV BRIDGE I looked down again at the river, but the bodies had been cleared away. The authorities might not be capable of feeding the city, but they still seemed able to keep it clean – clean of any evidence that might suggest they'd ordered troops to fire upon their fellow citizens at any rate.

But had all four of those bodies fallen victim to the regime? The wounds to the throat of the man I'd seen could well have come from a cavalryman's sabre, but they could equally have been caused by the teeth of a *voordalak* – of Ilya. It was impossible to know. And why only Ilya? From what I knew – from what I'd been told by Mama – vampires were as likely to descend upon a city in a pack as alone. They would still hunt as individuals, but they would huddle together once the sun rose, somewhere dark and safe, and brag about their exploits of the night before.

And whatever fate had befallen that man whose corpse I'd seen on the frozen river, there was another victim whom Ilya had most certainly claimed: that poor girl I'd seen him with. What had her choices been? She must have been starving, desperate for money to pay for food, probably not just for herself, but for her entire family. She'd offered up her body in exchange for enough to buy – what? – a loaf of bread or a few potatoes. But she hadn't guessed just how much she was offering when she gave herself to Ilya, nor how much he would take. I imagined what I would find if I went back to that courtyard close to the Yekaterininsky Canal. Would she still be lying there on those coal sacks, paler even than she had been before? Probably not. Like Tsar Nikolai's cronies, the *voordalak* was usually wise enough to clear up the mess that it left in its wake.

As I walked, I felt a trembling in my limbs. My cheeks were flushed with blood. An anger that I hadn't known in decades filled me. Strangest of all, I felt young again. My mother had raised me with a singular purpose: to hate vampires – to hate one in particular, but whatever I felt towards the individual, I felt towards the breed as well. I'd done my best in my later years to be a good man, to make a difference for the better, but now I knew once again what I'd known since I first suckled at my mother's breast. I knew the reason I was here on Earth – my purpose. It was to rid the world of the scourge of the *voordalak*. If it was only Ilya, that would suffice, regardless of his being Nadya's brother. But I hoped there were more, more than I could ever deal with, so many that I would kill them and go on killing them and never stop. Until they stopped me.

The mood passed, fading as rapidly as it had arisen. I was older now than then. I'd seen so much more of the world, and so much more killing. Now I knew better. The *voordalak* was a symptom, not a disease. Or if it was a disease it was a secondary infection that attacked a body already weakened by something far more deadly. In 1812 vampires had only dared come to Russia when it was debilitated by the pestilence that was Napoleon Bonaparte. In 1855 they had waited until the nation was on the verge of defeat. And now they had chosen the moment when Russia was at war with itself. When the tsar was weak – too weak to ever lead again – and when the people were battle-weary and starving and being struck down by the very police whose duty it was to protect them.

And yet I knew that it had been more than opportunism that had brought vampires to Russia. There had been a grander plan – a plan devised by the greatest and most dangerous vampire of them all: Zmyeevich, also known as Ţepeş and sometimes as Dracula. His quarrel with Russia – with the Romanovs – dated back to the time of Peter the Great. They had been friends. Pyotr had promised to let Zmyeevich make him into a vampire, but had reneged when the process was only half complete; Zmyeevich had drunk his blood but he had not drunk the vampire's. It meant that the Romanov dynasty was forever in danger. Zmyeevich could complete the process with any descendant of Pyotr and make him, or her, not just a vampire, but thrall to Zmyeevich's will. And if that Romanov were tsar, then all of Russia would be under Zmyeevich's dominion. The Romanovs knew what might happen to them – and feared it. Sometimes they even shared a part of Zmyeevich's mind, through the blood that they shared, and could see with his eyes.

But still the tsar remained human. Zmyeevich and his emissaries – Iuda among them, until the two had fallen out – had tried more than once to spring the trap that he had set with Pyotr, but they had always been defeated. My family had played no little role in that – Aleksei, Tamara and most recently myself. We had all paid a price, though mine was different from theirs. I still lived, but unlike my mother and grandfather there was Romanov blood running in my veins. And knowing that, I had quite deliberately drunk Zmyeevich's blood – one of several samples Iuda had taken from him years before when they worked together. It meant that for a time I too had been privy to the thoughts that passed through Zmyeevich's foetid consciousness. But even that brought with it the benefit that I could assist the Romanovs. While Zmyeevich's mind was bound to mine he had no power over any other Romanov of my generation – no power over one tsar, at least.

And soon there would be no tsar at all. Once things changed, once a decent, honest government took power, then Russia would have no need to fear vampires. For now, though, the danger was very real. Whether it was a question of 'they' or simply 'he' I did not know, but Ilya was the only one of them I knew to exist for sure, and so it would be with him that I would start.

But not just yet. It was mid-afternoon, still a few hours before dusk. The sun shone high in the sky – as high as it could in February in Petrograd. Ilya would be sleeping, protected from its rays, and I had little chance of guessing where. There must have been ten thousand tombs or more in and around the city – perhaps a hundred thousand. I couldn't search them all. And there was other business to attend to: the Duma.

I went home briefly and spoke to Syeva. Nadya had gone out. She worked at a kitchen most days, serving borshch to those who could find nothing to eat. It wasn't a recent thing. She'd started in 1915 – that was when we'd begun to notice the war back home. Nowadays there were always some they'd have to turn away, simply because they had no more food to give. I went up the stairs to the top floor and past the three rooms we used to the end of the corridor. There was a heavy padlock on the door there, to which only I had a key. I opened it and went inside.

I flicked the switch and the light came on. There were no windows to this room, but fortunately the generators were running today – it hadn't always been the case of late. Polkan lay down at the doorway, as if nervous of what lay within. I went inside. I'd never dared get rid of any of it, always fearing that the day would come. Here was everything I possessed that might be of any use in destroying a vampire.

Along one shelf stood Iuda's notebooks. When alive, and when undead, he'd been a scientist and had made detailed studies of creatures like himself. It had aided his understanding of them, and the books contained information that might be used against them. Here too was my *arbalyet* – a crossbow firing wooden bolts that might kill a vampire. In my hands it had only ever killed a human – a girl called Dusya who had chosen the wrong side. Over the years I'd looked into my heart and attempted to find regret over her death, but I could not. I recalled her pretty face and shining blonde hair, and that brought to mind the girl I'd seen with Ilya in the courtyard. Her hair might have shone too, if she'd had the opportunity to wash it. But now she never would. If killing someone like Dusya might offer the chance of saving someone like that girl, then there could be no room for sentimentality. But I knew that over the years I *had* grown sentimental.

There was various other junk in the room: a box full of Yablochkov Candles, arc lights intense enough to kill a vampire, as I had so happily demonstrated with Iuda. (Ordinary incandescent bulbs, like the one that lit the room now, had no power to destroy them. But the Yablochkov Candles emitted light across a broader spectrum and so could, as far as was necessary, imitate the sun.) There was a simple wooden sword, no more than a child's toy – and yet deadly to a vampire.

But none of these was what I had come for. It would be a risk to carry an *arbalyet* or a wooden sword around the city at the best of times, let alone now with guard posts at every street corner. I chose instead a weapon that had belonged to my mother. It was a simple walking cane, or so it appeared. I took it in my hand and leaned on it, testing that it could take my weight. It was sixty years old – as I was – but unlike me age had not weakened it. In terms of style, it was out of fashion, but that hardly mattered. I raised it up and held its tip in my left hand, gripping it tightly as I gave the shaft a firm twist. The cap came loose to reveal the sharp point that my mother had whittled all those years before. It would still be capable of its purpose – piercing a vampire's heart.

I put the cap back in place, then turned off the light and locked the door once more. I went downstairs and looked at myself in the hall mirror. I'd managed so far to walk without a cane – my legs were still strong. But the time would come soon enough. No one would think it amiss to see an old man carrying a walking stick. I went outside, leaving Polkan in the house, and set off for the Tavricheskiy Palace.

My route took me north, up to the Neva and then along the embankment to the east. The streets were busier now that it was mid-afternoon, and I was still outside the *cordon sanitaire* marked by the Neva and Fontanka. Whether the streets within it were calm and peaceful, I had no idea. I couldn't even imagine what it was they were trying to protect. The tsar was far away in Mogilev, to where the Stavka – the circle of ancient generals who pretended to direct the path of the war – had most recently been forced to retreat. It was probably a wise decision on his part. It was difficult to rise up against an absent dictator.

The Neva was still frozen and I could see figures running across the ice. The recent warmer temperatures wouldn't weaken it, but within a month the frozen surface would start to thin, and people would have to stick once again to the bridges. That would make the city easier to control. The French had waited until July for their revolution, but in Russia we knew these things were best achieved in the cold. On the Liteiny Bridge, its movable span swung open to one side to prevent anyone from crossing, I saw a group of soldiers. They aimed their rifles at the men who were approaching across the ice. They fired and one of the protestors fell. The others began to hurl rocks and chunks of ice, and soon they were safely under the middle span. But now they were trapped. If they emerged, they'd be shot down before they could even raise their arms to throw a single stone. I didn't wait to see what happened, but carried on towards my destination.

The river began to curve slightly northwards. I turned inland and then on to Shpalernaya Street, pressing my cane into the snow with every other pace, practising so that carrying it would appear natural. Soon I came to a wide gap in the blocks of buildings that lined the road, and I turned off on to the long crescent drive of the Tavricheskiy Palace. The name came from the old Greek term for the Crimea. When Potemkin had conquered the peninsula for his lover, the Empress Yekaterina, she'd had the palace built for him. It was an imposing enough structure, but in every aspect it reeked of 'second best'. It was not like the Capitol in Washington or Westminster Palace in London. Those places were built specifically to house the governments they contained. The Tavricheskiy Palace was just a convenient place to let the members of the Duma debate, while the tsar got on with the real business of government.

The entrance reminded me a little of the Izmailovsky Barracks, where I'd been earlier, but on a grander scale. Again there was a triangular pediment, this time with six equally spaced columns, but the whole thing was far more impressive, set back from the street and out in front of the main building itself, and almost twice the size of the Izmailovsky. There was a guard on the door, but they didn't bother to ask for my papers. They knew the members of the Duma by sight. Where, I wondered, would their allegiance lie, if it came to it? *When* it came to it. So far the Duma had taken the line that it was loyal to the tsar, and so there wasn't an issue, but soon we would have to make a stand, and our guards would have to decide whether their real duty was to protect us or to detain us.

It was almost five years since I'd first come here after the elections of 1912. After I'd returned from the war against Japan I'd become increasingly interested in the prospect of taking Russia along the path that Aleksandr II might have chosen, if he'd lived. I was still in the army, but my heart meant I was unfit for active service – and there were better ways I could be put to use. The military's newfound interest in aviation coincided with my own expertise and so I found that I rarely had to travel far from our aerodromes in Petrograd and Moscow. Standing for parliament seemed the perfect way to fill what remained of my time. Then, as now, I'd been a member of the Constitutional Democratic Party – the Kadets. In many countries we'd have been considered moderate – conservative even – but in Russia simply to favour a constitution was thought extremist. Of those represented in the Duma we were the tsar's best hope. The parliaments since 1912 had sat only sporadically, and achieved little. But now we sensed our moment had arrived.

I went through to the Convention Hall. The Duma wasn't in formal session, but the hall was still full. To my mind, if not to others, it was a beautiful place. It was filled with row upon row of desks, neat semicircles of them, seating for each of the assembly's 448 members, slightly raked, like a theatre auditorium. All around were galleries where members of the press or indeed the public at large could sit and witness the process of government. That was a new idea for Russia. In the past, however wise the decisions of our leaders might have been – and they were not all fools – they were still discussed in secret and announced to the people once a decision had been made.

And yet it was all pretence. The Duma had no power. It had no ministers, it could pass no law without Nikolai's approval and it was subordinate to a second chamber, the State Council. That was a far older body, established by Aleksandr I before he turned away from the path of reform. Half of the State Council was appointed by the tsar, so it tended to do his will. And if it didn't he could ignore it just as he ignored us.

But however little Nikolai allowed us to do, he did at least allow us to talk, and that was a new enough thing in Russia, and a dangerous one, particularly for the tsar.

We were talking now; everyone was. The whole chamber buzzed. Men stood in small groups, or sat at the rows of desks, half of them facing backwards so that they could speak to those behind. I pushed my way through to where I could see Nikolai Nekrasov, one of the vice-chairmen of the Duma and a fellow

Kadet. He was talking with two other men, both of whom I recognized: Prince Georgy Lvov, another Kadet, and Aleksandr Kerensky, a Trudovik, on the political left.

'Where the hell have you been?' hissed Nekrasov, covering his concern with a veneer of anger.

'I told you – I went to see what the mood was like on the streets.'

'That was yesterday.'

'What *is* it like out there?' Lvov seemed calmer.

'It's quieter today, but that's Sunday for you. Yesterday there were crowds everywhere. There were shootings, but not all the army has the stomach for it. The Cossacks are joining the people, defending them from the police. I saw it for myself in Znamenskaya Square.'

Nekrasov nodded. 'We heard. The whole city is militarized, supposedly, but who knows which side half of them are on.'

'Apparently the Pavlovsky Regiment has gone over to the people,' added Kerensky. 'Not just the rank and file; officers too.'

'And those that haven't are dead, killed by their own men.' Lvov sounded bitter.

'What's Nikolai doing?' I asked. 'There must still be regiments he can trust.'

'Perhaps there are,' said Lvov, 'but how can he know which? And it takes time to get men back from the Front.'

'He had over a hundred revolutionary leaders arrested this morning,' said Kerensky. 'Bolsheviks, Mensheviks, SRs.'

'Anyone from here?' I asked.

Nekrasov looked around. 'There are plenty of faces missing, but they might just be stuck out there, like you were.'

'All the bridges are blocked,' I said.

'It hardly matters who they arrest,' said Kerensky. 'The real leaders – Lenin, Trotsky, Kamenev – are all in exile. The ones doing the damage at the moment are nobodies. But there are too many for Nikolai to arrest them all.'

'He might still prevail,' said Nekrasov. 'The army's not fallen apart completely. A victory for Nikolai now and the tide could turn.'

'Or if he came and spoke to them in person,' suggested Lvov.

Nekrasov laughed, and I couldn't help but join in.

'Rally the troops behind him?' said Kerensky scornfully. 'His father maybe, but not Nikolai.' Kerensky talked like he knew a lot, but he couldn't have been more than about twelve when Aleksandr III died. I doubted he'd ever heard him speak.

'He wouldn't dare anyway,' said Nekrasov. 'What the people need is something to vent their anger on. He'd be it.'

'Nikolai Vissarionovich!'

The shout came from across the room. We all turned to see that it came from Mihail Rodzianko, the Duma's chairman, standing on the platform that was the focus of the chamber. He looked ashen, fear written unmistakably on his face. Despite his huge belly, he had an air of emaciation. Nekrasov obeyed the summons and went over to him. We stood in silence as the two of them and a few others held a whispered discussion, huddled in a circle. Then Rodzianko stood upright. He banged a book on the table in front of him to attract attention. A hush filled the room.

'Gentlemen.' Rodzianko's voice boomed across the hall. 'I have just received a pronouncement from His Imperial Majesty, Tsar Nikolai.'

I swallowed. Could this be it, the announcement of his abdication? Had it taken so little for him to abandon what his ancestors had fought so long to keep? The room became quieter yet as every man held his breath, each with the same expectation. Behind Rodzianko I caught Nekrasov's eye. His face was grim and he gave me a slight shake of the head. He had guessed what we were all thinking, and we were wrong.

'In the light of the ongoing civil disturbances, His Majesty has instructed that the Duma be dissolved. His intention is that we should reconvene when order has been restored – April at the earliest.'

He paused to let the news sink in, scanning his eyes across the chamber to gauge our reactions. A soft murmur of conversation began to rise, indicating he had given us long enough. He had only to draw a deep breath and it subsided.

'So, gentlemen, what do we tell him?'

It was not meant as a rhetorical question. While opinion varied widely across parties as to what the fate of the country should be, almost all adhered to the concept of the rule of law, and legally

Nikolai had the authority to prorogue the Duma. It would not be an easy decision.

For Kerensky, though, there was no such dilemma. I heard his voice whispering in my ear. 'What do we tell him? We tell him to go fuck himself.'

I didn't stay long at the ensuing debate. It seemed to me that the matter had gone beyond political niceties. Whether the institution of the Duma existed – whether the office of tsar itself existed – was not down to any decision that either we or he would take. It was down to the mood of the people, or that fraction of the people who had taken to the streets of Petrograd in the hope of changing their lives. But beyond that, I had more important things to do than help decide the fate of my country.

It was drawing dark now and any vampire in the city – one in particular – would be waking up.

I had few clues, other than where I had seen him last. But that was on the other side of the Fontanka and I would have to cross the defensive ring that had been thrown up around the city centre. The atmosphere simmered with a mood of anticipation. There were more people out on the streets than when I'd gone to the Tavricheskiy Palace earlier in the day, but they were quieter, grouped around fires that they'd built at street junctions. Pickets of soldiers still manned every bridge on the Fontanka. I skirted along it to the south as far as the Simeonovskiy Bridge, but then decided my best chance of getting through was via the Neva.

I went back north and stepped down on to the ice just opposite where the Nevka branched off, between the Liteiny and Troitsky Bridges. Like the Liteiny, the Troitsky had its moving span open. This gave me some slight advantage. The opening sections of both bridges were close to the left bank, where I was, and since sentries could not stand where there was no roadway to stand on, they were less likely to see me. The ice was almost abandoned now that it was dark. It was cold again, and it would be madness to light a fire on the frozen surface, so most had moved on to the land.

I crept forward furtively, hugging the wall of the embankment, and soon I came to what I'd been looking for: the entrance to the Lebyazhya Canal, one of the shortest waterways in the city. I could hear footsteps above me on the bridge at its mouth, which stood as a part of the Neva embankment, and prayed that no one looked down. I slipped under the bridge, finding purchase for my fingers against the brickwork and sliding smoothly and silently across the ice. Now I was inside the cordon. I carried on down the canal. Looking up I saw a few people, soldiers and civilians, walking around, but none looked down to see me. For the moment it seemed safer to remain as I was below street level, avoiding the crowds and following Petrograd's alternative network of thoroughfares. I passed under another bridge and was now on the Moika. To my left the Moika joined the Fontanka, just a stone's throw from my house, but I turned right, heading deeper into the heart of the city.

Down here it was difficult to keep one's bearings, with landmarks hard to see. Even when you could spot them, they were at strange angles. But there were fewer turnings to choose from and I knew that the next left would be the Yekaterininsky Canal. I carried on down there a little way and finally found some steps to climb back up. There were no soldiers around, and those few people who saw me clambering up from the level of the water seemed unperturbed. One even offered a gloved hand to help me to my feet. I stood up and took my bearings. I'd emerged just opposite the Church on Spilled Blood.

I looked across at it for a few moments. It was a foul building, for all that I shared in the sentiment of wanting to commemorate the death of my uncle. Russia had forever been torn between the east and the west, and nowhere was that better exemplified than in the two capitals. Here in Petrograd, Pyotr's gateway to the West, the architectural style was generally modern; European – but with a distinctively eastern twist. In Moscow, the old capital, it was uniquely Russian. The buildings of the Kremlin dated back centuries, to a time when Russia shunned Europe and shunned enlightenment. Both were beautiful cities, each in its own way.

But for every tsar like Pyotr or the first two Aleksandrs, who embraced what the West had to offer, there was a Nikolai I or an Aleksandr III, who rejected it and feared it. There was even talk that the current Nikolai wanted to return the capital to Moscow, though at the moment he had greater issues to deal with. But one way these tsars could display their distaste for the West was to impose the older style of architecture on Petrograd. Saint Vasiliy's in Red Square in Moscow was a beautiful church, built in the sixteenth century. Its coloured onion domes, though garish, fitted perfectly with its surroundings. The Church on Spilled Blood was a fake, designed to emulate Saint Vasiliy's. It was built at the wrong place and in the wrong time – in the wrong city and the wrong century; built by a spiteful tsar. Aleksandr III must have known, even as he commemorated his father, that his father would have hated what he was attempting. Let Moscow have Saint Vasiliy's but leave Petrograd its Saint Isaac's. And leave it its name – Saint Petersburg – too, while we were about it, for all we hated the Germans.

I turned away and went back into the courtyard where I had seen Ilya the previous night. I looked in the doorway where they had been, but there was no sign of the girl's body. It would most likely be revealed when the spring thaw came and the snow that had been blown into huge piles finally melted. I went back out to the canal. I'd get a better view from the other side, but it was a long walk to the bridges at either end. I considered climbing back down on to the ice and walking across, but my thoughts were interrupted.

It was less than a scream but more than a yelp, stifled before it really began – female, I guessed, though it was possible a man could make such a sound if shocked or scared. I looked around but could see nothing. It was quiet here, with few people about on either side of the canal. Opposite, on the corner of Inzhenernaya Street, a couple stood against the wall in an embrace. My mind wandered to thoughts of Nadya. How much would I rather be with her now, wrapped in her arms? I'd not explained the reason I would be returning home late tonight, but it wouldn't have been entirely shocking to her. I had long ago told her of the existence of vampires and of my family's battles against them. I had not one jot of proof to show her, but she had taken it all in her stride. Yet still I balked at revealing that her own brother had become one of them.

Across the water the man stepped back from his lady friend and she crumpled to the ground. He walked briskly away alongside the canal, heading south. I didn't see his face, but I knew. Two men passed him in the opposite direction. Moments later they saw the untidy pile that was his victim. One of them bent forward to examine her. It took him only moments to discover her wounds.

'Jesus Christ!'

The sound echoed up and down the canal, channelled by the tall edifices on either side, but I was already moving. Even if it wasn't Ilya, I was most certainly dealing with a vampire who therefore merited no less a fate. And the chances were that there was some connection between them. Following one would lead to the other.

I had no immediate opportunity to cross the canal and get closer, nor had I any desire to. This way it would be easier to track him without being seen, and if he did see me, he wouldn't be able to get at me so easily. The only problem would be if he decided to leave the canal and head east, away from me. Then I'd have to find the nearest bridge pretty sharply, or cut straight across the ice.

My first chance to cross came as the canal went under Nevsky Prospekt. The road was so wide that the waterway vanished completely. Those travelling along the prospekt might not even realize that they were on a bridge. Without the channel between us, it might have been more obvious to Ilya that he was being followed. But we were outside the Kazan Cathedral and the streets were thronged, just as they had been the previous day. There were soldiers, but faced by too many people for them to know what to do with. I hung back in the shadows and watched as the figure crossed the prospekt. Diligently, the vampire looked both ways, allowing me a glimpse of his features.

There was no doubt about it; it *was* Ilya. He carried on along the embankment. I followed, staying on the other side. I was almost at the spot where I'd seen the girl with the roses. The cathedral was built right up to the water's edge, but it was easy to slip between its tall columns and continue my pursuit. The canal turned right and then left again as we traversed the city. Ilya walked swiftly and I had no real need for subterfuge. There were plenty of others heading in the same direction as me, perhaps returning home now

65

that they realized things were settling down for the night; that the revolution would not be happening until tomorrow, or the day after that.

Finally Ilya abandoned the canal and cut through to the Haymarket. There was nowhere for me to cross the canal – I was midway between two bridges. I could only guess that from the Haymarket he would continue southwest along Sadovaya Street, otherwise why not leave the canal sooner? I ran forward, but a sentry was standing at the bridge. He didn't seem concerned with who was going past, but I'd rouse his suspicions if I was in too much of a hurry. I walked calmly until I was across, and then with a slightly greater pace down towards Sadovaya Street, hoping that Ilya had not gained too much ground on me.

He hadn't. Indeed I almost bumped into him as I emerged into the street, and so I decided to cross to the far side, if only to waste a little time while he got far enough ahead of me. He crossed to my side of the road near Saint Nikolai's Cathedral and so I dropped further back. Still we were inside the boundary defined by the Neva and the Fontanka. It seemed unlikely that his nest would be within that area, but so far he had been disinclined to leave it.

At last he turned south, towards the Fontanka, along Lermontovsky Prospekt. I could only presume he was unfamiliar with the city. Of all places to cross the Fontanka, this was the worst, since the bridge that had once taken the prospekt over the river – the Egyptian bridge – had collapsed years before, killing a number of men and horses. It had never been rebuilt. But as we approached, I realized that that was precisely Ilya's reason for coming this way.

The trapezoidal steel archway still stood where the foot of the bridge had once been, mimicking the stone entrance to some pharaoh's ancient tomb. A railing prevented pedestrians from accidentally falling in. There was a picket mounted, but consisting only of two men. I could just make out another two on the far side. There was no need for more – it was quiet around here. Ilya approached them, hailing them with words that I couldn't catch. It allowed him to get close and as he drew near the two of them stepped towards him, so that they were standing side by side. Ilya struck.

I heard the crunching sound almost before I realized what had happened. His hands had moved quickly, smashing their heads together. Given his inhuman strength there was little hope that either of them would survive. He hadn't bothered to use his most natural weapons – his fangs – but as I had seen, Ilya had already fed that night.

He didn't tarry. He dropped straight down on to the ice below. I moved forward a little to get a better view. Ilya was already across, looking up at the two guards on the far side. He leapt, his fingers and toes somehow managing to find purchase on the wall and launch him further. He grabbed the tails of the coat of the right-hand man and then fell back, silently taking his victim with him. Once down on the ice Ilya did use his teeth, swiftly dealing with the sentry – but not silently. The man had time to emit a brief scream. It was enough to attract the attention of his comrade, who looked downwards and saw what was happening. He jumped, his bayonet already aimed. It was an impressive manoeuvre – the blade pierced Ilya somewhere near his kidney before the soldier's feet even touched the ice. Against a human it would have been a devastating assault, but to Ilya it meant nothing. He turned with the bayonet still in him, causing the rifle to twist and wrenching it from the soldier's hands. He lunged forwards and bit him, again giving his prey a brief opportunity to cry out, but this time there was no one to hear. Within moments Ilya had climbed up from the river and was continuing on his way.

I briefly examined the two soldiers on the embankment, then lowered myself down on to the ice to take a look at the other two. All were dead, beyond help, but even so a part of me felt the obligation to do something – anything; to seek out their families and tell them what had happened, or to lay them out in a more decent fashion. But I didn't have time to linger. I looked at the high wall which Ilya had so deftly climbed to get out of the gully of the river, but it was too much for me. In my prime I might have managed it, but not today. I hurried along a little way and found a ladder fixed to the brickwork. Once over the river there were several directions that Ilya could take, and I knew I must hurry if I wasn't going to lose him. We were close now to the Izmailovsky Barracks and I wondered briefly whether he was returning to the fold of his former regiment, but as I looked around I could see that he was pressing south.

As I walked, just far enough behind not to be seen or heard, I began to marvel at my own inhumanity. There was nothing I could have done to save the woman that Ilya had killed when I first saw him, but I had just allowed four men to die, simply so that I could pursue him. If I had acted swiftly and thrust the cane I still held in my hand through his heart, then those men might have been saved. But it would not have achieved my goal. There was more than one *voordalak* in Petrograd, I felt certain of it, and so I had to find their lair. I felt the coldblooded resolution of my youth returning to me, a determination that had been inculcated in me by my mother. I could not be sentimental about those four soldiers, any more than I had been about killing Dusya. If I allowed Ilya or any of the vampires he shared his nest with to live, then there would be a far greater number of deaths on my conscience.

At the Obvodny Canal there were guards on the bridge, but they were letting people through unchecked. We were too far from the city centre now for them to care. Ilya turned along the canal, passing the Baltic Station and the Warsaw Station and then finally headed south on Zabalkansky Avenue. We were truly leaving the city.

I had some inkling now of where Ilya would be sleeping when the sun finally rose. He had not taken the most direct route, but he'd clearly known the best way out of the city, avoiding guard posts manned in such numbers that even he might be overcome. But now we were heading along a path that was familiar to me, that I'd traversed years before in very similar circumstances. Again I had been following a vampire. On that occasion it had been my uncle Dmitry. He had found a location that was most suitable for a vampire to sleep – why shouldn't Ilya come to the same conclusion?

I was proved right. Ilya turned off into the Novodyevichye Cemetery. Since I'd started following him, the moon had risen – it was almost full – and although it was dimmed by a thin layer of cloud I could see him making his way between the gravestones and sepulchres. Perhaps it would have been wisest to leave him there. I knew his resting place now, and I could return in daylight, safely to deal with him and however many others I found there. But it was a big graveyard; anything I could do to restrict the area I had to search when I came back would save time – and therefore lives.

I removed the cap from the end of my cane and slipped it into my pocket, holding the sharp point out in front of me. I crept in after him. Somewhere in the distance I could see the light of a fire, towards which he seemed to be heading. After a few minutes I lost sight of him, but I could still see the flickering flames and thought I could make out voices. I took a few more steps, and then decided I had gone far enough. I'd be able to get this far again in daylight; the remnants of the fire they had lit would show me precisely where they were. I looked over my shoulder to check that the path behind me was clear.

In an instant the fire went out. The moon still shone down, but it was not nearly as bright as the flames. I became aware of movement all around me, shadows dancing amongst the headstones – figures of men, though I knew they had long since ceased to be humans. I heard whispered instructions and laughter, and then I felt hands gripping my shoulders. I lashed out with my cane, but it was plucked from my fingers. I was shoved to the ground and then dragged face down by the ankles, grass, earth and stones rubbing against me. I covered my face with my hands.

At last we stopped and I was rolled on to my back. The fire was alight again – I don't know how they had managed to hide its flames. They stood all around me, in a circle. I didn't have time to count them. One bent forward, his face leering in front of me, fangs bared. It was Ilya. I tried to lift myself up, but another of them stamped his foot down on my right arm. A third copied him on the other side. The only chance I could see was to tell Ilya who I was and pray that some spark of humanity might remain in him, but I knew the nature of the *voordalak* too well to imagine it to be any real hope, and besides, his next words proved that he was already quite aware of my identity.

'This'll teach you to screw my little sister.'

He raised his head to strike and at that moment my eyes locked with one of those surrounding us. It was a tall figure with dark hair, aged about fifty, or at least he had been when he became undead. I couldn't fail to recognize him, but his brown eyes stared down on me with complete dispassion. Either he didn't know me or he didn't care. But I knew him.

It was my uncle, Dmitry.

CHAPTER IV

'FOR CHRIST'S SAKE, DMITRY, IT'S ME! MIHAIL KONSTANTINOVICH! Tamara's son!'

Ilya thrust the heel of his hand against my jaw, silencing me and forcing my head to one side, so that my neck was stretched out for him to bite. I felt his lips touch my skin, but then he jerked away. I looked up to see Dmitry standing closer, his booted foot still raised from kicking Ilya in the side.

'Let him go!' Dmitry's voice had the same timbre that I had known years before, but now there was an added authority to it. The vampires obeyed him instantly and I was able to sit up. He reached out a hand to help me to my feet.

'You're an idiot,' he said as I dusted myself down.

I wondered for a moment whether I should counter by telling him that he was an idiot for letting me live – that one day he would come to regret it – but it would have been churlish. And I wasn't sure it was even true. In the past we'd each had ample opportunity to kill the other, and yet we were both still here.

'I didn't think there'd be so many of you,' I replied instead.

He led me away from the group that still stood in a circle around where I had been lying and pointed to the plinth of an overturned statue near the fire. I sat down. 'Did you count *how* many?' he asked.

I looked over to them and totted up. They were shuffling away, uninterested now they knew they would not be feeding on me. Before I could complete the count Dmitry told me the number.

'Twelve of them,' he said. 'It seemed appropriate.'

'Appropriate?'

'In 1812 my father, your grandfather, recruited a dozen vampires to help him save Russia from the tyrant Bonaparte. Today I'm doing the same.'

'He went on to kill them – all of them.'

'All but one,' Dmitry reminded me. 'But that was a mistake born of ignorance. You and I understand these things better.'

'So you're going to save Russia?' My voice was scornful. 'Send the Boche scurrying home to Berlin?'

Dmitry gave the briefest of laughs. 'Germany isn't the enemy – not the real enemy. The Kaiser may be a tyrant, but that's for *his* people to worry about. We have our own tyrant to deal with.'

I could guess his meaning. 'Nikolai?'

Dmitry nodded. 'I take it then that you share my opinion.'

'Perhaps. I didn't think it was the kind of matter over which a *voordalak* could really have an opinion.'

'And why not?' He exaggerated his offence, but it was real enough. 'Perhaps when I was young – young as a *voordalak* – then all I was interested in was my baser desires. It's the same with the young of any species, though their desires may differ. And not all of us grow to be much different, but some do. Look at Zmyeevich. When he brought the twelve – the *oprichniki* – to Russia, his mind was on things greater than simply the craving to feed.'

'He wanted the throne – wanted revenge on the descendants of Peter the Great.'

'Absolutely. But my point is that his desire was beyond mere bloodlust.'

'His may have been, but the *oprichniki* had only one thing on their minds. How do you know your lot won't be the same? I've already seen one of them kill tonight.'

'We have to feed. But I know they will obey me.'

'The same way Zmyeevich knew? Because you exchange blood with them – and control their minds?'

A strange expression crossed his face. He lowered his jaw, but did not allow his lips to part. His eyes widened and bulged. I could not tell by the light of the moon and the fire, but I imagined he grew pale.

Finally he spoke. 'I would never do that again.'

I studied him. There was an indisputable sincerity in his words, and on his face. It was in a tomb in this very graveyard that I had witnessed him and the great vampire Zmyeevich exchange blood. It was I who had explained to him that it meant their consciousness would begin to merge. It would be the same process that bound Zmyeevich to the Romanovs, but the link would be far tighter, and quite irrevocable. In the end the stronger mind would be dominant. Neither of us had been in any doubt which of the two that would be. Dmitry had been fortunate to be able to tear himself away from Zmyeevich before his will was subsumed entirely.

I felt suddenly aware of the enormity of the moment. This was my uncle – my half-uncle; we both were descended from Aleksei Ivanovich Danilov, but Dmitry was his son by his wife, Marfa. I was his grandson by his mistress, Domnikiia. Even so, he was the closest thing I had to a family. More than that, he'd known Aleksei. My grandfather was my hero, but I had never met him. Even my mother had only spent a few brief hours with him. Dmitry was his son. And Dmitry had been born into a different time – a different world. 1807. He was a hundred and ten years old. Of his long strange life, I knew very little.

'Where did you go?' I asked. 'After . . . Zmyeevich.'

'As I told you I would, I went to America.' He spoke as if he'd mentioned it to me only the other day. Perhaps it seemed like that to him. For me it was over half a lifetime ago. 'The further I was from Zmyeevich, the safer I felt. I'd left Petersburg even before they killed Aleksandr. I landed in New York – just one amongst millions.' He smiled to himself. 'It was easier for me to get in than most. I travelled as a piece of cargo. Oh, but what a city! Have you been there?'

I shook my head. I was the least well-travelled man in my family. Aleksei had been to Paris, and now I heard Dmitry had gone even further. I'd made it as far as Vienna once, though to the east I'd been almost as far as a man can go.

Dmitry continued. 'The nation was scarcely a hundred years old. The French sent them a statue to commemorate it. It went up soon after I arrived: Liberty Enlightening the World. They believe that's what they can do, not like here, where we can't even enlighten our own children. I lived there for over twenty years; passed myself off as an American, although there were so many Russians arriving every day I could just as well have lived amongst *them*.'

'You fed, I take it.'

He laughed. 'Of course I did, and enjoyed it too. I don't need to justify myself to you, Mihail. I don't need to explain myself to you, because I cannot. You question how I can kill an innocent human, eat his flesh, drink his blood, but at the same time want the best for humanity? It makes no sense to you, but then you're a human. I'm not. Humans do far worse things. Those Russians I told you about, who came to America? Most of them Jews, fleeing their own country in fear for their lives, just because the tsar decided to blame them for his nation's ills. And worse than him are the millions of Russians who happily believed him, who turned on their neighbours of hundreds of years and burned down their houses, murdered them and sent them running across the world in hope of a safer place to live. And even those who didn't participate stood by and let it happen. Drinking a little blood hardly seems so bad, does it?'

It was a spurious argument. Not 'I am good', but 'you're just as bad'. It didn't absolve him of what he had done, and continued to do. But he was right, I had stood by and let it happen. Many of us had. 'Why did you leave?' I asked.

'I knew I'd have to one day. A vampire can't settle like a man does. There's no moment at which he can say to himself, yes, this is the place where I shall live out my days, because he knows that no end will come. I could have stayed longer in New York, or gone to another city. I travelled back and forth between Europe and America, unable to settle. I had no plans to return to Russia. The revolution of 1905 had already failed, and the best of Russia were those wise enough to abandon the country, like the ones coming to America.' He paused. 'That's what I thought.

'But then I found myself in Paris. It was the twenty-ninth of May 1913. I went to the theatre – a new place called the Théâtre des Champs-Élysées. It had only been open a month or so. It was a mixed bill – ballet. *Les Sylphides* was first, and I so used to love Chopin. There was some Weber and Borodin too, but the main event was a new work by Igor Fyodorovich Stravinsky called *Le Sacre du Printemps – The Rite of Spring*. You must have heard what happened.'

I nodded. 'It made news around the world.'

'The theatre fell apart,' Dmitry continued. 'There was always a divided crowd in Paris. The rich who sat in their boxes so they'd be seen, and the young, artistic types – *les bohèmes* – who adored anything that was new, however awful it might be. But then I heard that opening bassoon solo, so high up, quite wrong for the instrument, and yet so perfect, and I knew that this was as far from awful as it's possible to be. And yet there was laughter. And it wasn't just the music. When the curtain rose and the dancers stood there, their feet turned in as though they knew nothing of ballet. I understood the music better, but it was still all beautiful to me. But the audience wouldn't have it. They weren't there to see what was on stage, just to hurl abuse at each other. And then they got bored with that and started to shout at the orchestra and to throw things at them. The noise was so loud, I'm surprised they managed to keep going. I could see Nijinsky standing in the wings shouting the count at the dancers because they couldn't hear the music.

'Finally the police were called, and the worst offenders were taken away. It quietened down after that, but there was still some catcalling. In the end they applauded; demanded Stravinsky and Nijinsky come on stage to take a bow.'

'And what were you doing throughout all this?' I asked. 'With all that chaos around you, no one would have noticed a few drained bodies until it was all over.'

Dmitry didn't rise to the bait. I don't think he even noticed the bile I'd tried to inject into my words. 'I just sat there. I was enraptured. It was the most wonderful thing I had ever heard. When I became a vampire, I lost something, some ability to understand music; certain aspects of it – the emotion. I'd sat through *Les Sylphides* and remembered how much I used to enjoy Chopin – to listen to or to play – but now the sound was no more than pleasant. Chopin is so much about emotion. But there's more to music than that, and Stravinsky has it all. Maybe there's emotion there too, maybe I *am* missing something, but there's plenty to listen to without it. At the end I was on my feet, shouting and applauding. I saw it twice more before it went to London. There were still people laughing and shouting, but it was nothing like at the premiere.'

'And that's why you came back to Russia?' I asked.

'That's when I began to consider it. This was the greatest work of art I'd ever seen. All right, it was staged in Paris, but the conception was entirely Russian. The composer, Stravinsky; the choreographer, Nijinsky; the designer, Rerikh; the impresario, Diaghilev; all of them Russian. But they'd all left Russia, like those immigrants in New York. Like Chopin, for God's sake, a century ago. And I realized what Russia might be if her greatest minds didn't just leak away to the West. And I understood what I've always known, that the thing driving them away was the tsar. It doesn't matter which one. In 1825 I stood with three thousand comrades in Senate Square to stop the first Nikolai. We failed, and for a long time I believed we'd always fail. But things have changed. The world's changed. And for once Russia will change.'

I couldn't disagree with him. 'And that was four years ago,' I said.

He shrugged. 'Then the war started and things got difficult for everyone. Difficult for Nikolai too, which was a good thing. That lunatic *starets*, Rasputin, made them look like fools. I rejoined the army, stirred things up a bit, but there wasn't much I could do but wait – and gather together my little troop. I knew there would be a battle in the end, between the people and those still loyal to the tsar, and I knew that then we'd be able to help. And now it's started.'

He stopped, his story complete. I could think of nothing to ask him. Mostly his eyes had been fixed on the fire as he relived times past. Now he looked directly at me and smiled. His face was open, genuine and friendly, and I felt very much afraid.

'Which side are you on, by the way, Mihail? That of the people? Or do you remain loyal to the tsar? He is, after all, your cousin.'

There was no reason to suppose he would have forgotten who my father was. And clearly my life depended on the answer I gave. Here I was in the dark, sitting opposite a vampire, with a dozen others lurking somewhere near by. If I chose to side against them, I was doomed. But I had no need to lie.

'You're my uncle,' I said, 'and I despise what you've become. If Aleksandr II were still alive, I would have fought to save him, but not his son, nor his grandson.'

'You protected his son.'

'By drinking Zmyeevich's blood, you mean?'

Dmitry nodded. 'And thereby attracting to yourself the power that Zmyeevich can wield over the Romanov family just once in each generation.'

'The lesser of two evils. If Zmyeevich ruled over Russia then the reign of the tsar would seem like paradise. That's why, much as I hated Aleksandr III, I feared for his death. I couldn't protect his son, not in the same way. I knew Zmyeevich would come for him.'

'But now he will never come,' said Dmitry.

'Never,' I replied with a smile. 'A year before Nikolai came to the throne the curse that Pyotr brought upon his family was lifted.'

'You're sure Zmyeevich is dead?'

'I saw it with my own eyes. From the moment I drank his blood I began to see what Zmyeevich saw. Not always. Sometimes when he wanted me to. Sometimes when he felt an intense emotion, like fear as he died. It must be the same for you – you've shared blood with him.'

Dmitry nodded sombrely. 'Tell me what you saw.'

'You didn't experience it for yourself?'

He did not answer my question, other than to gaze at me with a sense of urgency and say simply, 'Please.'

I wasn't going to deny him; it was a memory that would be a pleasure for me to recall. I took a deep breath.

'I remember it very clearly. The twenty-fifth of October 1893. I was in Moscow, sitting in a tea shop on Tverskaya Street. It was early evening – the sun had just set, though it would not yet be dark everywhere in Europe. For several days before I had been experiencing glimpses and visions that I knew were not mine, but came to me from Zmyeevich. Nothing had been very clear, but I was aware that I – he – had travelled a great distance, first by sea and then by land and that we were going home – a destination that would soon be reached. But I'd experienced nothing for a couple of days.

'Suddenly, I awoke. I couldn't recall falling asleep. My last memory was of the table where I sat in Moscow. Now I was in total darkness, lying on my back. I was moving with great speed. The road I was on must have been rough as I was bumped and jostled around, but I did not care. I knew that haste was essential. My pursuers were close and if they could catch me they would try to kill me, but if I could only gain a little time on them, I would be safe.

'The cart went over some great bump and I was flung into the air. My cheek banged against something hard and rough – wooden. I put my hands up to brace myself and realized with horror that I was inside a coffin. No, not a coffin, simply a crate. That was why it was dark. This was a safe means of transportation. Outside it was still daylight, though it would not be for long. There was something soft beneath my back, something strangely comforting. I lowered my hands and pressed my fingers into it. It was soil – the soil of my homeland. I felt safe at the touch of it, though I knew it was a mere luxury – inessential to my survival. But it gave me comfort.

'I assessed my chances. I wasn't sure how many of them were pursuing me; perhaps six in total, though one was a woman and another old. And I was not alone. I listened. I could hear the sound of the wagon's wheels turning beneath me, and of the pounding hooves of the horses pulling it. Around me there were more horses, and riders, men that would be faithful to me. I'd hired them, local Szgany with instructions to take me home. I couldn't tell how many; perhaps a dozen. In the distance I heard the howl of a wolf, soon joined by another. They would protect me too, if they could reach me in time.

'But perhaps I wouldn't need protecting. The castle must have been close by now. If we could make it through the gates and inside then I would be safe. They might follow me in, but if they did, they would not come out again alive. And dark as it was inside the crate, I could sense that outside the sun was about to go down. We were in the Borgo Pass, and the mountains would be towering above us, meaning that the sun would set earlier than if we had been on the open plain. Once it vanished behind their peaks I would be strong again, and they would not defeat me, not six of them. Not sixty. But that was still minutes away, and I had to survive until then.

'I heard a shout outside. "Halt!" It was in English – two men speaking in unison. None of the Szgany could have understood what the word meant, but the fools stopped anyway. I heard their horses' hooves stamping against the ground to slow them, and felt the wagon come to a standstill. I waited. I could have flung myself from the crate and fought them there and then, but I was still weak from the daylight. I might even have found myself unable to prise the lid open. Better to let them cut through each layer of defence I had placed around myself. The Szgany, the wolves if they could reach us, even the wood of the crate might delay them by a few seconds, and then the sun would be gone, and they would wish they had let me be.

'I heard the sound of a lash against a horse's rump and a flurry of hooves and knew that the Szgany were preparing to defend me. Then there was the cocking of a rifle and all became calm again. My defenders were not armed with guns, but I knew they would fight with what weapons they had. One of them issued a command: "*Omorâţi-i!*" It was in a language I didn't understand, yet the meaning came to me clearly: "Kill them!"

'A battle ensued, though fists and blades were the weapons I could hear – my English pursuers regarded themselves too much as gentlemen to use rifles against a foe who was not equally armed. I began to doubt whether I would even need to rise up and lay a hand on any of them in my own defence. But I hoped that the Szgany would not be too brutal in their task, and that some of my enemies would still be alive once the sun had set so that I could bring death to them in the way which I would most enjoy, and which they would most abhor. I particularly hoped that the woman would survive. She was to be mine. I had already tasted her blood, and it was sweet.

'Then suddenly I heard two thumps in rapid succession and the wagon shook beneath me. Someone had jumped up on to it, their feet landing one after the other. I steeled myself, waiting for the lid to be ripped away, knowing the sun would fall upon me, but knowing also that, unlike most of my kind, I was strong enough to survive its rays. And moments later the sun would set, and I would be reinvigorated, and would kill whoever it was had dared to disturb me.

'But the lid did not open. Instead I felt the whole crate being lifted up. If there was only one of them doing it then his hatred of me had given him preternatural strength. I felt for a moment weightless as the crate and I inside it flew through the air, then we hit the ground, tumbling over and over until at last coming to a halt. I had landed in the same orientation I'd been on the wagon, lying on my back and facing the sky, though now the earth on which I had been resting was scattered everywhere. I heard a scream that sounded more as if it came from an Englishman than a Szgany. I hoped that I'd judged correctly. Still I waited. It was a matter of seconds now before the sun vanished from the sky.

'Then they were upon me. A chink of light appeared at the joining of the lid and the side as a huge steel blade slid between them. It was not intended to do me any harm, not yet, but as it pulled against the wood the gap widened and more light entered. I felt an instinctive fear at it, but it was weak and I knew it could do me no harm. Then the knife was joined by a second, this one with a smaller blade and entering further down, towards my knees. Together they strained against the lid, but it was nailed firmly in place. One knife alone would not have succeeded in opening it, but in combination they would do so eventually. With luck they would not need to. Once the sun went down then it would be I who would open the crate, smashing its flimsy lid with a single blow.

'But with each twist of the blades the chink of light widened. Now the gap was wide enough to reach through. Fingers penetrated the breach and began to pull. For a moment the nails resisted, but then with a tearing screech they gave way and the lid was thrown back. I had only an instant to take in my surroundings.

'It was snowing. The land all around was blanketed in white, and flakes were buffeted in the air. Above me – a thousand feet above me – towered my castle, the precipice of its walls unassailable from any of the mountains around it. I was so nearly there, and yet I sensed that there was something wrong. My home had been entered, desecrated, despoiled. Clearly to pursue me as I lay helpless upon the wagon had not been their only line of attack.

'Around me the battle had come to an end. I saw two of the Szgany with their hands raised, one allowing his sword to drop on to the ground. I could not see any further, but guessed that there were rifles aimed at them, and they had finally realized that they could not win.

'Two faces loomed above me. I recognized them both. One was the American, the other was the Englishman, the solicitor who had so cruelly abused the hospitality I offered him at my castle. Each of them held in his hand a knife. The Englishman's was an ugly thing, pilfered from one of their colonies in the east, with a long blade that curved inwards. The American's was more mundane, but I feared neither of them. The men exchanged glances and grinned with a shared lust to kill. Both raised their weapons, the Englishman's high behind his head, silhouetted against the mountains, and the American's hovering above my heart. But it was too late for either of them.

'At that moment the sun vanished behind the mountaintop. I felt strength flood into me; it would take only seconds for my potency to return and for my body to be revivified. A sense of triumph surged through me. My eyes widened and I began to smile, pushing myself up from where I lay.

'The two blades fell in unison. The American's knife pierced my heart. It was a fascinating sensation. A sudden burning, which almost immediately subsided as I began to heal. It was only steel, and could do me no harm. But the other blade was different. The Englishman was lucky. He brought it down on my throat and dragged it across, pushing down hard. Perhaps I was weakened by the blow to my heart, but the weapon cut deep, deeper than I could imagine. The man was filled with an insane hatred and vented it in his unquenchable desire to see my head severed from my body.

'And in that desire he succeeded. I felt little pain after the first incision, but he pushed and pushed and at last, with a slight click, he was through. My body was separated from me and I felt my face fall away. My senses abandoned me one by one and I could no longer smell, nor feel, nor hear, nor see. Nor could I taste my own blood upon my lips. And yet still I was capable of thought, of sensation, of memory.

'And then . . .'

CHAPTER V

'. . . I WAS BACK IN THE TEA SHOP IN MOSCOW. ZMYEEVICH WAS DEAD and I could no longer perceive his thoughts. It was quite a relief, I can tell you.'

I hadn't been looking at Dmitry as I spoke, but I raised my head to face him now. He was enthralled, transported, the very image of how I'd imagined him to be as he'd sat there watching *The Rite of Spring* for the first time. But it couldn't have been new to him.

'Didn't you experience it too?' I asked. 'Just like me?'

'I did, but not as you did. Whenever I began to see through his eyes I tried to push him away from me. I knew I'd be tempted to go back to him – wherever he was, whatever continents and oceans might separate us – and share his blood once more. I saw what you saw, but not as clearly. If I'd known it was to be a vision of his death, I'd have treasured the moment more.'

'You look as if you enjoyed hearing me tell it.'

'I did. I did. It's safe now; he's gone. I can't go back, however much I'm tempted.'

'Do you know what happened?' I asked. 'How he got to that point?'

Dmitry nodded. 'I can make a few guesses. You said they were English; Zmyeevich had good reason to go to England.'

'Which was?'

'That was where Iuda had hidden the things that he'd stolen from Zmyeevich, assuming Iuda could be believed: the last sample of his blood and, of course, Ascalon.'

'The sword that Saint George used to slay the dragon.'

'More of a lance than a sword,' explained Dmitry.

'Did Zmyeevich find it? In England, I mean?'

'Does it matter? Did he have it when he died?'

I searched my memories, but could find no trace of anything that might resemble a lance. I shook my head.

'I think you'd have known,' said Dmitry. 'It was very dear to him.'

'Why?'

'I never knew. He hid that from me. I asked him once, and he told me it merely had sentimental value.'

'That doesn't sound like him.'

Dmitry chuckled. 'Oh, you'd be surprised.'

'Maybe, but he went to a huge effort to get Ascalon back – you did too; digging down to the tunnels under the Armenian Church. It must have some real value – some power.'

'Even now Zmyeevich is no more?'

'I'd still feel safer to know where it is – to destroy it.'

Dmitry breathed in deeply through his nostrils. He shivered. 'Then you will have to do so without my help. I don't even want to be near it. It would remind me too much . . . of him.'

I didn't try to argue. I understood what an effort it had been for him to break away from Zmyeevich in the first place. We sat in silence for a few moments, then Dmitry spoke. 'Of course, if you do want to find Ascalon, you know who to ask.'

'Who?'

Dmitry looked at me, puzzled. 'Who else is left? Papa killed eleven of the *oprichniki* when they came to Russia in 1812. Now Zmyeevich is dead. That only leaves one.'

Now it was my turn to laugh. 'Iuda? No, Iuda's been dead even longer than Zmyeevich.'

'What?'

'He died the same day as Aleksandr II, at almost the same moment, down there in the chambers beneath Malaya Sadovaya Street, where Ascalon once was hidden.'

'How can you be sure?'

'Because I killed him.' I tried to control the pride that forced its way into my voice.

'That can't have been easy.'

I let my mind slip back. In the end it had been very simple: the mere flick of a switch to allow the flow of electricity through a new kind of arc light. But only years of preparation had made the final act so uncomplicated; years of research and experimentation – Mama and I working together – to find the most effective weapon against a vampire; years of investigation to track Iuda down under whatever alias he might be using; and finally months to close in on him, to lure him down to those tunnels beneath the streets of Petersburg – the very same tunnels in which Ascalon had once been hidden. He thought it was I who was walking into the trap, but I had merely been the bait to bring him down there.

I recalled Iuda's reaction to the bright light, as I had done so many times before, and the pleasure I had taken from it. He had been confused at first, not realizing the danger but sensing the discomfort that would gradually transform into pain and then agony. As his flesh began to smoulder he had tried to flee, but I was too quick for him. I cut the clothes from him using his own double-bladed knife, so that the light could permeate every inch of his skin. I'd watched as his limbs became dust and as his eyeballs burst into flame. But that was only at the end. Something else had happened, before that.

'He fought back,' I told Dmitry. 'Managed to bite me, but it was too late for him.' I remembered the sensation of his teeth penetrating my throat, of the blood being drawn from me. But that hadn't been the worst of it.

'He bit you? So . . . you shared his mind.'

'Briefly.' The memory of it was utterly lucid, undiminished after all those years – worse than the feeling of his teeth in me, worse than the sound of his lapping at my blood: the presence of his thoughts mingled with mine. 'It was strange,' I said, 'as though there were something very precise he wanted to communicate to me, something that didn't make sense, though I could understand the words as clearly as if he had been speaking to me.'

'What were they?'

'He said, "Tell Lyosha. It was . . ."'

'It was what?'

'That was all,' I explained. 'He died before he could say any more.'

'And by Lyosha, he meant Papa?'

85

'I always assumed so. It's a common enough diminutive for Aleksei.'

Dmitry nodded. 'It's how Iuda always used to refer to him.'

'Mean anything to you?' I tried not to sound too eager. Over the years I'd pondered what Iuda could have meant, but with no conclusion. I'd largely given up caring, but there was always the chance that Dmitry might be able to make some sense of it.

He shrugged. 'I don't know. "Tell Lyosha it was all my fault"? Seems unlikely.'

I chuckled. 'I've never come up with anything that really made sense.'

Dmitry slapped his hands against his thighs and then stood, as if suddenly ready for action. 'All in the past now,' he said. 'We should be worrying about the present. We're on the same side, Mihail; with regard to the revolution at any rate.'

I stood up and faced him. He was inches taller than me. 'We're hoping for the same outcome,' I conceded.

'And will we get that outcome if Nikolai orders the troops to gun down the strikers? Even if we do, should we ask them to make that sacrifice, if it can be prevented?'

'What do you propose?'

'We'll be out there. There'll be battles in the streets – there already are – we can turn them in the right direction. The deaths of a few reactionary officers could save hundreds of lives.'

I laughed loudly. 'Don't pretend you care.'

'What does it matter if I care? You do. That's why you'll help us.'

'Help you? How?'

'The same way Papa helped the *oprichniki*. Be our eyes and ears during the day. Devise our strategy. Use us as a weapon.'

I looked up into his eyes and could see nothing but sincerity. Or perhaps I simply saw nothing. But whatever his motivation, his logic was sound. He – they – could change the course of the revolution.

'I'll think about it,' I said. 'I'll meet you this evening. Not here, though.'

'No.' He thought for a moment. 'Beside the Bronze Horseman. Half past nine.'

It was an entirely appropriate location. I offered him my hand, but before taking it he reached down to the ground and picked something out of the snow. It was my cane – its sharpened tip still exposed. He examined it, smiling wistfully – a strange expression for a vampire holding something so clearly intended to bring about the death of its kind.

'This was your mother's,' he said.

I nodded.

'We had one each,' he continued, 'me, Tamara and . . . Iuda. It was me who thought of it. It would be ironic, wouldn't it, if it was this that did for me in the end?' He handed it back to me. 'Let's make sure that doesn't happen,' he concluded.

I took the cap from my pocket and placed it back over the tip. It was a symbolic gesture, but I would make him no promise. We shook hands and I departed, walking between the headstones as I tried to find a route to the road. Then one last question occurred to me. I turned back to see him still standing there, watching me.

I spoke loudly, so that he could hear me across the graves. 'You said we shouldn't ask the people to sacrifice their lives.' He nodded. 'What about you?' I asked. 'Would you lay down your life for the cause?'

He paused for a moment, but I don't think he needed to consider his answer. 'I've known for a long time that I would. When I stood in Senate Square in 1825 it was pure chance that I survived; many died around me. I thought I was the lucky one. But as I sat there, in that theatre in Paris, I knew that I was wrong. There's a story to *The Rite of Spring*. It's supposed to be based on a Russian folk tale, but you know how these things are – made up to suit the circumstances. But it rang true for me.'

'What happens?' I asked.

'In the second part, there's a group of young girls on the stage. They walk in circles until one of them is selected. She's the "Chosen One".'

'Chosen for what?'

'To dance.'

'Is that all?'

Dmitry gave half a smile. 'Yes, that's all. She dances. And she dances and dances, until she can dance no more. She dances, beyond exhaustion, until she is dead.'

I felt the urge to snigger, but resisted it. It clearly meant everything to Dmitry. He had one more thing to add by way of explanation.

'She does the one thing she is capable of – she dances – dances herself to death. And I'm prepared to do the same. I don't want to die, but I'll be happy to if I must. I used to be a soldier and now I am a vampire. There's one ability that those two have in common and that is to shed blood – to kill. And you know as well as I do that blood will have to be shed for this revolution to succeed. And I'm prepared to do it – to kill and going on killing – either until this revolution is complete, or until I am dead.'

It was the small hours of the morning by the time I got home. It was a long walk and I took it slowly, contemplating what Dmitry had said, and whether I should trust him – whether, indeed, I needed to. Could a vampire really be a patriot? Could a vampire be interested in anything other than the lust for blood?

The answer was simple – yes. Iuda was a vampire and had been interested in more, as had Zmyeevich. In both those cases their other interests had been in directions just as foul, if not fouler, than the desire to feed. Iuda's fascination was to learn, learn by experimenting on his own kind; Zmyeevich's yearning had been for power. But if Iuda was a worse kind of vampire then it was conceivable that Dmitry was a better kind. And if I were to consider what I knew of how they had been in life, then it made some sense that Dmitry would carry forward the traits he already possessed. And yet it was as a living man that he had chosen to become a *voordalak*. True, he had been tricked into it by Iuda, made to believe he was acting out of love – to be with the woman he loved – but the very idea should have been abhorrent to him. I would not have been so easily duped – neither would Aleksei.

It was an unnecessary dilemma. I would judge Dmitry by his actions. We had arranged to meet again that evening and I'd go through with the meeting and decide then what to do.

I skirted round the city to the east. This far from the centre all was quiet and still. It was only when I hit Nevsky Prospekt and walked in the direction of the Fontanka that anything unusual became evident. The bonfires were still burning to keep the crowds warm, though most were asleep now. I noticed a few men standing alert and on guard, ready if the government forces chose this moment to strike, but there was no sign that they would. In more than one doorway I saw couples copulating. Whether the act was voluntary, forced or paid for I did not know, nor just then did I care. I doubted my help would be welcomed any more than it had been by the girl I'd seen with Ilya, and the fate of these women would be nothing to what had befallen her.

There was still a formidable picket at the Anichkov Bridge, but I had no need to cross. I followed the course of the river and was soon home. I tried to unlock the door without a sound, knowing that Syeva would be up to welcome me if he heard. I managed without disturbing him. On the first-floor landing I noticed a light glowing under one of the doors. We hadn't used any of the rooms on that floor for years, but this one had been a bedroom. I went over and tried the handle, but it was locked, just as it should have been. The keys were downstairs somewhere, but it would mean waking Syeva and anyway, I was too tired.

I carried on up to our bedroom and went inside. I could hear Nadya's soft breathing. I heard Polkan's feet crossing the floor and felt his nose sniffing my hand. Once he had verified that it was only me he returned to his place beside the bed. I undressed and slipped in beside Nadya.

I woke up alone. I could see daylight glowing at the curtained window. I looked at my watch – it was after eight. I shaved and dressed quickly and then went out into the hall. Nadya was not in the dining room, but we rarely chose to have breakfast there. I went downstairs and found her in the kitchen, along with Syeva and Polkan. I went over and kissed her.

'You got in late,' she said.

I sat opposite her. I had hidden nothing of my life from her. I knew that neither the name nor the nature of Dmitry Alekseevich would be a surprise to her, but I didn't want to tell her I'd seen him again; not just now. Syeva placed a glass of tea in front of me.

It wasn't hot – it cost too much fuel to keep the samovar warm all the time. I took a sip while I decided what to say.

'I was at the Duma. Nikolai wants us to disband.'

'You're not going to, I hope.'

'I won't vote for it. I don't think many will.'

We sat in silence. Eventually Nadya spoke. 'Do you think it will be over soon?'

I wondered what she meant by 'over'. There were some who thought the French Revolution was still to be resolved. 'I think things will have settled down within a week, one way or the other.'

'People can't stand much more.' There was an edge to her voice. She wasn't far from tears. 'I was out there yesterday. There are families starving. And freezing.'

I reached across the table and squeezed her fingers. 'That won't be going away – not quickly. That's the war as much as the tsar.'

She stroked the back of my hand. 'We should do something.'

'We are. I am at the Duma. You are at the kitchen.' I downed my tea and then stood up. 'In fact, I have to go there now.'

She exchanged a glance with Syeva.

'I meant more than that. I was thinking. We've got spare rooms here, plenty of them. Perhaps we could take people in – just a few. The ones who really need it.'

We'd discussed it before, but things hadn't been so urgent then. The objection was still the same. 'It's not the rooms, Nadya, it's the food. We've barely enough to manage ourselves.'

'That's no excuse; we could easily work something out – make sure they knew they had to buy their own, or I could arrange something with the kitchen. And rationing's supposed to start on Wednesday.'

I looked into her eyes. I knew she was right. However much I loved to talk at the Duma about the plight of the poor, she was the one who actually faced them every day. And if we let out some of the rooms here, it would still be she and Syeva who dealt with them. But I wasn't going to rush into it.

'I'll think about it,' I said. 'I'll tell you this evening.'

I kissed her and quickly left the house.

*

The Duma had grown used to its own impotence. Nikolai had given us no power except the ability to talk, and so talk we did. Lvov made a fine speech, as did Kerensky and then a dozen others afterwards. I said nothing. There was no need. It was obvious from the first that we weren't going to obey the tsar and dissolve ourselves, but other than that there was little we could do beyond awaiting events. But the talking made our position clear – if we were in session then indisputably we still existed.

My mind was elsewhere: on Dmitry. We'd arranged to meet at half past nine, but the minutes ticked by slowly. I thought back to what Nadya had spoken of that morning. Suddenly it all made sense. She'd asked whether we would take in the homeless, but she was asking in retrospect. I remembered the light I'd seen under the door as I came home, and the look she had exchanged with Syeva that morning. She'd already found some waif and offered them our empty room. It mattered little. I'd already decided I'd agree to what she wanted.

We broke for lunch and I went back out to discover the mood in the city. Everywhere was crowded now. It was Monday, a working day and therefore a striking day. Yesterday the options had been to come out on the streets or to stay at home. Today the alternative to protest was to go to work. For most it was no choice at all.

But it wasn't just strikers; there were more soldiers out today too. Evidently someone had finally understood the seriousness of the situation and organized a full defence of the city. There were troops at every junction now, and the bridges were better defended. I could only presume it was the same across the city. But it was a double-edged sword. True, there were more soldiers on the streets, but what was just as evident was more uniforms amongst the protesting crowds. At the foot of the Liteiny Bridge I saw more than twenty men steal away from the picket, slip off their caps and join the crowd that moments before they had been facing. And with every man came a rifle. In the initial turmoil of revolution, the protestors had been poorly armed, but with each day, with each desertion, they became more of a force to be reckoned with.

At first I didn't see any shooting, but the sound of gunfire could be heard across the city. Usually the sporadic sound of a rifle, but occasionally the harsh, rapid pulse of a machine gun. It seemed more likely that such weapons were on the side of His Majesty, but I couldn't be sure. Whenever I looked at the expressions of the frightened soldiers who stood facing their own countrymen, rifles raised, the less I believed that they would be prepared to fire when the order came. I wasn't even sure that their officers would give the order, though I knew some would. Just as Colonel Isayev had said – was it only the previous day? – some of them had too much to lose to allow the tsar to fall.

It wasn't just crowds on the streets either. There were more cars and trucks than I'd seen on Sunday, though I doubted the drivers were very familiar with the workings of their vehicles, certainly not those of the automobiles. The motor car was a luxury item. Few people who owned a carriage would ever dream of sitting on the perch themselves and taking the horses' reins. Similarly the owners of a car would employ someone else to drive it for them – and call him by the French term 'chauffeur' to add a little class to his role. Now these same vehicles were being driven by striking workers. The trucks might well be driven by those who sat at the wheel as a part of their job, but there were enough inexperienced hands controlling the cars to bring an added danger to the city.

And both cars and trucks were horribly overloaded. The only ticket that seemed to be required to get on board was to be in possession of a gun, and so vehicles roamed the streets in imitation of giant hedgehogs, bristling with the muzzles of rifles, sometimes with bayonets fixed. If two or three of them could get organized enough to make a joint charge on one of the soldiers' lines then they would easily break through. This was a very different revolution from the one in which a little girl offered a bouquet of roses to a Cossack captain.

I went back to the Tavricheskiy Palace. Nekrasov accosted me almost as soon as I entered the chamber.

'Have you heard?' he asked. He didn't wait for an answer. 'They've ordered troops back from the Front. General Khabolov is leading them.'

'When will they be here?' I asked.

'Tomorrow? The day after? At the very least it will restore some order.'

'I doubt that. There's plenty of troops out there already. The problem is that they're going over to the other side in droves. If you see that as a problem.'

'However this ends, order has to be maintained.' Milyukov, the founder and leader of our party, had come to join us.

'How can there be order?' I asked. 'There's no one in charge.'

'His Majesty is on his way back now, by train.'

'Back here?' I was astounded.

'To Tsarskoye Selo,' Milyukov explained. It just showed how little Nikolai understood. Tsarskoye Selo was the tsar's out-of-town retreat and had been for centuries. It was thirty versts from Petrograd. It was the perfect symbol of Nikolai's isolation from the people.

'Does he have any idea what's going on here?' asked Nekrasov. 'They've started throwing open the prisons.'

'Who has?' I asked.

'The mob. This morning they burned down the Lithuanian Castle and I've just heard they've torn open the doors of the Kresty.'

Milyukov emitted a curt laugh. He'd been an inmate of the Kresty Prison for a while, as had many others in the Duma. It was a fate I'd been lucky enough to avoid, so far.

Nekrasov clearly understood what he meant, but had other concerns. 'It's not just politicals that they're letting out, though, is it? There's common criminals too.'

'It's going to be pandemonium out there,' I said. 'The police and the army are dealing with the crowds – those that haven't gone over to them. And there are more guns out there than there are in the trenches. If this doesn't stop, the city will tear itself apart.'

'Leaving it ready for the Germans to march right on in,' said Nekrasov grimly. 'Much easier than fighting their way here like men.'

'I've heard they've got their own agents out there,' I said, 'acting as agitators.'

'I know for a fact they've been funding the Bolsheviks for years,' said Milyukov.

'Even so,' I said, 'it isn't *just* down to the Germans.'

Nekrasov seemed distracted. He was looking over my shoulder, across the Convention Hall. Quite a crowd had assembled at several of the doors, looking out into the corridor. We went over. 'What's happening?' asked Milyukov.

I didn't know the man who replied. 'They've let them out of the Peter and Paul. They've all come here.'

'Who was in there?' I asked.

'A load of Mensheviks they arrested last month,' said Milyukov. 'The Central Workers' Group, or something. But why have they come here?'

It was better that they were Mensheviks than Bolsheviks, but only marginally. The two socialist factions had split as long ago as 1904 over the question of whether the revolution – when it inevitably came – would be led by a broad party membership or by a professional elite. Neither was exactly a vision of democracy, but the Menshevik idea of widespread support was closer – and it looked as though it was their version of revolution that was coming to pass.

I shouldered my way through the crowd and was eventually out in the corridor. There were hundreds out there, some of them, like me, members of the Duma, but others were pouring into the building. No one seemed to have the remotest interest in the Convention Hall. Instead their goal was in the opposite wing of the building. I went with the flow, but we soon came to a halt outside Meeting Room 12 of the palace as the throng tried to squeeze itself through the doorway. There was little chance that half of those trying would fit in.

I felt a hand on my shoulder, pulling me to one side. I turned. It was the Bolshevik Yelena Dmitrievna. 'I wouldn't bother,' she said.

We stood tight against the wall, allowing the crowd to heave past us. 'What's going on?' I asked.

'They've had an election. They're forming a council: "The Soviet of Workers' and Soldiers' Deputies".'

It was a common enough word, one that had been used for centuries to mean all kinds of committees and assemblies. During the revolution of '05 they'd formed all over the country, soon to be put down again. But there was something about the way Yelena said 'soviet' that imparted to the word a significance it had not held before.

'On what authority?' I asked. 'Who do they represent?'

She nodded towards the window opposite. 'Haven't you been out there? What authority is there other than that? They represent workers and soldiers. They *are* workers and soldiers.'

'Do they intend to rival the Duma?'

'I don't think they know what they intend.' She smiled. 'But that will change. The Duma's had its chance. See where you've brought us to?'

She was right, but it wasn't too late. And Milyukov had been right too: there had to be order. I couldn't see how the tsar could survive for long now, but there would be a struggle for power once he fell. For my part I knew I'd prefer it to be the Duma rather than this Soviet that was in the ascendant. The Soviet had been elected by the workers, and the workers wanted revenge.

I turned away from Yelena and began to push my way against the tide, trying to make it back to the Convention Hall. I heard her voice shouting behind me, crowing. 'Your friend Kerensky knows which way the wind is blowing. He's joined them.'

I didn't bother to find out more. It took me a full ten minutes to get back to the Convention Hall. The place was in uproar. I found Milyukov again. 'You've heard what's happening?' I asked him.

He nodded. 'We have to act, or we could lose power to them.'

'What are you going to do?'

'We can't waste time discussing things in full assembly,' he said. 'We've formed a group. We're calling it the Interim Committee.'

I looked at him quizzically.

'The Interim Committee of Members of the State Duma to Restore Order and Relations with Individuals and Institutions. We're taking charge. Rodzianko's the chairman, but Lvov's on board, and Nekrasov and Kerensky.'

Any amusement I might have experienced at the preposterously longwinded title vanished with the mention of that last name. 'Kerensky? I just heard he joined the Soviet.'

'I know. He says he's acting as a vital conduit between the two bodies. But I'm more concerned about you, Mihail Konstantinovich. I've been asked to see if you'll join the Interim Committee.'

I thought about it for a moment, then shook my head. It struck me too much as a grab for power. On the one hand I could see the necessity in present circumstances, but I found it hard to envisage them returning control to the full Duma when things got better. Admittedly Prince Lvov was a member, and I trusted him unquestioningly, but Kerensky was an opportunist, as today's events had shown. And Milyukov himself had changed his position too often over the years for my liking. 'That's best left for men like you,' I told him, hoping he would take it as a compliment.

'Will you at least join the delegation then?'

'Delegation?'

'His Majesty may not be here to take charge, but his brother Grand Duke Mihail Aleksandrovich is. We're going to ask him to become temporary dictator – of the capital, not the country, but it amounts to the same thing.'

'How temporary?'

'Long enough to calm things down, so that *we* can come to a decision without fear of being lynched in the streets.'

'Why should the people obey the grand duke?' I asked.

'The army might. Mihail's seen real action – got medals to prove it. He stands a better chance than we do. And you're an old soldier – you might help convince him of that.'

This time I agreed. It sounded like the best hope of bringing stability to the city that I'd heard in several days. 'All right, I'll go with them. Where are we meeting him? Isn't he still in Gatchina?'

Milyukov shook his head, then slowed the movement to a furtive glance around him to ensure he would not be overheard. He lowered his voice. 'His Imperial Highness arrived at the Warsaw Station at six o'clock this evening. You are to meet him at the Mariinskiy Palace as soon as possible. There's a car waiting for you.'

'Who else is coming?'

'Rodzianko – a few others.' He laughed. 'Whoever makes it to the car before it sets off.'

I took the hint and headed outside. The corridors had quietened down, but I was unprepared for the sight that faced me at the front of the palace. There must have been five thousand there. It was then that I began to understand – and to fear – just how powerful this Soviet might be. There had never been such crowds when the Duma had been sitting. Our own guards were trying to hold them back, but were vastly outnumbered. So far things seemed good-humoured. I pushed my way through to the car. Rodzianko was standing up, looking for me. He shook my hand then pushed me inside. We set off.

The route we took was not the most direct, but the driver clearly had some idea of where the trouble spots were, or where they had been when he'd last come this way; the crowds were in constant turmoil. We went down to Znamenskaya Square where the car turned. I caught a brief glimpse of the hippopotamus and then we were driving up Nevsky Prospekt. We couldn't move quickly. There were two cars in front of us, and they themselves were slowed down by the crowds that slowly parted to make way. On the corner of Liteiny Prospekt I saw a lorry that had crashed into a lamp post, bending it to 45 degrees. It could only have happened minutes before. The driver was still inside, turned round and kneeling on his seat to remonstrate with the dozen or so men loaded into the trailer behind him. He was obviously drunk. It wasn't the only such accident I saw in the city. Inexperienced drivers enjoying the generous amounts of alcohol that had been liberated from shops and private cellars meant that collisions were inevitable.

At the Anichkov Bridge there was a heavy guard, but Rodzianko showed them his papers and we were allowed through. From there on things got worse. The strikers and protestors who'd made it through the cordon and into the city centre were inevitably the most determined and therefore the most radical. And now they were trapped, with no way to get out again. Groups of them hurled stones and ice and flaming bottles at the patrolling soldiers. Near the Kazan Cathedral I heard the sound of a rifle firing. A man in the crowd, both arms raised above his head ready to hurl a paving slab into a mounted brigade, fell as the bullet hit him.

I looked around, but could not see who had fired. Another shot rang out. This time I managed to follow the sound. It came from the top of the building opposite. There were snipers up there. The crowd scattered and our driver accelerated along the street. I looked back behind us. More shots were coming down from the offices. Those in the crowd who had guns fired back, but there would be no clear target for them.

As we approached the end of Nevsky Prospekt the car slowed to a halt. I looked out to see what the problem was, and found myself gazing straight down the barrel of not one but about a dozen machine guns. They were obviously intended to defend the Winter Palace and the Admiralty, but they did more than that. Nevsky Prospekt was the widest and busiest street in Petrograd. If the crowds decided to march down there, there'd be room for tens of thousands of them. And that machine gun nest had a clear view, all the way down. It could end the revolution with a single, bloody, brutal act. That was if the soldiers behind those guns were prepared to fire, but I doubted their superiors would have chosen anyone they didn't trust for that particular duty.

We turned down Gogolya Street, but there were still crowds slowing our pace. At last the familiar bulk of Saint Isaac's emerged from behind the buildings and we turned back across the Moika to pull up outside the Mariinskiy Palace. There were crowds here too, and soldiers, though more of the latter and fewer of the former than there had been at the Duma. The car quickly became engulfed by the mob, eager to discover who we were and what we were doing here. I made the mistake of getting out on the side away from the palace entrance. The others were wiser, but even so the guards had to drive a wedge into the people with the butts of their guns to allow a passage through.

Then I heard shots. I don't know who fired first, but there was soon a gun battle going on. The crowd scattered, most to get away from danger, but some to find a better vantage point to fire from. I was carried with them, over to the Moika embankment. I looked back to see Rodzianko and the others make it safely into the building, though whether they would be safe inside, I couldn't tell. I could have tried to join them, but my heart had never really been in the mission. From the moment I'd heard the location I'd had an ulterior motive not too far from the front of my mind. I needed to get into the centre of the city – to Senate Square. What better way to get past the sentry posts than as part of an official government delegation? I looked at my watch. It was after nine already. I didn't have much further to go.

The shooting had subsided now, and people were beginning to come out of hiding, most of them again bravely gathering outside the palace. I went in the opposite direction, across Saint Isaac's Square and towards the cathedral. I passed the statue of Nikolai I on horseback, but scarcely bothered to look up at it. I rounded the cathedral to the west then crossed Senate Square. Now that I was out of the car I was able to notice the smell in the air – the mixture of smells. It was repellent; a blend of every human excretion. Piss, vomit and shit – they were all there. The people had turned Petrograd into a giant cess pit. And underneath it all was the scent of the thing which helped to cause all the others: the scent of alcohol.

I arrived at the statue of Peter the Great – the Bronze Horseman, as Pushkin had christened it. It completed the trio of mounted tsars that, according to some, guarded Petrograd from its enemies. Pyotr here, Nikolai I in Saint Isaac's Square and Aleksandr III in Znamenskaya Square. But they were too busy looking outwards – for foreign invaders – to have observed where the threat would really come from.

'It's quieter than I was expecting.'

I turned. It was Dmitry. Ilya was at his side, along with another of them. I looked around. The square wasn't as busy as elsewhere in the city. But it was hardly abandoned. There were a couple of fires lit between us and the cathedral, where people were warming themselves, and along the quay there was traffic in both directions.

'What *were* you expecting?' I asked.

He walked towards me. The other two remained where they were. 'I thought people might make a stand here; out of . . . nostalgia.'

'This isn't the same as 1825,' I said. 'Don't be fooled into thinking it is.'

'The tsar's army is shooting his own people. That's the same as before.'

I couldn't argue with him. 'What can you do to help?'

'You tell me. That was the plan, I thought.'

I considered what I'd seen. There was the machine gun nest on Palace Square, but in truth it wasn't doing much harm. The very sight of it kept people at bay, and so there was no need for it ever to fire. There was another threat, though, which had actually killed people, and which a vampire might be very well suited to deal with.

'They've posted snipers,' I told him. 'I saw some on Nevsky Prospekt, on top of the Singer Sewing Machines offices, but I'll bet there're others elsewhere. They're impossible to deal with from street level.'

'Let's go then.' He seemed keen.

We walked back pretty much the way I had come in the car. Ilya and the other *voordalak* hung back, following a few paces behind. In my life, I had not encountered more than a handful of the creatures, and all of them had been of reasonable intelligence. But these two fitted better with the descriptions I had heard – albeit at third hand – of those original twelve *oprichniki* that my grandfather had first encountered. They were base and surly, scarcely more than animals. With the *oprichniki* I understood the reason for it. They had exchanged blood repeatedly with Zmyeevich and their free will had been consumed by him. But Dmitry insisted that he was not doing the same with these, and I was convinced that the idea revolted him. Perhaps these two were witless simply because they had been witless in life – and yet that did not describe the Ilya I'd known. Either way it didn't sit well with the idea that they shared Dmitry's higher goals. They were here simply to feed.

We kept away from the machine guns in Palace Square and soon found ourselves in the colonnade of the Kazan Cathedral. We weren't the only ones there: a crowd of several hundred sat in fear. A few aimed rifles, but did not bother to fire. Beyond, Nevsky Prospekt was empty. I could guess the reason, but I asked one of the armed men. By his uniform he was a boatswain.

'Snipers,' he said. 'Up on the roof. They've got us pinned down.'

'How many?' asked Dmitry.

'Four maybe. Hard to say.'

Dmitry smiled at me. 'I was hoping for more,' he said.

He gestured to Ilya and his comrade, indicating that the three of them should separate. They went in opposite directions, staying in the shadows of the cathedral's two curved arms. When they were almost at the street Dmitry began to move. He took a more direct route, across the square and out to the roadway. The other two shadowed him and all three arrived on Nevsky Prospekt at the same time. There were shouts from the crowd calling them fools, but nobody made a move to stop them.

The snipers above must have been at a loss as to what they were doing, and held their fire. But when Dmitry was about halfway across a shot rang out, followed by another. Dmitry turned back towards us, his arms spread as if to make a bigger target, and shouted. 'Missed!'

That may have been true of the first bullet, but with the second I'd noticed the slight judder of his body as he absorbed its momentum, and the little puff of dust and fibre at his shoulder where it had entered. Another shot was fired and all three of them ran towards the building, more for show than out of any real fear. The other two went down the streets on either side, but Dmitry chose a frontal assault.

The building wasn't a difficult one to climb – decorative ridges in the stonework made for convenient hand- and footholds – but Dmitry's ascent was far swifter than any human could have managed. He held his body close to the wall, and moved upwards like a lizard on a rock. I could only assume his two comrades were making a similar assault at the sides of the building. Now the shouts from the crowd were of encouragement, not warning. At last one of the snipers realized what was happening and came forward to shoot straight down at Dmitry, but a hail of bullets from our own gunmen forced him to step back.

Soon Dmitry reached the top of the wall and disappeared over on to the roof. Then nothing, for about two minutes, save for occasional sounds that might be taken for a scuffle. At last a body fell. It hit the ground half on the pavement and half on the road, bouncing very slightly before lying still. As one the crowd rushed forward. Within seconds they were upon the corpse, kicking at it and pummelling it with the butts of rifles and whatever else came to hand. If it bore any of the tell-tale signs of a vampire's bite, they would be lost amid the deluge. But there were, at the sailor's guess, another three snipers up there, along with three hungry vampires. I didn't suppose the remaining bodies would be thrown down for quite some time.

I headed home. Dmitry had done well. How many had those snipers already killed, and how many more would they have killed if they hadn't been stopped? Compared with the losses in the war, it was nothing. And even though it was my own countrymen who had died here, this too was a war: a war for the freedom of a nation. Even so, I'd have preferred them to have died from a bullet wound than from . . . that.

I took a fairly direct route, sticking to the side streets and staying close to the cover of buildings, but there was no more trouble. The only guard post I had to get through was on the Fontanka, just opposite my house. I showed them my papers and they let me through. They were trying to keep people out of the city centre, not in it, and when they saw how close my address was, they accepted I had reason to be there.

I put my head round the kitchen door when I got in. Syeva was at the sink, washing some clothes, leaning forwards oddly to keep some of the weight off his bad leg. Polkan was asleep on a rug near by. It was odd of him to be down here and not at his mistress's side.

'Evening, sergeant,' I said.

He turned to me. 'Good evening, colonel. Would you like your supper now?'

'When you're ready.'

I went upstairs. In the excitement of the day, I'd forgotten the more domestic issue that I had to face – the fact that Nadya had taken in a lodger. There was no light from that room on the first floor tonight. I carried on up. In the living room there was a roaring fire. Nadya wasn't sitting in her usual seat, but instead was facing the door. I could tell she was not alone. Over the back of the other seat I could just see the top of a head – a wisp of blonde hair.

Nadya looked up as I entered. 'Misha . . .'

'It's all right,' I replied, 'I worked it out. We've got plenty of room; we shouldn't keep it to ourselves.'

She smiled at me and I suspected that she was not merely pleased with my acquiescence, but happy to have manipulated me so effectively in getting her way. 'In that case I'd like you to meet Anastasia.' She stood and held out her hand towards the other chair.

I walked across the room as the figure in the chair began to stand too. It was a girl, young – fifteen at most. Her blonde hair shone in the dim light. It had been washed since I last saw her, as had her face. Even so, there was no mistaking her.

It was the girl I'd seen in the courtyard, selling her body to Ilya.

CHAPTER VI

'HOW DO YOU DO, ANASTASIA?' I SAID.

'How do you do, sir?'

I looked in her eyes for any hint that she recognized me, but saw none. That meant little. She couldn't have seen my face for more than a moment, and if she had, she might want to do everything to conceal the fact of where and how we had met – not least from Nadya.

'Where did you find her?' I asked Nadya. I realized after I'd spoken how rude it was of me not to ask the girl herself, but it was too late.

'Just round the corner,' Nadya replied, 'on Gagarinskaya Street.'

'Have you no family?' I asked Anastasia herself this time.

She shook her head. 'Papa went to fight the Germans, and then Mama died.' Her simplistic way of speaking didn't sit well with her age, or the obvious intelligence of her face. She was putting it on to rouse sympathy – but that didn't mean what she said wasn't true.

Any questions I chose to ask were only surrogates for the one foremost in my mind. Why was she here, and not lying dead beneath a blanket of snow as a result of her encounter with Ilya? Her name seemed entirely appropriate: Anastasia – it meant resurrection. One obvious answer could easily be dismissed. I knew from various sources, not least from Iuda's notebooks, that the process of transformation from human into *voordalak* was not one of minutes or even hours. After the necessary exchange of blood in both directions, death would still come to the victim. Many of them would be buried, as would any corpse, and only weeks later claw their way out of their grave. There had not been sufficient time for Anastasia to have been transformed. Somehow, she had survived.

'Colonel?' Syeva's voice interrupted my thoughts. I looked to see what he wanted, but rather than standing at the door, he walked across the room before speaking to me. He seemed to be attempting to conceal his limp, which only made his gait more unusual than ever. I wondered if he had something confidential to say to me, but once he was close his announcement was mundane.

'Your supper's ready, colonel.' After he had spoken he turned away from me, and I realized why he was behaving so strangely. His eyes were fixed upon Anastasia – she hadn't been visible from where he was at the door. It was understandable. She was a pretty girl. All the same, I felt a sudden urge to be protective of him. If he'd been my son, she wasn't the kind of girl I'd like him to know.

'I'm going to bed,' said Nadya. 'We've already eaten. Anastasia, I'll walk you downstairs.'

'I can do that,' said Syeva quickly.

'I know the way, thank you,' snapped Anastasia. She calmed instantly. 'Please, I don't want to be any bother.'

She walked to the door. Syeva quickly limped over to hold it for her, even though it was already open. At the threshold she turned. 'Thank you both for letting me stay. I'll find somewhere of my own soon, I promise.'

She left. Syeva hovered. He was going in the same direction, but he'd been told not to accompany her, and so he had to leave a respectable gap between them. He didn't wait long. By my estimation – and, I presumed, his – he would be close enough to be able to watch her as she descended the stairs.

Nadya headed for the door too. 'I won't be long,' I said.

I went to the dining room and ate what Syeva had put out for me: more black bread and a bowl of thin broth. It didn't take me long. I went downstairs and tapped on Anastasia's door. I heard the sound of the lock turning, and then her face appeared.

'Can I have a word?'

'Of course.'

She stepped back, opening the door. I went inside. The room

was much as I remembered it. There was an iron bedstead, which had been made up. A chair and a table had been brought from somewhere else in the house. Anastasia had already changed into her nightdress. She sat down on the bed. I'd have felt more comfortable if she'd chosen the chair.

'Madame Primakova said you'd be happy for me to stay here, Colonel Danilov.' I wondered if she had deliberately chosen to emphasize the mismatch between our surnames; to remind me that I could not take the moral high ground.

'And she was absolutely right. I'm quite happy about it. But there was one thing I wanted to ask you.'

'Yes?'

She looked up at me with innocent eyes. I tried to think of a way to broach the subject. 'Don't you recognize me? From Saturday night?'

Her gaze fell to the floor. 'I hoped you hadn't remembered me. Please . . . don't tell Madame Primakova.'

'I won't – of course I won't. What's important is that you're safe. But I need to know what happened.'

'What happened?' She seemed to have no idea what I was talking about.

'After I . . . left.'

Her face flushed a deep crimson. 'You want me to tell you what he—?'

'No. No. God, no.' I felt my own face match the colour of hers. 'I just mean: how did you escape?'

'Escape? I didn't need to escape. I let him do what he'd paid for, then he did up his trousers and went on his way.'

It was unpleasant language to hear from a girl of her age, but understandably she was trying to terminate the conversation. She'd realized that the more she managed to embarrass me, the sooner that end would come.

'He didn't try to hurt you?'

'What? You mean with the knife? That was just playing. Some of them like that. Anyway, if he'd gone too far, it wouldn't be me that got hurt.'

I scarcely noticed her move her hand, but an instant later she was holding a switchblade, open and pointed towards me.

The time it had taken her to reach under her pillow and fetch it couldn't have been much longer than it took for the spring to extend the blade to its full length. Clearly she knew how to defend herself, but such a weapon would be no use against a *voordalak*. She'd undoubtedly had a very lucky escape that night.

I didn't press the issue any further. 'Just remember,' I said. 'You never have to go on to the streets and do that again.'

'I know,' she said. 'I have a place here now. Thank you.'

I was halfway back up the stairs before I realized the double meaning of what she'd said. She couldn't have been serious, but if she'd meant it as a joke then it demonstrated that she had extremely quick wits, and extremely poor taste.

I quietly got into bed beside Nadya. I could tell she was awake, but I waited for her to speak first.

'You don't mind her staying, do you?' she asked.

'You could hardly leave her out there, could you – even at the best of times?'

She cuddled me. 'I knew that's what you'd say.'

'But it's still food that'll be a problem. Two more mouths to feed.'

'Two?'

I pinched her on the arm. 'Don't play dumb.'

'You noticed then?'

'It's not obvious, but it's showing. How far gone do you think she is?'

'Three or four months, I suppose. She's so young, it's hard to tell.'

I could only wonder what we'd let ourselves in for.

The following day I went to the Tavricheskiy Palace again. If anything the crowds outside had grown, but they seemed harmless, at least for the time being. We were not the enemy and the people who gathered here did so more in the hope of being the first to hear any good news than with the intent of forcing their will upon those inside.

But what now might I mean by 'those inside'? For eleven years the palace had been the home of successive Dumas – ours was the fourth to be elected in that time. All of them had proved utterly ineffectual in guiding the nation. And now at this turning point in history, when we had the opportunity to wield at last the power that the people had given us, we had a rival: the Soviet. In a sense it had a greater authority than we did: it had been elected by the people who were making the revolution, the workers and soldiers of Petrograd. But that was just the point. The job of a government wasn't merely to do right by those who elected it, it was to do the best for everybody. I wasn't convinced that the members of the Soviet would appreciate the point. I wasn't sure all the members of the Duma did either.

I elbowed my way through to the building without too much trouble. On a table in the hallway was a pile of newspapers, a title I'd not seen before:

ИЗВѢСТІЯ

Izvestia. That one word – 'The News' – boldly summarized a more longwinded title: *The News of the Petrograd Soviet of Workers' Deputies*. They'd got to work quickly, but they had dozens of secret presses all over the city. Nikolai tried to have them closed, but others popped up just as rapidly. I glanced through it. It had reports of what was going on across Petrograd. There was plenty that I hadn't heard, but nothing that surprised me. It made little attempt at neutrality, and why should it? It rejoiced at every victory by the people and denounced every act of oppression by the authorities. There was nothing there that I could disagree with. It called the Duma 'feeble', and even with that I could find little fault. The tone was distinctly Menshevik, but that was to be expected, given the make-up of the Soviet. The Bolsheviks had had their own paper for a while. They'd called it *Pravda* – 'The Truth'. Both factions opted for a title that delivered the same simple certainty to readers. Why should there be any need for doubt that what they were reading was the truth? *Pravda* had been banned even before the war started. I doubted it would take long to re-emerge.

The Convention Hall was chaotic. There were various groups engaged in their own debates, but there was no order to it as there should have been at a time like this. I saw Rodzianko, sitting at the focus of the room in his formal position as chairman. He was alone and silent, gazing glumly into the hall, but seeing nothing. I went over.

'Mihail Vladimirovich,' I said.

He turned to me, but took a moment to take me in. When he did, his face suddenly broke into a smile.

'Mihail Konstantinovich. Thank God you're safe. What happened to you?'

'After the shooting started I got separated from the rest of you. I couldn't get back across the square.' I didn't need to mention that I'd had better things to do. 'What did His Imperial Highness have to say?'

Rodzianko's face returned to its former despondency. 'The Grand Duke won't do anything without consulting his brother. We talked for a while, then he went to General Belyayev's house to try to contact the tsar.'

'There's a telephone line to him?'

Rodzianko shook his head. 'A Hughes Telegraph.'

'And what did His Majesty say?'

'He said to carry on as if everything were normal, or something that amounted to that. Grand Duke Mihail thinks he'll be in a better position to act once he reaches Tsarskoye Selo, but it'll be too late by then. He's as good as lost his capital already.'

'It's as bad as that?'

'There's a few areas that are still putting up a fight against the mob.' He gave a harsh laugh. 'Areas! That's a nice way to put it. A few buildings, if I'm honest. The Winter Palace and the Admiralty, of course. And the General Staff building. Oh, and the Astoria Hotel. No one who can afford to stay there's going to be happy to see the Romanovs fall.'

I don't know whether Rodzianko had been conscious of it, but it was a grave admission. He wasn't just worried about Nikolai losing power – now it was the whole dynasty.

'So what are you going to do?' I asked.

'I've sent my own message to His Majesty. I'm waiting for a reply, but it's hopeless. And the worst of it is, it won't be us who take over. It'll be them.'

I understood perfectly what he meant, but to emphasize the

point he jerked his head in the direction of the other wing of the palace, towards the Soviet.

I spent most of the day in the Tavricheskiy Palace, wandering between the city's two centres of power. The Executive Committee of the Soviet sat in the left wing of the palace; the Interim Committee of the State Duma remained in the right wing. It was probably a good reflection of their politics. The use of 'left' and 'right' dated back to that other revolution – the one in France. Ours seemed a very different affair: a distant echo of the French Revolution, a ripple that had taken more than a century to cross Europe, but the path was clear. The French Revolution, Bonaparte, the Decembrists, our humiliation in the Crimea, Aleksandr II's reforms and assassination, and now this. There were other steps in between, and at every stage Russia – not just the tsars, the people too – had ignored the opportunity to take a different path.

The discussions of both these committees, from what little I could gather, were on the question of restoring order. In truth, only the Soviet had the ability to do so. The Interim Committee issued an order for soldiers to return to their barracks, but it was ignored. The men out in the streets were afraid they'd be punished for mutiny, and besides, they had no trust in the Duma. They'd created the Soviet and now they looked to it for leadership. But it wasn't in the interests of the Soviet to have peace and calm return to the city – not yet. If that happened while the tsar was still in charge, even nominally, then what would have been achieved? Nikolai must have known he had lost, but by clinging on to power he was simply prolonging the turmoil. Even that did him better justice than he deserved. The idea of him clinging on to power gave the impression of some activity. Burying his head in the sand was a more apt image.

Outside the palace the mood of the crowd was still peaceful, but I didn't want to bet on it staying that way. I went home early, before darkness fell. The streets seemed calmer now, though they still teemed with people. Thankfully no one was firing on them at the moment. It was as Rodzianko had said: there were just a few pockets of resistance remaining, and none of them was in this part of the city. I wondered how much of it could be put down to Dmitry and his comrades. They'd been eminently effective against the snipers, but now that the streets were silent I feared for where their attentions might turn.

The door of the house was locked. I was glad of that. I imagined Nadya and Syeva safely within, with Polkan faithfully at their side. For a moment I forgot our new houseguest, but even before I'd opened the door I realized that Anastasia would be there with them too. As I turned the key I heard noises on the other side of the door which I presumed to be Syeva rushing to unlock it from the inside and save me the trouble. But I didn't feel him pulling at the door in response to my push. When it was open, the hall was empty. The sound I'd heard had been Polkan's claws scrabbling against the wood of the stairs as he came down to greet me.

'All alone?' I asked him.

He stood his ground a few feet from me, his tail swishing from side to side. I went over to the kitchen and he followed. I looked inside, expecting to see Syeva, most likely asleep, but the room was empty. I went back out to the hall.

'Anyone home?' I shouted. There was no response. I tried not to be concerned. Both Nadya and Syeva had reason enough to be out, and as I'd seen for myself, the streets were safer than they had been for days. I cared less for where Anastasia was, though I'd feel happier, for our sakes rather than for hers, if she was not alone in our house. Perhaps Nadya had taken her to help at the kitchen.

I went upstairs, Polkan running ahead of me as ever. I looked into the living room and confirmed that there was no one about, then went to the bedroom and sat on the bed to take off my boots. I put on some slippers and then wondered what to do with myself. I wasn't used to being home alone. Even to do nothing other than sit quietly, if Nadya was there, felt like a good use of my time. The best thing that I could do was to wait.

I stood up and it was then that I noticed it. It was on the dressing table, left as though for me to find. I walked over and gazed down at it.

It was unmistakably Nadya. Her face stared directly out at me from the paper, smiling in that way she managed to do without actually needing to raise the ends of her lips. It was a simple drawing, charcoal on paper, but I could only be impressed at the skill of execution. She was reclining on a settee, probably the one in our living room, though little attention had been paid to its details. Nadya was the entire focus of the work. She was naked, her arms raised behind her head, pulling her breasts into more shapely mounds than those in which gravity attempted to make them lie. She looked beautiful, but there was no attempt at false flattery. Her belly sagged a little, revealing that hunger had not affected us as much as it had many in the city. The hair under her arms and between her legs was wild and unkempt. This was quite unlike the classical nudes of the Hermitage. There was nothing in it that I hadn't seen before, nothing that Nadya wouldn't willingly show me were I to ask, and yet seeing it here, through the eyes of another, recorded in permanence, added a certain excitement.

And I was in no doubt it was through the eyes of another; it was no self-portrait. Nadya was fascinated by art and had often tried drawing for herself, but was the first to admit that she had little talent. There was always the possibility that whoever had drawn it had not been working from life and had, beyond Nadya's face, been using their imagination, but too many details were accurate for that to be the case. I knew every inch of her – every blemish and birthmark – and it was all here. There was no signature, but there were not many candidates for who could have drawn it. Syeva was an impossibility – his hands would have shaken too much. And that left only one other. Clearly Nadya was not ashamed of it; as far as I could tell, she had left it out for me to discover.

And yet as I looked down at the undoubtedly beautiful drawing, a sense of familiarity came to my mind. Obviously I recognized Nadya, but there was more to it than that. Perhaps it was the expression on her face or even the style of the drawing itself that reminded me of something or someone I had seen before. It wasn't unlikely. I'd known other members of Nadya's family; perhaps there was some trait that they shared, that I'd noticed here for the first time.

But there was another, more sinister possibility. Not all of my memories were my own. I had shared Zmyeevich's mind, if only for a few years, until he died. Might I be recalling something I had seen through his eyes, or even something that he had witnessed years before, which had infiltrated my memory? It wasn't a pleasant idea at the best of times. Now I had to worry about why on earth the image of the woman I loved should feature in the memories of a monster such as that.

'What do you think?'

I turned. Nadya stood at the door. She looked quite, quite different from the picture I held in my hand. The only flesh visible was her face, and moments later her hands as she removed her gloves. Every other inch of her was covered to protect her from the cold outside. Her cheeks and the tip of her nose glowed in the sudden warmth of being indoors.

'It's beautiful,' I said. 'Anastasia's work, I take it?'

Nadya nodded. 'She's talented, isn't she?'

I put the drawing down and went over to kiss Nadya. I felt her arms squeeze me around the waist. 'Inspired, I would say.'

She giggled and slapped me on the shoulder.

'How ever did she persuade you?' I asked, stepping away.

Nadya sucked her lower lip and then smiled. 'You know, I'm not really sure. She started out just doing a portrait. Look.' She went over to the dressing table and opened a drawer to take out a similar sketch, but this time only of her face.

'But this isn't the one you left out for me?'

She gave me a look of condescension. 'Did I make the wrong choice?'

I shook my head, then sat down on the bed, indicating she should join me. She frowned, sensing I had something important to tell her. I was going back on what I'd said to Anastasia, but Nadya deserved to know the truth.

'I saw Anastasia,' I said. 'A few days ago. Before you took her in.'

'Really, where?' Nadya was trying and failing to sound casual.

'Near the Yekaterininsky Canal. In a courtyard. In a doorway. She was . . . working.'

'Working?'

If I'd been talking to a man I would have had no qualms about being direct. 'She's the girl I told you about. They don't carry yellow tickets any more.'

'Oh!' she said quietly, understanding. She looked down at the floor, lifting her toes up in the air as if she were inspecting them. 'Well, I suppose the city's never been short of moths – more so now.'

I hid a smile at her use of the euphemism. I didn't know who had coined it, but you only had to notice the way they gathered around streetlights to see the connection.

'It explains the baby, I suppose,' she continued. Then she brightened. 'All the more reason that we should have taken her in, though, wouldn't you say? To keep her safe from all that.'

I nodded. Nadya was probably right, though I suspected she might have felt very differently if I'd told her precisely who I'd seen Anastasia with.

I went out again to meet up with Dmitry, at the same time and in the same place as the previous night. This time he had come alone.

'Just you?' I asked.

'Looks like it.'

'So now you trust me enough to come along without anyone to protect you?'

He laughed, genuinely. 'You think I'm afraid of you?'

'Just a joke,' I acknowledged.

'I'd have thought you had better reason to be afraid of me.' He paused for a moment in thought. 'And yet you don't seem to be.'

'I'm a good enough judge of character to know you wouldn't harm me – not out of simple hunger, anyway. I've known that for years.'

He raised an eyebrow. 'Perhaps I've just never been that hungry.'

I ignored the barb. 'So where are the others?'

He shrugged. 'Somewhere in the city – or still in their graves. I'll find them when I need them.'

'I thought you were in charge.'

'Not always. That's why we'll have to leave the city as soon as this is over.'

'And feast on peasants instead?'

114

'We have to sustain ourselves. But in a city, with so many people, there's a temptation to do more than that.'

'Only a temptation?'

'I lived in New York. I managed to resist, mostly.'

I knew there was little point in trying to judge him by human standards. I changed the subject. 'You did good work with those snipers last night.'

He smiled wistfully. 'It felt right – the climb before the kill. Natural.'

'It's quieter tonight. Nothing much for you to do.'

He looked at me gravely. 'Men will die tonight, whatever you tell us. Their throats will be ripped open and their bodies drained of blood. I may abstain, but I can't stop the others – not all of them. It will ease your conscience to know that those who died were our enemies, rather than chosen at random.'

It wasn't really a threat – more a simple statement of fact. But he was right; these creatures were not a weapon one could easily lay aside when it was unneeded.

'You know the Astoria?' I asked. 'The hotel?'

He nodded curtly.

'There's still a few holding out there.' I felt like Judas, but just like Judas I believed what I was doing was right. I didn't mention the other buildings that were still showing resistance. They were essentially military establishments, obeying orders from those above them. Once the officers changed sides, so would the men.

Dmitry emitted a brief laugh. 'You remind me of my Uncle Dmitry.'

'*Your* Uncle Dmitry?' He was my uncle, but I'd never been aware that he himself had an uncle of the same name.

'Not technically an uncle, but I called him that. Dmitry Fetyukovich Petrenko – one of Papa's comrades in the Patriotic War.'

'And how am I like him?' From what I'd heard of Dmitry Fetyukovich I didn't think I was going to like the comparison.

'Didn't you know? It was he who invited the *oprichniki* to Moscow, fully aware of what they were, having seen them in all their dreadful glory when he served in Wallachia. He just thought of them as a weapon; like a cannon – you point it at the enemy

115

and fire. And if the weapon is slightly more distasteful than a cannon, what difference does that make?' He spoke as though he were merely thinking out loud, quite unaware of how his words turned the knife in me. 'How do you feel about gas attacks at the Front? What do they call it . . . vomiting gas – chloropicrin – like Brusilov used at Lutsk?'

I didn't have to think. I'd long ago come to a conclusion on that. 'They're a necessary tool if we're to win the war.' I heard the words on my own tongue and understood how easy it was for him to compare me to Dmitry Fetyukovich.

'But a dirty, underhand trick when the Boche use them, I suppose?'

I wasn't going to be so parochial. 'They have their war to win,' I replied.

'And you have yours. Or in fact you have two. The one against Germany and the one here in Petrograd. And in neither does the choice of weapon matter, as long as you win.'

He was right, and so was I. He understood my motivation perfectly, but I knew my reasoning was valid, and would lead to the greater good.

'I'll see you tomorrow,' I said, then turned and left. I heard Dmitry's voice call after me.

'Remember what happened at Loos.'

I ignored him and headed home.

The journey didn't take long. I circled south to avoid any fighting, and to avoid seeing any of what Dmitry might achieve at my behest. I understood perfectly well what he had meant. In 1915 at the Battle of Loos the British had used their own gas of choice – chlorine – for the first time. But the wind had been blowing the wrong way and the gas had drifted back to the British trenches, choking and killing soldiers of the side that had launched it. It was the same with Dmitry and his comrades, just as it had been with the *oprichniki* a century before. It was just a matter of when the wind would change, of anticipating it and knowing that then would be the time to act.

The only question was, why was Dmitry telling me this, telling me what he was eventually bound to do? Chlorine gas didn't turn to the British generals and warn them of its own fickle nature.

At home there was no sign of Syeva, but it was late and he'd most likely gone to bed. I went upstairs. Polkan poked his head out of the door of the living room as I approached, then turned back inside. Nadya stood as I entered. As if caught in the act of something. I could see that she had been crying. On the table beside her chair there was a pile of torn-up paper. On one of the fragments I could make out three toes, drawn in charcoal, and I realized it was Anastasia's sketch of her.

'What's wrong?' I asked.

She tried to speak, but couldn't. Instead she threw herself against my chest and sobbed silently. I held her tight and said nothing, waiting until she was ready to speak.

'I saw her,' she said at last, not moving from my embrace.

'Anastasia?' It seemed like a reasonable guess.

I felt her head move against me as she nodded.

'Where?' Perhaps 'doing what' would have been a more apposite question.

'After you left. I was standing at the window, looking to see if Syeva was coming back.'

'Is he still not home?'

'I haven't seen him all day, but that's not important. I saw a man leaving the house – a soldier.'

The sudden fear gripped me that it might have been Ilya again. 'Who? Did you recognize him?'

'That hardly matters, does it? I came out and looked over the banister. Anastasia was just coming back up from the front door. *She'd* let him out.'

I could guess the implication, but it was by no means cut and dried. 'It could just have been . . .' I searched for a sensible possibility but could find nothing that didn't sound inadequate, '. . . a friend of hers.'

She laughed caustically.

'So what shall we do?' I asked. 'We can't throw her back out on the street.'

'We should talk to her. Both of us. Now.'

I thought for a moment, but no better ideas occurred to me. I held the door for her, letting her lead the way in the hope that she would take the lead again when it came to speaking to Anastasia. We went down the stairs to the first floor, where we could see a light shining under Anastasia's door. Nadya knocked softly.

There was no response. She tapped her knuckles against the wood once again, harder this time, but with the same lack of reply. I banged against it with the base of my fist, producing a loud booming that would have awoken anyone inside.

'Anastasia!' I didn't shout, but the sound was just as loud. Years of addressing the Duma had taught me how to make myself heard. But still nothing came from within.

Nadya turned the handle. The door was not locked. She pushed it open, but stopped after only an inch. She turned to me. 'Let me go first. She may not be decent.'

I took a step back and Nadya went inside. After only a few seconds she called out calmly, 'Misha!'

A sudden feeling of dread filled me and I strode across the landing to go into the room. As soon as I entered I saw that my fears were quite unfounded. Anastasia's bedroom was empty.

CHAPTER VII

WE CHECKED HER ROOM AGAIN THE FOLLOWING MORNING and found it was still unoccupied. But she had certainly been there – or someone had. Where the bed had been neatly made the previous evening, now it was rumpled. Whether she had slept there alone or with company I did not know. I didn't mention the possibility to Nadya, but I couldn't doubt she would have thought of the idea herself.

More concerning was the continued absence of Syeva. It had been two nights now since either of us had seen him.

'Perhaps they're together,' suggested Nadya.

'Eloped, you mean?'

'Something like that.'

'They've only known each other a few days.'

Her eye glinted at me and I recalled just how rapidly our first acquaintance had descended into the consummation of a passion that neither of us had suspected could be roused so quickly – and we'd been adults. Syeva and Anastasia were still children, however much they might have seen of the world in their brief lives. But while Syeva's attraction to the girl had been unmistakable, I couldn't see why he would leave us without a word.

'Did she show any interest in him?' I asked.

Nadya shook her head. 'Not that I noticed. But she'd have tried to hide it from us, wouldn't she?'

It was possible, but I had a darker explanation, which I kept from Nadya. The streets out there were dangerous. I didn't know how many had been killed at the hands of government forces, or even by the protestors, but there was little chance that families or employers would be notified of a death. And there was another way that people were dying out there. A boy like Syeva was no military target, but I didn't expect all Dmitry's comrades to be as assiduous as he claimed to be.

There was nothing to be done but wait and hope that either or both of them returned. I went to the Duma again. As I walked through the streets I sensed an air of stalemate. There were even more people out there now than there had been over the previous days, but on the other hand there was very little for them to do. Whatever complaints they might have, who were they supposed to address them to? No one was there to represent the tsar. There were no more loyal forces to stand in the way of the protestors – not that I saw on my short journey to the Tavricheskiy Palace – and so no one to become the object of their anger. I could only count it to the good. The more peaceful this revolution, the better its chance of producing a stable government in its wake. And on a more personal note, if Syeva was out there in the city, then there was a better chance that he was safe.

A crowd was still congregated outside the Tavricheskiy Palace. I wondered how many of them understood the difference between the two sources of power that lay within: the Duma and the Soviet. Did they see us as distinct, or did they see us as linked by the only belief we held in common – opposition to the tsar? I'd have liked to believe that, though I couldn't help but notice how much bigger the crowds were now that the Soviet had come into being.

I went through the main entrance and walked down the hallway, along with dozens of others, most of whom I did not recognize and doubted whether they had genuine cause to be here. We came to the point where the corridor split and we could choose to head for the left or right wing of the building. I made my way to the Duma, but I was in a minority. In the Convention Hall the first person I saw was Nekrasov. Beside him was Konovalov, also a Kadet. Before I could greet either of them Nekrasov handed me a piece of paper. It was dated that day, 1 March 1917, and headed 'Order Number 1'. I read it quickly.

*To be immediately and fully executed by all men in the
Guards, army, artillery and navy and to be made known to
the Petrograd workers.*

*The Soviet of Workers' and Soldiers' Deputies has re-
solved: . . .*

It went on to list seven instructions, all of which took power
away from officers and handed it to local committees of soldiers
or sailors, who in turn would report to the Petrograd Soviet.

'What do you think?' Nekrasov asked.

'They had to do something after Rodzianko ordered the troops
back to barracks.'

'It's not as though any of the troops obeyed.'

'Exactly,' I said. 'That was mutiny – God knows where it might
lead. Better to give them some order – any order, as long as they
obey it. Otherwise they'll be a law unto themselves.'

'You think they'll obey this?'

'It hardly asks much of them, does it?'

'It says they should obey the Duma,' said Konovalov.

I laughed. 'Like hell it does. It says they should obey the Soviet,
and if the Duma happens to concur, that's not a problem.'

'They'll be happy with the last two points – soldiers should be
treated like human beings and officers shouldn't be treated like
gods.'

'If Nikolai had granted them that much ten years ago then we
wouldn't be here now.'

Konovalov nodded in agreement, but Nekrasov was more scep-
tical. 'You think so?'

'Who can tell? I know one thing for sure.'

'What?'

'We're no longer at war with Germany.'

Nekrasov grabbed the paper back off me and looked at it again
as if searching for something he'd missed. 'It doesn't say that here.'

'It says all weapons are under the control of the battalion committees. They don't use the word "soviet", but it's the same thing.
I'm not saying the war's over, but it's not us fighting it any more.
It's them.' I nodded towards the other side of the building, to
where the Soviet sat.

'I'm not sure it's going to be "them" and "us" for too much longer,' said Konovalov.

'What do you mean?'

'In the early hours of this morning they sent a delegation over to negotiate with us on forming a provisional government.'

'Are they serious?'

'Rodzianko's taking it seriously. Of course, it'll mean nothing until Nikolai makes a move.'

'He's still at Tsarskoye Selo?'

Nekrasov answered before Konovalov could speak. 'He never arrived. The train couldn't get through. He's still on board as far as we can guess.'

'And while he dithers, the Soviet grows stronger.'

'It's not like that. We'll bring them into power, but we can control them. They give us what we need – influence over the workers and the soldiers. Once we've got that, we can forget about the Soviet itself.'

It sounded very simple, but I couldn't help remembering one spring, when I'd been growing up in Saratov and Mama had shown me a cuckoo's egg in the nest of a tree pipit. We watched the chicks as they grew. From the start it was obvious that one of them was different – bigger for one thing, and therefore stronger. It got the lion's share of the food its adoptive mother brought, while her own offspring starved.

I pictured the Duma and the Soviet as being in the same relationship. We would happily feed it, but in a few months' time it would have grown to four times our size – four times our strength – and we would be able to do nothing to control it. But if we didn't help it out now, neither of us had any chance of survival.

I went home at lunch time. I knew that Nadya would be worried, and I couldn't deny that I was concerned myself, primarily about Syeva. Still he didn't come to greet me as I entered. For that matter, neither did Polkan, who was busy scratching at the wall near the kitchen door. I went through, shouting, 'Sergeant!', but he wasn't in there either. When I came out I saw Nadya on the stairs. She must have heard me call.

'No sign of either of them,' she said. 'I asked at some of the shops near by, but no one has seen him, though how they know who's queuing outside I have no idea. Polkan!' She snapped at the dog, who was still intent on destroying the already threadbare wallpaper. 'He's been doing that all morning,' she explained.

'I'll go out this afternoon and look for him.'

'He could be anywhere.'

I paused. I didn't want to tell her where I intended to look, but I had to be honest with her for once. 'I meant the morgues.'

She looked away from me. Polkan turned his attention once again to the wall.

'I'm not giving up hope,' I went on. 'Far from it. But at least we'll know, one way or the other. What's *wrong* with him?'

I meant Polkan, not Syeva. The dog was whining now, and snuffling at the skirting board.

'Probably just a dead rat. This place is filled with them.' She said it as though she blamed me for the rats. Or perhaps I just imagined that, for the simple reason that I blamed myself. Our home was my responsibility. I could have afforded a better place for us, if only I'd had the time to bother with it. But I was suddenly gripped by a concern more profound than the matter of rodents in the wall spaces.

I went through to the kitchen and to the other side of that same section of wall. It was thick here, more than the width of a mere few bricks. There was a good reason for it. Nadya joined me, sensing my urgency, but Polkan was too concerned with what he had smelled to follow us. There was a large wooden cupboard against the wall. I opened the door so as to get a better grip on the side, then started trying to move it.

'What are you doing?' asked Nadya.

'You remember when we moved in? What was behind here?'

She took a moment to think, then began to help me. Thankfully the paucity of food supplies in the city meant that the cupboard was almost bare. We couldn't lift it completely, but managed to walk it a few feet away from the wall. I looked at the space behind.

It was just as I remembered it: a rectangular frame, much like a picture frame, a little wider than my shoulders and at the level of my chest. But within there was neither a portrait nor a landscape, just a pair of wooden panels, meeting in a tight seam halfway down, with tarnished brass handles on each. It was a dumb waiter, installed long before we took up occupancy of the house. We'd known we'd never be hosting the grand dinner parties for which such a device might be useful. We'd not even bothered to see if it worked.

I grasped the two handles and tried to pull them apart, but they wouldn't budge. I looked around to see if there was some kind of catch, but found nothing. I felt Nadya return to my side, though I hadn't noticed she'd gone. She handed me a big, solid kitchen knife. I slipped it into the ridge between the two shutters, forcing them apart enough to allow it to enter. I pushed it in up to the hilt and then began to lever the handle up and down. I was reminded for a moment of my vision of Zmyeevich's death, the twin blades prising my coffin lid gradually open. With each motion the doors parted a little further, until I could at last get my fingers between them. Now I was able to grip properly, and with only a little more effort they began to slide open. I could feel the effects of the hidden gears which linked them together, whereby in moving one upwards the other was pushed down.

Now that same frame bounded merely a dark, open, empty space. I could smell whatever it was that had caught Polkan's sensitive nose. I glanced at Nadya and saw that she had noticed it too. She blanched and held her curled fingers to her nostrils, stepping back. It was undoubtedly the smell of decay. I'd known it more than once on the battlefield. But it was surprisingly weak, and therein lay some slight hope. A dead body would have produced a far stronger stench, certainly after two days. Perhaps it *was* merely a rat.

I could see that the cart was not on this floor. The back wall was dark and stained. I peered forwards tentatively, in part out of fear of what I might see, but also a little out of the knowledge that somewhere in the shaft above me hung the cart, unused for years, perhaps ready to fall. It wasn't far to look down, only to the level of the floor. It was too dark to see much. At the bottom there was a crack of flickering light, from the same direction that I heard Polkan's snuffling as he pushed against the skirting board and revealed its shoddy construction.

'Fetch me the torch, would you?' I'm not sure why I whispered the instruction. Nadya went away and returned to me seconds later, handing me the heavy yellow cylinder. It lay somewhere between a novelty and a practicality. A paraffin lamp would have provided better light, but not as quickly, and within the space of a few years the new technology would have utterly surpassed the older. I liked to be among the first to try such things out. And besides, I had good reasons for my penchant for electric light.

I twisted its brass end, pushing the contact of the bulb against the connection to the battery. I was pleasantly surprised to see the clear, yellow light that shone from it. It had been months since I'd last used it, and the batteries had a tendency to decay. I shone it down into the base of the lift shaft, then looked, fearing what might be revealed.

There was nothing – not the crumpled, pathetic human body that I had expected, nor even the squalid remains of a starved rodent. I heard Polkan whine, louder through the thin wall between us than via the kitchen door. I scanned the torch beam over the small rectangle that marked the bottom of the shaft. There were cobwebs and a few vague, tiny shapes that might have been dead flies or woodlice, but nothing else; just the flat, uncarpeted floorboards, much the same as those beneath my feet.

Except for the dark, grim stain that seemed to spread from the centre of them.

There wasn't enough light for me to be able to tell, and if it had been there any length of time it would have faded, but I felt for sure that the stain was red. I twisted and tried to look in the other direction, up the shaft, but it proved impossible. I could shine the light up there, or direct my gaze up there, but not both at the same time. If I'd been younger it would have been no problem. Even so, I caught a glimpse of something.

I handed the torch back to Nadya and at the same time gave her a simple instruction. 'Get out!'

'What?'

'Please. You don't want to see this.'

'You've found something?'

'No, but I'm going to. And you're not going to like it. Leave it to me, please.'

She moved away. I didn't check to see where she'd gone, but

I knew it wouldn't be far. I'd done my duty in warning her. She couldn't blame me for what she saw. I reached to the side of the shaft and found the two thin ropes I'd been expecting – one to go up, the other down. I tried the nearer one, but it wouldn't budge. The other rope moved with surprising ease, and the cart began to descend, the squeak of its motion with each pull signalling its approach. It didn't have far to come, but I stopped before it even reached the hatch in the kitchen.

Syeva's hair stood on end. His eyebrows were raised, his eyes gazing up towards them. His nostrils were wide, like a pig's snout. A few teeth were revealed between his parted lips. It was a bizarre expression, but easily explained by the fact that Syeva was hanging upside down; every feature of his face was distorted by the gravity that pulled at it from quite the opposite direction to what was normal. It also meant that the wound to his neck gaped open as a wide bloody mess, like an additional smile above his own pallid, lifeless lips.

I heard a gasp from behind me. Nadya had not done as I told her. I hadn't expected her to.

'Help me get him out, for God's sake.'

She came closer again. Her hands moved towards Syeva's dangling body, but dared not touch him.

'Pull the rope,' I said. 'Lower him.'

She went around to the other side. I put her hand on the same rope that I'd been holding, then I reached inside and grasped Syeva by the shoulders. Guiding him outwards, his forehead caught on the lip of the hatchway, bending his head back. I tugged it free, but could move him no further.

'Now,' I said, and Nadya began to pull on the rope, lowering his body and allowing me to draw it out through the hatch. Eventually only his shins and feet remained inside. I was supporting his whole weight, cradling him with my arms beneath his shoulders and knees. He wasn't stiff – rigor mortis had begun to fade – but he wouldn't move any further. I looked over and could easily see the reason. His bootlaces had been tied together and hung from a hook which was screwed into the bottom of the cart. It must have been there for years, for carrying extra loads, but it had never been intended for this use.

'Get him free,' I said.

Nadya looked at me and then at the dumb waiter. She swallowed, but reached forward and unhooked the laces. Now I was able to move him. I laid his body out on the kitchen floor. I heard the sound of Polkan trotting into the room, but Nadya pushed him out and closed the door.

'So that's what it looks like then?' she said.

'What?'

'The bite of a vampire.'

I'd only once before seen such a wound close to – in a mirror when looking at my own neck, at the bite marks left by Iuda. But it was not a good example – death had prevented him from doing the damage of which his kind was truly capable. The wounds at Syeva's throat were certainly too ragged to have been caused by any knife, and the flesh had been eaten away in precisely the manner that Mama had told me, and that I'd read about for myself. The pallor of his skin showed just how little blood there was left in him. It might easily be explained by the fact that he'd been hanging upside down, except that the stain at the bottom of the shaft was too small for that to make sense. Even so, while it might have been a reasonable conclusion for me to draw, it was a leap of intuition for Nadya.

'What makes you say that?' I asked.

'You deny it?'

'No. It seems pretty clear to me.'

'You knew before you even found the body,' she said. It was not a question.

'I didn't know for sure,' I protested feebly.

'We're both sure now.' She went to a drawer and fetched a table cloth which we laid over Syeva's body. I closed his eyes before covering his face. 'You'd better tell me everything,' she said.

'One thing first. We need to go upstairs.'

She looked at me, puzzled.

'There's two of them missing,' I said.

Her hand went to her mouth as she realized what I meant; the shaft ran the entire height of the building, and if one body hung beneath the cart, another could easily be resting on top of it. She dashed out of the room. I followed, but remembered to close the door so that Polkan could not go and investigate what we had found. She was in Anastasia's room before I was even halfway up the stairs. We were directly above the kitchen. Here nothing covered the doors to the dumb waiter. Nadya already had them open and was peering down into the darkness. Her body was very still. Then suddenly she stood upright.

'Give me the torch,' she said.

I handed it to her and she bent back through the hatchway. She scanned it beneath her, then twisted to look upwards. Finally she emerged once again.

'Thank God,' she whispered.

'Nothing?' I asked.

She shook her head, then went over to sit on the bed. 'I think you'd better tell me what this is all about.'

I sat beside her and took a breath. 'It's Dmitry Alekseevich, my uncle. He's in Petrograd.'

At the sound of his name she blanched. It was understandable; however much she was reconciled to the idea of vampires as creatures from my past, it was another thing for such creatures to become a reality of our present. I told her how I'd met Dmitry, about the other *voordalaki* with him, about his ambitions to aid the revolution and my assistance to him. I missed out the fact that one of those other vampires was her brother. There was no need.

'You're a fool, Mihail Konstantinovich,' she said when I'd finished. 'How could you have trusted him?'

'You think Dmitry did this?'

'Does it matter? Him, one of the others. They probably followed you here and saw something they couldn't resist. Two young innocents. God knows where we'll find Anastasia's body.'

I laughed harshly and saw the tear that it caused in Nadya's eye. 'That's not what's happened,' I said as gently as I could. 'I haven't told you everything. You remember I said I saw Anastasia selling herself in the street. Well I did see her, but not with a man. She was with one of Dmitry's vampires. For a while I wondered how she survived, but now it's obvious. He wasn't trying to drink her blood, any more than he was trying to screw her. They were just together because they're the same type of vile creature.'

A sudden further realization flashed before me as to what

might have been happening when I saw them together. I'd not had time to look properly, but who was I to say that behind them in that archway, under those sacks, there didn't lie the body of their shared victim, some other child, as innocent as Anastasia had once appeared, fallen victim to the same life that she pretended?

'It can't be,' whispered Nadya.

'What if we find others?'

'Others?'

'She's been bringing men here, you said so yourself. What if some of them don't leave. There's more places than the dumb waiter to hide a body in here.'

'Then find them and ask me again.'

I didn't relish the idea, and I wasn't convinced Anastasia would be so foolish as to hide too many bodies so close to one another. I changed tack.

'Have you ever seen her in daylight?'

She thought for a moment. 'I couldn't swear to it, but that doesn't prove anything. I don't see you that often until well after dark.'

I turned to her and looked into her beautiful brown eyes. 'You know it's true, Nadya.'

'Do I? Do I really? I know it enough to do what? To kill her? To drive a stake through her heart? To cut off her head?'

It would have sounded like the voice of reason but for the edge of desperate panic. I understood her well enough to see through the façade. It was hope, not reason, that made her reject what seemed so obvious. Even so she was right; I couldn't be certain. I didn't need to be.

'It doesn't have to come to that,' I explained. 'There's a way to prove it and deal with her, all in one.'

'A witch trial? If she floats she's guilty; if she drowns she's innocent?'

'Quite the reverse,' I said. 'But first we've got to deal with Syeva.'

'You mean—' Her face contorted in horror.

'What?'

'You think he might . . . end up as one of them?'

The prospect hadn't even occurred to me. If he were to be

transformed into a *voordalak*, the process would take weeks. And I knew of no sure method to prevent it. Perhaps the corpse should be dealt with in the same way as a living vampire: beheaded, or a stake driven through its heart. I had no idea, and doubted I'd be able to bring myself to do it. But it seemed unlikely. The fact of his death was one thing, but the way that Anastasia had left his body, hidden, dangling, gave no hint that one day she hoped to have him stand by her side as a fellow creature of the night.

'No. I think she killed him purely to feed.'

'*She?*' Nadya asked pointedly. I didn't bother to respond.

I got hold of some sheets, then went downstairs and wrapped Syeva's body in them. I went to a drawer in the kitchen to get some string to tie it in place, but couldn't find any. Bizarrely I almost shouted for Syeva, feeling sure that he'd know where it was kept. I looked around the kitchen and could see him everywhere, preparing food, washing, carrying out all the tasks he'd so happily done for us over the years. I could hear his voice calling me colonel. I sat down at the table and buried my face in my hands.

It can't have been many minutes before Nadya roused me. She didn't comment on the tears on my cheeks, and neither did I say anything about those on hers. She was dressed to go out. 'We'll take him to the mortuary at the military hospital,' she said.

'I need string.' It was an everyday item, but the words came from my lips as a desperate plea.

Nadya remained calmer. She looked through the drawers and found some and we made a reasonable job of tying the shroud so that it didn't fall away.

'You want me to carry him?' I asked.

'Only to the street. I'll ask Vera Glebovna if we can use her cart.'

She went ahead of me. I carried the body out to the hall and put it down, then shut Polkan in the kitchen. Syeva had never been a big lad, but I felt exhausted from just that short walk. Even so, I determined to carry him with dignity. I opened the front door and lifted him up again, then walked out on to the street. Nadya was just returning from the gate to our neighbours' yard, dragging a two-wheeled trolley behind her. It was an old-fashioned-looking thing in a city of so many motor cars, but it would suffice.

We walked down the snow-covered streets pulling Syeva's body behind us. Few of those we passed bothered to cross themselves, though there could be no doubt as to what the shape laid out on the wooden platform was. It was only to be expected. These people had troubles of their own, and there'd been enough death in the city to tire the arms of even the most devout. But I couldn't help feeling there was more to it. Everything that was happening, this whole revolution, was about people getting what they needed here and now. It was understandable that that would lead to some forgetfulness regarding the world to come. Some of the more outspoken figures – in exile, mostly – insisted upon it. And how could we complain? We were breaking every taboo by bringing him through the streets like this.

We went over to Liteiny Prospekt and across the bridge to where the hospital stood, overlooking the river. It was busy, both as a hospital and as a mortuary, but a combination of my papers and the generosity of my donation to their funds meant that we could find a place for him. The doctor took a glance at his wounds and drew breath through his teeth.

'We've seen a few of these,' he said.

'Really?' I tried not to sound too interested. Nadya scowled at me, reminding me of my connivance in Dmitry's activities.

'What do you expect?' the doctor continued. 'They've let everyone out of the prisons. I'm not saying there weren't people in there who shouldn't have been, but there were enough of them that were thugs and murderers. It's not enough for them just to kill, they have to mutilate the body – leave their mark. There was a case in London, thirty years ago. It was women then, but—' He looked at Nadya and saw the expression on her. 'I'm so sorry,' he said. 'I wasn't thinking.'

'We'll have a funeral arranged in a day or two,' I said, though I wasn't convinced we could achieve anything so quickly, if at all.

We went back the way we had come, but at the corner of Solyanoy Lane Nadya turned off to go into Saint Panteleimon's. It was where we worshipped, when we bothered. She went more often than I.

'I'll see if I can arrange something,' she said.

'Do you want me to . . . ?'

She shook her head. 'You have other things to do.'

She was right. I hurried home and went straight up the stairs to the top floor. I was exhausted by the climb, but had no time to waste. It would be dusk in less than two hours. I went to the door at the end of the corridor, then froze in horror.

The padlock was open. It still hung from the hasp, but would require no key to remove it. I looked close and saw the twisted metal of the mechanism that had once held the shackle in place. It would have taken some sort of jemmy to break it, and even then an enormous amount of strength – inhuman strength.

I considered what to do. Almost every weapon I had to deal with a vampire was in that room. If Anastasia – I had no doubt it was she who had broken in – was still in there then I was lost. I had only my cane, with the cap that covered its wooden tip, but I'd left that downstairs by the door. But then I realized my immediate fears were groundless. The broken lock had been put back in place. That could only have been done from the outside.

I walked forward and plucked the lock from the hasp, then opened the door. As I'd concluded, the room was empty. I flicked on the light and looked around, trying to deduce what she had been doing here – what might be missing. To my relief the items I was after were still there, in a box in the corner: my Yablochkov Candles. They were what I'd been thinking of when I'd told Nadya I had a way both to test Anastasia and to destroy her if she proved guilty. The light from these lamps would do nothing more than dazzle a mortal human, but they would reduce a vampire to dust in minutes – seconds if I used enough of them, and I had over a dozen.

I looked around the room in more detail, trying to remember what had been where. There was no reason to suppose she had taken anything. Perhaps she had just been exploring. Even to a vampire a casual look at this place would not scream out that everything here was dedicated to its destruction. A crossbow could be used to kill many creatures. The wooden sword might be just a toy. And why should any vampire realize the danger of arc lights such as the Yablochkov Candles; to my knowledge they had only been used twice, and neither victim had survived to warn his brethren.

Then I saw what was missing: on the bookshelf – all of Iuda's notebooks. I'd stolen them from his rooms at the Hôtel d'Europe, decades before, and had learned from them everything that he had discovered through his experiments on vampires. As soon as Anastasia read them, she would understand that I knew far more about her kind than she might have guessed. But there was still some hope; the books were written in English. It seemed unlikely that a girl of her age and background would be able to read the language. I stopped myself, shaking my head at my own ridiculous logic. She was a *voordalak*. However old she might appear, what did I know of her age and background? The very fact that she'd taken the books indicated she had some interest in them.

I picked up the box of Yablochkov Candles and went back down to Anastasia's room on the first floor. When I was very young, Mama and I had proved their effectiveness on a *voordalak* we'd captured. Back then we'd got our power from a Gramme generator which Mama had to crank by hand. With Iuda I'd used a bank of Leclanché cells. Times had moved on. Petrograd now had its own electricity supply. It would make my life easier.

It didn't take me long to rewire the lighting of Anastasia's room – my changes didn't need to be well hidden. One switch would, as ever, turn on the single incandescent bulb above the bed. It would do her no harm; the light it emitted was of the wrong wavelength. I hid a second switch behind the chest of drawers near the door. It was just a small knife switch in the electrical cable, not fixed to the wall. It would do the job, but I'd need to be careful – the exposed metal meant I risked an electric shock. I tested one of the Yablochkov Candles and it worked fine. Ideally I should have checked them all – they were decades old – but such was their design that they could only be lit once, after which it took a lot of effort to re-prime them. I inspected them all visually and they seemed in order. I wired them in parallel so that even if one failed, the others would still function.

It took me less than an hour. I have to admit I enjoyed the work. Spending an afternoon designing circuits, stripping wires and connecting components reminded me of my days in the army as a sapper. Whenever we had a problem with the wiring in the house (which was often) I always made sure to fix it myself rather than hire someone. I probably understood electricity better than most of the tradesmen in Petrograd who claimed it was their profession. When I'd finished I looked at my work. There were eight of the candles around the room. If any one of them worked it would be enough to kill Anastasia – presuming she was a vampire. If not then I could simply ask her if she liked the new lights I'd put up for her. I also searched the room top to bottom, and anywhere else I could think of in the house, but there was no sign of Iuda's journals – nor of any other victims. I made sure to remove the key from the door. The entire plan would be foiled if Anastasia were able to lock me out.

Nadya returned before I'd finished. She looked in briefly at what I was up to. When everything was ready I called her down and explained to her what I'd done and what the effect would be – both if Anastasia were a vampire and if not. I showed her the switch and told her to be careful not to touch the bare metal.

'You expect me to do it?' she said.

'Only if I'm not here when she comes back.'

'You only have to go to the Duma during the day. She won't come then.'

'I have to go out this evening.' I spoke softly, as if it would change the meaning of the words.

'What?'

'I have to speak to Dmitry.'

'Why?'

'To find out what he knows about Anastasia.' I knew I sounded irritated, and that wasn't fair. I certainly had to see Dmitry, but it was me, not Nadya, who had brought the situation about.

'When?'

'Around half past nine. I'll make sure it doesn't take long. Did you arrange the funeral?'

She nodded. 'Friday – first thing. That won't take long either.'

As darkness drew in we went upstairs. We looked out over the banister for Anastasia's arrival, though we'd have heard her anyway. I realized I should have wired it so the switch was up in our room, and so the whole thing could be done remotely. But I knew that in my heart I wanted to see the *voordalak* die. It had been too long since the last time.

When I left for my appointment with Dmitry she still had not come. I tried to go over the details again with Nadia of what to do, but she told me she understood.

It didn't take me long to get to Senate Square. The city was much as it had been the previous night: busy, but quiet. A mood of anticipation hung in the air. Dmitry's tall figure was already waiting when I arrived.

'How did it go at the Astoria?' I asked.

'We went there, but it hardly seems worth it. There's a handful holding out who are loyal to the tsar, but nobody's trying to deal with them. It's all but over.'

'So you'll leave?'

'When Nikolai's gone. Even then it will be more of a withdrawal than a departure.'

'What do you mean?'

'Every revolution will need protecting after the event. There'll be those who want to return things to the way they were. If they try too hard, we'll stop them.'

'And in the meantime?'

'We'll leave the city, as I said.'

I paused. I didn't want to ask about Anastasia too directly. 'How many of you are there?' I asked.

'A dozen, plus myself. I told you.'

'All male?'

He nodded.

'Are there any other vampires in the city?'

He looked at me thoughtfully for a moment, then smiled. 'Apparently. A woman.'

'You know then?'

'I only know what you've just told me.'

I emitted the briefest of laughs, mostly at my own stupidity. 'She's called Anastasia Eduardovna Agapova.' Nadya had told me her full name – the name that Anastasia had given her. None of it could be trusted. Dmitry shook his head. 'She's young, or looks it – fifteen at most. Blonde.'

'If she's in the city, I've not seen her. To be honest, I don't think I've ever met a vampire that young.'

I decided to play my trump card. It was the only one I had left. 'One of you knows her – Ilya. I saw them together.'

Dmitry's nostrils flared. 'You're sure?'

'That's why I followed him – and found you. Seems they're not quite the loyal band you thought they were.'

'I'll talk to him.'

'I'd rather you didn't – not for a little while.'

He looked at me quizzically, then seemed to understand.

'There was one other thing about her,' I said. 'She looks as though she's pregnant. Is that possible?'

'Don't Iuda's books have anything on that?'

I wasn't going to tell Dmitry they'd been stolen, but in truth, and perhaps surprisingly, there was nothing on the subject in them. 'Not the ones I have,' I replied.

'As far as I know, she couldn't have conceived as a vampire.' He spoke carefully, choosing his words. 'That really is an impossibility.'

'So she got pregnant as a human? But she's only a few months gone.' Absurdly I felt more pity for her to know she had so recently been one of us.

'I don't think it works like that,' said Dmitry. His caution was becoming palpable, but then his mood lightened. 'But as I say, I'm no expert.'

'I don't suppose it makes much odds.'

'To what you have planned for her?'

'Exactly. So you don't have any objections?' It hadn't been my intention, but suddenly it seemed as though I was asking Dmitry's permission.

'At your killing one of my kind? I can hardly complain, can I?' He gave a smile that reminded me – however friendly the manner in which we communicated might be – what a monster he truly was. 'You've not raised a finger to stop me killing dozens of yours.'

He walked across the square in the direction of Saint Isaac's. I fingered the cane in my hand. I could easily have chased after him and plunged its sharp point into his back. If I'd been lucky I might even have taken him by surprise. But, despite what he was, it would still have made me a murderer – and it wouldn't have made his words any less true. I would kill a vampire tonight, but it wouldn't be an act of petty malice. It would be an act of justice – an execution. It would be just as it had been with Iuda.

I hurried back across the city. I was glad to have spent so little time talking with Dmitry. It was a terrible thing for me to have left Nadya to perform what should have been my onerous duty, but I had been away less than an hour, so the likelihood was that Anastasia had not returned. And even if she had, Nadya was as capable as I of operating that switch and reducing the creature to ashes. Perhaps that was my real concern – that I wouldn't be there to see it.

I walked along the Neva and then headed inland to follow the Moika, taking me through the Field of Mars. There were bonfires dotted about and I could see the shadows of men and women around them, keeping warm. Still the city waited – waited for Nikolai to act, one way or the other – to give up power or to send in troops that would enforce it, if he could find any who would obey him. As I walked I couldn't help but notice what a playground the place would be for any *voordalak* who chose to come here. How easy would it be for him or her to wander amongst those sparse crowds, passing themselves off as a likeminded citizen and then finding some dark shadowy corner in which to pounce? Dmitry might have had nobler intentions in coming here, but it couldn't have been difficult for him to raise recruits. It had been the same in 1812. They waited until mankind was weak – weakened on its own stupidity – and then came to pick off whatever easy victims they could find. They were vultures, not hawks. Scavengers. Maggots feeding on the flesh of Petrograd's corpse.

It was as I crossed the foot of the Lebyazhya Canal, separating the Field of Mars from the Summer Garden, that I noticed something was wrong. Here the path turned a little and I could see all the way to the corner of our building, overlooking the Fontanka. Or I should have been able to see it. On this side of the river the electric streetlamps were shining. They were perhaps a little dimmer than usual, but still cast plenty of light to see by. But at the line of the Fontanka that light came to a sudden halt. I didn't know precisely how electricity was routed around the city, but it was divided into sectors. With the strikes and the lack of fuel, sometimes sufficient power could not be produced. That could have various possible effects. One was that the whole city would dim; bulbs still glowing but less intense – the light they cast almost brown. Alternatively an entire sector might lose its supply completely. That was what had happened tonight.

Our house, our street, and the whole area around were without electricity. And electricity was the only weapon I had given Nadya to protect her.

CHAPTER VIII

I COVERED THE DISTANCE HOME IN LESS THAN A MINUTE. THERE were still troops supposedly on guard on the bridge as I crossed the Fontanka, but they had long since stopped trying to prevent people crossing in either direction. The difference in atmosphere on the other side was instantly noticeable. The darkness was like a curtain. The moon would not rise for another few hours. I could see the flickering lights of candles behind some windows, but they cast no useful light on to the street. It was only a little way from the embankment to my front door, but already any benefit I had of light from across the river had gone. I ran my fingers over the painted woodwork, feeling for the keyhole. Soon I was inside.

I could hear my own breath rasping in the darkness of the hallway. I held it, and then heard the pulsing beat of my heart. The short run had exhausted me. Even if it hadn't there was no possibility of my being able to run up the stairs. Inside it was totally dark. I would have to feel my way. I removed the protective cap from my cane, ready for what I might encounter, but then I used it for a quite different purpose. I held it out in front of me, sweeping it slowly from side to side as if I were a blind man, which for the time being I was. Soon I felt it tap against the wooden pillar at the foot of the banister and moments later I had my hand on the rail.

Now my progress was faster. The banister rail continued unbroken all the way up the building. I had merely to keep in contact with it to find my way to the top floor. I glanced in the direction of Anastasia's door as I passed, but could see no light. Even a candle would have shown up in the utter blackness that enveloped the house, as was demonstrated when I reached the upper landing. A dim glow seeped out from under the living-room door. I silently opened it, and went inside.

The scene beyond would have appeared, to most observers, quite natural – a perfect representation of domestic tranquillity. There was a candle on the table and two more on the mantelpiece. A single log glowed in the grate. I walked in a little further. Polkan was asleep on the hearth rug. Nadya was in her usual chair with her back to me. In her hands she held a book, but as I moved further into the room I could see her eyes were not on it. They looked across the room to the other chair, where Anastasia was sitting. She was sketching. I couldn't see what was on the paper. The only hint that something was amiss was the whiteness of the tips of Nadya's thumbs as she gripped the book so tightly that it seemed she might be about to rip it apart.

'Good evening,' I said.

They both looked up at me. Anastasia seemed a little startled, but Nadya appeared calmer. I doubted it was anything other than a façade.

'Good evening, colonel,' said Anastasia. She looked me up and down. I realized I was still carrying the cane, its sharpened tip exposed. Luckily I held it as one genuinely would a cane, and so the point was close to the ground, lost in the shadows with any luck. She certainly didn't react to it. I leaned over and kissed Nadya on the cheek, though my eyes never left Anastasia. Neither did Nadya's.

'We were just keeping each other company until you got home,' Anastasia continued. She stood up and showed the drawing to me. 'Do you like it?'

I took it from her and glanced down at it. It was Polkan, sleeping in just the pose that he currently occupied. It was very good – as good as the sketch she had done of Nadya – but I didn't allow my eyes to linger over it for long. I offered the paper back to Anastasia, attempting a smile of approval.

'No,' she said. 'Keep it.'

She gathered up her pencils and her pad and made for the door. She turned before opening it. 'Goodnight, both of you.'

I stood, frozen, and listened to her feet on the stairs, then the faint opening and closing of her bedroom door. I turned to Nadya, ready to cling to her as she threw herself into my arms and sobbed in relief that the terror had passed, if only for the moment. But no such embrace came; neither did tears.

'Why the hell didn't you kill her?' she hissed.

'What?'

'That's what it's for, isn't it?' She batted the cane with her hand, knocking it from my grasp. The sound of it clattering on the floor woke Polkan, who looked up at us, but didn't move. Clearly Nadya's terror had banished any pretence she'd made of giving Anastasia the benefit of the doubt. I was less certain, but then I hadn't been sitting there with her all evening.

'Yes,' I said, keeping my voice low. 'That's what it's for. But it's as effective on a human as on a *voordalak*. It was only this morning you wanted me to make sure – one way or the other. We'd be sure enough if she was sitting there now in that chair, with a stake through her heart and her body still intact like any normal person. That's why I was going to use the lights.'

'You didn't think about the power cut, though, did you?'

'No. No I didn't.' I silently cursed my stupidity. 'Did she say anything?' I asked.

Nadya shook her head. 'Nothing important. She asked after Syeva.'

'Did you tell her?'

'Of course not! We don't have a chance if she knows we suspect her.'

'You don't think she does?'

'I don't know. But when she was sitting here, waiting, it was almost as if she was toying with me. As if she knew how afraid I was, and the only reason she didn't kill me was to prolong the pleasure she got from that.'

It didn't sound unlikely from what I knew of the behaviour of vampires. 'You seem very certain of what she is,' I said.

'I was, when she was here. But it was just a feeling. You're right; we have to be sure. It's not your fault the power workers are on strike.'

We went to bed. I locked the door and put a chair up against it.

Then I locked the window shutters too, remembering how easily Dmitry and his friends had climbed the walls of the Singer building – how Anastasia might do the same. I held my cane in one hand and pulled Nadya close to me with the other. I tried not to fall asleep, but I did.

I was awakened by a bright light. It took me a moment to realize what it was: the single bulb that hung from the centre of the ceiling. The power had come back on, and I'd deliberately left the light on so that I'd know when it did. I looked at the clock. It was almost half past three in the morning. The cane was still held loosely in my hand. I got up. Nadya was already half awake from the light and as I moved she raised her head to look at me.

'I'm going down to deal with her,' I said.

'I'm coming with you.'

There was no point in me trying to forbid her. I removed the chair from the door and unlocked it. I could have turned on the stair light, but that might have given Anastasia warning of our approach. Instead I lit a candle. Polkan tried to come with us, but I shut him in the room. As we went downstairs I felt Nadya close at my back. It wasn't long before we reached the door of Anastasia's room. I decided I wasn't going to take any risks. I could have knocked on the door, or called to her, or simply turned on the regular light to see if she was there, but any of them would have given her the chance to escape, or worse, to counter-attack. My plan was simply to move the switch and activate the Yablochkov Candles. And then we would know.

I softly turned the door handle and pushed. There was the tiniest squeak of the hinges, but I doubted it could wake anyone. I only needed to open the door far enough to reach in and operate the switch. I could see it behind the chest of drawers, the brass glinting in the candlelight. I reached forward, at every moment expecting to feel the steely grip of her hand on my forearm, dragging me away from my goal and into the room to the horrible fate that awaited me. I had to turn my head away to extend my arm to its full length. I tried to picture the exact position of the switch, knowing that if I touched the wrong part of it I would feel the shock of the current flowing through my hand. At last my fingers felt the insulated rubber tip. I moved my thumb beneath the wooden base of the switch and squeezed, pulling the lever down against the contact.

The pause as the arcs formed – a mere fraction of a second – was just perceptible and then the room was flooded with light. I stood and flung the door wide open, stepping inside the room, all fear lost now that it was filled with the brilliant illumination. All, that is, but the fear of embarrassment. If Anastasia were not a vampire, merely the unfortunate girl that she appeared to be, then this sudden interruption of her night's sleep would require some explanation. It took a few seconds for my eyes to adjust to the new brightness, but when they did they brought only a sense of disappointment.

The room was empty. Anastasia was not there. I maintained the briefest hope that the light might have destroyed her so quickly and so utterly that all remains of her had vanished, but it was an unconvincing idea. There would have been some noise. There would be marks of burning at the place she had been; on the bed or on the carpet. And that particular smell – unpleasant in its character but delightful in its association – would hang in the air. I could still remember from when I had killed Iuda, and the vampire we had experimented on before that.

'It was never that likely she'd be here,' I said. 'At this time of night, she'll have better things to do.'

'It makes you wonder why she needs to come here at all,' said Nadya. It was a question that had already occurred to me.

We sat in the bright light until dawn, just in case she came back and we would somehow be able to trick her into the room, but there was no sign of her.

I spent the first part of the Thursday morning rigging up a new set of lights in Anastasia's room, just the same as I had done before. If I had time I'd be able to repair the ones we had used the previous night, so that they could be switched on again, but for now I still had enough in the box. I kept two back, just in case things went wrong again, but next time I promised myself I would be more certain that Anastasia was there before I threw the switch. We did one other thing. Together Nadya and I carried down the mirror from her dressing table and put it on the table in Anastasia's room. It was hinged into three sections, like a triptych. We angled it so that from the door reflections of most of the room would be visible. It would be an additional way for us to determine her nature. Then there was nothing more to be done, not until nightfall – and neither was there any danger. I once again went to the Tavricheskiy Palace.

'I never trusted Kerensky.' Those were Nekrasov's first words to me when I arrived. It seemed like the wisdom of hindsight – I'd never known him express any doubts about his colleague in the past.

'What's he done?' I asked.

Nekrasov glanced around then took me to a corner of the room. 'He accepted a ministry – Ministry of Justice.'

It was a simple enough statement, but there were half a dozen reasons why it made no sense whatsoever. 'Nikolai's appointing ministers?' I asked.

Nekrasov scowled and shook his head. 'His Majesty's in no position to appoint anyone. I'm talking about the government after he's gone.'

That only raised further questions. 'With Kerensky as a minister. So the Soviet is trying to form a government?'

'No, that's the thing. The Soviet's promised to give us its support – just as long as whatever we do "corresponds to the interests of the proletariat", whatever that means.'

I had a good idea what it meant – they'd support it until they felt strong enough to take power for themselves. 'Kerensky's just hedging his bets,' I said.

'That's how I see it. He's told the Soviet it's the only way he can ensure the release of politicals, and they seem to have bought it.'

'And who's in charge? Milyukov?'

Nekrasov shook his head. 'He's the real power broker, but he knows the Soviet would never stand for him being in command, and he had to make sure Kerensky didn't get the job.'

'So?'

'Our new Prime Minister is Georgy Yevgenyevich Lvov.'

I clicked my tongue. It was a surprise, and a gamble. Lvov

was a fair man and had more chance than anyone of doing what was right by all the people of Russia. But he was no politician – he was too honest. Men like Kerensky and Milyukov would run rings around him.

But there was something else Nekrasov had said which concerned me. '"*Is*"?' I asked.

He shrugged. '"Will be", if you insist. But it won't be long. Rodzianko has been on the Hughes Telegraph all night talking to General Ruzsky.'

'Ruzsky's with Nikolai?'

'They're stuck on the imperial train, somewhere near Pskov. It sounds as though Rodzianko's convinced Ruzsky that Nikolai's got to go, but it's a question of whether Ruzsky can persuade the tsar himself.'

'If everything that's happened can't persuade him I doubt a solitary general will be able to do much.'

'From what I hear, everyone's giving him the same message. There are telegrams arriving from generals all across the Front.'

I breathed deeply. It was hard to take in. Nekrasov was younger than me, but even for him the idea would be difficult to get used to. I said it out loud. 'And so soon Russia will have no tsar.'

'Well, there'll be a tsar – Aleksei II – but he won't have any power. Even so, not much fun for a boy of twelve.'

'I can't see the Soviet standing for a constitutional monarchy.'

'They don't think it's worth the battle. It's only a provisional government, until there can be elections. That's when they'll decide on a constitution.'

'How soon?'

'Before the year's out – though Christ knows if Aleksei will last that long.'

It was an unnecessarily harsh thing to say about the boy, but that didn't make it any less true. I'd never heard the specifics, but we'd all noticed how carefully the tsarevich was treated by his family, how they protected him from anything that might injure him. The tsarevich had some horrible disease whose details were kept hidden from his people. Many who knew more than I were surprised he'd lived as long as he had. But even if Aleksei did die, there would still be a tsar. He might not have any brothers, but there would always be someone, however distantly related. That was how dynasties worked.

'What did you get, by the way?' I asked. 'In the cabinet?'

Nekrasov's lip curled slightly. 'Transport.'

I tried not to smirk.

I spent the remainder of the day at the palace, talking to members of the Duma and to those members of the Soviet that I knew. The story was much the same as Nekrasov had told me. Few could take in the enormity of what was happening, or that it had all started just a week ago with the protests on International Women's Day. But everyone knew that it had really begun long before that – before many of us were born. And yet still there was the sense of impotence – of waiting for events to unfold. Nikolai still reigned, even if he did not rule, and his last proclamation would change everything. Now at last, though, there was a palpable sense of anticipation.

I went home in plenty of time for sunset. As I pushed through the crowds outside the Tavricheskiy Palace I picked up snatches of their conversations. From what I could make out, they were little aware of how quickly events had begun to move. But they understood enough to know that this was where they should be to be the first to hear any announcement that was made – not at the Winter Palace, nor the Mariinskiy Palace, where the State Council sat. No one bothered to ask me if I knew anything – I didn't look important enough for that. I thanked God for it.

'No sign of her, I suppose?' I asked. Nadya was sitting in the kitchen when I arrived.

'Of course n— No. No sign.' I understood why she'd corrected herself. 'Of course not' meant that it was impossible to have seen Anastasia, because it was daylight and because she was a *voordalak*. That was a presumption we should not leap upon.

'I won't go out to see Dmitry tonight,' I said. 'Not any night, till this is finished.'

She reached across the table and squeezed my hand. 'What if she never comes back?'

'She will,' I said. The confidence in my voice was not without reason. She'd taken Iuda's journals. Even if she hadn't yet managed to read the English or have it translated, she would soon. And then she would have to come, to find out how much I knew about her and her kind.

'I couldn't stand it,' said Nadya. 'If we never knew.'

'I'll wait outside tonight,' I said. 'Across the street. That way I won't miss her.'

'And what do you expect me to do?'

'Go upstairs. Lock the door. Wait.'

'And if you're dead in the morning?'

'Then you'll have the satisfaction of knowing you were right.' It was a horrible thing for me to say. She stood up and then snapped her fingers to instruct Polkan to follow her. She'd got to the door before I could summon the good sense to call after her. 'I'm sorry. That was a stupid thing to say.'

'I didn't leave you much choice, did I?'

She left. I waited half an hour or so, then went upstairs to the living room. I touched her shoulder and felt her fingers squeeze mine, then I went to sit opposite. The sketch of Polkan was still there. I crumpled it and threw it on the fire. It uncurled in the heat and I watched the paper blacken, so that the drawing itself became black on black, before finally crumbling to nothing. Time passed slowly. Never before could I remember being so impatient for something of which I was so afraid. When I'd killed Iuda, I'd known little fear. It had been a confrontation that I had sought all my life. This new confrontation had been thrust upon me. It was unfair – and not just on me. When I'd known I was to face Iuda I'd been very careful to ensure I was not loved, that there was no one who could ask, 'And if you're dead in the morning?' I should have left things that way.

Even as the thought passed across my mind I rejected it. I looked up at Nadya and could feel the tear forming in my eye. There was no conceivable reason for me to regret the years I'd spent with her. Whatever misery I might bring her because of this, it was more than compensated by the joy I felt to be sitting in the same room with her for just a moment. It might be selfish for me to balance my joy against her misery, but love is selfish, whatever lovers might say.

She saw that I was looking at her and raised a questioning eyebrow.

'I love you,' I whispered.

'Then come back.'

At last the light outside began to dim. I flicked the switch on the wall and the light in our room came on. The generators were working for now – but who could say when that might change?

'I'll go down,' I said. 'Lock the door behind me.'

She came over and kissed me goodbye. She had turned away before she spoke. 'I love you too.'

I went downstairs, pausing only to go to the kitchen and get hold of the electric torch. I checked that it was still working and slipped it into my coat pocket. If the power did fail again, I didn't want to be completely without resources, though this diffuse light would only give me the ability to see a *voordalak*, not to kill one. I went out across the street. Looking up at the high window I saw Nadya gazing down. I gave her a cheery wave, then moved on. The only place to hide was inside the doorway of Saint Panteleimon's. It was some way down the street, but I could see our door, and a long way in both directions. The priest would come to lock up sometime, but by then it would be darker, and I'd be able to hide in the shadow at the side of the church. In the morning it would be open again, and Nadya and I – and almost certainly no one else – would go in to attend Syeva's funeral. With luck his death would have been avenged by then.

It was almost ten o'clock when she came. As I'd expected, the priest had closed up and I'd been forced to move. The street wasn't empty, but wasn't busy, either. Thankfully, the lamps above my head continued to glow, showing that we still had electricity. The downside was that it might make it easier for her to see me, but then if she was a vampire she'd do just as well with only the light of the stars.

She came from the direction of the Fontanka, but I couldn't tell whether she had crossed the bridge or come along the embankment. Like most in the city she was dressed for the cold – a heavy overcoat and a fur hat – a hat Nadya had lent her. It might have been hard to recognize her, but her diminutive figure betrayed her age, and the glint of golden hair emerging from beneath the hat was unmistakable. I shouldn't have been surprised that she was not alone.

148

It was a man – a soldier, though not an officer. In the gloom I could not see enough of his uniform to make out his regiment. He had his arm around her. Evidently she was posing as a prostitute to lure victims. Perhaps she did not even have to go that far. With the collapse of civilized normality over the last few days, there were plenty of women giving it away in the streets for nothing. But of course Anastasia didn't have to do it in the streets. We'd given her a room. It would have been bad enough if she had been using it as a place to take clients; but she had no clients, only victims. That would end soon.

They paused at the door and the soldier turned into her, rubbing her face and neck as if about to kiss her. She giggled and pushed him away, but with little conviction. She unlocked the door and they went in.

I raced down the street. Little respect though I had for a man who would pick up a girl like that, with only the basest of thoughts on his mind, he did not deserve the fate that awaited him. If I was quick I could save him. But at that moment I heard shouts and laughter and a crowd of men appeared from around the corner. There were more than twenty of them – some soldiers, others workers. They were no different from any others I'd seen over the last few nights – no more and no less drunk – though they appeared in higher spirits. I tried to get in front of them to get to the house, but they cut me off. I pushed my way through, but felt a shove to my chest and found myself sitting on the snowy road.

'How do you like it then, *burzhooi*?' shouted one of them. 'You have to let *us* pass, now.'

I'd heard the word '*burzhooi*' before. It was a bad pronunciation of 'bourgeois' – hardly a term that applied to me, but outside of the writings of intellectuals like Lenin and Trotsky it was simply an expression of animosity for anyone they thought had once had a better status than they. I lay still. I was lucky they were in such a merry mood, or I might have got a beating. As they passed one of them unshouldered his rifle and aimed it at me. I'd scarcely even taken in what he was doing before the moment had passed. He made the sound of an explosion with his mouth and jerked the gun as if it were recoiling, then laughed and continued on his way. If he had fired I would not have been the only man to die so trivially over the last few days.

Once they'd passed I was back on my feet and over at the door. Anastasia had locked it behind her, but I had my own key and it took only moments to get through. The light on the stairs was switched on – a final confirmation that we had the electricity we needed. I slipped off my shoes so as to make no sound, then silently climbed the stairs up to Anastasia's room.

A figure stood on the landing above me. For a dreadful moment I thought it was Anastasia, aware of the trap that awaited her and now preparing to turn the tables on me. But it was Nadya. I signalled at her to go back upstairs, but she shook her head. I made another gesture for her to stay where she was and she seemed prepared to comply. Just as I had done in the early hours of that morning, I took hold of the door handle. I could see the glow of the regular light at the bottom of the door. That was to the good – it would make it easier to see the switch.

For some inexplicable reason I counted silently to three, then swiftly opened the door.

The scene beyond was just what I had expected it to be, yet still it filled me with terror and revulsion. They were kneeling on the bed, facing each other, both stripped to the waist. I could see them from the side. Anastasia was close to the man, her breasts pressed flat against his chest. The bulge of the child in her belly was clearer than it had ever been. Their arms were at their sides, but their fingers were lightly entwined. The man's head was tilted back, his mouth opened wide in a silent scream of terrifying intensity. The cause was plain to see. Anastasia's mouth too was wide open, her lips pressed against his neck. I could see the trickle of blood running down to his shoulder, as it pumped from him faster than she could drink it.

She must have heard me, for she raised her head and looked at me. Her eyes radiated excitement and pleasure, and a strange sense of victory. The man's blood was smeared over her lips, cheeks and chin, as well as across his own neck, centring on the two dark holes where her teeth had penetrated his skin. I glanced in the mirror – as if further confirmation were needed – and saw nothing. Anastasia appeared to be about to speak, but I had no interest in what she might have to say. I reached out in the direction of the switch, knowing that eventually I would have to look at what I was doing, but for now unable to tear my eyes away from Anastasia's.

Then a hand gripped my wrist. I looked in horror to see that it was Nadya, standing beside me. I tried to fathom why she should be preventing me from doing what we had planned together – what we both knew to be so necessary. Then she spoke.

'Let me,' she said.

Her other hand was already on the switch and she didn't wait for my confirmation before closing it. The immediate effect was just the same as it had been the previous night. The room was filled with illumination. This time, because the main bulb had already been on, it took only moments for my eyes to adjust.

Anastasia's reaction was quicker. I don't know how she so readily sensed the danger from the lights, which must have been quite unknown to her, but in an instant she had grabbed a blanket from the bed and thrown it over herself as a shield from the rays. It would be a matter of little effort for me to go and rip it away from her, and a pleasure to watch as her body swiftly decayed, but for the moment I was distracted.

Anastasia was not the only one in the room to be affected by the Yablochkov Candles. The man – her victim – reacted in a way that was thrillingly familiar. The only other two vampires I had seen die this way were exposed to just a single candle and their deaths had been agonizingly – gratifyingly – slow. Here the same process was compressed into mere seconds. It was the smear of blood at his neck which erupted into flame first. I had long known that their blood was the thing most sensitive to light. His exposed skin followed suit moments later, blackening and then shrinking and peeling away to reveal the muscles and organs beneath. These didn't even have time to burn, but simply transformed into a grey dust which for a moment occupied the space in the air where his upper body had once been. His legs and midriff were protected by his trousers and were not so instantly destroyed. They fell forward on to the bed and began to smoke as the light penetrated them from the opening at the top, where he had effectively been cut in two. The dust of his upper half, buoyed by the air, fell more slowly and the echo they had left in the shape of his body smoothly dissolved to nothing.

The whole process had caused hardly a sound to be emitted, but now the silence was broken by the shattering of glass and the splintering of wood. A cold breeze suddenly filled the room. I looked and saw the window smashed. Hanging from the remnants of the frame was the blanket that Anastasia had used to protect herself. I ran over and looked down on to the street. There she was, splayed out in the snow, face down, her hair cascading over her naked back. I could see wisps of smoke rising from where the light had caught her. From what I could make out, most of her left hand was missing, but that would soon regrow. A few passers-by were already forming a circle around her. Some approached to see if she was dead, others looked up at the window from which she had fallen – and therefore at me.

But before any of them could do very much she was on her feet. Upon some leftover human instinct she raised her arms to cover her naked breasts. I could clearly see that only the thumb of her left hand remained. The rest of it must have been exposed as she clutched the blanket to her. She looked up at me, but her eyes showed no hatred, merely that sense of victory I had witnessed before, though stronger now.

Then she ran.

CHAPTER IX

I WAS OUT ON THE STREET IN SECONDS AND RUNNING IN THE DIRECtion she had gone – back towards the Fontanka. I clutched my sharpened cane in my hand. It was only when I reached the Panteleimonovsky Bridge that I noticed Polkan running beside me. He should have been safely locked away with Nadya at the top of the house, but they'd both proved to be as disobedient as each other.

I stood on the bridge and looked around, fearing that the chase was cold already, but then I saw her. She had got down on to the ice and was running – or trying to run – along the surface of the Moika. Her gait was a pathetic, shambling limp and I could see that her left leg was shorter than the right. It too must have been burned in the light. Like her fingers, it would regrow, but slowly under the stress of her escape. I needed to catch her while she was weak.

I found an iron ladder fixed to the wall and climbed quickly down to the level of the river, then ran as best as I could after her. My winter boots had cleats to prevent me slipping in the snow and they gave me reasonable grip on the ice. Polkan could find no way down, but kept level with me on the embankment.

The route that Anastasia was taking was by no means certain. Even if she decided not to climb back up to street level, there were many branches in the network of rivers and canals she could choose to take. When I'd seen her she had already been beyond the mouth of the Lebyazhya Canal, but then the Moika kinked to the right and she was out of sight. The next point for her to turn off was along the Yekaterininsky Canal. I looked down it, but it ran dead straight for almost a verst and was well lit. The only place to hide was behind the slight protrusion of the Church on Spilled Blood. It was a possibility, but if I'd been in her shoes I'd have stayed on the Moika which here began a curve to the left that I knew would eventually take it through a full semicircle. Even if she kept only slightly ahead, it would be a long time before I caught sight of her again. She must have understood that much herself, and therefore that would be the way she would go.

By now I had slowed to a walk – I'd be flattering myself even to apply an adjective such as brisk. I followed the curve of the river round, with ever decreasing confidence that I would be able to find her. Whenever I glanced up I could see Polkan, but he was no bloodhound and his only interest seemed in keeping close to me. As I walked I considered what I had seen in Anastasia's room – and what I had not seen. I'd taken a brief glance in the mirror to confirm that she had no reflection, but I'd also seen nothing of the man she was with on the bed. I'd scarcely had time to take that in before I saw a much clearer proof that he was a vampire – his destruction by the light of the Yablochkov Candles. It was beyond doubt; Anastasia had been drinking the blood of a fellow vampire – and I was certain that later, had events not interceded, he would have drunk hers.

I'd witnessed the same thing years before between Dmitry and Zmyeevich, and I knew the consequence. If two vampires exchanged blood then their minds would gradually become one – and the stronger mind would take control. That could only ever have been Zmyeevich. But in this case who possessed the stronger mind: Anastasia or the *voordalak* she had been with? The answer was obvious enough. When I had first seen her she had been with another *voordalak*: Ilya, Nadya's brother. What I'd witnessed then was just what I'd seen tonight. Anastasia could hardly be handing over possession of her mind to two of them. It must have been she who was doing the taking. I remembered how I'd asked Dmitry about Ilya's seemingly brutish character – how like the *oprichniki* he was. That was easily explained if he and Anastasia had been exchanging blood for long enough. And Ilya wasn't the only one of them who had displayed that base, bestial attitude. How many others of them might Anastasia be trying to control? The vampire

154

she had been with tonight had been dressed in the uniform of a soldier. Could he have been another of Dmitry's elite brigade?

If so, what was her reason for it? It could be for simple pleasure, but I felt sure it must be more than that. She wanted power over other vampires – at least two of them, perhaps more. Was she trying to take over from Dmitry, to take them away from his command? She must have known of him and what he was doing; she'd have learned that from Ilya. Or was she working *for* Dmitry? I had no reason to trust him when he said he didn't know her. Perhaps after his own experiences he was too squeamish to exchange blood with them for himself. It might be easier to take control of them through her. But it would be a risk; how could one *voordalak* ever trust another? It was all speculation. I was confident that I understood what Anastasia had been doing, but I had little concept as to why.

I was close to the Hermitage now. To the right another branch of the canal network – the Winter Ditch – led directly to the nearby Neva. Again I had to put myself in her shoes and guess whether she would go that way for the greater chance of freedom. On the other hand, ahead lay the Pevchesky Bridge, so wide that it was more of a tunnel than a bridge. It was the perfect dark, dank hideaway in which a *voordalak* might lurk and allow its wounds to heal.

Polkan made the decision for me. He stood with his hind legs on the embankment and his forepaws resting on the railing, barking into the darkness beneath the bridge in front of me. It was undoubtedly her domain rather than mine, but she was weakened and this might be my only chance. I reached into my pocket and drew out the torch, twisting it to turn it on. The light did not penetrate far into the shadows. I scanned it from side to side, then took a few steps forward.

'I'll warm those up for you if you like, sweetheart!' The shout, from somewhere above and behind me, was followed by a salacious laugh, which was instantly echoed by others. There was nothing special about it – the nights were full of such catcalls, with so many out on the streets and so much drink inside them. Even so, it was enough to distract me slightly from peering into the darkness, and make me wonder what the man might have meant. I tried to push it from my mind, afraid that any lack of attention would make me vulnerable. But then suddenly I understood.

I turned and saw Anastasia climbing up the embankment. A man – I guessed the one whom I'd heard – was reaching down to help her, leering at her naked breasts. I could see her bare foot, its toes finding purchase in the gaps between the heavy stones that kept the river in its channel. Clearly that wound had healed. She was reaching up to the man with her left hand. He was about to grasp it but then his face fell. He muttered the words 'Jesus Christ' and stepped back from the railing, leaving Anastasia hanging there with an outstretched arm. I could now see what he had seen; that her fingers were still not fully formed. Her thumb and little finger reached out for help, but there was nothing between them – they were merely a pincer, like the tail of an earwig. It meant she could not climb as well as she might have. It was my chance to strike.

I ran across the ice and leapt up to grab her ankle. She was taken by surprise and couldn't maintain her grip. We both fell back on to the ice, skidding across to the middle of the river. She was on her feet quicker than me and at the next moment was standing over me. She cut a bizarre figure, though none the less terrifying for it. Her body was as puny as it had ever been, and semi-naked as she was, she might have appeared utterly vulnerable. One foot was booted, the other bare. I could only presume that the light of the Yablochkov Candles had caught her around the calf and completely severed one leg, boot and all, which had now regrown. Her hand was still mutilated, but even now I could see three tiny, wiggling stumps of fingers which had not been there before. Her face was still smeared with blood and she bared her fangs to reveal more. Her eyes bore down on me with anger and hatred as she prepared to pounce.

I held the point of my cane out towards her, bracing the other end against my chest. It was enough to make her wary. She stepped to one side and I ensured that the sharp tip followed her. I pushed against the ice with my feet and gradually slid across to the other side of the river, but she walked forwards and kept a constant distance from me. Behind her, on the bank, I could see spectators gathering, but no one tried to intervene. They must have been wondering what to make of it.

When Anastasia finally made her move it was swift and devastating. She threw herself sideways, her hands stretched out towards the ice as if she were about to perform a cartwheel. But instead of swinging her legs over her, she let them scythe horizontally, catching the cane just above where I gripped it and knocking it from my hand. Then she pushed off with her hands and almost bounded the few feet towards me. From somewhere I heard a cheer; the watching crowds were impressed by her move. In an instant she was on top of me, her hands on my wrists pinning me down, her mouth open and bloody, her eyes searching my throat, seeking out the point at which she would bite. I kicked out, trying to shake her off me. Despite her strength, she was no heavier than a living child of her age would have been, and so I was able to move my body with surprising ease. It was enough to distract her, if only slightly. However, she had a solution.

She raised her knee sharply between my legs. The pain was excruciating, but it didn't stop me hearing the laughter of our audience. I saw stars before my eyes and felt the urge to vomit. It lasted only moments, but it was enough for her to push my chin back and lower her face towards my neck. I felt her tongue against my skin.

Then, suddenly I was free. She had rolled away from me, to the right. I looked and saw her on her back, a white figure pressing her into the ice, just as she had held me down. Its teeth were at her throat just as hers had been at mine. It was Polkan. I don't know how he'd got down on to the ice – perhaps he'd simply jumped – but he had taken Anastasia entirely by surprise. It didn't last. With a sharp twist of her body she hurled him through the air and against the wall. He let out a brief yelp, but was up again in an instant and bounding back towards her, greeted by enthusiastic shouts from the crowd. She was already on her feet, but his impact knocked her down again – he must have been almost as heavy as she was. He continued past her, unable to get much grip, but eventually he turned to face her, snarling.

By now quite an assembly had formed around us, watching the fight. They were on both sides of the river, leaning against the railing and looking down as though we were in a bear pit. No one did anything to stop us. Perhaps if I were to gain the upper hand then someone would come to the defence of the innocent young girl, but it seemed unlikely. I tried to stand, but did not have the strength. My chest was tight and my breathing short. However bravely Polkan might attempt to defend me, he could only fail. Then it would be merely a question of whether it was Anastasia or my own weak heart that ultimately did for me.

Polkan ran towards her, gaining speed as he did and preparing to leap and knock her down once again. Then I saw the glint of something in her hand. It was the switchblade she had shown me in her bedroom. She held it low as if she were in a street fight, ready to drive it upwards under her opponent's ribcage. It wasn't a tactic that required much adaptation if that opponent happened to be a dog. Polkan had no idea of the danger and continued his charge.

I shouted to him, 'Polkan!' but it made no difference. He launched himself from the ice and flew through the air towards her. The moment his paws left the ground, when it was too late for him to alter his motion, she stepped to one side – no human could have timed the manoeuvre so precisely. As he went past her hand jerked towards him and I heard him yelp again. He hit the ice without any attempt to place his paws and slid until his body came to a natural halt.

Anastasia turned again to me and began to approach. She folded the knife closed and pocketed it, baring her teeth once more. At that moment the ice shook, as if some heavy weight had landed on it. I saw nothing, and could only guess it had happened behind me. Anastasia most certainly saw it. She froze, but only for a moment. Then she turned and fled, the disappointed jeers of the crowd around us ringing in her ears. She headed down the Winter Ditch, towards the Neva. I didn't have the strength to follow, nor the inclination.

I was still unable to get to my feet. I could scarcely breathe except in short, painful rasps. I swivelled myself around on the ice to see what was behind me. I shouldn't have been surprised; it was Dmitry. Even if she had never met him, she had seen him through the eyes of Ilya and others. He was a huge man; she would not have stood a chance against him in a fight.

'That's her, I take it,' he said.

I tried to speak, but my lungs would not respond. I reached into my coat and searched for my silver pillbox. I found it at last and took out a tablet, slipping it into my mouth. Dmitry came over and grabbed the collar of my shirt, hauling me over to the edge of the river so I could lean back against the wall. It must have been an odd sight, but the audience had already begun to disperse. Nothing was going to live up to what they'd just witnessed.

'What are those?' Dmitry asked.

'Pills – for my heart.' I was pleased that the power of speech had returned, though I immediately regretted revealing my weakness to him. He sat down beside me, leaning against the wall as I was.

'Do you recognize her?' I asked.

He shook his head. 'Does it matter? There's probably vampires from all over Europe in Petrograd at the moment. It's easy pickings. When humanity is at its lowest, we come to feed.'

I knew it wasn't as simple as that. Anastasia had been feeding on other vampires, not on humans – not solely on humans. But Dmitry seemed to have admitted to something else. 'With the exception of your noble self?' I asked.

'I've still fed,' he said.

I didn't respond. I didn't have the strength. I looked over to where Polkan lay.

'But I believe I've done some good,' Dmitry continued.

'Good?'

'Things could have been a lot worse. Thousands more might have died if we hadn't come.'

I let out a curt laugh, which hurt my chest. 'There's still time,' I said.

He looked at me quizzically. 'I take it you haven't heard, then.'

'Heard what?'

He chuckled. 'And you a member of the Duma.'

'What?' I insisted.

He got to his feet and looked up at the stars, and at the tall buildings that loomed over us. He breathed deeply, though he had little need to. Then he looked back down towards me.

'It's over,' he said. 'Nikolai has abdicated. We're free.'

OCTOBER

CHAPTER X

'YOU'RE ON A LIST.'

'What do you mean?' I asked. 'A list of what?'

'Don't be an idiot, Mihail Konstantinovich.' Yelena Dmitrievna's voice sounded distant over the telephone line, even though she was just a few versts away. 'The first thing they'll do is round up anyone they think might be dangerous. It's only a matter of days before we make—'

She stopped mid-sentence. 'Yelena?' I raised my voice and spoke closer to the mouthpiece. 'Yelena?'

I rattled the switch from which the earpiece normally hung, more out of irritation than because it would achieve anything. The line had been cut.

I wasn't entirely surprised. A lot had happened since the February Days, not least that I'd had a telephone installed in our house. The Bolsheviks were far more powerful now than anyone had thought they ever could be. Their leader, Nikolai Lenin – not his real name – had returned from exile in April and then gone to hide in Finland. He'd only recently returned to the city again. Trotsky had been back since May. Together they'd managed to turn the Soviet into an instrument of Bolshevik power. The party itself was now based at the Smolny Institute, of all places – a former girls' school attached to a convent, a little way to the east of the Tavricheskiy Palace. That's where Yelena Dmitrievna had been calling from.

It wasn't in any way beyond the Bolsheviks to cut telephone lines if they couldn't get what they wanted by more democratic means – but they were unlikely to disable communications to their own building. Of course it could have been I who was cut off. I wound the handle of the telephone rapidly. It reminded me of the detonators I'd used when I was in the sappers. It was the same mechanism, but to a different end.

'Number, please?'

I hung up the earpiece. It had been unlikely they'd bother to cut me off. I was nobody – nobody at all since the Duma had been disbanded. Even so, I was important enough to be on a Bolshevik list, according to Yelena. I should never have spoken out against Lenin. It had done no one any good, and could do me a lot of harm.

But if it wasn't the Bolsheviks who had cut the telephone lines then it could only be the government – still the Provisional Government. Whatever the upheaval since the tsar's departure, some things hadn't changed.

The abdication hadn't quite been the end of the Romanov dynasty. Originally Nikolai had thought to hand the throne over to his son, the sickly Aleksei. But he'd been told that he himself would almost certainly have to live the rest of his life in exile and so would be parted from the boy. He couldn't face that and instead named his brother Mihail as his successor. Some people pointed out that this was unconstitutional – the tsar had no right to nominate who would replace him. But what did that matter in such times? We could make up the law as we went along. Mihail was an experienced soldier and he'd seen the rioting in Petrograd at first hand. He knew that accepting power would be a poisoned chalice. He turned it down. The reign of the Romanovs came to an end. Russia was, by default, a republic. Syeva was one of the first to be buried in land that he could truly call his own.

I almost wished Zmyeevich were still alive, just so that he could see his chances of ruling Russia decay to nothing, much as his own body had. He would still have been able to transform any Romanov he chose into a vampire, sway to his will, but what would that gain him? Currently Nikolai Aleksandrovich Romanov's dominion encompassed just one large house in Tobolsk. He could not even leave its grounds without permission.

But the fall of the Romanovs had not brought any real gains to Russia. We were still at war, though we had no means to fight.

We were still hungry, but had no means to feed ourselves. Lvov had struggled on as Prime Minister until July. Then there were more protests in the streets and troops were called out to stop them. It was called a counter-revolution, but no one took that idea seriously. Most of us thought that the Bolsheviks were stirring things up in order to seize power, but in the end they didn't act. It wasn't that they didn't want to – they just weren't ready. They were better prepared now.

Kerensky took over from Lvov and revealed himself to be as self-interested as we'd always suspected. Within a month there was more trouble. The Supreme Commander-in-Chief of the armed forces, General Kornilov, mounted an assault on the Soviet, but it was easily rebuffed. Some saw it as an attack on Kerensky, but others suggested that Kerensky was in cahoots with Kornilov and had decided that the Soviet was now a threat to him.

Kerensky held on to his position, but was weakened. He promised elections and to hand over power to the resulting Constituent Assembly, but the date kept changing. We'd elected the so called 'Pre-Parliament', but that had only assembled a few weeks ago. I doubted it would prove to have much worth. To cap it all, Kerensky had moved himself and the Provisional Government into the Winter Palace. Nobody missed the symbolism of it.

And all this time the Bolsheviks had been growing stronger. For the people – the soldiers and workers who had made the revolution – the Soviet was *their* parliament. And it wasn't just the one in Petrograd. There were Soviets in cities and towns all over the country now, elected, representing the people at a local level. It was Lenin who had coined the phrase: 'All Power to the Soviets'. Within the Soviets, it was all power to the Bolsheviks. And in case that didn't work, they had men infiltrating the factories and the army and the navy, all ready to make sure the people acted correctly when the time came.

They didn't even bother to hide it. The Bolsheviks in the Petrograd Soviet had formed a 'Military Revolutionary Committee' which claimed authority over the garrison in the city, and just yesterday over the Peter and Paul Fortress. Kamenev, one of Lenin's few opponents in the party, had written an article in *Novaya Zhizn* arguing that now was not the right time for a *coup d'état*. But why even write the article if nothing was being planned? Everyone knew it was coming, but no one had the first idea how to stop it. Now, though, it seemed Kerensky had acted. He'd had the phone lines cut. I could only imagine he'd be closing down the Bolshevik presses as well.

As for my own problems, I'd seen neither Dmitry, nor Anastasia, nor any vampire, as far as I knew, since our fight on the ice of the Moika. Dmitry had been coming to find me after I'd failed to show up at Senate Square. I'd been lucky his path took him along the Moika. We'd spoken for a little while. I told him what Anastasia had been doing, and he grimaced at the thought of one vampire sharing its blood with another. But he'd assured me that he would keep his promise – that now the revolution was done he and his men, those of them he could trust, would leave Petrograd. He also told me that he wouldn't go far. There was always the risk of counter-revolution. He'd stay close enough to the city to come to its aid if the need arose. Part of me just wished he'd leave us alone, but I knew how powerful an ally he could be. We might have needed him in July, when the Provisional Government was close to toppling. Perhaps he came, but he wouldn't have been able to do much in the height of summer, with only six hours of darkness. Now the nights were drawing in again. It wasn't winter yet. There was snow, but it didn't settle. The rivers and canals still flowed as water.

I went upstairs, checking as I did the new switches and the new lights. A hundred years before – more like two hundred – a Russian peasant would have bedecked his home with garlic and crucifixes to keep the *voordalak* at bay. Nowadays people knew better. Most thought they knew better in that they believed there was no such thing as a vampire. I simply knew that garlic and crosses were no defence. It had taken me a while to find enough Yablochkov Candles to have one in every room. They weren't as popular as they used to be. In some places I'd had to use other types of arc light. I could make a good guess that they would be as effective, but they were untested. Each room now had a second switch. If Anastasia came back then it would take only the flick of a finger to send her to her death, or flying out of the window again to safety. We'd never had cause to use them.

'I'm going out,' I said.

Nadya looked at me. She could tell something was wrong. 'Has she . . . ?'

I shook my head. 'Nothing to do with that. Politics.'

'Is something happening?'

'That's what I'm going to find out.'

She began to stroke Polkan, taking comfort from his calm and warmth. He'd been lucky to survive, so the vet said, both that the knife missed his heart and that the wound hadn't become infected. Even so, he didn't have much movement in his left foreleg now. He could get about the house, but we never went for long walks any more.

I went downstairs again and was soon outside. Superficially it was reminiscent of February – except for the weather. There were groups of workers and soldiers milling about, looking for something to protest at. Among them, though, was something new: men in dark leather coats. It had become almost the uniform of the Bolsheviks out on the street. The fact that the proletariat they purported to represent could never have afforded such a garment didn't seem to matter – equality came to some before others. Just as with Kamenev's letter, there was no secrecy to it. These men were there to lead the people, to rally them in support of the Bolshevik party. For now there was nothing to do, and so they waited.

The reason that they had chosen to wait here, on our street, soon became clear. It was only a short walk to the Panteleimonovsky Bridge but once again – just as in February – it was guarded. There were probably fewer men in the army loyal to Kerensky than there had been loyal to Nikolai, but he had managed to find some. They would be all over the city – and those bridges that could be raised would have been. Now, with the water below flowing, guarding the bridges would be more effective than it had been in February, but the strategy still had the weakness that it relied upon the loyalty on the pickets and their willingness to fire upon their own countrymen. In February they had not proved faithful to a regime that had stood for three centuries. What allegiance would they show to one that had been around just seven months?

Fortunately a member of the Duma – even though that body

no longer existed – was better respected now than he had been in February, and so my papers saw me across the bridge. Within the cordon the city was not much different from outside. There were groups of factory workers, mostly accompanied by a distinctive Bolshevik leader. Kerensky had acted too late. He'd have done better to withdraw those men he trusted to a tighter perimeter. But even so, that would only defer the end.

I followed the Moika, taking almost the exact same route I had when pursuing Anastasia; the only difference was that I stuck to the embankment. As I approached the Pevchesky Bridge I glanced down to the spot where we had fought. The dark turbid water flowed swiftly under the bridge, out towards the sea. It was hard to imagine that we had been able to stand there. And yet in no more than a month or so the surface would be solid once again. I turned away from the river and into Palace Square. Now it became clear that Kerensky's mind had been following a similar path to my own. He knew he wouldn't be able to hold the bridges. His plan was to make a stand here, at the Winter Palace. There were armed men out in the square and I could see figures at the windows too. It was hard to divine what purpose they might serve. If the Winter Palace were surrounded and isolated then Petrograd – and hence Russia – was lost. I could only guess that troops had already been recalled from the Front and that the hope was to be able to hold out until they arrived. But the army at the Front was as Bolshevized as anywhere, and there was little doubt as to whose side they'd be on if and when they arrived.

As I crossed the square and got close to the façade of the palace I noticed that I had been mistaken in the term 'armed men'. It turned out that the majority of them were women. At the gate the sentry who inspected my papers was one of them. She was in a military uniform, though I didn't recognize it. Her pretty face peeped out nervously from beneath an oversized woollen cap. Next to her stood a boy – a cadet by the looks of him. He was half her size. It was laughable to imagine either of them on the battlefield.

'What regiment are you from?' I asked her.

'First Petrograd Women's Battalion of Death,' she said earnestly.

I'd heard of it, but its formation was a sign of how terribly things were going at the Front and how badly we needed anyone to replace our losses. And it wasn't just casualties; sickness and desertion were having as great an impact on our numbers as did enemy operations.

'Your country is very proud of you,' I said as I walked past her.

I'd been inside the Winter Palace a number of times since Kerensky had moved the government there, but before that only once, back in 1881, when I'd come here to visit my father Konstantin and his brother, Tsar Aleksandr II. I could hardly claim that the place was familiar to me. This time I made my way to the office of Aleksandr Ivanovich Konovalov. He was one of the few original members of the Provisional Government to still be in the cabinet. He had two roles: Kerensky's deputy, which he loathed, and Minister for Trade and Industry, which, given his background in the textile business, he quite enjoyed. He'd not done too badly out of the war or the revolution. He'd always been good to his workers – comparatively speaking – and done so out of conscientiousness. But it did lead to the benefit that his business was far less hit by strikes when they came. Today he sat morosely at his desk, gazing into space. He smiled when he saw me, but it was unconvincing.

'It's started then?' I said.

He nodded. 'Phone lines cut, presses closed, the city locked down. And now we wait for them to make a move.'

'Why now?'

'The Soviet Congress starts tomorrow. Delegates from Soviets all over the country are already in the city.'

'So?'

Konovalov sighed. 'When the Bolsheviks take over, they'll need to legitimize their regime. Obviously they've got the Petrograd Soviet in their pocket. But if they can get approval from all the delegates – or most of them – it'll make it harder for anyone to object. It'll buy them time if nothing else.'

'You don't think we'll be able to stop them?'

'I'm not sure that's the plan. The idea is just to scare them off. They can only try it once. If they fail then we can deluge the country with propaganda about how they attempted to overthrow the legitimate government. But they have to try – and that's a risk for them. That's why they bottled it in July. It's much easier for them just to sit there and claim that we're the counter-revolutionaries.'

'That's ridiculous.'

'Is it? Not to the people out there. You know how much they hate Kerensky – especially now he's moved in here. They're calling him Napoleon.'

'Napoleon did a lot of good for France,' I said.

He gestured outside with his head. 'Go and tell them that.'

'So the defence here is just for show?'

'If you can call it a defence.'

'How many?'

'About three thousand.'

'Can they be relied upon?'

'Maybe. Problem these days is the more reliable a soldier is, the less capable he is.' He searched through the papers on his desk until he found what he was after. He summarized it for me. 'We've got two companies of Cossacks – that's something, I suppose, though if they're as loyal to us as they were to the tsar, we're in trouble. The rest are cadets – just boys.'

'And the women?'

He laughed. 'Well, at least *they'll* be faithful to Kerensky. They're his pet project – but only because he couldn't recruit anyone else after February. And they don't have soldiers' committees, so there's a chance they're not Bolshevized.'

'Can they fight?'

'We'd do better to send them to the German barracks to spread the pox.' He paused, then shook his head vigorously. 'That was a stupid thing to say. They're doing their best.'

'Even so, it's hardly a long-term plan, is it? If the Bolsheviks hold back this time, it's only because they're waiting for a better chance.'

'There is one hope,' he said.

'And what's that?'

'The Germans might invade.'

There was another hope, though a slim one, and certainly not one that I could mention to Konovalov. I spent a few more hours at the Winter Palace, but heard much the same from everyone. Not many were as forthright in discussing the prospect of a German occupation as he had been, and I doubted he really meant it. It was an insoluble dilemma for any Russian patriot. We couldn't give in to Germany and the central powers – that would be defeatist. But Russia was so debilitated by the war that it was ungovernable until a peace settlement was reached. We'd harboured some hope of a military victory in the summer – with the so-called Kerensky Offensive – but it had been a failure. Now if he sued for peace his failure would be complete. Only the Bolsheviks had a policy to end the war, but their idea of a 'just peace' was a pipe dream. The Germans had no reason to give us anything in a settlement. And the Bolsheviks had most to fear from them. Not so long ago Germany had been bankrolling Lenin and his party, but that had been a temporary arrangement. They backed whichever side was weaker – not out of love for the underdog; simply because it would destabilize the country. But in the end they'd act true to form. They'd restore Nikolai. The war would prove to have been a minor spat in comparison with upholding the Divine Right of Kings.

What the Bolsheviks really hoped for was a socialist revolution in Germany – across the whole world. Then, so they saw it, there'd be no need for war at all. I didn't know much about German politics, but from what I'd heard it didn't seem likely. Russia's best chance was if the rest of the Entente powers could defeat Germany quickly, and give us an opportunity to put together a stable government. But they hadn't managed it in three years. There were the Americans in there too now, but it would still take time. Time was something we didn't have, and Trotsky, Lenin and the rest knew it.

I went home and ate with Nadya, then waited till late into the evening. Then I went out again to make a rendezvous in which I might be the only participant. Even so, I had to try it. It seemed like a better hope of saving the revolution than the Women's Battalion of Death could ever be. I got there early, around nine o'clock, and stood beneath the Bronze Horseman. Dmitry had said he would return to Petrograd if the revolution came under threat. We'd not said explicitly that we'd maintain our previous meeting place and time, but it was a chance worth taking.

The biggest question was whose side he would be on. He'd said he'd come back to fight counter-revolution, but that certainly wasn't the Bolsheviks' aim. They wanted to go further than most of us had ever dreamed, and their propaganda was that it was Kerensky and the Provisional Government who wanted to turn the clock back. I couldn't entirely disagree, but even that would be better than life under men like Trotsky. 'We must put an end once and for all to the Papist-Quaker babble about the sanctity of human life.' I'd heard him say it in the corridors of the Tavricheskiy Palace. I was neither a Papist nor a Quaker, but I didn't much like the kind of religion he seemed to preach.

But as to Dmitry's view, I simply didn't know. He might regard me as an enemy of the revolution, in which case I had little hope of surviving our meeting. But his beliefs had been forged a century before. I could see very little that the Decembrists and the Bolsheviks had in common.

'I thought I might find you here.'

Dmitry stood at the edge of Senate Square, his back to the Neva, the lights of Vasilievskiy Island forming a backdrop. He was flanked by two figures. I recognized one of them from our first encounter in the Novodyevichye Cemetery. I had no doubt they were both *voordalaki*. Dmitry walked towards me, leaving them where they were. They hung their heads and muttered to each other, then one giggled childishly. The other quickly followed suit. I couldn't help but remember what Anastasia had been doing and the effect it could have on the mind of a vampire.

I led Dmitry further away from them, along the embankment, until I was confident we were out of earshot. 'Are you sure you can trust them?' I asked.

'What do you mean?'

'Ilya wasn't the only one I saw with Anastasia, remember.'

'But neither of these two?'

'Of course not.' The only other vampire I'd seen her with was dead.

'I think I'd know if they were disloyal to me.'

I could hardly argue with him. 'What have you done about Ilya?'

'We've parted company.'

172

'Is he in Petrograd?'

'Not if he's got any sense. And it's not only him that's left me. That's one reason I trust these two. They've stuck with me.'

'And why are *you* here?' I asked.

'You know why. Because the revolution is under threat.' I still found it hard to believe that that was his real interest, but I could not deny the passion in his voice.

'And who's threatening it?'

He'd been stooping slightly, down to my level, so that we wouldn't be overheard, but now he stood upright with a smile on his lips. 'I was rather hoping you could tell me.'

I paused. If I was to win Dmitry as an ally, I'd do well to choose my words carefully. On the other hand, Dmitry was too wily to be fooled by anything less than absolute candour. 'The Bolsheviks are a threat to everything we've achieved,' I said.

'That rather depends on what you think you've achieved. As far as I'm concerned you've got rid of Nikolai. I don't see that the Bolsheviks are going to bring *him* back.'

'Lenin won't call himself tsar, but he won't be much different.'

'And Kerensky will? He already seems very comfortable in the Winter Palace.'

'He's an ambitious man,' I said, 'and a vain one. But he doesn't have the strength to be a dictator.'

'Then he's bound to be replaced by a stronger one. Why should I try to prevent the inevitable?' The question wasn't rhetorical.

'It's obvious, isn't it? Remember when you told me about *The Rite of Spring*; about how those great Russians – Stravinsky and the rest – couldn't stomach actually living in Russia?'

He nodded warily.

'Well do you think they're more likely to come back under Kerensky, or under Lenin?'

He gave a slight smile. 'I'd come to much the same conclusion myself.'

'Do you have a plan?'

'Until we know exactly what *their* plan is, it's hard to counter it. The best option may simply be to scare them – and that's easy.'

I didn't like the way he said it, nor the images it brought to my mind. And anyway, I wasn't convinced it would be the most effective tactic. If they shied away from acting now, they'd only try again later. As Konovalov had suggested, if we could defeat them, we might be rid of them for ever.

'Hardly noble, though,' I said.

'What would be?'

'To defeat them in open battle.'

'Where?'

There was only one place. 'The Winter Palace – that's the last stronghold the Provisional Government has.'

'And that's where the Bolsheviks will attack?'

'Where else?'

'Soon?'

'It has to be.'

'And what if it happens during the day? We can be no help to you then.'

I shrugged. I knew as well as he did, there was no answer I could give him.

He looked out across the Neva. 'I bet that's got something to do with it.' He pointed as he spoke.

'The *Avrora*,' I said.

'You're sure?'

I nodded. I wasn't a naval man, but I'd learned enough fighting the Japanese. The silhouette – three funnels and two masts – was unmistakably a Pallada class cruiser. There'd only been three built. One had been sunk and the other captured. That only left the *Avrora*. Since the revolution she'd been under the control, like many other ships, of her own revolutionary committee. And that meant she belonged to the Bolsheviks.

'She's in a good position to fire on the Winter Palace,' I said. It was stating the obvious.

'I'll see if I can find out how they plan to use her. We'll meet here same time tomorrow – unless it's already kicked off.'

'Very well,' I replied.

He seemed to be waiting for me to leave, but I remained still, looking out across the river at the ship. He turned and went back to his two comrades. The three spoke for a few moments in soft voices, occasionally glancing in my direction. Then they departed. One of them headed in the direction of the Admiralty, while Dmitry and the other went across the square towards Saint Isaac's. I waited until they had disappeared from view, then set off myself.

The easiest route home was the way I had come, walking along the bank of the Neva until I could turn in and follow the Moika. It would allow me to take another look at what was happening at the Winter Palace. But I had a more immediate concern. I was not alone. It wasn't easy to pick them out amongst the hundreds that were walking through the city, but I'd acquired an instinct for it.

There were four of them – two groups of two – perhaps with others that I hadn't spotted. One pair was behind me, the other to one side. Those two must have picked me up somewhere around Palace Square. The last thing I wanted to do was lead them to my house, so I turned on to Nevsky Prospekt. I didn't make any attempt to lose them, not at first. It would be easier if they thought I had no suspicions, so I would let them stay with me, if only for a little while.

The immediate question was who they were. It could have been Dmitry, or the *voordalaki* that followed him, but it seemed unlikely. For a start, there had only been three of them, not four, and although I couldn't see the faces of my pursuers, none of them had Dmitry's unmistakable build. That didn't mean he couldn't have sent others to follow me, but I couldn't see what reason he might have for it.

Another possibility seemed more likely – Yelena Dmitrievna had warned me of it. I was on some sort of Bolshevik arrest list. I'd not expected them to make any move until their coup began, but perhaps this was the first sign that that was precisely what was happening. The four men weren't wearing the distinctive leather coats of Bolshevik thugs, but even they understood that there were times when it was better to be covert.

It's not difficult to follow someone down Nevsky Prospekt. It runs in a dead straight line for almost three versts. It was busy tonight, with both traffic and pedestrians. The city felt very different from how it had in February. People were going about their business. The rich could still afford to eat out and to go to the theatre. The poor were still obliged to serve them. In February not a soul in the city – not even a cat or a dog – could have been unaware that something momentous was about to take place. Today that knowledge was limited to a select few. The Bolsheviks knew it and the Provisional Government knew it, along with a few others such as myself. The government could change tonight – perhaps it already had – and no one would notice any immediate difference. The transfer of power from Kerensky to Lenin might raise as little interest from the people at large as had that from Lvov to Kerensky. As long as it wasn't the tsar, nothing else mattered. I could only hope that would prove to be true.

The men following me had dropped back and spread out, two on either side of the prospekt. I'd left it long enough and now was the time to be doing something about them. I could have dodged down a side street, but if they knew the city they'd soon be able to find me. There was no chance that I'd be able to outrun any of them. My approach was much simpler.

As I approached the corner of Sadovaya Street I saw a tram waiting at the stop. I'd passed others along the way, but I had to get the timing just right, and this one was in the perfect position. There were two people waiting to get on – a man and a woman, together as far as I could judge. I stopped and stepped beneath one of the arches of the colonnade of Gostiny Dvor, pretending to light a cigarette, even though I'd never smoked. I made sure I didn't vanish completely – that would have raised the alarm with them. I just needed a pause, to time my next move.

The couple were on the tram now and the bell rang. That was my signal to move. I ran from the colonnade and across the pavement. The tram was already in motion when I leapt on to it. I managed to grab a rail to steady myself. A few of the passengers looked up disapprovingly to see an old man being so foolhardy, but none of them stood to offer me a seat. I looked back in the direction I had come from and saw two figures break into a run, but they couldn't catch the tram as it rolled smoothly away. I'd still need some luck; trams didn't always outpace pedestrians. But as long as we weren't held up at a checkpoint I should be all right.

We only stopped twice before reaching the Fontanka – once to pick up and once to set down. On the bridge stood the usual sentries. If we were detained for any length of time, I'd have to get off rather than give my pursuers the chance to catch up. But even that risked rousing the suspicion of the guards. As it was they scarcely gave us a second look. Their concern was with who was coming into the city centre, not who was leaving it. A pair of eyes peered in through the windows from under a peaked cap, but then we were waved through. I stayed on till we were at Znamenskaya Square, outside the Nikolaievsky Station. Even then I waited until the carriage had just begun to set off before stepping down on to the street. I went into the station and looked back up Nevsky Prospekt, but I saw no sign that they'd kept up with me.

I crossed back over the square, glancing at the hippopotamus statue that still stood there, and then made my way up Znamenskaya Street. At the first opportunity I turned off the thoroughfare and began to meander home. Finally I turned into Panteleimonovskaya Street, coming from the eastern end, away from the river as I had done for all those years when returning from the Duma. It was deserted now. The crowds of workers that had been here when I left had dispersed. As I got closer to the house I could see that ahead there was no longer a picket on the bridge, and so anyone coming this way would be able to get through to the centre of town. I couldn't guess whether they'd been recalled, overwhelmed, or had simply abandoned their post.

It was only when I'd passed the church, and beside it the last side street before home, that they revealed themselves. Ahead two figures emerged, one coming around each corner and standing still. I kept going for a little while, wondering whether I would be able to make it to – and through – my door before they got to me. They made no move. I stopped and turned. The other two were there – not close to me, simply waiting at the junction I'd just passed. There was no escape for me. My only chance was my own front door. I wondered if they knew that. Had they been following me, and chosen this as the best place to trap me, or did they already know that I lived here?

I began to walk again, feeling in my pocket as I did for the key, so that I could get in as quickly as possible. Ahead of me two women turned to come down the street, but one of my pursuers sent them quietly on their way. Still I couldn't be sure whether they were vampires or Bolsheviks. If the former, perhaps I could lure them into the house and then destroy them with the light that

I had at my command, or use my cane against them. If the latter, at least I would be able to barricade myself in. If the coup failed, they might not be in a position to come for me again. If it succeeded I had little hope anyway.

My fingers settled on the cold hard metal of my keys. I sifted through them in my pocket, still walking at a gentle pace, until I found the correct one. I glanced towards my door, judging how far I would have to run, imagining inserting the key into the lock, so that when the time came I would not fumble.

It was a mistake. One of them must have realized what I was thinking. The two in front of me began to sprint forward. I broke into a run too, not bothering to check what the others behind me were doing. The two in front were smart; one was heading straight for me, the other for the door, to cut off my path. I had the slightest advantage, but it was my only hope.

I pushed on harder and reached the door. The key was already in my hand, stretched out in front of me, but it was too late. A fist came down on my forearm and the keys slipped from my fingers, hitting the pavement with a brief jangle. One of the men ran into me from behind, throwing me against the heavy wooden door. A pair of hands grabbed my coat and turned me around to face them. His strength was enormous. He lifted me off my feet and I felt my body hit the door once again, this time my back. I kicked and flailed my fists, but I knew there was little hope.

'Get his wrists,' one of them shouted. 'Hold him.'

The two on either side obeyed and I found my arms pinned against the door. Another squatted and I felt him holding my feet. The one who had issued the orders did nothing. He looked into my face and I recognized him for the first time. The question of whether these were vampires or Bolsheviks was answered. It was Ilya. He bared his teeth, though he didn't seem about to bite. Instead he raised his hand and put it to my throat, pressing hard against it with all his weight behind him, cutting off the flow of blood to my brain. My vision started to blur.

And then I felt the strangest sensation as I – as all of us – began to fall backwards.

CHAPTER XI

MY HEAD HIT THE WOODEN FLOOR BEHIND ME, DAZING ME even more than Ilya's hand at my throat. Even so, one sensation was clear – a bright, blinding light, directly above me. I heard screams – at least two different voices, maybe more – and the hands that had been holding my wrists and legs and throat suddenly let go their grip. The scent of the burning flesh of a *voordalak* reached my nostrils.

Then another pair of hands, smaller and weaker, gripped me under the arms and tried to drag me away.

'For God's sake, help!' It was Nadya's voice. I wondered who she was talking to, but realized that it could only be me. I pushed against the ground with my arms and legs, noticing that my feet still felt strangely constrained. It was more down to Nadya than me, but I managed to move a little way. That was enough. She let go of me and ran round to the door. She gazed outside for a few seconds, but I could not see at what. Then she slammed it, locked it and bolted it. She leaned against it, her hands behind her back, staring upwards, gasping for air. In the intense arc light she looked like an angel.

I lay still, as breathless as she was. I thought of reaching into my pocket for my pills, but realized I didn't need them. My heart could be fickle in its weakness. I closed my eyes. For a minute I heard nothing but the sound of our harshly drawn breaths. Then I felt her beside me. I opened my eyes.

'Can you get up?' she asked.

I pushed myself into a sitting position, then drew my legs under me. She held my arm and I managed to get to my feet. I tried to

179

take a step but lost my balance and almost fell. I looked down at my feet.

'What the devil?' For some reason I spoke in a whisper.

With Nadya's help I hobbled over to sit on the stairs, then examined my legs more closely. There was a rope tied around them – or half tied. The knots were not tight or complete. Evidently they'd been interrupted in the middle of it when Nadya had opened the door and turned on the light. I undid the knots and threw the rope into a corner of the hallway.

'Why on earth would they do that? Why not just . . . ?' I hesitated to raise the concept with Nadya.

'Why not just kill you, you mean?'

I nodded, but she had no answer.

'Let's go upstairs,' she replied instead.

I rose to my feet again. Unthinking she went over to switch off the light.

'No,' I said. 'They're still out there. It'll keep them away – for tonight.'

We went up to the top floor. I could hear Polkan scratching against the living-room door, where Nadya had shut him in. Once we went in he seemed unconcerned, and lay down beside the hearth. Nadya poured me a brandy, then one for herself.

'How did you know they were vampires?' I asked.

'What?' She seemed absent-minded. 'Oh, I didn't. I didn't *know*, but what else would they be? Even if they were just thugs, the light might have scared them off.'

'You got down quickly. I assume you heard the fight.'

'No, I was watching for you. I always watch when you go out to see . . . him.'

'Dmitry?'

She nodded curtly. I recalled all those times earlier in the year when I'd gone to meet Dmitry. When I returned she'd always been sitting in her chair, pretending all was well. We fell into silence. I tried to make sense of what had happened – most particularly of why they had tried to tie me up. And why strangle me? It couldn't have been to kill me – they had teeth for doing that. It could only be that they wanted me unconscious.

'I recognized him, Misha.' She blurted it out like a confession.

My lips began to form the word 'Who?' but there was no point in playing the fool. Her own brother had been standing at the door, his hand at my throat. 'Ilya, you mean?' I said instead.

She nodded. 'I opened the door and you fell through, along with the other two. And he just stood there. He had a smile on his face. His hand was outstretched, as if he was about to greet me. For a moment I forgot what was happening. It was what I'd hoped for all these years; that he'd come and knock on the door and say that he forgave me. Or not even that, simply that he didn't reject me; that he was my brother and that he loved me, whatever I'd done.

'And then his face began to change. It was as if he'd come to this house at random, and hadn't expected it to be me who opened the door, and when it was he couldn't hide his look of disappointment. But it wasn't that, of course. It was the light. His skin was weak. It began to fall from his cheeks. He pulled back his hand to shield himself, but the hand wasn't there. What was left of it was blackened and burning. Then he ran, and so did the rest of them.'

'I should have told you,' I said.

She looked at me, blinking. Her eyes were wet, but no tears spilled down her cheeks. After a few seconds she laughed, but there was no humour in it, only bitterness.

'Don't be a *prostak*, Misha. I've known as long as you. Almost as long. I've always been just a few days – a few hours behind you.'

'But . . . how?'

'You mentioned his name, remember? Back in February. You told me about how you'd seen a girl – Anastasia, it turned out – selling herself to a soldier. And then all out of the blue you asked me about Ilya, as if it was quite unconnected.'

'It might have been.' It was a feeble attempt to defend myself, but I felt affronted, as though I'd been tricked.

'Not the way you said it. There was this tiny pause when you spoke his name, as if you were afraid you'd been caught out in a lie.' She giggled. 'It was just the same with me whenever I said your name in front of my husband.'

'But that didn't mean he was a . . . a *voordalak*.'

'Not straight away, no. Then I just thought you'd stumbled

across my brother getting his pleasure by screwing a pregnant girl in an alleyway. When I learned what she was, and worked out what he was, it was somehow . . . better.'

I felt the urge to shout at her, to walk over and shake her, slap her across the face and talk some sense into her. How could being a *voordalak* be better than anything? It was a certainty that Mama had brought me up with, that she'd somehow inherited from Aleksei. It was one step away from the romanticism that could make some people actually want to become a vampire, to cheat death and live – exist – like that throughout eternity. It was precisely the maudlin foolishness that had led Dmitry himself to follow exactly that path.

And yet Dmitry was the counter-argument to all that. However much I might loathe the *voordalak* as a concept, however much I might be revolted by the knowledge of how he gained sustenance, when I met him face to face I could only regard him as – insane though it sounded – a fellow human being. Whether I liked him or trusted him I wasn't sure, but he was not a creature on to which I could pour the revulsion that I so sincerely felt for his kind. But none of that was of any concern to Nadya. If she chose to find solace in the fact that her brother was the victim of some external evil and not a weak-willed man who was happy to indulge his carnal desires, then who was I to attempt to disabuse her?

'Let's go to bed,' I said.

We went out on to the landing and into our bedroom. Here it was darker, seemingly darker than usual in contrast with the stark, soulless whiteness that the Yablochkov Candles brought to the rest of the house. This was the only room that I'd left free of them. We made love for the first time in several weeks, and I felt closer to her than I had done for months – since I'd first lied to her about my encounter with her brother.

The arc lights had burned out by the time we got up. They only lasted a few hours, but a few seconds was usually long enough for the purpose to which I put them. I replaced them with new ones, feeling certain that we would need to protect ourselves again.

I spent most of the day at home, as I generally did now that the Duma was no more. It had been less than a month, but already retirement was making me lazy. I'd turned sixty since the revolution and was beginning to feel my years. When the Duma was dissolved I'd felt sure I'd want to stand in the elections for the Constituent Assembly when they happened. Now I wasn't so convinced. Nadya still worked at the kitchen most days, and so my time was my own. Polkan was company enough.

I'd tried to telephone Yelena and the Smolny Institute, but the line was still down. I managed to get through to a few friends, but none of them knew very much. There was a rumour that Lenin had returned from Finland and had managed to get across town in disguise the previous night to join his comrades in the Smolny Institute. I'd been walking not far from the route he must have taken. Perhaps I'd unwittingly walked past him. I'd only seen him in pictures, but his most prominent feature was his bald head. That would be easy to hide with a wig or a hat. There was a vague connection between us. His real name was Vladimir Ilyich Ulyanov. He'd become political when his elder brother, Aleksandr, had been hanged for a failed plot to assassinate Tsar Aleksandr III. The attempt had been planned for 1 March 1887 – the sixth anniversary of the murder of Aleksandr II – by a group that continued to call itself the People's Will, even though it had little direct connection with the original organization. I'd been a part of the original People's Will back in 1881, though I'd escaped the arrests afterwards, thanks to my illustrious father. But if I'd managed to do what I should have done, and prevented my uncle's death, then Aleksandr Ulyanov might not have been hanged and Vladimir Ulyanov might never even have bothered to come up with the alias of Nikolai Lenin.

Nadya came home and we ate together. We both knew that I had to go and speak to Dmitry, but that didn't stop either of us from worrying.

'What if they come after you again?'

'Dmitry's the only chance I have of stopping that. They used to be under his command. He might have some idea what they're after.'

'It might be a trap.'

'I'm as safe going out as I am staying here. They know where I live. All they have to do is hang around outside until there's a power cut, and then we're both in trouble.' She paled. It was harsh of me to point out that the danger was to both of us, but she knew as well as I did that I was doing the right thing. I was merely curtailing the argument.

'What are you taking?' she asked.

'I've got my cane, and a wooden sword. And an *arbalyet*.' I'd been in the storeroom upstairs for half the morning, gathering what weapons I could – cleaning and preparing them. None was as effective as the Yablochkov Candles, but those weren't portable. On the other hand, there were still areas of the city lit by arc lamps, which I could use as a safe haven and perhaps even as some kind of weapon. 'I'll take my sabre too,' I said as an afterthought.

'You'll look like something out of the last century.'

'I'll hide it under my coat.' I'd already constructed a loop of cloth which I slung over my shoulder, allowing the pommel of my sword to nestle unseen in my armpit. I can't have been the first to come up with the idea.

'Did you find any of the . . . the things you lost.'

I shook my head. After Anastasia had gone I'd discovered that more than I thought was missing from that room. Iuda's notebooks for sure, but a couple of other things too, both of which I'd stolen, at different times, from Iuda. It was hardly theft, though – Iuda had had no right to either of them. One item I'd taken from the pocket of his jacket, after the body it surrounded had crumbled to nothing. It was a ring in the form of a dragon, with a body of gold, emerald eyes and a red, forked tongue. It had once been Zmyeevich's. Somehow Iuda had got it from him, then I had taken it from Iuda and finally Anastasia had taken it from me. I cared little for its loss.

The other item – strictly items – were more personal. They were six little bones: two distal phalanges; two intermediate phalanges; two proximal phalanges – the bones of the two smallest fingers of my grandfather's left hand. They'd been severed in a gaol in Silistria in 1809. Somehow Iuda had got hold of them, but he had no right to them; neither did Anastasia. I was Aleksei's heir, and they were amongst the few things I possessed that could make me feel directly linked to him, however macabre they might be.

I'd looked for them again today, but I was in no doubt that she had them. I reached into my shirt and allowed my fingers to touch two further items that never left me. One again was a link to my grandfather: an oval icon depicting the Saviour, hanging from a silver chain that had once broken and been retied. Aleksei had been given it by his wife – not my grandmother – when he set out to fight Bonaparte. He'd given it to his daughter, my mother, Tamara, who had given it to me. The second item around my neck was similar, but instead of depicting Christ it displayed the picture of someone I loved far more dearly and trusted far more deeply – Nadya.

There had been a time when I'd worn a different pendant around my neck: a locket containing twelve strands of blond hair that had once belonged to Iuda. After I'd killed him, I'd seen no reason to keep hold of them. I'd waited till the spring thaw and then hurled the locket into the Neva, along with his double-bladed knife.

Nadya noticed my instinctive action and tried to smile. She knew how much the icon of Christ meant to me. I hoped she understood how much her image meant too.

I set out in good time to meet Dmitry at half past nine. I wanted to go to the Winter Palace on the way and see if they'd improved their defences. Tonight the city seemed utterly normal – a typical autumn evening in Petrograd. It was only as I started getting close to the palace that I noticed things begin to change. Here once again there were groups of workers, but they were not simply loitering, looking for somewhere to protest. These were men of the Red Guard, a militia formed after the revolution – in Petrograd, Moscow and other cities – for the protection of the Soviets. Now it was the military wing of the Bolshevik Party.

Groups the size of platoons – they were too shoddy to genuinely be described by a military term – were assembled in the backstreets around the Winter Palace, waiting. They made no attempt to stop me, or anybody, but it was clear by their presence that Lenin and Trotsky would be making their move tonight.

I crossed Palace Square and quickly checked out the defences. At first glance they were unchanged from the previous day – armed men and women all along the front of the palace, facing out into the square. But perhaps on reflection there were one or two fewer of them. And I could see no marksmen at the windows as I had before. It was the same girl on guard as yesterday. She recognized me and let me in with a nervous smile, not even bothering to look at my papers. Worse still, she didn't check my knapsack. I'd walked straight into the heart of the Provisional Government carrying a sabre and a crossbow. They didn't stand a chance.

Konovalov wasn't in his office, but I asked around and soon found him, in a first-floor room that overlooked the Neva. He was alone, standing with his back to me, taking long intense drags on a cigarette. He was staring out of one of the tall windows, framed with velvet curtains that must have hung here for decades. I went and stood beside him. He gave a slight nod to acknowledge my arrival. I followed his gaze. There was only one thing he could have been looking at: the *Avrora* – still moored on the far bank of the river. The six-inch barrels of her guns were pointed towards us.

'It'll be tonight,' I said.

'Looks like it.'

'I don't think she's your biggest worry.'

'Really?' He seemed uninterested.

'There's troops of Red Guards waiting to make a move.'

'How many?'

'A few thousand maybe – but they're a rabble. You've got three thousand to see them off.' In truth the women and boys guarding the Winter Palace were as untrained as the Bolsheviks outside. Only the Cossacks had any real experience.

'Three thousand? More like three hundred now.'

'You've had casualties already?'

'No, no casualties. Merely desertions.' He tutted. 'That's unfair. We can't even feed them. Most of them have gone in search of a half-decent meal. But they don't come back.'

'What's Kerensky going to do?'

'Kerensky? He's scarpered.'

I could only laugh.

'He went this morning,' Konovalov continued. 'He couldn't even get hold of a car. In the end he just sent men out to "requisition" one. They stole it from outside the US embassy. It was still flying the Stars and Stripes when he left in it.'

'Where's he gone?'

'God knows.'

'Who's in charge?'

Konovalov laughed. 'In charge of what?' Then he relented. 'Officially it's Kishkin. From charities minister to dictator in a day. And tomorrow – who knows?'

He fell silent, staring out of the window and down to the river, looking at nothing in particular. I took a step closer to the glass, so that I could see down to the embankment below us. The wide ledge outside blocked my view, but I could make out the figures of men moving past, swiftly and purposefully, as if they had been deployed. On the ledge I noticed a little chip of missing stone that looked to me as if it had been caused by a bullet. But it was not recent; the edges were worn smooth by time. It was the remnant of some previous battle here – but the building would receive fresh scars before the night was out.

'Why don't you leave?' I asked.

'We decided, collectively – the final act of the Provisional Government – to make a last stand. Anyway, where would we go to? You should go, though. You might still have time to get out.'

I hadn't been planning on staying. I shook his hand and then left. I went down to the palace's central courtyard, but instead of going back out on to Palace Square, I looked for one of the more humble exits on the western side. I found one. The sentry was a cadet of about fifteen. The door was open and he was happily chatting to the group of Red Guards who stood outside. They could have got past him at any moment, but the order had not come yet. I stepped out into the street.

'What do you think you're doing?' It was one of the men outside who asked. His accent wasn't local.

'I'm leaving.' I hadn't meant to inject quite such a sense of cowardice into my words, but my response got a huge laugh from all of them. I began to push my way through and was offered no resistance. I felt the pat of several hands on my back, congratulating me for my apparent desertion.

I glanced over at the Palace Bridge. It was lowered again now and that could only mean the Red Guards had taken it – it was to their advantage to allow more troops to come in from the north of the city. I decided it was best to get to Senate Square by skirting around the Admiralty to the south rather than going along the embankment. Suddenly from behind me I heard shouts and laughter. I looked. One of the Red Guards had been hoisted on to the shoulders of another so that he could paint a message on the palace wall. He'd just finished. It was large enough for me to read.

Down with the Jew Kerensky! Long live Trotsky!

I could only smile to myself, but not, I supposed, for the same reasons that they laughed. What did they think Trotsky was? A Buddhist?

I made it to Senate Square unmolested – nobody gave a damn about someone walking away from the palace. The square and the embankment were busy with workers, some loitering with no real sense of what to do, others – Red Guards – clearly better organized. Dmitry was already there, accompanied by the same two *voordalaki* that had been with him the previous night. I looked at them more carefully than before, but neither had been among those who had followed me.

'Any news?' he asked.

I jerked my head to indicate that he should come away from his lackeys.

'You can speak in front of them,' he snapped.

I had no choice – and I had no specific reason to think that these two were not loyal to him. 'Last night,' I said, 'after I left you, I was followed and attacked. There were four of them – vampires.'

'Vampires? The very fact you survived would suggest not.'

'Don't underestimate me. I'm the grandson of the three-fingered man, remember? And it was me that killed Iuda.'

'Touché. But why does it have anything to do with me?'

'One of them was Ilya Vadimovich. The rest might well be your other . . . deserters.'

'Did any of them survive?'

'All of them, I think.' It was a comedown to have to admit it after my earlier bravado.

He raised an eyebrow, but let it pass. 'What did they want with you?'

'I don't know, but they didn't want me dead. They were trying to grab me.'

'Ilya's not smart enough to think beyond his next meal, unless he has someone telling him what to do.'

'Exactly. Anastasia.'

'You think they'll try again?'

'Why not?'

Dmitry considered for a moment. 'When you go home tonight, I'll send these two with you just in case.'

I eyed the vampires. To me they were indistinguishable from the four who had attacked me, whatever faith Dmitry might place in them. And even if they were the sweetest-natured creatures in the world, I did not want *voordalaki* at my side.

'I'll take my chances,' I said.

'If you insist. Anyway, we have more important matters to concern us. What's happening at the Winter Palace?'

'It's surrounded. Most of the guards have run off – as has Kerensky. I don't know why they don't just walk in and take it.'

'They're waiting,' said Dmitry.

'For what?'

He walked over to the river's edge. The road along the embankment wasn't empty, but what traffic there was was at a standstill. The two *voordalaki* stuck close to him – closer than I'd seen before, as if he or they had decided there was some extra need for his protection. He pointed across the river. 'They have control of the Peter and Paul Fortress. Its guns are trained on the Winter Palace, just like the *Avrora*'s. The signal to attack will be a red lantern that they're going to raise up the flagpole. At the same time the *Avrora* will fire a blank round, so that those who don't see the light will still know. Then they'll attack.'

'How did you find all this out?'

'I can be very persuasive.' He smiled as he spoke, just enough to reveal his sharp white teeth. 'They've already taken the Mariinskiy Palace – God knows why.'

'That's where the Pre-Parliament sits. It's the only legitimate power in the city – unless you count the Soviet. You're sure they're in control there?'

'I saw it for myself.'

'What were you doing there?'

He looked down into the water, embarrassed. 'I went to the

theatre,' he confessed. 'Not for a performance – just to take a look at the place.'

'The Mariinskiy Theatre?' He nodded. I remembered following him there one night, years before, thinking he was going to feed, only to discover that his sole purpose had been to play the piano.

'I couldn't have got a seat anyway,' he continued. 'The place was packed. All the restaurants are busy too. No one's got the faintest notion what's happening around them.'

'Possibly. Or perhaps they understand too well, and know they have no hope. What would you have done on the *Titanic*? Jumped into the sea, or gone to the restaurant for one last good meal?'

'I *was* on the *Titanic*,' Dmitry replied. 'And I had a very good meal.' One of the vampires standing beside him sniggered, but I had no reason to think it had been meant as a joke. 'Do you know what's playing at the Mariinskiy?' Dmitry asked.

'I've no idea,' I said, trying to give the impression that neither did I care.

'It's *Boris Godunov* – Shalyapin's in the title role. It seems fitting, don't you think?'

'I suppose so.'

My agreement didn't stop Dmitry from explaining. 'The tsar who came to power after the fall of the Rurik dynasty. He was an *oprichnik* himself, you know; a real one – one of Ivan the Terrible's bodyguards. Brought stability to a turbulent nation.'

'Not for long.'

'The Time of Troubles, you mean? A necessary period of adjustment until Mihail Romanov came along and brought three centuries of prosperity – for some.'

'And that's where we are now? With Kerensky as Godunov? Or maybe that was Lvov. And Lenin as Mihail I?'

'Lenin, or Trotsky, or whoever comes after them.'

It seemed he was trying to tell me something – that he had made up his mind and that he now saw in the Bolsheviks the best hope for Russia.

'And what about the False Dmitrys?' I asked. 'Where do they fit in?' During the Time of Troubles three men had come forward claiming to be Ivan's lost son, Dmitry, heir to the throne. All were lying.

Dmitry raised his eyebrows, understanding the connection I was making with him. 'Don't accuse me of falsehood. I'm merely fickle. At my age, it's difficult not to be.'

'One of those Dmitrys actually became tsar.'

He laughed. 'Not my ambition, I assure you. I'm not that fickle.'

He gazed out across Senate Square, looking not into the distance, but into the past, when he'd stood on this very spot against Nikolai I, along with thousands of his fellow soldiers. Aleksei and Iuda had been here too, but for other reasons. I could understand why Dmitry would hate that tsar – and any tsar. The cannon had been lined up in front of Saint Isaac's, from what I'd heard. Nikolai had given the order and they'd fired upon the ranks of his own countrymen.

An explosion shook the ground we stood on, but it hadn't come from the direction of the cathedral. It was behind us. I whirled round. Even Dmitry's companions appeared momentarily shocked. Only Dmitry himself was calm. He turned slowly. I'd already guessed where the sound had come from – the *Avrora*. Because the shot had been a blank it was even louder than a standard round. It would have echoed across the whole of Petrograd – telling all that the Bolshevik coup had begun.

I looked over to the Peter and Paul Fortress, but I couldn't see any sign of a red lantern. Even so the guns there had begun firing on the Winter Palace. It was laughable. The fortress's weaponry was ancient – it hadn't been needed to defend the city for centuries. Their range wasn't even enough to reach the far bank. The cannonballs splashed harmlessly into the water. If they'd brought up just one heavy gun from the Front they could have ripped the palace open with a single round. But that wasn't the point. This was a show of strength – it would be the men on the ground who did the real work. The *Avrora*'s guns would have been devastating, but she remained silent after her first signal.

The effect on those around us was instantaneous. At the sound of the ship's gun, almost everyone in the square had begun to move in the direction of the Admiralty and beyond it to their true destination – the Winter Palace. There were far more of them than was necessary. Those defending the palace were outnumbered a hundred to one, but it would mean thousands who would be able to say to their grandchildren, 'I was there.'

Soon there were only a few of us left – me, Dmitry and his comrades, and a handful of stragglers. Even if Dmitry had been minded to help defend the palace, there would have been little he could do. He might kill a few Red Guards, but to no avail. It was better to let history take its course.

I held my hand out to him. 'I won't come again,' I said. 'I'm not sure I'll be free to once—'

I stopped mid-sentence. Dmitry looked at me, puzzled, but I was no longer looking at him. That handful of stragglers had diminished now to just four figures – familiar figures, one of whom I recognized very clearly. It was Ilya. I nodded in his direction and Dmitry turned to look. He showed no surprise at what he saw, but paused a moment or two before speaking.

'Ilya Vadimovich. I thought I told you to leave Petrograd.'

Ilya ignored him; instead he turned to face first one, then the other of the two vampires that still flanked Dmitry. 'Louis,' he said to the first, and then 'Riccardo. It's time for you to choose. Whose side are you on?'

He didn't wait for an answer, but instead walked past them and Dmitry, coming straight towards me. The one he'd called Louis moved first. He thrust his hand upward, faster than I could really see, catching Ilya in the chest. The impact sent him sailing through the air to land on the pavement. Riccardo glanced at him and then seemed to make up his mind. He raised his fists, with the look of someone who knew how to box, and approached the nearest of Ilya's cohorts. Dmitry strode purposefully towards the other two.

The odds weren't too badly against us. Three *voordalaki* against four – and Dmitry was bigger than any of them. I wasn't completely defenceless either. I didn't think my *arbalyet* would be much use in a fight like this, but it took me only seconds to have my sabre in one hand and my cane in the other, its sharpened tip exposed. It had been time enough for Ilya to get back on his feet. He lowered his head and charged in the direction of Louis. Louis did likewise. A collision between two men at that speed would have cracked both their skulls, but I was eager to see what the effect would be on vampires. It was not to be. Ilya's move had been a ruse. He slowed a little, letting Louis come to him, and lowered himself even further. When the impact came Ilya rose quickly and it was Louis's turn to be hurled through the air. But Ilya had been aiming more precisely. Louis careered over the wall of the embankment and landed in the Neva with a splash. It would take him precious minutes to return to the fray.

Ilya now began to march towards me. To his left Dmitry appeared to be doing well enough in subduing the two he had taken on. I held my sabre out wide to my right, ready to swing it at Ilya's neck, but perhaps it would prove unnecessary. Riccardo had managed to fell his opponent with an almighty punch. The creature lay dazed on the ground – I couldn't guess how long it would take him to recover. Meanwhile Riccardo was on course to intercept Ilya before he could reach me. He still had his fists raised in that classic pose, but as he approached Ilya he grabbed him by the shoulder and forced him to turn and face the fight.

Ilya did turn, and quickly, and at the same time he reached under his coat for something. It was not an object that I would have expected to see a vampire carrying, but it demonstrated that he had come prepared. It was a wooden sword, much like the one I had in my knapsack. It was simply fashioned – just a sharpened wooden stake with a short handle lashed to it – but perfectly effective. Riccardo was fast, but not fast enough. The blade went under his guard and straight into his heart. Ilya didn't even stay to watch his opponent's remains crumble to nothing. His attention was turned once again to me.

I raised the cane a little, making it clear that I knew how to use it. He stopped, standing just far enough away to be out of my reach. He could have come closer and I still wouldn't have attacked. I knew that I had to sever his head completely with my sabre, and that would require the middle of the blade.

He walked a few feet to one side, and then the other, prowling like an animal, as if trying to find a way round. I made sure that the points of both my weapons followed him all the way. Behind him I could see that Dmitry was now in trouble against two of them, but there was nothing I could do. Then suddenly Ilya seemed to give up. He relaxed from his predatory pose and stood upright. He spoke, but I could make no sense of his words.

'Oh, go on then.'

Too late I realized that he wasn't even talking to me. Four of them had not been enough to deal with me the night before, so why should there be only four this time? From behind me a fist came down heavily on my forearm, knocking the cane to the ground. Ilya lunged forward, aiming his heel close to its tip. I heard it snap as it sank down into the mud. I still had hold of my sword and began to turn, judging the threat from the rear to be the greater, but it was too late. Now the hand grabbed my wrist. Ilya took hold of the blade and twisted it harshly. It drew blood, but the force was strong enough to wrench the hilt from my grasp. I fell backwards and found myself gazing up at the statue of Pyotr; more specifically at the face of the serpent that writhed beneath his horse's hooves. Then I saw nothing. I felt dirty cloth against my face, covering my eyes and sucking into my mouth as I breathed.

Finally I felt Ilya's hand squeezing my throat, just as he had done the night before, cutting off the blood that my brain could not survive without. But this time there was no one to come to the rescue. I slipped into oblivion.

CHAPTER XII

I T WAS NOT AN UNFAMILIAR SITUATION. WHEN I CAME TO IT WAS dark, but I could make out some illumination. The sack was still over my head, tied around my neck, but not so tightly that I couldn't breathe. It had been the People's Will who had done this to me before, years before. They'd kidnapped me and interrogated me, leaving my head covered so that I could not see who I was dealing with, not until the very end, when they had accepted me as one of their own. That had made some sense; this did not. If Ilya had simply ripped out my throat and sucked my life from me, that would have been reasonable. Evidently he wanted more from me than simply my blood – and that could only be worse for me.

My hands were tied behind my back, but my feet were free. There was no point in trying to escape, though. I was not alone. Around me I could hear voices, in several directions, but I could not make out what they were saying. It told me something about where I was: a large indoor space – echoing. My guess was a church.

'What are you going to do with us?'

As when I'd been a captive of the People's Will, the first voice I heard was a familiar one. Indeed it was the exact same voice: Dmitry's. Then, though, he had been in charge. I doubted that was the case now.

'With you? Nothing. It's him we want.' Again it was as before. This second voice was female, and familiar, but it was not the voice of the assassin Sofia Lvovna. It was Anastasia.

'And what do you want with *him*?' Dmitry asked.

'You'll see, soon enough. In fact, why not now? Wake him.'

A booted foot kicked me in the side.

'I'm awake!' I shouted. 'I'm awake.'

'Stand him up.'

I felt a hand under my armpit, pulling me, and soon I was on my feet. I was prodded in the back and walked forwards a few steps until another hand restrained me.

'Let him see.'

Fingers fumbled at the back of my neck, and then the sack was pulled off. I twisted my head from side to side, partly to take in my surroundings, partly to stretch the muscles in my neck. I knew immediately where I was. I was standing just feet from the point where the fatal bomb had been thrown at my uncle, Aleksandr II, in 1881. His legs had been blown to tatters and he'd bled to death. He had died at the Winter Palace – with the future Nikolai II, then just twelve years old, watching on – but this location had taken on a greater significance as the site of the brutal act. They erected a memorial to him here, a shrine – the Shrine of the Blessing of the Lord, officially. I could see it from where I stood: dark jasper columns topped with a canopy of serpentine, embellished with topaz and gold. Within were the paving stones on which Aleksandr had fallen and a section of the railing that edged the canal. I'd heard that bloodstains could still be seen on those stones, but I'd never had the desire to look. Before long they had built a church to house the shrine. Where once there had been a vast crater – caused more by the first bomb, which had failed to kill the tsar, than the second – now stood the Cathedral of the Resurrection of Christ; the Church on Spilled Blood.

I'd been inside before, more than once. In my opinion it was a building better viewed from within than without. While the exterior tried to mimic the far more ancient Saint Vasiliy's in Red Square, the interior had none of its labyrinthine complexity. It was a single, open chamber. Every inch of the walls was decorated with mosaic – saints with their golden halos glittering, even in the dim candlelight. Four great columns stretched up to a ceiling that seemed unnecessarily high for so small a nave, but which in the middle reached even higher, into the central cupola. I could not see from where I stood, but I knew that on the inside of that dome the mosaic of Christ Pantocrator looked down, blessing all who prayed beneath him. If he had the choice, he would not have blessed today's congregation.

Dmitry was seated on the floor, leaning against one of the pillars. There were manacles on his wrists, connected to each other by a chain which stretched around the column. A circlet of iron was fastened around his neck. It too was attached to a chain. If he had been held by mere ropes he might have stood a chance, but clearly those who had bound him understood the horrendous strength of the *voordalak*. And why not? – they were *voordalaki* themselves.

There were six of them altogether. Four were sitting idly around the nave, one on the steps leading up to the Beautiful Gate, which they had opened – a sacrilege in itself. I recognized three of the faces from earlier. Another was at my side; it was he who had removed my mask. The sixth, Ilya, stood in the centre of the church, directly beneath the dome and the mosaic of Christ. Beside him was his mistress.

Anastasia looked older than when I had known her before, but it was an illusion. It was partly down to her posture – she was the only source of authority in the building – to her clothes and also because she was wearing make-up. But beneath it I knew she could not have aged a day since I had first seen her, seeming to all the world a frightened child. But that too was an illusion – in truth she might be decades old – or centuries. One small, almost irrelevant matter was cleared up. The bump of her pregnancy was no larger than it had been before. Just like its mother, her unborn child was frozen in time.

'Untie his hands,' she said.

Behind me I felt the pressure of a blade against the ropes that bound me, then I was free. I raised a hand to my face and rubbed my cheek and chin. There was a practical purpose to it; I felt very little stubble – I could not have been unconscious for more than a few hours, if that.

'Thank you,' I said.

'Don't,' she replied. She signalled to two of the others, who walked over to two of the four main columns, diagonally opposite each other, and picked up ropes that had been bound around them. Then they came over to me. They tied my wrists with the

197

two ropes, which trailed loosely across the geometric patterns of the marble floor. Then they went back to the columns, and behind them so that I couldn't see what they were doing. Whatever it was had an immediate effect. The ropes began to tighten and I was pulled into the middle of the church. There was little point in offering resistance. Soon I was standing on the circle of black marble – shot with browns and whites – that marked the very centre, gazing upwards like a great eye, zigzag circles of orange and pink radiating from it. Above me, far above, was the Christ Pantocrator, both hands raised, each forming the symbol of the *troyeperstiy* – two fingers folded down in preparation to make the sign of the cross. On the three visible arms of the cross on his halo were written the Greek letters 'O ω N' – omicron, omega and nu, meaning 'The one who is.'

I could move a little, but not much. My arms were stretched out horizontally, as if I were being crucified, but thankfully I didn't have to bear my weight on them – not so far. Dmitry was directly in front of me, as unable to move as I was; he did not look me in the eye. I turned my head to see Anastasia, but she walked around me until she was standing between me and Dmitry. In her hand she was carrying a flimsy exercise book.

'You recognize this?'

I had done so instantly, but I said nothing.

'You should. It was in your house – not that it belonged to you. It was the property of a fascinating man by the name of Richard Llywelyn Cain. He made it his life's work to study and understand our kind, and even became like us. He tortured and killed more vampires than any human in history – far more than your grandfather ever did, and *he* managed a few. But Cain learned a lot about us – information that could be useful to friend or foe. And then, about forty years ago, he simply disappeared. His last known whereabouts were in this city and then – nothing. Not a hint of his existence on the face of the Earth.'

'I killed him,' I said.

She tilted her head to one side and smiled. 'Really? We suspected as much. One of you was bound to kill the other. That then was the first great service you performed for us.'

Her use of 'us' and 'we' was quite deliberate and I could tell that they were not intended to include the vampires who now so happily served her. I couldn't help but remember a conversation I'd once had with Dmitry, years before in a cellar beneath Senate Square, when he'd also talked of 'we'. But the other half of the partnership then could not be the same as whoever Anastasia was referring to. Then it had been Zmyeevich, and he was long dead. I felt a shiver run through me. It was 25 October; twenty-four years to the day since I had witnessed – had experienced – his death.

'Let me read you something of Cain's work,' Anastasia continued. She flicked through to a page she had marked and began to read out loud. The text itself was in English, and that was the language she spoke in. As far as I could tell her accent was perfect, better than anything I'd ever been able to achieve, even though I spoke the language fluently.

'"On Anastasis.

'"I have recently heard of a legend not uncommon among Wallachian vampires, though less widespread elsewhere, which, if true, would add another level to the bond between a human and a vampire in the circumstances of the Romanovs and Zmyeevich, or indeed any other pairing where the human's blood has been drunk by the vampire, either directly or through descent . . ."'

She paused and looked at me intently for a moment, then returned to the text.

'". . . either directly or through descent, but for whom the process of induction has not been completed. I have long known that if the vampire were then to die there is still the possibility (as I am the living proof) that induction may be achieved, but equally the human, if left unmolested, may go on to experience a natural death. However, it seems that under certain conditions the human may be susceptible to drinking the vampire's blood not to the end of themselves becoming transformed but of bringing about a form of parousia with regard to the dead creature. This seems to be a very ancient story, going back to before the time even of Zmyeevich's human existence as Ţepeş, and I can find no vampire who has been eyewitness to it. However, it is an intriguing possibility and clearly an apt subject for experimentation, when circumstances next permit."'

She looked at me, smiling. 'He could have put it more simply, couldn't he?'

I didn't respond.

'And what's wrong with plain English? Why all this Greek? "Anastasis" and "parousia". Still, I suppose that's the way he was brought up. You know what they mean, I take it.'

I nodded. They had made no sense to me when I'd first read them, but over the years I'd dissected every word of Cain's – Iuda's – writings, and it hadn't taken me too long to discover what those two meant. In the end they amounted to the same thing. Parousia was the more obscure. Literally it meant the physical presence or arrival of a person, but it had a frequent and specific use in the gospels. Seventeen times it was used to refer to the arrival of one particular individual, Christ Himself, and not to His arrival into Jerusalem, nor even His entry into this world at Bethlehem. All referred to His second coming, after He had already died.

The word 'anastasis' had a more simple, direct translation. It was the root of the name Anastasia. Tsar Nikolai had chosen it for his youngest daughter, but I couldn't help but suspect that the Anastasia who stood before me had chosen it for herself, in honour of this time and this place, which – to her as much as to me – must have seemed the moment of her destiny. The entire concept could be expressed in a single word, which I spoke out loud, hoping to hide my fear at its import.

'Resurrection.'

'Very good. So perhaps you'd care to summarize what Cain, in his tortuous, roundabout way, is trying to say?'

'He's saying,' I replied, 'that he's heard a rumour that, if true, would mean that even though Zmyeevich is dead, he might be resurrected, with the help of a member of the Romanov family.'

Dmitry gasped. He had more than most to fear from Zmyeevich. I was less concerned. I'd understood the meaning of what Iuda had written for a long time and there were so many steps to be completed along the way that its realization seemed preposterously unlikely, even if it was indeed anything more than a rumour. But the fact that Anastasia seemed to believe it unnerved me.

'It's quite a concept, isn't it?' she said.

'A myth,' I replied.

'A myth? Like the three-fingered man?'

'What do you know about that?'

'More than you'd think.' She put down Iuda's journal and walked out of my view for a few seconds. She returned carrying a leather bag – a sort of satchel. 'It was a three-fingered man, your grandfather, Aleksei, who freed dozens of vampires that Cain had been holding captive at Chufut Kalye. He became something of a legend amongst our kind, but its basis was entirely true. We honour him for that, if not his other actions. Look!'

She reached into the satchel and brought out a small, flat piece of wood, no bigger than a book. She hugged it close to her, hiding one side of it, and approached me. When she was only a few feet away she held it out, so I could see the side she had been concealing.

I recognized them instantly: the bones of my grandfather's two missing fingers – the ones she had stolen from our house. They'd been mounted on the wood somehow, in just the position they would have been in life. The shape of the living fingers had been drawn around them in pencil, which continued to outline the entire hand, as if waiting for the remaining bones to be added. There was one other addition, one other item that had been stolen from me. Zmyeevich's ring was there too – the golden dragon. Its emerald eyes gleamed at me in the candlelight. Its red tongue stretched forward as if trying to taste the air. It was mounted just as would be expected, on Aleksei's ring finger.

'Zmyeevich wore this ring for as long as anyone knew,' Anastasia explained. 'Some people think it has magical powers – rings are often supposed to. Even I half believed that when I placed it on Aleksei's dead finger, the flesh might begin to regrow – Zmyeevich's flesh on your grandfather's bones. What might that have been like, I wonder – the intertwining of Danilov and Țepeș? But nothing came of it, so perhaps we shall never know.' She put the mounted bones back into her bag.

'Zmyeevich must have made quite an impression on you,' I said.

She smiled briefly, but could not disguise the look of genuine melancholy that crossed her brow. I might even have caught a glimpse of a tear in her eye, though it was probably my imagination.

'Oh, he did. I'm sure he made an impression upon you, though not in the same way – you are not a *voordalak*. But for someone like, say, Dmitry here, he was the greatest creature that ever walked the Earth. I was devastated when they killed him – but not despondent.'

'You don't stand a chance of bringing him back.'

'Don't I? As you said, the first thing I need is a Romanov. Zmyeevich drank the blood of Peter the Great, and now all Pyotr's descendants are ripe to fall under his dominion. That's why I came to Russia. Pyotr's line has been fruitful, and there are plenty of Romanovs to choose from. Even an illegitimate child would do, but how could one be sure of his parentage? My first idea was to get at that little weakling Aleksei, the tsarevich. I got close to him, after a fashion. By the end that lunatic Rasputin would do whatever I told him. But they killed him before we could get what we needed.

'And then you stumbled across me and Ilya together, you remember? Just over there.' She pointed vaguely over my shoulder. 'You think Ilya didn't recognize you? Didn't tell me who you were? He had no idea how much you might be able to help, but I wasn't going to forget all that Zmyeevich had told me about you; and he told me so, so much. After that it was easy enough to find out where you lived, and then to make sure your mistress Nadya discovered me, shivering in the snow, and took me in. You think I wouldn't have killed you both on the first night if I hadn't had a far greater purpose in mind for you?'

I closed my eyes briefly. It shouldn't have come as a surprise to me – why else would I have been brought here?

'Mihail Konstantinovich Danilov,' Anastasia continued. 'And not just a Danilov, but a Romanov too. There's no doubting it. You demonstrated the fact very clearly to Zmyeevich when you swallowed his blood and stole his chances of ruling over any of your Romanov cousins. You'll do very well for what Cain described. You should regard yourself as honoured; to be the one chosen for a moment such as this.'

Dmitry let out a sound that was half a sigh, half laughter. I understood what he was thinking. He had spoken of the 'Chosen One' when telling me of *The Rite of Spring*.

I still thought Anastasia was overreaching herself. 'Cain described nothing,' I told her. 'He talked of a legend, no more. Even if it's true, you've no idea how to carry it out.'

'Oh, but I have. Zmyeevich himself understood the process perfectly well. That word Cain used – "parousia" – it was very apt. In the Bible it generally refers to the second coming of Christ, but there's one passage where it describes the arrival of someone else: the Man of Sin; the Lawless One. Who else could that mean but Zmyeevich? He explained the formalities. It has to be on consecrated ground.' She paused and looked around her. 'The sacrifice, the chosen one, need only be of the correct bloodline – he can be willing or unwilling. He must be bled and his blood mixed with that of the vampire to be resurrected. Then half that mixture must be burned and half drunk by the sacrifice himself. Some ancient words must be spoken. And then the reincarnated body will appear.'

'How can you be sure?' asked Dmitry. 'Sure you've not missed something?'

Anastasia laughed. 'Oh, Dmitry Alekseevich – you're just what he said you were. A believer. Zmyeevich understood. It's not a question of what is needed, but what can be discarded. He'd never seen the ceremony performed, but he had unearthed several texts on it. He felt confident that it could work, but he knew how superstitious even vampires can be. Some of it – most of it – is undoubtedly nonsense, but which parts? The burning of the blood? The location? The recitation? Why take the risk? If we include every detail, then we can guarantee to have those pieces which are essential.'

'There's one piece you don't have,' I said. 'Zmyeevich's blood.' Even as I spoke, I felt I was on thin ice.

Anastasia turned away from me and began to wander around the nave, staring up at the mosaic walls and arches. 'I didn't know Zmyeevich for long. I met him when he came to England. He shouldn't have come. He didn't understand just how resourceful we English can be. I had so little time with him, but I grew to admire him – to love him. But his journey wasn't simply a whim. He had to visit England. Dmitry knows why.'

She turned and looked at Dmitry, who gazed up at her for a few moments. It seemed to be reverence rather than defiance that delayed his response. 'Iuda had taken two things which belonged to Zmyeevich. As far as we knew he'd hidden them in England – somewhere.'

Anastasia picked up the story. 'Cain had two properties in England: one in London, on Piccadilly, the other in a town called Purfleet. Zmyeevich came to take back what was his, but he never managed it. After his death I succeeded where he had failed.'

'And what was it that Iuda had stolen?' I already knew.

Anastasia reached into her bag again. She brought out another piece of wood, but of a quite different shape. This was cylindrical; about a foot long. One end was sharpened to a point, while the other was roughly splintered as though it had been broken over someone's knee to separate it from a longer shaft. It was unmistakably the tip of a spear. Its wood was darkened with age, but even darker stains were still visible on it.

'Ascalon,' whispered Dmitry. His eyes were wide.

'Ascalon,' Anastasia repeated. 'The spear with which Saint George slew the dragon, the relic that Zmyeevich kept always close to his heart, until it was stolen from him.'

'Why not use that to bring him back?' asked Dmitry. I scowled at him – she didn't need our help.

'That would be a different magic,' she said. 'One of which we have no need. Ascalon is merely . . . his. I shall be proud to have the honour of giving it back to him when he returns.'

'And what was the second thing you found in England?' I asked. I saw no reason to delay the inevitable.

'This,' she said. At the same moment she fetched from her bag a glass vial, small enough that I could have hidden it in my closed fist – though her dainty hand would not entirely have concealed it. Inside was a thick dark liquid – unmistakably blood. She held it close to my face. There was a label on it, written in the Latin alphabet. 'Read it,' she said.

'Zmyeevich.' The handwriting was unquestionably Iuda's; the same as in his notebooks.

204

'Cain must have taken this sample from Zmyeevich in 1825, when they were allies and trying to convert Aleksandr I to their cause. He took many samples – he'd found a way of preventing the blood from congealing. This, as far as I know, is the only one that remains. You destroyed one of them yourself when you drank it.'

'It tasted rancid.'

She smiled. 'Then what is to come will be even more unpleasant for you than I'd hoped. Cain was meticulous – a true scientist. I broke into his house on Piccadilly, disarmed his traps and finally entered his inner sanctum. There were more notebooks there, and shelf upon shelf of blood samples, each neatly labelled with the name of its source. I was afraid that at any moment Cain would return and prevent me from taking this precious blood, or worse destroy it – destroy the last earthly remnant of Zmyeevich's existence. But I didn't know then what I know now – that you had killed Cain years before. Did you ever think you would live to regret it?'

'I don't regret it. So what if you manage to bring Zmyeevich back? He won't thank you for it. You'll have raised him from the dead only to look upon what he can never have: Russia. For two centuries his only desire was to rule the tsar and thereby rule the nation. Well he can do what he likes to the Romanovs now. They have no power. Everything Zmyeevich ever wanted is lost to him.'

'We'll let him be the judge of that, don't you think? England overthrew her king, and then begged to have his son restored. And much the same happened in France, for a while at least. Nikolai lost Russia because he was weak and inconstant, like his ancestor Pyotr. With Zmyeevich's help he can be a powerful tsar once again – or if not him then his son, or any of them.'

'You think Russia will accept a tsar again?' asked Dmitry.

Anastasia's eyes gleamed, making her appear again more like a young girl. 'Let's find out, shall we?'

I didn't even see her move, but in an instant she had her switchblade open in her hand. She signalled to Ilya who picked up from the floor something I couldn't see. Both of them approached me. Ilya was carrying a small granite bowl. My coat and jacket had been removed before I'd come to, but I was still wearing my shirt. Anastasia tugged at the front of it and the buttons popped away. Then she held on to the collar and cut across the chest and along the arm, splitting it open. She repeated the action on the other side and the shirt fell away to the floor. She had been clinically precise, ensuring that at no point did the blade cut my skin. That was not to remain the case for long.

Ilya held the bowl under my bare forearm, still kept outstretched by the rope. Anastasia rested the blade of her knife against my skin and began to press hard. Even so the skin did not break, not until she dragged the blade swiftly downwards. I winced. Blood spurted out under pressure, splattering across the marble floor, but then began to flow more smoothly. Ilya managed to catch most of it. I wondered why they had chosen to use a knife rather than their teeth, but I thought it wiser not to ask. Soon there was plenty in the bowl – more than in the vial containing Zmyeevich's blood. Anastasia already had a strip of cloth to hand and used it to bandage the wound. A red stain spread across its surface, then came to a halt. I could feel the vein throbbing beneath, but it was enough to stop me losing any more blood.

'We don't want you dying on us, now do we?' clucked Anastasia.

She took the bowl from Ilya and held it under her face, inhaling it as though it were a warming broth. She dipped her forefinger into it then opened her lips to press it against her tongue, dragging her finger downwards to leave a slight stain across her chin.

'Tasty,' she said.

She walked over towards the iconostasis and put the bowl down in front of it. Then she took the vial. She held it up to a candle, judging how much was in there, then bent back down to the bowl, tipping a little of its contents away, which cascaded down the steps. Now she uncorked the vial and poured Zmyeevich's blood into mine. She picked the bowl up again and swilled it around to mix the dark liquids together. Again she held it close to her face, but this time she did not taste it. She glanced around her five accomplices. 'You all ready? You know what to do?'

There were general nods and murmurs of affirmation, but one of them, the one who had come at me from behind, had a question. 'Where will he appear?'

'I don't know. The writings aren't clear on that.' She was

flustered at having to reveal her ignorance. 'But don't worry – you won't mistake him. Fetch the vessel.'

Ilya came forward carrying an ornate chalice. It looked to me like the sort of thing from which I was accustomed to drinking communion wine. It could have been pilfered from any church – most likely the one in which we stood. Anastasia poured half the contents of the bowl into it, then returned to the iconostasis, placing the bowl in front of the altar, in the arch of the Beautiful Gate itself. She took another vial from her pocket and poured a little of its contents into the blood. The she turned to face me.

'Begin!' she commanded.

Ilya came towards me with the chalice, offering it to me as if to drink, but I kept my mouth firmly shut. They might have as much of my blood as they needed, but they had no more of Zmyeevich's to waste. If they had to force it down me, I might be able to make sure enough fell on to the floor. But they had clearly thought about it and weren't taking risks.

One of them grabbed my hair and pulled my head back. Another had his hands on my jaws, prising them apart. For a human it would be an almost impossible achievement, but his vampire strength made it easy. He held them open while Ilya poured the liquid into my mouth. I tried to shake my head from side to side, but the grip was too strong. I flicked my tongue back and forth, but could only displace a few drops. I felt fingers squeezing my nostrils closed. I tried not to breathe, and managed for perhaps half a minute, but then I could resist no more. I used my tongue to push the liquid away from the back of my mouth, to keep my airway clear, but it was impossible. Finally I made the decision – I would suffocate rather than swallow the revolting draught. But nature was stronger. My body rebelled against my will, and at last I swallowed, a moment later taking in great whoops of air.

It had become darker. I looked around to see Anastasia in the process of extinguishing all but a few of the candles. The cathedral was notable for having been built from the beginning with electric light, but evidently this ceremony required something more sombre. As she said, she had no idea what was necessary to the ritual and what was adornment, so she had to follow every detail she knew to the letter.

She plucked one candle from its holder and went back over to the altar. She held the candle close to the surface of the liquid in the bowl and it erupted in flame. Sparks leapt on to the stone floor and smoke billowed upwards. Whatever chemical had been in that second vial had made the blood burn readily. She walked back, positioning herself at the halfway point between me and the burning blood. Around us the five vampires prowled anti-clockwise, outside of the pillars to which I was lashed. I could imagine them as wolves around a campfire, fearful of the flames but hungry for the flesh of the humans who sat beside it. Again I was reminded of what Dmitry had told me of *The Rite of Spring*, and I wondered whether he would be judging how this awful but genuine rite lived up to the fakery he had witnessed in a Parisian theatre.

Anastasia began to speak.

'*Simili modo, postquam cenatum est, accipiens et calicem, iterum gratias agens dedit discipulis suis, dicens, "Accipite et bibite ex eo omnes. Hic est enim calix sanguinis mei novi et aeterni testamenti, qui pro vobis et pro multis effundetur in celebrationem peccatorum. Hoc facite in meam commemorationem."*'

I didn't speak much Latin, but I knew enough to work out that this was the text used in the West for the sacrament of the Eucharist, or some obscene variation of it. The *voordalaki* circling around me began to chant in soft voices.

'*Mortem tuam annuntiamus, Domine, et tuam resurrectionem confitemur, donec venias.*

'*Mortem tuam annuntiamus, Domine, et tuam resurrectionem confitemur, donec venias.*

'*Mortem tuam annuntiamus, Domine, et tuam resurrectionem confitemur, donec venias.*'

I tried to prepare myself for what was to come. The metallic taste of blood – my own and Zmyeevich's – still clung to my tongue. I could feel the liquid in my stomach, but I couldn't tell whether the sensation of nausea that had begun to fill me was a physical reaction to it, or merely the result of my knowledge of what it was. I looked into the darkness of the church and the world around me began to blur. The processing figures of the vampires became just dancing shadows, revealing and obscuring the light of the candles beyond them. The faces in the icons on the walls began to stare at me, and then to laugh. The white beards of the saints vanished to become long moustaches of iron-grey that hung from beneath arched nostrils. Every one of them – male or female – had been transformed. I flung my head back to look up at the face of Christ on the inside of the cupola, but it too had distorted into the image of Zmyeevich.

Anastasia had been silent for a while, but now she began again, louder this time, repeating the words she had spoken before. '"*Accipite et bibite ex eo omnes. Hic est enim calix sanguinis . . .*"' Beneath her the *voordalaki* continued their sinister mantra. I looked beyond them into the shadows of the church and saw a tall figure, whose face I could not make out. I could not see his eyes, but I knew they were staring at me, burning into me. He began to pace slowly forward.

I looked down at Dmitry, but he didn't notice me. His eyes flicked around the room, looking to discover what the effect of the ritual would be, but from what I could glean from his expression, seeing nothing untoward. The blood in my stomach burned in sympathy with the portion that had been separated from it and was being consumed in fire before the altar. Anastasia began to recite again, shouting this time. I looked back at the dark figure. Still it seemed to approach, without ever getting closer.

Then the nave became fractionally darker. Anastasia turned away from me and walked up the steps towards the Beautiful Gate. She looked down. The bowl was no longer alight. She picked it up and shook it and it spluttered briefly with flame and sparks, but they quickly vanished. Its fuel had been consumed. She held the bowl high in her hand and let its contents fall on to the altar, but all that descended was dark, powdered ash which dispersed in the air. I could tell from her face that this was not a part of the rite – this was the act of a disappointed woman, unable to comprehend the fact that her magic had failed.

The *voordalaki* saw it too. One by one they drew to a halt. The chanting stopped. I looked at the faces in the mosaics and all were as they should be, benignly looking down on me. The figure in the shadows had vanished – if it had ever been there.

'Shit!' said Anastasia.

'Where is he?' asked Ilya. He looked around, as did the others. If they hadn't been so totally under her thrall I might have suspected they were mocking her.

'It hasn't worked,' she spat.

'I told you,' said Ilya. 'He has to die. It's obvious.'

'It's not obvious at all.' Then she calmed. 'But it was always a possibility. It's the only chance we have.' She walked towards me, her knife already in her hand. Although the ceremony was over, my stomach still burned, worse now than it had before. I glanced down at the bulge of the child she carried and felt a sudden, all-consuming despair at the thought that this whole ceremony might have succeeded to the extent that it had left me in a similar state. The pain inside me grew, as if some monster lay within, clawing to get out; as if Zmyeevich had been conceived anew and was now desperate to be born.

Anastasia held the knife low, ready to stab me in the heart, but I felt certain now that she would do better to slash my belly open and unleash whatever was inside me. The pain was so great I was tempted to beg her to.

And then the church was filled with light. There was a shout from behind me.

'There they are. I told you. Fucking *burzhooi*.'

I tried to turn and look. They'd come in through the main door and turned on the electric light. They were only Swan bulbs, too dim to do the vampires harm, but the brightness was enough to startle them, dazzling them momentarily. A crowd of perhaps thirty poured into the nave – Red Guards by the look of them. At their head was Louis – Dmitry's henchman, whom I'd last seen being flung into the Neva. He made straight for Dmitry, trying to release him, while the others engaged the five *voordalaki*. They could have little idea what they were facing, but with such overwhelming numbers they might stand a chance – particularly if Dmitry was free to join them.

No one paid any attention to Anastasia. She had been momentarily fazed by the invasion, but now she turned her attention back to me. I could understand her reasoning. If my death would bring Zmyeevich back, then now might be her last chance. She drew back the knife.

Then Louis appeared between us. Anastasia's knife plunged into his stomach, but to no effect. He swung at her with the back of his hand and sent her across the church, smashing into the iconostasis. He turned to face me. I tried to speak but could not; the pain in my stomach was beyond endurance. I pulled at the ropes to indicate he should free me, but he focused on something behind me and his face dropped.

He just managed to form a shout. 'Look out!'

Then something hard and heavy hit me on the back of the head. My vision blurred. I tried to force myself to remain standing, but the agony in my stomach was already overcoming me. I slumped forwards, dangling from the ropes, and for the second time that night collapsed into unconsciousness.

CHAPTER XIII

'DOMINIQUE.'
I heard the word and realized moments later that I had spoken it myself, though I had no concept as to why. I opened my eyes. It was dark, but not pitch black. I sensed that I was indoors. The back of my head throbbed. I lifted my hands to rub my face, but felt that they were restrained. I pulled again and found that I was not bound tightly. There were ropes tied around my wrists, but fixed to nothing at the other end. My arms were hindered only by the weight of them dragging across the cold stone floor. I touched my head where the pain was, and realized it was better to leave it alone. I rubbed my face and eyes. My skin felt strange, but I could not place what was wrong with it. I was almost clean shaven, which suggested I hadn't been out for very long. As my arms came into contact with my chest I realized that I was naked from the waist up. My right forearm was bandaged. I looked in all directions, taking in my surroundings.

I was in a church. I didn't recognize it, but then I was hardly familiar with all the churches and cathedrals in Petersburg. Who could be, with so many of them? It was an assumption even that I was in Petersburg, though it seemed likely. That was where I had been, as far as I could recall. My memories – particularly those of the immediate past – felt vague; distant.

There were only a few candles to light the nave, but they were enough to see the mosaic icons that covered every inch of the walls and pillars. It was an impressive piece of work. I was lying in the very centre of the building. Columns soared above me, up to a cupola from which the image of Christ stared back down, unnerving me. I sat up. Around me the floor seemed uneven; undulating in the flickering candlelight. I felt for the ropes around my wrists and tugged at them, but they would not yield. I unpicked the knots with my fingers and threw the ropes to one side. I stood.

The reason for the strange shape of the floor became clear now. There were bodies, seven of them, strewn about the place. Two were on the steps leading up to the iconostasis. One was sprawled over the gate of some little chapel or shrine directly opposite – and therefore presumably to the west. The others were on the floor. I examined them; five had the unmistakable signs of having been killed by the teeth of a vampire. Of the others one had a broken neck and the other a stab wound to the heart. I also came across two empty sets of clothes – both men's – from which a little dust escaped as I kicked them. It seemed that in whatever battle had taken place between men and vampires there had been casualties on both sides. I could only count myself lucky that I was not among them.

I grabbed the shirt, jacket and overcoat that had belonged to one of the vampires and shook them to clear as much of the dust as I could. There was a hole in the cotton where a wooden blade had pierced the creature's heart, but it wouldn't be seen and the outer clothes were intact. I felt an unaccustomed distaste at the prospect of donning clothes that had so recently been worn by the undead, but on looking around the chamber could see nothing better. I put them on, then looked for a way out. Typically the main door would be to the west, away from the altar, and in this church it was no exception. There were windows high in the walls, but no light penetrated. That probably meant it was night, but they might have been curtained or painted over. I opened the door only a fraction at first and felt a cool breeze flow through. Still there was no sign of daylight.

I opened the door wider and stepped outside. It was certainly night, but not as dark as I had expected. The streetlights seemed brighter than usual, but that was not an immediate concern. I tried to sense exactly what time it was, but I could not. Sometime in the small hours was all I could guess. I looked around me. This certainly felt like Petersburg, but I could not fathom where exactly I was. I turned to look back at the church from which I'd emerged. Perhaps it might be more familiar to me from outside than it had been from within.

It stirred memories, though the place it reminded me of was in a quite different city – Moscow. And despite the similar style, there were obvious differences between this and Saint Vasiliy's. This, it seemed to me, was a poor imitation. I walked around it and eventually, on the far side, discovered that it had been built to abut a long, straight canal. Now at last I recognized where I was.

It was most definitely Petersburg. This was the Yekaterininsky Canal – the northern end of it, close to the Field of Mars. I felt a strange sense of comfort wash over me, a feeling of familiarity that managed to soothe the unease I'd been experiencing since I had awoken. I walked a little way along the embankment and then turned to look back at the church. That was one thing that was neither familiar nor comfortable. It should not have been there. That was more than the assertion of my memory. The church simply didn't fit. It stuck out into the canal, which had clearly been narrowed at one point to accommodate it. No one would ever have reason to build a church there – no architect would ever consider it. But beyond that was the simple fact that a church did not exist at that particular location in the city. I'd walked alongside the canal often enough to know.

Two possibilities, both implausible, came to mind. The first was that this was not in truth Petersburg, but some counterfeit, assembled like a Potemkin village with the intention to deceive. If I were to go to one of the buildings on either side of the canal and knock on its door and go inside, I would find that there *was* no inside, that they were empty façades, constructed only to confuse. Tsaritsa Yekaterina had never bothered to inspect the illusions that Prince Potemkin had created for her. Perhaps I would, but not yet. The whole idea was preposterous. Why create so accurate a facsimile and then ruin everything by putting that church there?

The other explanation was only a little more credible: that I had been unconscious for far longer than I'd guessed – for a matter of years rather than hours, long enough for that building to have been raised up from nothing. It would have taken years; decades. And still that didn't explain why it was built in so preposterous a location, forced upon an embankment where it simply didn't fit. Even so, it was the best explanation I could come up with for now. I tried to recall what I had been doing before I lost consciousness, but could remember nothing beyond an overarching sense of pain and fear.

The embankment was empty of people, but even if there had been anyone, I wasn't sure I would have approached them with a question such as what year it was, or who was tsar. How could I trust their answer? If this whole city was a fake, then wouldn't those who populated it be creations also – actors trained to maintain the deception? I'd do better to behave as I had always done and rely upon my own wits. I would unearth the truth, once I had gathered sufficient evidence.

I walked on alongside the canal. Ahead of me I could see the lights of Nevsky Prospekt, and from what I could make out the slight movement of people and carriages. A man brushed past me, running towards the prospekt. He slowed for a moment and turned, walking backwards so that he could address me.

'Come on! The palace has fallen. It's a free-for-all!'

He turned again and raced away from me. I wondered what he could mean. There must have been two dozen palaces in the city, but in the absence of any qualification, and based on the direction he was heading, I could only guess he meant the Winter Palace. And if *it* had fallen, then surely Russia was in the midst of an invasion, or even a revolution. Was the tsar in residence? Had he been captured? I broke into a run, following the direction the man had gone. Within a minute I was at Nevsky Prospekt. I came to a halt, breathing heavily. I should have been able to cover that distance without even raising a sweat, but I felt an aching in my lungs, along with an unfamiliar sensation in my chest. It was the pounding of my heart – whatever this fanciful world was that I had awoken into, it was not only the city that had been altered by it. So too had my own body.

The prospekt was busy, considering the time of night. The general flow was towards the Winter Palace. Individuals, couples and small groups – many of them carrying rifles. A few came from the other direction. Two soldiers – a sergeant and a lieutenant – passed me carrying a huge painting between them, horizontal like a table. The canvas was face down so I could not see what it was of, but the gilt of the frame hinted at its value. It was obvious where they had taken it from, and it only served to prove what I'd already been told. The Winter Palace was open to all comers, to take what they wanted.

I had no interest in such booty, but I was fascinated to discover what was happening. Whatever circumstances had led to me being here in this strange yet familiar city, I was privileged to have arrived at just this moment – a turning point in history. Perhaps I'd even be lucky enough to witness the tsar – whoever that might be – emerge from his former home in chains. Whether the extinction of the Romanov line would prove to be to my advantage or otherwise, I was unsure, but if it was to happen, I would delight in being there to see it. I set off along the pavement, walking now, wary of the apparent limitations of my body.

Then, from behind me, I heard the most bewildering of sounds. It was a low growl – as if from some great dog – steadily rising in pitch, lasting longer than a dog or any animal could have maintained without drawing breath. Then at last there was the slightest break in the sound, only for it to begin again back at its lower frequency, smoothly rising once more. It was getting closer. No one else on the street seemed even to have heard it. I stopped and turned.

It was, as far as I could suppose, a carriage, but unlike any other I had ever seen. Its shape was unusual, but its purpose was clear from the fact that it carried seven people, some standing, others sitting. Two of the men had rifles, which they fired without aim into the air. There was no roof to the vehicle, but it had windows at the sides. The wheels were smaller than I would have expected to see on a coach of that size, allowing it to sit closer to the road, but that was not the strangest thing about it. What marked it out from any carriage I had seen on Nevsky Prospekt before, or on any road, was that it had no horses.

I realized now that decades must have passed to which I had been quite insensible. Whether I had been in some way unconscious or had actually been transported through time, I could not guess. The concept of a horseless carriage was not new to me, but for more than a century – according to my perception – such things had been confined to run on rails. Building a steam locomotive that could travel along an ordinary road was not impossible, but had been determined quite impractical. And yet this thing was not like any steam engine that I had ever seen. Where was its funnel? Where was its firebox or its boiler? And that sound that had first drawn the vehicle to my attention was nothing like what I would expect from a steam engine.

The carriage sped past. I turned my head to follow it and soon it was receding into the distance. It left in its wake a strange smell, a smell which I realized had been hanging about the city since I had awoken, but was stronger closer to its source. It was the smell of burning, but not of either coal or wood, more like paraffin, but even that was not quite right. It was another thing I would have to investigate.

I walked onwards, trying to work out how much time must have passed – with me oblivious to it – for such changes to have taken place. The position of the Romanovs had always been precarious and for the people to turn against them might have taken only months. To build the church in which I had found myself would have been the matter of a decade or so. But for that carriage to have been invented – and to have become so commonplace that no one but me had even turned to marvel at it – would have taken far longer. Was this 1920? 1930? 1940? I couldn't guess. I could only lick my lips in anticipation of what further wonders were to be revealed to me.

217

Before long I was at the end of Nevsky Prospekt. Ahead of me was something else new – a bridge that I had not known before stretching out across the Neva – but it was of no immediate concern. I looked across Palace Square and saw a scene of chaos. There were fires blazing, men, women and children drinking and singing, soldiers standing doing nothing. I walked over towards the palace. At the main entrance there had been some sort of barricade built, but it had long since been breached. A chain of men – like ants who had found a basket of food – went back and forth from it, taking pieces of wood and furniture to use on the fires. Others went through the gap and into the palace, while still more came out of the building carrying what loot they could find.

I stood and looked up at the higher windows. Many of them were broken. Inside I could see figures running back and forth. A face thrust itself out through one of the broken panes and shouted across the square, but I couldn't make out the words. A little closer to the building I saw a figure standing like me with his head raised, gawping at the sight before him. I went over and stood near by, close enough to note the stench of alcohol that hung about him. My hope was that he might offer some information of his own accord; any question I asked risked my being regarded as a madman. I waited a few minutes, but he said nothing. In the end I had to speak.

'Did they put up much of a fight?' I said. It was as neutral a question as I could think of.

'Hardly,' he grunted. 'Kerensky had already made a run for it. The rest of them didn't have much stomach.'

The name meant nothing to me. I could only presume that Kerensky was some kind of senior minister – the tsar's right hand, much like Speransky or Arakcheyev had been. But I wasn't concerned with bit players.

'And what about . . . the tsar?' I asked, managing to suppress my instinct to say 'His Majesty' in time. If this was, as it seemed, a revolution, then I didn't want to appear part of the old guard. At the same time, I wondered why I cared. It was becoming ever clearer to me that I wasn't myself.

'Nikolai? Why should he give a fuck? He's lucky to have got out when he did.'

The man walked away. In his hand he carried a bottle of cognac, of a quality and price that would more usually find itself drunk at a table than in the street. From his coat pocket I caught a glint of gold. It wasn't just brandy he'd taken from the palace. Evidently the emperor had already fled, but now I knew his name. My memory was quite clear on matters of history; there had been a Nikolai in direct line to the throne – Nikolai Aleksandrovich. If he was now tsar then I could make a guess at the year. If he had lived into his eighties, it could already be 1950. If his father had died at, say, sixty it could be as early as 1905. It was an enormous timespan; the method was less helpful than I'd anticipated.

Then I saw something that might be of far better use: a sheet of paper blowing across the square, quite possibly a newspaper. I chased after it. The wind dropped and the paper settled down on to the cobbles. I reached out, but it was off again. I ran, but found myself unable to keep going for any longer than I had before. Eventually the paper caught against one of the pillars at the foot of the Aleksandr Monument. I managed to grab it.

It was the front page. The title was *Pravda*. I hadn't heard of it, but that hardly mattered. The first thing I read was the date: 23 October 1917. It couldn't have been more than a few days old. That meant a gap of decades since my last memories – vague though they were. I could recall emotion more clearly than events, and the one emotion that seemed to overwhelm me was fear; fear that I was about to die. No, more even than that. I hadn't been *afraid* that I was going to die – I *knew* it. My fear had been at the punishment to come. And if I had died, then there was only one explanation for my current state. I had been resurrected. I had not merely slept, like those creatures once entombed beneath Chufut Kalye, nor had I travelled in time. I had died and had been recalled to life.

But then another thought occurred to me, bringing a smile to my lips. In facing death I had feared what was to come, feared that the stories of a vengeful God and a just Hell were more than fables taught to frighten children into obeying their parents, and men into obeying their kings. I had feared, like so many, that the innumerable sins of my earthly existence would be weighed in the scale and that I would be found wanting. It was for that reason that so many chose the immortality of the vampire, not because they wanted to live for ever, but simply so that they might put off the day of judgement. But now I knew better. I had visited that undiscovered country and returned, but while there had found it to be an empty place – a place of oblivion, not punishment, and as such it was nothing to fear. I did not plan to return there quickly, but I knew now that no action of mine on Earth would ever need to be accounted for in another place. I could live an existence untrammelled by fear of reprisal. I doubted it would make much difference to my behaviour.

There was more than that, though, to be gleaned from the newspaper. I quickly read the articles and began to make some sense of what was going on. The tsar had fallen some time ago – months at the very least – and had been replaced by a Provisional Government of which this Kerensky was the head. The nation was at war with an alliance of Germany, Austria-Hungary and, inevitably, the Ottomans. The war had been going on for years, starving Russia, but Kerensky had insisted on continuing with it. His main rival was a party called the Bolsheviks, who now accused Kerensky of being about to allow the Germans to occupy the city of Petrograd in hope of propping him up in power. It took me a moment to realize that this Petrograd was just a new name for the very city in which I was standing – Saint Petersburg. By the time I'd finished reading the four pages of newspaper I had in my possession, I felt somewhat confident that I could pass myself off as informed. I knew, though, that I had to be wary. The paper made no attempt to disguise the fact that it held a particular viewpoint, one that chimed with the opinions of the Bolsheviks. I did not want to appear to be throwing in my lot with either side until I was sure which had been victorious.

There was nothing more to be done here. I crumpled the

paper and cast it aside, leaving Palace Square to the east, along Millionaire's Street. Here too there were signs that a barricade had been built and destroyed. I pressed on. I still wasn't sure how long it would be till dawn, and in that time I needed to find a safe, dark place to sleep. And there was something else I needed. I had begun to feel the pangs of hunger. It was a sensation not quite as I remembered it, but compelling none the less. It had been decades since I had last fed, but that was hardly relevant. It was an interesting question to ponder: when a man was resurrected from the dead, was it with a full belly or an empty one? But then hunger wasn't the only reason to feed – there was the pleasure of it too. I would find some quiet street or sleepy household, and there I would indulge myself.

I turned on to the Moika embankment, looking all the time I walked for a place where I might find the blood I was beginning to crave. I was doubling back on myself, but perhaps that was for the best. I needed to return to the church; if anywhere held clues to how it had come about that I was alive at all, then it would be there. Even so, memories sent scurrying by the trauma of the event were beginning to creep back into my mind. Regarding the question of how I had come to be resurrected a simple and intriguing answer occurred to me: because I had planned it. That in itself didn't get me very far. For any man to embark on so audacious a scheme would require a quite uncommon degree of both intelligence and fastidiousness. It sounded entirely the sort of thing that I would have attempted. I tried to imagine how I might have achieved it; if I could not remember the events then perhaps trying to recreate them in my imagination would be of some help.

Behind me came the sound of running footsteps; some looter, no doubt, fleeing the palace with his spoils – probably drunk too. Perhaps that would make him incautious. I would let him pass me and then follow. I could almost taste his blood on my lips. He was close to me now, but it was still wisest to let him go by. Then I felt a hand on my shoulder, turning me.

'My God! You're alive!'

I looked at his face and the most unusual sensation swept over me: a sense of relief at no longer being alone. I had lived longer than the span of any human life and had adapted to the changing world with ease. But with this sudden leap into the future I found myself in a state of utter isolation. I sought neither friends nor companionship, but as I realized now, any creature will from time to time seek comfort in the familiar. And this face was familiar – he had once been a friend, though I had no reason to suppose he was any such thing now. He did not appear a day older than when I had last seen him, but why should he? He was, like me, a vampire.

'Yes, Dmitry, I'm alive.'

He stood uncomfortably for a moment, as if considering whether to embrace me, but in the end he decided against it. I desperately tried to assess him. His tone of voice expressed both less surprise and more pleasure than I might have expected. We had been friends once – allies even – but he decided long ago to turn away from me. Why then should he be so happy at my resurrection? More than that, though, he had not seen me for almost forty years; 'My God! You're alive!' could only be regarded as understatement. And yet I was not foolish enough to suppose that my new-born comprehension of our circumstances was in any way better than his.

'One of the Red Guards shouted out you were dead. I should have checked for myself, but I wanted to get after Anastasia.'

I could only relish the challenge of having to process so much information, and yet respond as if it all made sense to me. Clearly he was describing events of which I had no memory, and yet which he seemed convinced we had shared. Perhaps this was not a case of time travel or resurrection, but of simple memory loss; but not *that* simple – it would have to have been over a period of decades. And yet my memory was certainly hazy, even as to events before that. The term 'Red Guards' I understood from my brief look at the newspaper. But they had been formed for less than a year, so clearly Dmitry was referring to something relatively recent. The name Anastasia meant nothing to me, though it evidently should have.

'Did you catch up with her?' I asked. It seemed like the most obvious response.

He shook his head. 'She was fast, and the streets are busy. They all went in different directions, but I tried to stick with her.'

'I'm sure you did your best.'

'Do you think she'll be able to try again?'

'Who can say?' I despised myself to hear such platitudes on my lips, but I knew I had to remain noncommittal.

'There must be more of Zmyeevich's blood – somewhere.'

And that was when it all began to make sense to me. Now my mind began to race. Vague memories became more substantial. A sense of pride began to fill me – pride at my own ingenuity. I fell silent, deep in thought.

'Mihail? Are you all right?'

'Yes, yes, I'm fine. I was just thinking – about the blood.' I hadn't missed the name by which he'd called me.

'You think Iuda might have hidden away other bottles of it in London?'

'Let's hope not.'

'We're assuming, of course, that it did fail.'

'What do you mean?'

'I've been thinking. They were looking around for some kind of apparition – for Zmyeevich to materialize somewhere. We all were. But no one knew where to look. They were expecting something spectacular, but what did they know? Who's to say he didn't appear in some dark corner. Or even just outside the church, rather than just inside it. It's only a few feet to the embankment – what do stone walls matter with something like this?'

'Wouldn't you know if he'd returned?' I asked. 'Wouldn't you sense it?' It was a pleasure to toy with him.

Dmitry breathed in deeply again, as if scenting the air. 'No,' he said, but with little conviction. 'I don't sense him. But if he is newly born – possessed of a new body – then perhaps I can't feel his presence. Perhaps I wouldn't even recognize him if we stood face to face.'

I was forced to suppress my laughter. '"But their eyes were

holden that they should not know him,"' I said. He looked at me, puzzled. 'When the disciples first saw Christ after his resurrection,' I explained.

His expression didn't change. I realized my mistake – the more I spoke, the less likely it was that I sounded like who I was supposed to be: Mihail, whoever he was. I knew I should say as little as possible. Thankfully Dmitry let it pass.

'If he has returned, he'll reveal himself soon enough.' He paused, contemplating the prospect. I hoped I would be there to witness it when he finally discovered what had happened. He looked up at the sky. 'It'll be dawn soon. I have to go. We'll meet tomorrow – usual time and place.'

I had no idea what he meant, but I wasn't going to shatter the illusion he had about me, not just yet. I felt sure I'd be able to track him down when the time came.

'I'll try my best,' I said.

He gave me a brief pat on the arm, then departed. I set off in the other direction. I too needed to find a place to sleep before dawn came. But I also needed to feed. I turned away from the river and on to Moshkov Lane. It was quiet here. I looked up at the windows on either side, wondering which I should climb up to, but then by chance hit upon a far more convenient way to slake my thirst. I tripped over something on the pavement.

I looked back. It was a soldier – just a *ryadovoy* – he was stretched out, his head propped up against the wall. Beside him was a bottle of sherry, almost empty, held lightly in his hand. He was dead to the world. There would be little pleasure in it, but at least his blood would sustain me. And it might be wiser to pick a safe target until I was more familiar with my new state of existence. I looked around, but there was no one else about. I knelt down at his side and shook him. He groaned, but did not come to. I pulled aside his collar and lifted his chin so that the pale flesh of his neck was exposed to me. Despite my hunger I felt no appetite for the blood that flowed through him, but I was wise enough to understand that I needed sustenance. I leaned forward, letting my lips touch his skin. The smell was foul. He hadn't bathed for days, and there was the hint of vomit about him – presumably his own. Even so, I opened my jaws wide and bit.

I did not experience, as I had anticipated, the warm, revitalizing gush of blood running over my tongue. I tasted nothing but the rancid tang of his filthy skin. I bit harder, but still his flesh did not yield. I might as well have been sinking my teeth into a dirty leather boot. I simply did not have the strength that was required, nor did my teeth have the sharpness. I pressed my jaws together harder still, and the man screamed, pushing me away from him. At that moment I did taste blood, but it was not the rush I would have expected – merely a few drops. Even they brought me no pleasure. I knelt upright. The man turned on his side; the pain had not been enough to bring him fully to consciousness. I could feel fragments of his skin between my teeth and on my tongue, and was revolted by them. A distant memory returned of a time before I had become a vampire, when I had tasted the blood of a fellow human and had been revolted at the very concept.

I stood and ran, spitting the morsels of flesh from my mouth as I did. All that had once seemed natural to me was now alien. I was not the creature I had been. If I could not drink the blood of a human, then how was I supposed to live? I raced onwards, past doorways and shop windows, then suddenly I came to a halt. I had sensed a movement beside me, as if someone were running next to me. I went back and understood what I had seen.

In one of the windows there was a mirror. It wasn't for sale, but was positioned so that customers could see the back of a particularly fine frock coat. I had caught a glimpse of my own reflection as I ran past. I hesitated. On the one hand, this was my opportunity to find out who this Mihail was that Dmitry had recognized in me. On the other, I was well aware that the only way that the image of a *voordalak* could be reflected was in a special kind of glass that would reveal his true form – and perhaps send him mad in the process. I had seen it once myself, though only briefly. But I was hardly a *voordalak* any more. My inability even to drink the blood of an insensible drunk proved that. What other characteristics had I lost?

I stretched my hand out to one side and saw its reflection. It appeared perfectly normal. I took a step sideways and saw the whole length of my arm. One further step, and I could see my face.

It was certainly not the face I had seen staring back at me the last time I had looked into a normal mirror, when I was still a man. Years had passed, but as a vampire my appearance should not have changed. This was simply not me. I was looking into the eyes of a man of about sixty years. He was clean shaven. His hairline was receding, but it had not gone far. His hair was grey and tightly curled, with sideboards well down his jaws. It was difficult to tell in the dim streetlight, but his eyes were dark, probably brown. He was tall, but not as tall as I had been in my own body.

I touched his face – my face. Earlier I had wondered if this entire city might be an illusion designed in some way to bewilder me. This too could be some conjuror's trick, but every movement that I made was copied by the figure that stood before me in the mirror. There could be no mistake.

I peered closer at the face and some stirring of recognition began to move within me. If I had known him, then it must have been when he was a young man – in his twenties or thirties. I considered the name that Dmitry had used to address me – Mihail – and realization came to me in a flood.

I recognized the face before me, not just for itself, but for other faces I knew – relatives of the man whose physical body I had usurped. There was his grandfather, even his uncle with whom I'd only minutes before been speaking. This was Mihail Konstantinovich Danilov; a man in whose veins ran both the blood of the Danilovs and that of the Romanovs. And that blood ran in my veins too. I'd heard tell of the possibility, of the existence of a ceremony, but I'd had little idea of the steps that must be taken, or whether they would really work. But evidently this Anastasia had discovered more. She had taken my blood from the house in London, and found in Danilov an appropriate sacrifice – one whose blood I had imbibed, but who had not tasted mine. And it had worked. She had given me new life – taken Danilov's body and handed it to me. I tried to imagine who she might be. It was not a name I recognized, but it was most likely an alias. Dmitry had given no description, and there were many women over the ages who had been happy to assist me – even to lay down their lives for me.

And yet Anastasia was quite unaware of what she had achieved. She had been expecting – as they all had, based no doubt on biblical obsession – a bodily resurrection; a new being created from nothing to accommodate a soul which fluttered helplessly in the void. Why, though, go to the effort of creating new flesh where flesh existed already? Despite her ignorance I would have to find her and thank her. There was still much of what she had done that she didn't understand.

High on one of the rooftops above me a bird began to sing. Others immediately joined it. Dawn was almost upon us. Clearly my new body was very different from that of a normal vampire, but I wasn't about to take risks. I needed to find a dark place to rest. I looked around me and saw peeking over the top of a building the colourful onion domes of the church in which I had first awoken. It would make a good enough place to sleep, for one day at any rate.

It took me only moments to get there. Inside, all was as I had left it. The bodies remained unmoved. I chuckled to myself, pretending to look around as they must have done for the dark moustached figure that they had been expecting. What they had got was something quite different. I considered where it was best to lie down and sleep. There were more windows in this building than in the older churches which it mimicked. I remembered Saint Isaac's, remembered the fight I'd had there and the way that its windows allowed in so much of the sun during the day. It would not be safe for me to sleep in the nave. I found a door that led down into some kind of cellar – it could hardly be described as a crypt. It would do to keep me in darkness, and gave me a chance of being undiscovered if anyone came in. Soon I would find somewhere better.

I lay down on the hard floor and closed my eyes, but sleep would not come. I was too thrilled by the possibilities that this new life presented me. Memories of my death were beginning to come back to me. Though painful, it had been swift and I'd had no opportunity to regret. Now I was in a privileged position. I had died and I had returned. True, the same could be said of any vampire, but what I had achieved was different – was unique. I could only marvel at it, which meant I could not sleep.

I must have been lying there for about an hour when it happened. It began very slightly with me wiggling the fingers of my left hand. I raised it to my face and watched them flexing in the dim light. Then I stood up. It was a perfectly normal thing for me to do. The only remarkable feature of the action was that it took place completely without my intent. I walked back to the stairs and up once again into the nave, all without any volition on my part. Indeed, I made every attempt to stop myself, but there was no struggle to be had. My mind was not connected to my limbs. I was a passenger in my own body – in the body I had purloined.

Inside the church, daylight was shining through the windows, though none of it as yet reached down to the floor. But I did not linger. I strode over to the door and stood there momentarily. I knew full well what I was about to do, but could conceive of no way of stopping myself. I grasped the handle and opened the door. Then I stepped outside and allowed my body to be swathed in the light of the bright morning sun.

CHAPTER XIV

ICOULD SCARCELY FEEL THE RAYS OF LIGHT UPON MY SKIN. IT WAS late October and in Petrograd in the early morning the sun had little intensity. My most powerful sensation was one of disappointment – disappointment that I was still alive and not reduced to a billion fragments of dust to be blown through the city streets on the breeze. The one consolation to be drawn from my survival was to confirm what I'd already learned from my inability to drink human blood and the fact that I could see my reflection in a mirror: physically I was not a vampire.

I had been conscious since the moment I had awoken in the early hours in the Church on Spilled Blood. I had been able to perceive every incident that occurred as I walked through the night. I had heard every word that was spoken to me and every reply that I offered. But more than that, I had been able to perceive every thought that passed through the mind that had taken possession of my physical being. Every vile notion had been as clear to me as if it had been the product of my own consciousness. But I was no more than an observer. I could not shape those thoughts, nor could I delve into the memories that undoubtedly must belong to the spirit that possessed me. If he chose to recall a past event, then I would share the act of reminiscence, but the decision was not mine. And in his shocked state of rebirth, his memory was nebulous – but it was enough for me to know him.

As little as I had control over what thoughts he brought into my head, neither could I participate in the choice of what he did with my body. More than once in my life I have awoken from a dream and found myself for seconds or even minutes quite incapable of movement. It's a not uncommon experience – though a frightening one, especially the first time. There are stories that put it down to evil spirits sitting on the victim's chest, but I favour the more modern explanation – that whatever bodily function it is that keeps us from thrashing about and physically enacting our dreams hangs over for a few moments into wakefulness. But this was far worse. Not only could I not move; another mind could move me. As we had walked through Petrograd I had been able to conceive of stopping, or running, or raising a hand in the air, just as I have done every day of my life. But none of it had any effect. The other will was ascendant. When we had been talking to Dmitry I had shouted and screamed at him, trying to warn him, trying to tell him the truth, but none of it had any more effect on the world than a passing whim which idly crosses the brain and is then forgotten. I don't know if my thoughts made any impact on that other mind, but it did not seem distracted by them.

When I finally saw my own face in the mirror it was something of a relief to know that this was still my body and that the other mind was the invader – the cuckoo's egg laid in the nest so many years before which now had hatched. Had my consciousness been transferred to the body of another, then what would have been my prospects? Dmitry's reaction to me had given me some hope, but it was a joy to see in the mirror that I was physically the man I had always been.

And then I had lain down beneath the church. I'd felt a sense of sleepiness that I hoped affected both of us, but I tried to resist it. It was a desperate hope but I wondered whether, as he slept, I might gain control once more. I don't know how long it took, but I continually tapped my fingers against the ground, or attempted to; at first it was no more successful than any other motion I had tried. Then I'd felt it – my fingertips touching and releasing the cold stone. Soon I'd discovered that I was in complete control of my body once more. For a heady moment I hoped that the possession had left me completely, but I searched my mind and soon found it.

As far as I could make out it was not fully asleep but dormant, in much the same state as I had been for the last few hours, I supposed. I couldn't perceive its thoughts but sensed only its presence. It lurked there, waiting its moment. It reminded me of the Petrograd Soviet, sitting there for all those months in the opposite wing of the Tavricheskiy Palace. Now the Soviet had taken over completely – I'd learned that much from our wanderings of the previous night. I would not allow the same to happen to me.

I knew the one thing that he feared, though I worked out as easily as he had that, this being my body, it was unlikely to react to sunlight in the same way as that of a vampire. But if it did, then that was a sacrifice I would happily make. Even if my body was unharmed there was the chance that the light might simply purge me – destroy that part of me that was vampire and leave the remainder cleansed. Even if it had no effect, the impression of terror that I sensed lurking in a dark corner of my brain was a pleasure to experience.

I walked out of the church and headed north towards the Moika. When I reached it I stopped and leaned on the railing, looking down into the water. I was pleased once again to see my own reflection staring back at me, however fractured and distorted by the rippling waves. I examined my mind again, wondering if that other possibility had come true and the light of day had chased away the monster within me. For a moment I felt hope, but I soon found my lodger – the same quiet presence I had recognized before. The terror it had felt when I first stepped into the light had been piercing, but now it had calmed to almost nothing. We both knew that sunlight could not harm us.

I'd realized who he was some time before he had understood whose body it was he now occupied. But then I had two advantages over him; I could listen to his musings as they ran through my head and I knew what had taken place in the hours and minutes leading up to his awakening. Even so, to know his thoughts did not immediately reveal his identity; people do not continually repeat their own name at the front of their mind.

At first I'd been quite bewildered, but it took me only minutes to come to the most obvious conclusion. Anastasia's intent had been to raise Zmyeevich from the dead; what could be more likely than that she had succeeded? I was in no doubt that the mind which controlled me was that of a vampire. By virtue of my Romanov descent, Zmyeevich possessed my blood and now Anastasia had forced me once again to drink his. It was just the situation that Iuda's notes had described.

But as the night wore on I'd become less and less convinced that it was Zmyeevich. I knew Zmyeevich. For twelve years I *had* shared his mind – albeit occasionally. I had witnessed his death through his eyes. While the personality that sat beside mine shared some of Zmyeevich's characteristics – the arrogance, the lust for blood, the contempt for humanity – it had none of the haughty pomposity of a minor European noble who liked to style himself as 'Count'. This creature's arrogance – his belief in his own superiority – came to him not as a right with which he was endowed by virtue of his lineage, but as a prize he had fought for every day of his existence using the one gift that he had been born with and which he had cultivated at every opportunity: his intelligence. I knew him better than I knew Zmyeevich, though I had never shared his mind, not for more than a moment. I knew him because I had studied him from birth; I had been brought up to hate him, brought up to kill him. And I'd succeeded, though it seemed now that even death was not enough to overcome him. Moreover, he was the only other vampire, apart from Zmyeevich, who had carried my blood in his veins, which he had drunk from me in his very death throes. He had died just a few minutes' walk from here, but through luck or, so he seemed to think, his own design, he had come back, using my body. I ought to have recognized him from the first instant, but I did recognize him now, and with absolute certainty.

It was Iuda.

Anastasia's rite had gone perfectly, just as she had planned, but there were a few things she could not know. One was that Iuda had drunk my blood. It had seemed such a futile thing to do on his part, as the Yablochkov Candle burned into him, but I'd been in no doubt he did it with precise intent. It seemed like a ridiculous longshot, but Iuda knew how to play the odds. The other side of things was even easier to comprehend. The blood that Anastasia had mixed with mine and then burned was supposed to have been Zmyeevich's. Why did she believe it to be his? Because Iuda had said it was. He had written the name Zmyeevich on the side of the

232

vial, a vial which in truth contained Iuda's own blood. It was so simple. I'd been taught the lesson at my mother's knee: never trust a word Iuda says, nor what he writes, nor even what he thinks. I'd do well to remember that last one. Anastasia should have been aware of them all, but evidently had little experience of Iuda.

I looked along the Moika. It was only a few minutes' walk home to where Nadya would be waiting for me, worried. I'd been away all night, and she knew there were vampires out there after me. But I couldn't go to her for fear I lose control of myself once again. At the very least I should send her a note saying that I was safe, but if I even went to the door I might suddenly be gripped by the impulse to go inside. I shouldn't even be thinking about our home – to do so would reveal its location. Who could guess what Iuda might do with the knowledge?

I turned in the opposite direction, back towards the Winter Palace. My personal concerns were not the only matters of interest today. Last night the Provisional Government had fallen. The most likely outcome was that the Soviet would take over, controlled by the Bolsheviks, but I couldn't be certain. I needed to find out more.

Palace Square was quieter than it had been. There were Red Guards on duty at the palace gate, but they seemed more disciplined than those I had encountered before. There was no flow of looters in and out of the building, though that might have been down simply to there being nothing further to loot. On the corner of the square a man in a leather coat was handing out leaflets to passers-by. I went over for one. It took only moments to read:

Къ Гражданам России.
To the Citizens of Russia.

The Provisional Government has been deposed. State power has passed into the hands of the organ of the Petrograd Soviet of Workers' and Soldiers' Deputies – the Military Revolutionary Committee, which heads the Petrograd proletariat and the garrison.

The cause for which the people have fought, namely, the immediate offer of a democratic peace, the abolition of landed proprietorship, workers' control over production, and the establishment of Soviet power – this cause has been secured.

Long live the revolution of workers, soldiers and peasants!

Oddly it was dated at 10 a.m. the previous day – around sixteen hours before the Winter Palace had actually fallen. It only went to show that this was no spontaneous uprising; the whole thing had been carefully planned. I wondered how much of what was listed was what the 'people' had actually fought for. The thing they really wanted was food in their bellies. If the abolition of landed proprietorship, workers' control over production, and the establishment of Soviet power helped with that, then so be it, but none were things that had been widely demanded until the Bolsheviks had put the thought into people's heads. Peace was another requirement, but that wasn't quite what was being suggested. Instead we had 'the immediate offer of a democratic peace' – the Germans would laugh in our face.

And there was no mention of the one thing that Russia really needed, that most of us in the Duma had spent our political lives striving for; no mention at all of democracy.

'Are they going to move the Soviet in here then?' I asked the man with the leaflets.

He seemed taken aback for a moment. I realized that there was little prospect that either Lenin or Trotsky had taken him into their confidence about such things, but it went against the aura of petty authority that came with the leather coat for him to admit he did not know.

'We're not going to make the same mistakes Kerensky did,' he replied. It was his own assessment, but probably an accurate one.

I went round the side of the palace to the Neva. Here I had expected to see greater signs of the previous night's assault, but the state of the building on the side facing the river was little different from the front. Many of the windows were broken and the plaster was in tatters. In two places there were gaping holes in the walls, undoubtedly caused by shells from the *Avrora*, but nothing like what the ship could have done with a full-blown barrage. It would have been pointless destruction, considering how incapable the Provisional Government had been of defending itself.

I followed the Palace Quay to the east. If the Winter Palace was no longer the seat of authority, then either the Tavricheskiy Palace or the Smolny Institute would be – and of those two I had a good idea where the true power lay. The Military Revolutionary Committee might have been formed as a part of the Soviet, but it was Lenin who ran it from the Smolny. Lenin was our new leader.

As I walked alongside the river another sensation gripped me. I was hungry. I hadn't eaten since the previous afternoon. My path along the river took me close to home. It would be easy enough to slip in there and get something to eat. With luck Nadya wouldn't even be home, and I'd be able to defer the moment when I had to face her and tell her the truth. I pushed the thought quickly from my mind. I'd buy myself some food. I reached into my pocket, but found that my wallet wasn't there. It wasn't even my coat. I remembered I had – Iuda had – picked this up in the church. It wasn't a huge issue; I had plenty of money at home and—

Again I tried to suppress the thought, to find alternatives to smother it. My own overcoat should still be at the Church on Spilled Blood. With luck no one would have pilfered it. It was certainly worth a try. I turned back the way I'd come and before long came to the Field of Mars. That would be the shortest route. In the distance I could just see the highest dome of the church as I approached it for the third time in less than a day.

It seemed an uninspiring plan to me. I had no desire to sample Nadya's home cooking – much as I was curious to meet the lady herself – and I had no reason to suppose that Danilov's wallet, even if we found it, would contain sufficient funds to provide for what would be my first meal in almost four decades. I stopped walking and emitted a slight laugh. It was longer than that. We were not considering a feast of human blood. It now seemed clear to me that whatever the state of our minds the body in which they resided was entirely human and must be fed as a human. We would sit and have food cooked and served for us. It was closer to a century since I had indulged in that sort of pleasure. It deserved the finest restaurant in Petersburg . . . in Petrograd. And I knew precisely where that was. Things couldn't have changed that much, could they?

I began walking again, and only then realized it. I *had* stopped walking. I *had* emitted a laugh. I was in control again. I tried to determine what had caused the transition. When Danilov had managed to take back his body beneath the church I'd thought it was because I had been attempting to sleep. That didn't seem to be the case here. Perhaps the fact that I had been considering food – so bodily a concern – had returned the body to me. But Danilov had been thinking of eating too. Perhaps our body preferred my plans to his.

I knew that I must take advantage of what time I had. At any moment the process could reverse and Danilov could once again be taking us to a pitiful meal at some humble tavern. With the application of a little thought I would find a way to exclude him permanently from participation in any of the choices as to what we did and where we went, but I could not do it straight away. And I would have to be circumspect. Just as he attempted to hide his thoughts from me, so must I do likewise. If I worked out a way for one of us to take full possession over this lump of flesh, I would have to make sure that it was I who received the benefit of it and not he.

For now, though, I would eat. I continued in the direction of the Church on Spilled Blood. I wondered if Danilov had realized the recent reversal of our fortunes, but presumed he must have. I didn't go inside, but continued alongside the canal before turning down Italyanskaya Street. Soon we were at one of the many side entrances of the Hôtel d'Europe. I stood close by, leaning against the wall, waiting for the door to be opened. I wondered for a moment whether subterfuge was necessary. Danilov might be a recognized and regular customer. He was, as I understood it, a member of the Duma. I knew what the word meant, but I could only guess how significant an institution it had been in this new Russia. In any other nation a member of parliament could have found himself the best table in the best restaurant simply by walking in through the front door. But if I knew Russia it would take more than being merely elected to be granted

236

the rights and benefits of the elite. And anyway, I was hardly dressed in a manner that would be welcomed.

There had been a time when I myself had been a customer at this hotel, with permanent rooms that I could do with as I pleased. It was Danilov who had tricked his way into them. Would they recognize his aged face now, if any of them were left from back then?

The door opened. Two women emerged. They were surprisingly well-dressed for hotel staff, but they were leaving by a side entrance, so I could only assume that was what they were – unless like me they were thieves. They walked in my direction and I began to walk too, towards them. They were talking with each other and hardly noticed me and so it was easy to catch the door before it closed. Inside was a kitchen. I was pleased to see that it was busy; as with all revolutions the rich still needed to be fed, regardless of the system of government. No one noticed me enter. I walked calmly to the far door, knowing from years of experience that an aura of confidence was the best way to go unnoticed. Beyond I found myself in a corridor which ended in a junction. I tried to orient myself towards the main entrance and turned left. We passed a service staircase, but I didn't want to go upstairs – not yet. After a few more turns I could hear the hubbub of the lobby getting closer. The passageway ended in a curtain rather than a door and I could tell that the voices came from immediately beyond.

I peeped through. I was just behind the main desk. There were two of them attending it – both occupied in dealing with guests. The one closest to me turned and hung up a key on a rack that I could not see, but which must have been on the same wall as the archway through which I was now looking. The keys would be in easy reach. I waited until both guests had gone. The two members of staff stood quietly, looking out into the lobby; they would see nothing that went on behind them. I moved quickly, stretching out my arm until I felt the shape of a key and then plucking it off its hook. I did the same thing a second time – in one room I might not find everything I needed.

I must have made a sound. One of the two men turned, but I had already withdrawn my hand. I pulled away from the curtain and waited, but he didn't come through. Two keys – two rooms – would be enough for me. I looked at the numbers: 332 and 334. I went back to the stairs I'd passed and climbed them to the third floor. The door from the drab stairwell emerged on to an opulently decorated corridor. Things had changed since I stayed here, but it was still the epitome of luxury. I found room 332 and knocked on the door. The fact that the key was at the desk suggested that the guest was out, but I didn't want to take any risks. Danilov's body seemed too feeble to put up much of a fight if it came to it.

There was no reply. I used the key to let myself in and then locked the door behind me. I could tell immediately from the clutter on the dressing table that the room was occupied. The bed was made, which meant that the chambermaids had already done their work – I wouldn't be disturbed by them. There were two wardrobes. The first contained only women's clothes, but the second was filled with gentlemen's attire. I took out a jacket and looked at it, trying to judge its size – and mine. I searched the pockets, but found nothing. In the wardrobe were another jacket and an overcoat. In the coat pocket I found a money clip containing several hundred roubles. I realized that I had no idea what that was really worth, but judging by the quality of the room this was a wealthy man.

I went to the bathroom and stripped off my existing clothes. I didn't have time to bathe, but I certainly needed a shave. I looked at myself in the mirror, more closely than I had in the street. I could see obvious traces of Lyosha, and of Tamara, the mother of this latest Danilov. There was a cutthroat razor in the cabinet, and plenty of soap. I lathered up and began to shave. It is one of the incidental by-products of their nature that a vampire is able to shave entirely without the assistance of a mirror. It is a skill born of necessity; we cannot see our reflections and yet sometimes we must pass ourselves off in society. Thankfully the occasional cut as we are learning quickly heals.

As with everything I had experienced over the past few hours, I revelled in the simple pleasure of shaving with the assistance of a mirror. I did cut myself slightly, on the chin, but enjoyed even that as a new experience – a long-forgotten one, anyway. I wondered whether I should go further. I had in my hand a razor and a body under my complete control. Why not mutilate Danilov now? He would be fully aware of what was happening as the blade cut into his flesh, aware that the scars would never heal, aware that it was his own hand which had done this to him. But I still had need of this body myself – for the time being. I would defer such pleasures until I had discovered a way out. I contented myself merely to shave off his ridiculous sideboards.

I dressed in clothes from the wardrobe. They were a close enough fit. Fashion had changed considerably since 1881, but I had to take it on trust that whoever was staying in this room did not step outside each day to the ridicule of those around him for his preposterous dress sense. I pocketed the money, and also the razor. I looked around for a watch, but could not see one. Presumably it was in the possession of its owner. A clock on the mantelpiece told me it was a little after noon. Lunch beckoned.

I went out and locked the door. I was tempted to take a look inside room 334, but there was nothing more that I needed for now. I was hungry. I went back downstairs, this time revelling in the grandeur of the main staircase, and into the restaurant.

The newspaper I'd read told that the starvation of the working people was caused by the decadence of a rich few. I suspected there was more to it than that – not least the war – but it would be an easy conclusion to draw on seeing the menu here. I began with caviar and a glass of champagne – a 1914 Dom Perignon. I was tempted to chat to the sommelier as to how it compared with the 1821 – the last glass I had drunk before today – but it was better to keep a low profile. Moreover, I'd noticed a certain surliness in all the staff that would have earned their dismissal in my day. They were happy to take my money, but they displayed no gratitude for it. Such was the nature of a revolution.

I followed the caviar with steak and a claret. I asked for it to be cooked *bleu*, hoping to get something close to my more familiar diet, but in the end found it a little too raw for my taste – or for the taste of Danilov's body. I remembered that when human I'd never been particularly keen to have my food undercooked. I'd always been revolted by the feeding habits of the *voordalak* and on the rare occasions that I'd been forced to emulate them I'd scarcely been able to keep myself from retching. I managed to finish the steak and rounded the meal off with a *vatrushka*, which had always been a favourite of mine.

I paid the bill with the money I'd taken and, once I'd received my change, decided I'd be generous with the gratuity, knowing that I might well come here again. I counted out the coins and placed them on the table.

Don't. They're not keen on tips any more.

I looked around to see who had spoken, but there was no one there; besides, the voice had been too clear – quite separate from the noise of the dining room.

Since the revolution they've insisted they just get paid a fair wage for what they do. They think tipping undermines their dignity.

It was not spoken words that I was experiencing, but thoughts. And they could not be my own thoughts, for two reasons. First, I had not brought the words voluntarily to my mind and second, I could have no idea of the facts I had just revealed to myself. Already the nature of my *ménage* with Danilov was changing. Even though I was still in charge of the body, he could make his thoughts known to me – that was assuming he had done it willingly. I tried to communicate with him by thought alone. 'Can you hear me?'

He gave no response. It proved nothing. In the same circumstances I would have remained silent, if only to discomfort my opponent. Even so, I took his advice, and put the tip back in my pocket.

I left the hotel and walked along Nevsky Prospekt. I felt replete. The hunger I experienced in a human body was of a different nature to that which I had known as a vampire, but

240

the sense of satiation was identical. I was contented, relaxed, lacking any immediate ambition. The wine had helped too. On a street corner was a boy selling newspapers. I bought one for three roubles, which seemed an extortionate price. The boy looked me up and down with a sneer. When I saw the title of the paper, I understood why.

Рабочій и Солдатъ
Worker and Soldier

I didn't look much like either. The front page consisted solely of a declaration issued by the Petrograd Soviet and addressed 'To Workers, Soldiers and Peasants'. It covered much the same ground as the leaflet Danilov had read earlier, though in more detail. It made some mention of the democracy that he had found so lacking, even going so far as to talk of 'introducing complete democracy in the army', which I was certain the Germans would be pleased with. It ended with a warning of counter-revolution:

The Kornilov men – Kerensky, Kaledin and others – are attempting to bring troops against Petrograd. Several detachments, whom Kerensky had moved by deceiving them, have come over to the side of the insurgent people.

Soldiers, actively resist Kerensky the Kornilovite! Be on your guard!

Railwaymen, hold up all troop trains dispatched by Kerensky against Petrograd!

Soldiers, workers in the factory and the office, the fate of the revolution and the fate of the democratic peace is in your hands!

Long live the revolution!

Kerensky's was the only name I recognized. It might well be true, but equally it would be convenient for this new revolution to have an enemy to face in its early days.

Despite my feelings of contentment, I knew that I had to plan for the future. Russia would not be an easy place to live in once these Bolsheviks really began to tighten their grip on it. I would do well to get away as soon as possible. But to decide where to go, I needed to learn more about this war and which countries were involved. If the Germans were as close to Petrograd as I had read, then the whole of Europe would be in turmoil. We were back in the days of Bonaparte.

If I had still been a vampire, things would have been different. That, though, raised a philosophical question: was vampirism a state of the mind or the body? Clearly there were corporeal aspects to it, and for me those had been lost for the present. But in my mind was I now as I once had been? Was I again Richard Cain, son of a Surrey rector, who had gone to Oxford and achieved some little fame for his studies of the wildlife of the Crimea? It was a moot point – for me more than for the majority of my kind. I had possessed the mind of a vampire long before I acquired the body of one. There might be those who if they found themselves in my shoes would rejoice at having the opportunity to undo an act of utter folly, but I was not one of them. I would treat this as a holiday. I would take what pleasures I could while I had possession of this human body – I had already indulged in food and wine – but I knew my goal must be to become once again a creature of darkness.

And then I could imagine no finer country on the planet to inhabit than one in the state of turmoil into which Russia would surely descend. Why else had Dmitry come here?

Why, indeed? He had seemed on remarkably good terms with Danilov when we'd met, but that might have been a ruse. He was a melancholic soul at the best of times, as might be expected from one who became a *voordalak* for reasons of love. But perhaps over the years he'd learned to accept his sorry condition. Perhaps the blood he had exchanged with Zmyeevich had given him some idea of how a vampire should truly live. I would have to speak to him.

I tried to remember his words of the previous night. 'We'll meet tomorrow – usual time and place.' I had no idea what that meant, but I could assume I hadn't missed the appointment. It was mid-afternoon now, a few hours before dusk. Dmitry would be unable to meet anyone until then. The rendezvous could be any time during the hours of darkness – at any place in the city. It would be impossible to guess, but with a little mental agility it would be simple enough to find out.

I turned off Nevsky Prospekt and on to Great Konyushennaya Street where, by coincidence, Dmitry had once lived, with his father, Lyosha, and his mother, Marfa. It was where I had screwed Marfa, knowing Lyosha would find us there. But all I needed now was somewhere to rest. Just as I recalled, there was a bench.

I sat down and, as seemed fitting for the body of a sixty-year-old man after a heavy lunch, tried to sleep.

I would dearly have loved to sleep too, but at the first opportunity I stood up, pleased to be once again in command of my own body. As before I'd been fully aware of Iuda's every thought and action. I had been as surprised as he was when my thoughts had broken through to him in the dining room of the Hôtel d'Europe – and over such a trivial matter. I'd not been attempting to communicate with him; quite the reverse – I'd simply been trying to make something of my miserable state by crowing at his ignorance of the modern world. I'd somehow responded to his thoughts, but then managed to retreat into silence, like a snail hiding away inside its shell.

But now, like Iuda, I needed to make plans. I knew his ultimate intent – to make himself once more a *voordalak*. What that might mean for me I could only guess. From what I could gather, he had little idea either. Would his soul dominate in a body that was once again in a form that befitted his degenerate mind? Would I be destined for ever to witness each foul act that he perpetrated? Worse than that, would I not just witness it, but experience it? At lunch today it was Iuda who had willed his hand each time it lifted the fork to his lips, but I had tasted the food just as distinctly as he had – and enjoyed it too. Would I come to appreciate all his pleasures, or forever be revolted by them? I could only hope for the latter.

Perhaps my consciousness would simply wither and die once it found itself in the body of a vampire. It would be a blessed release for me, though it would mean the ultimate failure of my life's work. I thought I had killed Iuda decades before. Now through me he would live on as a vampire, taking my body and with it my reputation.

There was another possibility, though, that we would share possession of my vampire body, as we did my human body now. In that case he was doomed. It would take only moments, once I was in control, for me to walk outside and bathe myself in blessed sunlight, just as I had done this morning, but with infinitely greater success. It was not the perfect solution, but ultimately it would mean victory, and at a price I was more than willing to pay.

I checked myself, remembering that Iuda was eavesdropper to my every thought. I should be cautious in revealing my plans, and yet how could I make plans, if I did not think them? Anyway – in this case it was a strategy that I ought to be pleased for him to comprehend. It would make him think twice about becoming once more a vampire.

And why did I need to wait? If suicide was a viable tactic after we had become a *voordalak*, then why not before? I reached into my pocket and felt the smooth nacre of the handle of the razor that Iuda had put there. It wouldn't be too difficult for me to open up the blade and then open up one of my own veins. Or if not that, there were other ways. There were plenty of tall buildings in Petrograd. Unlike those in the West, my church preached that suicide was not in every case a sin. Surely in these circumstances God would forgive me? And anyway it was hardly suicide. My intent was to destroy Iuda – my death would be what Aquinas had regarded as a secondary effect.

But another way would be better. If I could find a means of killing Iuda that would leave me unharmed then I would take it. At present, though, I had no idea how that might be achieved. Perhaps the answer lay in Iuda's journals. Perhaps it was in his mind – if so there was a chance he would let it slip. But I had read his notebooks and seen nothing relevant. Anastasia knew more than Iuda did. It was she whom I should seek, though I had no idea where to look. There was still the possibility that she was looking for me.

244

I felt the desire to speak to Dmitry. Even if there was nothing he could do to help my situation, it would do me good to be able to share it with someone. But would he be inclined to help me? Would I even get the chance to speak with him? If it was Iuda who spoke through my lips, then there was no end to the lies he might tell. And I knew that Iuda was keen to see Dmitry. The easiest course of action was to do precisely the opposite of what Iuda desired. I would stay away from the rendezvous with Dmitry – stay away from Senate Square entirely and—

I thought I heard laughter. If it wasn't Iuda jeering at me then it was the voice of my own doubts. Now Iuda knew the location of our meeting. Thankfully he didn't know the time: half past nine. The same laughter echoed through my mind again. It was impossible to keep any idea from entering my brain once the train of thought had been embarked upon. So now Iuda knew the time and place. If my legs chose to obey him at the appropriate moment, then we would go to see Dmitry. If my lips chose to obey him, then he would be able to convince Dmitry of anything.

But I had one chance. Even if my legs were subject to Iuda's will, they were still bound by the laws of nature. They remained the legs of an old man and had a limit to the speed at which they could move. If I could get far enough away while I had the chance then there was nothing Iuda could do to return in time.

I began to walk. I turned down Nevsky Prospekt and carried on swiftly. As I crossed the Yekaterininsky Canal I reached into my pocket and flung the remains of the money I'd stolen into the water, keeping just a few kopeks. At the next opportunity I spent them, jumping on a tram and paying the fare to get me to the Nikolaievsky Station. Dusk had fallen by the time I arrived. I carried on along the prospekt on foot, in the direction of the Nevsky Monastery. I didn't know the area beyond – it would be interesting to see. I still had much further to go to ensure I could not make it back in time.

I was past the monastery and almost at the river when I turned around and began walking back into the city.

CHAPTER XV

DANILOV WAS RIGHT ABOUT THE FRAILTY OF HIS BODY. I walked back up Nevsky Prospekt with the same determination that he had walked down it, judging that he knew better than I how much strain his muscles could take. In the end it was not his legs but his lungs that began to register pain. I slowed down a little – there was plenty of time.

Danilov was right about other things too – most of all about my ignorance. I had no idea what would happen if this body became that of a vampire. It might even be *his* soul that took back the reins of power and mine that was cast out. And yet still I craved the strength that I had known as a *voordalak*. I felt the desire to hunt and kill and feed running in my veins. It was a base, animal urge and I was wise enough to know that I should not yield to it unthinkingly.

It was irritating that he had thrown away the money. He'd forgotten to get rid of the hotel room keys – though now I'd brought them to his attention I was sure that he would at the next opportunity. Anyway, their loss would have been discovered, so they were of little value.

I was at Senate Square in plenty of time. I didn't know precisely where we were supposed to meet, but it was a small enough area that I could patrol it. I went over to the embankment and looked out across the river. A grey battleship was anchored opposite. It must have been the *Avrora*, judging by Danilov's contemplations as to whether she had fired upon the Winter Palace. I turned and walked in the other direction, catching glimpses of the dome of Saint Isaac's through the trees. They were the same trees as last time I was here, though they had grown tall in the intervening years.

'Nice get-up!'

Dmitry had been standing beside the Bronze Horseman. He'd seen me as I walked across the square. For a moment what he said made no sense to me.

'What?'

He looked me up and down. 'The clothes.'

'Oh, these. I thought I'd better make use of them. I don't think there'll be much call for Sunday best now *they're* in charge.'

He seemed to accept it as an explanation, if he was even interested. 'Have you found anything out?' he asked.

We couldn't have been very far from the exact spot where the three of us – Lyosha, Dmitry and me – had stood on 14 December 1825, along with 3,000 soldiers preparing to defy Nikolai I at the outset of his reign. I knew that Dmitry would remember it too – when we'd been friends he'd been obsessed by it. It was the formative moment of his life; and of my life too, in a quite different way. I'd been human then, though not for very much longer. Lyosha had chased me out on to the river – frozen then, not like today. I could picture him, standing on the quay, his arm outstretched with a pistol in his hand. He fired and hit me, then came down and pretended to comfort me as I lay dying in his arms. But I cheated him, and cheated death too. I drank the blood of a vampire who had already drunk mine. I did die, but I rose again as a *voordalak*. I hoped Danilov was experiencing my memories, that they reminded him how like his grandfather he was. Both had killed me. Both had seen me return from death.

But it was Dmitry that I was more concerned with just now. I had nothing to tell him, but I needed to tease from him everything he knew. 'I went back to the church again to look around,' I said. 'I thought if Zmyeevich had appeared there might be some sign – but I couldn't find anything. The bodies hadn't been moved. What happened?'

'You were *there*, weren't you?'

It sounded like an accusation, though it was clearly not

meant as such. I was becoming paranoid, which was probably wise. 'I was hit over the head, if you recall. I can't remember anything after that.' I smiled. 'And what went before is a little hazy.'

'After they grabbed us here,' Dmitry explained, 'Louis must have managed to climb out of the river and follow us to the church. He saw what was happening and realized he'd need help. He found a troop of Red Guards. I don't know what he said, but he clearly got them to follow him.'

'You've not spoken to him?'

'They got him. It was Ilya, I think; ran him through with his wooden sword, but not before Louis had managed to get me out of my chains. You were already unconscious by then. One of the soldiers had realized his bullets were useless and had started swinging his rifle like a club. Caught you on the back of the head. I managed to take out a couple of Anastasia's converts with a sword. Then she told them to run.'

I still needed to find out who this Anastasia was, but I didn't want to reveal my ignorance. And clearly Dmitry had something more important to tell me. His face became dour.

'Mihail,' he said. 'She took Ascalon.'

'Ascalon!'

'Don't you even remember that?'

I suppose I shouldn't have been surprised. If Anastasia had managed to break into my house in London and steal the vial of my blood marked as Zmyeevich's then she could easily have found Ascalon too. 'Vaguely,' I said. 'Tell me everything she said about it.'

'There wasn't very much, to be honest. As far as she was concerned it was just—'

'—a sort of holy relic. I don't think she has any idea—'

'No!'

I threw my arms into the air as I shouted, doing everything I could to shock Dmitry into silence. It was effective. He took it calmly, but didn't say any more. The look on his face was one more of amusement than surprise. I took a step towards him and spoke rapidly and precisely.

'Dmitry, listen to me. I may not have much time. The ceremony *did* work, but it was not Zmyeevich who was resurrected, it was Iuda, and he didn't return in his own body but in mine. He's here now, in my head. Sometimes he comes to the fore, sometimes I do. Just then it was him you were speaking to; now it's me, Mihail. When we met last night by the Moika it was him. Be very careful what you tell me, because he'll hear it too.'

As I'd spoken his eyes had been fixed on mine, but now they fell to the ground as he considered what I'd said. When he finally spoke, it was not to dispute my words in any way.

'But how? Why should Iuda come back and not Zmyeevich?'

'The blood that Anastasia discovered – Iuda had taken a vial of his own blood and labelled it as Zmyeevich's.'

Dmitry fell silent, taking in what I had told him. 'So it would have worked?' he said at last. 'If it had been the right blood then I'd have been standing here talking to him – to Zmyeevich?'

'I'm not sure which would be worse.'

Dmitry ran a hand through his hair. 'It was him that told me – Iuda. In 1881 he said he'd hidden Zmyeevich's blood in London. He must have known that I'd tell Zmyeevich. How can he have been planning it for so long?'

'I don't know. The problem now is to get him out of me.'

'You're sure it's him?'

'I know him better than anyone.'

'Perhaps that's just it,' said Dmitry softly.

'What?'

'I've heard of cases . . . illnesses . . . where the mind plays tricks.'

'You think I'm mad?'

'No, no of course not.'

I considered the idea. On face value it was clearly wrong. Iuda's presence inside my skull was as much a certainty as the fact that I could see or hear or taste. But what did that mean? I could think of no objective test that would distinguish whether Iuda really had been resurrected in me or whether my own mind had created an imaginary Iuda for its own devices. As I'd said, I knew Iuda better than anyone. The first part of my life had been dedicated to his destruction. Could it be that I, in some way, missed him? Had I recreated him, having destroyed him, just to fill the void that he had left? But why leave it forty years? It seemed unlikely, but then so did what I believed to have happened.

'Either way, I need to get rid of him.'

'And he needs to get rid of you,' Dmitry pointed out.

I nodded. 'So we have to be extremely careful. Don't tell me anything that might be of help to him, unless it's absolutely necessary.'

'Like Ascalon.'

'Exactly.'

'Even if you ask me to?'

'You can't trust that it's me asking.'

'There must be a way to tell. Can't we work out some sort of signal?'

'Whatever we decided upon, Iuda would know.'

'What about something you knew before. Wouldn't that work? Something that happened between us, that he wouldn't know about.'

'It might.' I smiled. 'Though my memory isn't what it used to be.'

'What about a different language – one that you speak but he doesn't?'

'We know he speaks English, Russian and French fluently – and others. We could try German, but I bet he's comfortable with that too.'

'Don't worry – we'll work something out.' Dmitry completely failed to sound reassuring. 'There is one thing you might want to know.'

'What's that?'

'I've discovered where Anastasia is sleeping. I went back to where I lost track of her last night, then hung around. I saw Ilya going . . . in.'

'Is it close by?'

'Do you really want to know? Do you really want *him* to know?'

I thought about it, but I could see no other way forward. The only alternative was inaction, and that would be unendurable. Moreover, it might give Iuda time to make his own moves.

'Yes,' I said. 'I have to.'

'And how do I know that's you talking?'

'*Weil ich es sage.*'

'Not good enough, I'm afraid, Herr Cain.' Dmitry thought for a few seconds, then broke into a smile. 'Has he had a chance to read much since he's been back – to learn anything of world events since he died?'

'A couple of newspapers, but not much.'

'Good. In that case, what did Roald Amundsen do in 1912?'

For a moment I was dumbfounded, but then I began to laugh.

'Well?' asked Dmitry.

'He reached the South Pole.' Just at the mention of it I felt a yearning to see Polkan, and by extension Nadya.

Dmitry nodded. 'I don't think *Pravda* is still covering that, and so I don't think Iuda could know it. And you definitely want to know about Anastasia?'

'I do.'

'Actually, Iuda should be pretty familiar with it. She and the others are sleeping in the tunnels underneath Saint Isaac's.'

'She can't be.'

'Why not?'

'Because—'

'Because what?' asked Dmitry.

'It just seems unlikely, but if you've seen it you must be right.' I had no idea what Danilov had been about to say. Clearly he had a better idea of what had happened to the passageways that ran beneath the cathedral than I did, just as he had a better idea of world events. I felt a certain thrill at the news that the South Pole had been conquered and realized how much more I needed to catch up on, both out of curiosity and for the practical reason of being able to defeat Dmitry in his little tests. Perhaps I should do some reading; mug up on what had been happening. Someone must have published *The History of the World Since 1881*. It was a smart idea of Dmitry's to test me that way. Better than Danilov's. *Ich habe perfekt Deutsch gesprochen.* Perhaps I shouldn't have let him know that.

'Where did you see Ilya getting in?'

Dmitry turned towards the cathedral. 'I'll show you,' he said. 'This way.'

He set off, but I didn't move. There was little point in me hiding from him, not just yet. In future it might prove useful, but that would be made even more convincing if I was honest with him now. He noticed that I wasn't behind him and turned back, looking at me impatiently.

'It's been a long time, Dmitry Alekseevich,' I said.

He understood in an instant who I was. 'When did you change?' he asked.

'A few seconds ago.'

'When you stumbled over your words?'

I nodded. Perhaps it would have been better for him not to know that. He might recognize it again on a future occasion.

'I can only admire your planning.'

I smiled. I was tempted to indulge his misconception, but Danilov would instantly know I was lying and would tell Dmitry soon enough. 'People never seem to understand,' I explained. 'One doesn't make plans – not over a timescale of half a century anyway. One makes moves. How could I have known that swapping my blood for Zmyeevich's would end in this? Or guessed that when I drank Danilov's blood in the last throes of my existence it would be he that was chosen to act as the channel for Zmyeevich's resurrection? And do you imagine that if I'd planned things then it was my intended outcome to end up as lodger in the body of a feeble old man?

'My approach has always been to do merely what is interesting; what might lead to outcomes that I can turn to my advantage. And you'll agree that for people to mistake my blood for Zmyeevich's is interesting. To create in Danilov a living man who owes a debt of blood to both myself and Zmyeevich is interesting. You may think I'm lucky that those two happenstances have fused and then blossomed, but that's because you don't see all the times when what I've done has come to nothing. My father had a single view of how he would make a success of himself. He failed. I learned from him to be diverse in my ideas. Some of them fall on good ground and bring forth fruit.'

His lips curled with suspicion, but it hardly mattered whether he believed me.

'I'd still like to see where Ilya went,' I said.

'I was taking Mihail, not you.'

'You were taking us both, and you still shall be. The only difference is which one of us will be doing the talking – and on that I think you should count yourself lucky.'

'Come on then.'

We walked over in the direction of the cathedral. There was much that I wanted to learn from Dmitry, but Danilov had put him on his guard. I began with something inconsequential. 'An interesting idea of yours that I might be simply a figment of Danilov's imagination.'

'Now that I've spoken to you, I doubt his imagination would be able to achieve something quite so loathsomely convincing.'

'You mean he's not clever enough?"

Dmitry didn't reply. Moments later we were at the foot of the steps leading up to the north portal. We went up them and inside. I felt a strange reluctance to enter which I fought to repel. It could only be described as fear. It was inside this church that I had done battle with Zmyeevich, and lost. I thought I had him on my territory, but I had underestimated him. Alone among vampires he had the strength to survive the sun's rays falling on his skin. I did not. He had dragged me into the sunlight that shone through the cathedral's windows. All but the most miserable remains of my body had been destroyed, but it had been enough for me to survive and to regrow. I had been a vampire then – that was what made me vulnerable to the burning sunlight, but also what gave me the power to heal. Being human again brought both advantages and disadvantages.

'I followed him in through the south entrance,' Dmitry explained. 'I guessed he'd go over there.' He pointed to his left, to a mosaic icon of Saint Paul. 'That's the way you showed us down. But instead he went this way.' Dmitry led me to the right and to a doorway from which a spiral staircase ascended to one of the towers. 'I presumed he'd have to come back down again, so I waited, but he never did.'

'But you said they were sleeping *under* the cathedral. That way leads upwards.'

'A vampire is hardly going to spend the day up there. Even if they could find a dark place, it just wouldn't feel comfortable – you know that as well as I do. Anyway, we'll soon find out.' He began climbing the stairs.

'Don't be a fool, Dmitry,' I hissed.

'What do you mean?'

'It's night. They'll be awake, if they're here. Or if not they'll come back and we'll be trapped.'

'I can handle them.'

'You may be able to, but I can't. Look at me. I'm an old man.'

'What do you propose?'

'I'll come back tomorrow, when it's light.'

'I won't be able to help you then.'

'I understand that, but the daylight will be a far better ally for me.'

'I'll come at dusk then. I'll meet you in Senate Square.'

'Thank you.' I offered him my hand. It seemed natural when I did it, but it took him by surprise. Even so, he accepted it. We walked back outside and went our separate ways.

I had reasons beyond the matter of the protection of daylight to wait until morning. It was essential that I spoke to Anastasia without Dmitry being present. If he were there I feared he might point out certain discrepancies between my version of events and the truth. There was always the possibility that Danilov, if he got the opportunity to speak, would tell her the same as Dmitry, but I hoped by then he would realize that for the time being our interests coincided.

But that was for tomorrow. Now I genuinely needed sleep. It was not simply a requisite for the mind, but for the body as well. I hoped that would mean that Danilov was in the same condition. I could go to his home – I'd already discerned from him precisely where it was – but I decided against it. It would take some skill to bluff so well as to convince the woman who shared his bed. I would need to study him further. And besides, it was a long walk and there were plenty of places nearer where I could stay. The Hôtel d'Europe was one, but they would have discovered by now that the keys were missing and might recognize my face.

I went back across Senate Square and then along the English Quay to the Nikolaievsky Bridge. There was a picket on duty, but they didn't stop me or ask for papers. Soon after I passed them I heard a shout of '*Burzhooi!*' which I took to be directed at me, but whose meaning I could make no sense of. I knew that I was a little too grandly dressed for this socialist utopia. Once on Vasilievskiy Island I turned back east towards the university. Student lodgings would be rather humble for me, but I knew where the larger houses were that some of the professors lived in – or had in my day.

I looked up at the tempting high windows of many of them. That would be the safest way to slip inside, but climbing the smooth vertical face of a building was a vampiric skill, not a human one. In a way I was pleased. I'd always been happier using my wits.

I chose a house in a quiet street with no lights in the windows and pounded on the front door with both fists as if trying to knock it down. My aim was to conjure an image of frantic desperation. I paused for a few seconds and then began again. At my next pause I heard footsteps approaching, but I recommenced knocking to maintain the deception. A light came on and a moment later the door was opened by a man in a dressing gown.

'Thank God!' I panted. 'Thank God you came. Please – may I come in?'

I didn't wait for a response, but pushed through the open door. My playacting had been enough to ensure he offered no objection.

'What the devil's happened?' he asked, genuinely concerned.

I was bending forwards with my hands on my knees, pretending to catch my breath. I raised my left hand towards his, signalling that he should give me a chance to recover. A moment later I sprang. I put my hand to his mouth, covering it, and pushed him back against the wall. In the same movement I had the razor out of my pocket and open. I dragged it across his throat and blood spurted out under the pressure of his beating heart. While I no longer had the stomach actually to drink, I was pleased to discover that I could still enjoy the more cerebral pleasures that the moment offered: I could enjoy his sense of utter surprise, his fear, his pain. Ultimately I could enjoy his death. I took delight at the sight of the blood staining the wallpaper on the other side of the hallway, I could even imagine it rolling over my tongue and trickling down my throat, although the reality of it would have made me vomit. There are many things which a man will relish in his imagination but whose reality would disgust him. I had the benefit of knowing that I had once been capable of drinking blood, and would one day be able to do so again.

I let go of his head and his corpse slid to the floor. I closed the front door rapidly and turned the key that was still in the lock. I looked at the man's face, trying not to be distracted by the crimson stains on his nightclothes. By my estimation he looked more like an academic than a domestic servant. If that were the case, and he had answered his own door, then it would indicate he had no servants. By his age I guessed there would be no children at home either. I couldn't be certain, but with luck there would be only his wife – his widow – to deal with, if that.

There was a flight of stairs leading up from the hall and I could see further light at the top of it. It was only then that I realized that the whole place was lit electrically. Technology really had moved on, though none of what I'd seen was in the field that really interested me, that of biology. It would be fascinating to catch up. At the time of my death Charles Darwin's remarkable book *On the Origin of Species* had only just been published and had not yet received the acclaim I felt it deserved. How much further might men have taken those ideas by now? And how many had applied those ideas to the vampire? With luck I would be the first.

I went upstairs. There was one door open on the landing from which I could hear the irritating rasp of somebody snoring. I looked inside. It was a woman, asleep on the left side of a double bed, whose right side had the sheets thrown back.

Undoubtedly it was the man's wife, her sleep undisturbed by my activities downstairs. I shook her until she was just awake enough to know what was happening to her, then dispatched her in much the same way I had her husband.

It didn't take me long to check the rest of the house; there was no one else. In the kitchen I found plenty of food. I couldn't be bothered to cook, but there was some ham and a whole plate of blini that were quite enough for me. I didn't have much desire to sleep in a bed stained with the blood of the old woman, but I found another room across the landing. The single bed there was made up, which worried me that someone else might live here, but the sheets smelled as though they had been on there for a long time. Perhaps this was the bedroom of an adult son, who never came home to visit his parents in their dotage. He had missed his chance.

I slipped into the bed and was asleep in seconds.

I held my index and middle fingers together and checked that they would just fit between the flats of the two blades. The spacing was perfect. I finished binding the twine around the handles and tied it off. Then I held the thing up to the light, admiring my work.

It was revoltingly familiar: two parallel blades, an inch apart, sprouting from what seemed like a single handle, the lower edges of the blades razor sharp, the upper edges with jagged teeth. It was Iuda's unmistakable knife, the one he had used, when human, to mimic the wounds caused by a vampire's teeth. Over the years there had been many versions of it – and I had just constructed the latest.

I hurled it across the room and against the wall, hoping that it would smash, but it was too well made. It bounced off the plaster-work and fell to the floor intact. I looked around me. The kitchen drawers had been pulled out and tipped on to the floor. There was all kinds of junk in there; I noticed an electric torch, much like the one I had at home, though it wasn't that which Iuda had been after. Each one of the knives he'd found was piled upon the table, of every type that could be imagined. Iuda had been search-ing meticulously for what he wanted. Even so, the two knives he had used were not quite identical; one of them was a little broader and longer than the other although he – I – had compensated for the length by offsetting the alignment of the handles.

Evidently I had awoken after he had, though by how long I did not know. He'd had time to do this, but what else? More concerning was the fact that even when I had awoken, I had continued for minutes to carry out the manual task that he had set my body. I only hoped that if the undertaking had been something less mundane than this I would have realized and stopped sooner.

I stood up and went through the door. It opened on to the hall. One thing Iuda had not done that morning was clean up. The man's body still lay there, across the passageway, his head propped up against the skirting board. The dry blood caked his chest and stained the walls and carpet. I'd been able to do nothing to prevent it. The previous evening, when I'd shouted at Dmitry to stop him talking to Iuda, I believed I had managed to take control of my body through the overriding force of my will. But here, much as I had tried to do the same, I had been unable to take command of a single limb – a single finger. The longer Iuda remained with me, the more I would lose power over myself. Or perhaps it wasn't that. Perhaps, deep down, the life of a stranger just wasn't important enough to me.

I went upstairs and looked in at the bedroom. The woman's body was just as I had left it. My gut tightened and I turned to one side to vomit. It felt good, despite the discomfort. It was a bodily reaction, not a mental one, and it told me my body was still mine and not his, if it responded to death in so human a way. I looked at the mess I had produced. I could still see flecks of undigested ham. I was glad to have expelled them – they were what Iuda had eaten, not I.

This could not go on. These crimes were mine. The law would see it like that, of course; there would be no discussion as to whose mind was in control of the hand that had wielded the razor. But at any moral level I was just as responsible. I should have found a way to stop this. I'd even enjoyed some of it. I'd admired the way Iuda had sneaked into the room at the Hôtel d'Europe and burgled it. I'd done much the same myself, once. I'd taken pleasure in the lunch we had eaten with our stolen money. Was this so very different?

I felt the sudden urge to make amends. I saw the face of the dead woman staring at me, her head hanging limply to one side. I saw the mess that I'd made when I threw up. I had an inescapable duty to perform, but it seemed only fair that first I should tidy up. I could not change the past and make it so that the people who loved this old couple would not come here and find them dead, but the least I could do was to ensure that their home did not seem quite so despoiled.

But it was too great a risk. Iuda might return to me at any minute and the opportunity would be missed. It was more important that this should not happen again than that I should attempt to make pathetic compensation for what I had already done.

I went to the stairs, going up not down. I knew the layout of the house perfectly – Iuda had checked every nook and cranny the night before. Soon I was up in the garret. It was cold and a little damp; used only for storage. The walls sloped inwards slightly, undecided as to whether they were really part of the roof. There was a window looking out on to the street. I pulled it up. Outside was a ledge wide enough for me to stand on. I climbed through, wondering if I should sit first and contemplate this, consider whether there was any alternative. But I knew time was my enemy.

I stood and looked down. It was four storeys to the pavement below. It would undoubtedly kill me, or cripple me, and even that would be enough.

I knew I had only seconds. I tried to think briefly of everything I loved, thought of them together. I formed an image in my mind. Polkan at the side of the chair, my mother seated in it, young and healthy, not as I had last known her, and Nadya standing beside, her hand on Mama's shoulder. I wished I had longer to enjoy it, but I did not.

I stepped forward.

CHAPTER XVI

MY LEG DID NOT MOVE. I TOOK A STEP BACK. THIS TIME MY body complied with my thought. I had understood Danilov's intent from the moment he began climbing the stairs, but only when we had been on the very brink of death had my attempts to resist him borne fruit. And so it seemed that while Danilov's will could not prevent us from killing others, mine could prevent us from killing ourselves. I suspected that it would always be so. It was not that my will was stronger than his – not yet – merely that at some level beyond the depths that either of us could perceive there lay an instinct for survival that when it came to it chose to obey me and not him – chose life over death.

I climbed back in through the window and closed it, then went down to the kitchen again. I reclaimed my knife from where Danilov had hurled it. I also picked up the electric torch he had noticed. I would need light where I was going. I examined it to see how it was operated, but could make no sense of it. It was something I would have to learn from Danilov. I slipped it in my pocket along with the knife.

There was still some food left and so I finished it off. I was hungry again after losing the contents of my stomach, but beyond that it made a point to Danilov: whatever he could do with our body, I could reverse. The same, though, was true contrariwise. Anything I could do, he could later counteract. Our lives might become singularly unproductive. We would have to work together, but that could only be achieved if we had a common goal. The only outcome that would be acceptable

260

for both of us would be for me to acquire my own body. Not my original body, but one of which I could have the exclusive use. I knew Danilov was aware of my thoughts and hoped that he could accept the possibility of this compromise, if only for the time being. But he would know, as I did, that neither of us was to be trusted. We might settle for the amicable solution of our mutual survival, but we would each be indifferent to the destruction of the other.

But the first step towards any solution to our problems was to gather information, and I knew where it could be found. I left the house without any plans to return – the food was gone and the likelihood was that the bodies would be found. I'd changed my suit of yesterday for something a little more sober from the professor's wardrobe. It didn't fit quite as well, but would be more appropriate for life in the new Russia.

I took a different route back to the heart of the city, just in case I was recognized, crossing the new bridge near the Winter Palace, then turned back towards Saint Isaac's.

It was as I walked along the Admiralty Quay that I realized it was I who was once again holding the reins of my body. I considered breaking into a run, taking Iuda by surprise and hurling myself into the wide blue waters of the Neva, but I knew it was foolish. I sensed, as he had done, that he would always be able to prevent my suicide. Certainly an attempt to drown myself would prove futile. Even if he didn't prevent the initial plunge into the waves, he would have plenty of time to swim back to shore.

And he was right too that there were better solutions to our problem, though he misjudged me in what I would find acceptable; it would be pointless not to admit it. If he were to find some other body as the dwelling place for his soul, then the question arose of what happened to the previous occupant. I would not tolerate the death of another – or, worse, another being forced to live the dual life that I now suffered – merely to alleviate my discomfort. And if he did manage to reanimate some cadaver whose former spirit had no further use for it, then I would make it my duty to ensure that the duration of the second life of that body was mercifully short. I had killed Iuda in 1881. Why did he suppose that I would not try to do the same again now?

But with regard to our immediate course of action, I was in agreement with him. We needed to find Anastasia. I didn't even break step, but carried on along the quay in the direction Iuda had been heading. Perhaps a sharp-eyed observer might have noticed a change in my gait or posture, but it would have been nothing remarkable. I carried on, then turned across Senate Square and entered the cathedral through the same door we had used the night before.

It was a little busier than it had been then. There was no service taking place, nor any sign of a priest, but a few people were silently praying in front of the iconostasis. They were probably wise to do so now while they still could. I'd heard nothing definite, but from all that I'd read about the Bolsheviks their belief was that religion was merely another way for those in power to perpetuate their control over the poor. What place could prayer have in their new society – indeed, who would need it once a perfect state of human existence had been achieved? It wouldn't last, though. They tried it in France during that revolution, and soon realized that God was the only tyrant from Whom most people did not want to be freed.

I realized now that I had a problem. I had no idea how to get down to the chambers below. There was only one route I had ever known and it was unlikely to be of much use. I went over to the corner of the nave, beside the entrance to the Nevsky Chapel, and looked up at the mosaic of Saint Paul. It hadn't changed since I had first stood there as a young man. There was no one near by. I reached out and rested my thumbs against each of the saint's big toes, trying to remember the precise location of the mechanism. I quickly found it and pushed. The switches were stiffer than I remembered them, but eventually yielded. The panel swung open, but I looked beyond to see what I had suspected – what I had been told by my father.

Where once the passageway had stretched out ahead and into darkness, now it managed only a few feet – ending abruptly in a brick wall that appeared both new and solid. I leaned forward and put my hand against it. It felt quite impenetrable. After the murder of Aleksandr II I'd spoken to my father, the late emperor's brother Konstantin, and told him everything I knew – of the tunnels beneath Malaya Sadovaya Street and of those here. He had promised to ensure that they were sealed, that no one – neither man nor vampire – could ever make use of them again. He had been as good as his word, but he could only seal the entrances he knew about.

Dmitry had shown us the spiral staircase that he had seen Ilya use. I went over to it and began to climb up. I didn't get far. The way was blocked by a locked iron gate. I could only presume Ilya had a key. I went back down. No doubt there were other paths to the tunnels below, but I was not aware of them. Iuda was and he had come here with confidence that he would find a way. He had helped to design the building, a century before, and would know every hidden entrance to the passageways below. I needed his guidance and I could only wait for it.

I sat down on one of the wooden chairs that faced the iconostasis and tried to empty my mind. Then I remembered that there was a favour I needed to do for Iuda. I reached into my pocket and took out the electric torch. It switched on in the same way as my own, by twisting the metal cap at the bulb end. I turned it on and off twice, so that he would get the idea, then put it back in my pocket. I relaxed again, waiting for him to come, but he remained lurking in the dark shadows of my mind, unwilling or unable to take centre stage. I bent forward, as if in prayer, though I could find no words to offer the Lord. If He was there, He knew my predicament. He didn't need my pleas to tell Him what to do.

I sat for almost an hour, then stood, crossed the nave and went back outside.

The gate across the spiral staircase was a new addition. Evidently Konstantin had known more than his son supposed and realized that there were other routes to the world below. Or perhaps he was just being circumspect. Either way, his precautions had proved fruitless. Somehow Ilya, or Anastasia, had got hold of a key. If we had been able to get beyond that gate then we would have eventually come to a short corridor, paved with flagstones. Levering up the third one along would

263

have revealed an iron ladder, no doubt rusted by now, leading down. How Anastasia knew all that I could only guess. It would have taken her weeks of investigation. Perhaps Zmyeevich had discovered something. He'd known about the entrance through the icon of Saint Paul. He'd slept here for several nights. He could well have explored further and told Anastasia of what he had learned.

I would have to use a more humble entrance. I went round the cathedral to the south side, looking on to Saint Isaac's Square. I walked across the grass until I was close to the cathedral wall. The iron manhole cover was still there, just as I remembered it. I pulled it up and went down the staircase beneath. The stench of the city's sewers flooded over me. It seemed fouler than when I had last been here; no doubt as the city had grown so had the amount of filth they tried to wash away. But there were other explanations. Then I had been in no good state to perceive anything. After my battle with Zmyeevich it was to here that I had been forced to slink and lick my wounds – to grow back a body from almost nothing. And I had been a vampire. Compared with the nostrils of a human my senses had then probably been more acute, but also less discerning – less repelled by the knowledge of what caused those odours.

But it was not the sewers that I wanted to inspect. Back then I had crawled here from one of the tunnels beneath the cathedral. Today I would make the reverse journey. I got the torch out of my pocket and imitated Danilov's actions in turning it on. It worked. I shone the beam around the chamber, then walked along a little way until the wall turned sharply left. I pointed the torch up into the shadows where the wall and the ceiling joined. Even then it was difficult to make out: a dark gap, the height of just three or four rows of brick, at the very top of the wall. I turned off the torch and put it back in my pocket, then raised both arms above my head.

I jumped, grabbing the top of the wall as I did and pulling myself up, trying to get my whole arm over. It was too high. I fell back and waited a few seconds to catch my breath. Then I tried again; this time I made it. I got my right arm over the wall and held on with my left. The tip of my boot scraped against the bricks as I tried to raise it, and finally I had it resting on the top of the wall, able to take the majority of my weight. Again I took a few moments to rest, hanging there with one leg dangling vertically below me like the pendulum of a clock. It was not a comfortable position, but it required no real energy to maintain. Once I was recovered I pulled myself up completely and slipped into the recess at the top of the wall, scarcely big enough to house a human body.

It was pitch dark without the torch, but I knew my way. I crawled forwards and soon the gap in the wall by which I had entered was replaced by solid brick. A few feet later the wall on my right opened up, yielding to empty space. On this side the arrangement was just the same as on the other: a recess at the top of the wall, scarcely noticeable. I felt a slight breeze in my face. I could have continued further, pushed open a small grille and found myself in the nave again, almost at the point I'd come from. But I wouldn't have been able to get through. The gap was too small, and yet that was the way I had escaped; the few bones and organs of my body that remained had slipped through quite comfortably. I could scarcely believe that with my one remaining hand I had pulled myself along this tunnel, my fingernails clawing against the brickwork. But the terror I felt at the thought of Zmyeevich catching up with me was ample motivation. Today, though, I had a different route to take.

I switched the torch back on and lowered myself down. The passage was long and straight, going directly under the nave from the southwest corner to the northeast, and a little beyond. I followed it quickly. Another corridor joined from the left – that was the way Ilya would have come once he had descended that ladder. All the way the path had been sloping downwards, but now finally it came to an end with a curved stone wall – the outside of the shaft of another spiral staircase. It was not, however, complete; there was a gap at one side, narrow, and about half my height. I crouched down and slipped through to find myself facing the underside of the staircase, at the very bottom.

I braced my back against the wall behind me and pushed at the stairs. They swung forward easily, pivoting on the spindle of the spiral itself. It was no surprise that the mechanism was still working so well. This was the route that Ilya and Anastasia must take each time they entered or left, so it was well used.

I closed the hidden door behind me and the bottom four steps were soon indistinguishable from those that rose above them. Up there was the brick wall we had found behind the icon of Saint Paul. Ahead of me stretched a passage that led to the main chamber of this warren. That was the direction I took.

It ended in a wooden door. I was well beyond the foundations of the cathedral now. I reached for the handle and opened it. It was not locked. The room I entered was entirely familiar, despite the changes that had been made to it. This ancient chamber had been unearthed when the foundations of the cathedral were being dug; it had been easy for me as a senior figure of His Majesty's secret police to ensure that it was buried again, leaving entrances of which only I was aware. The arched ceiling was about twice my height, supported on eight brick columns, lighted candles fixed to each of them. I switched off the torch. In the centre of the space, where a ninth column might have been expected, was a raised circular structure, looking a little like a well, which in some sense it once had been. I went over to it. At one time it had been filled with water, fed by the Neva itself through a pipe that stretched out beneath my feet. But things had changed. There was no pool here now, just a pile of dirt and bricks and rubble that had been used to block off that particular route of egress. More of Konstantin's work, I suspected; we were fortunate his men hadn't noticed the secret door at the foot of the staircase. On the walls there had once been cupboards containing my work – books and samples. They were gone too – the cupboards as well as their contents. I wondered why he hadn't just caved in the whole chamber and the passageway that led to it. But that would have been dangerous. Somewhere above us stood the statue of Peter the Great, mounted on its colossal stone pedestal. It would not have been a pleasant omen to see that sinking into a gaping hole in Senate Square, though a portentous one.

At the far end of the chamber lay two coffins, side by side, both closed. I went over to open them. The first was empty. In the second lay a male vampire, sleeping. I didn't recognize him. I lowered the lid gently back into place. It would be better not to wake him. What I had to say would convince Anastasia, I felt sure, but the others might not even let me get as far as speaking to her. She wasn't here. Still, there were plenty of other places within these tunnels where she might be found.

I turned to go and search them, but did not need to. She was standing in the doorway, watching me with an expression of detached amusement on her face. I felt suddenly cold. My blood seemed to drain from me and my stomach felt as though I had eaten a rock. I staggered backwards, almost tripping over the coffins, finally finding the wall behind me and leaning against it for support. She looked just as beautiful as the last time I had seen her. Her flaxen hair shone even in the dim candlelight, cascading over her shoulders. Her eyes still retained the glint of mischief that I had known as a boy. It must have been 125 years since I had seen that face. That she was the woman that Dmitry had referred to as Anastasia I had no doubt, but I knew her real name. Involuntarily I spoke it.

'Susanna!'

Whatever surprise I might feel at the fact that she was here, now, in Petrograd, one thing came to me as nothing more than a confirmation of what I already suspected: she was a vampire. And that was entirely my fault.

She had been my first love, and my first lover. Our sole physical encounter, lying between the pews of my father's church, had always been a pleasant memory, but it had had one troublesome side effect. She had fallen pregnant. Young as I was, that didn't fit in with my plans, and I knew I had to get rid of them both. Fortunately I had the means to do it. Even as our exertions on the floor of the church created new life, so beneath that floor, in the crypt, I kept a prisoner

267

– a vampire, the first I'd ever encountered. His name was Honoré, or more formally Honoré Philippe Louis d'Évreux, Vicomte de Nemours. I'd managed to trap him, and to study him, and kept him nourished by occasionally feeding him one of my school friends. But I'd never imagined I would do that with Susanna, not until the wretched baby came along.

I'd lured her down with the promise of discovering something fascinating – her curiosity was almost as insatiable as mine – and let her walk in there, quite unwitting. I remembered the white of her dress disappearing into the darkness. Then I'd heard the sound of Honoré pouncing, and I'd locked the gate and run away.

But that was not the end of it. I didn't know much about vampires then, not compared with what I've learned since. I understood that they could transform humans into their own kind, but I hadn't determined how. The very last time I went down to visit Honoré, to let him free in exchange for his promise to kill my father, I saw her. Behind him, in the gloom, I'd caught a glimpse of the pale, delightful face that had once smiled down on me in the moment that our bodies became one flesh. I'd suspected it to be a figment of my imagination, spurred on by my guilt – I'd hoped that it was.

Now, however, I was sure. There she was, standing in front of me, the same as the day she died – the day I had killed her. And she would have no reason to regard me with anything but hatred. My only hope was to stick to my original plan – though now the danger I faced if that plan failed was greater than ever. I tried to think how *he* would behave. I'd already made the mistake of calling her Susanna – I'd have to stick with it. I opened my arms widely, welcomingly, and then spoke.

'Susanna! You are a genius.'

She was clearly taken aback. 'What?'

I took a step forward. 'I understand. I understand. I'm still unrecognizable in this ridiculous body. But look through that and you will surely recognize me.'

She narrowed her eyes, assessing me. 'You've got quite a nerve, Mihail Konstantinovich.'

'Is that whose body this is?' I pretended to be thinking for a moment. 'Not Mihail Konstantinovich Danilov?' I laughed heartily. 'Well, I suppose it could have been any Romanov, but somehow it seems fitting that it was him.'

'What the hell are you talking about?'

'The ceremony. My blood. The anastasis.'

'The ceremony was a disaster. I did it all wrong.'

'No, Susanna, you did it beautifully. I have returned, just as you hoped. I am he. I am Zmyeevich. I am Ţepeş. I am . . . Dracula.'

She stared at me for several seconds, then began to clap her hands slowly. 'You almost had me,' she said.

I took a step towards her, my arms reaching out, pleading, but I felt myself suddenly restrained. Someone had grabbed my shoulders from behind and pulled me back. The vampire in the coffin had awoken and was ready to protect his mistress.

'Kill him,' she said brusquely. As she spoke an expression of pain crossed her face. She put her hand to her stomach and turned away. I felt the vampire's hand at my chin, forcing my head up as he prepared to bite.

'If you kill me, you'll regret it for ever,' I shouted after her, scarcely able to move my jaw. 'Think about it, Susanna. You know it's me. How else would I know your real name?'

She paused and turned back to me. 'Anyone could know that.'

'You never told Danilov that, though, did you?' I was guessing, but I felt I was on solid ground. 'You told me years ago. You think I'd forget it? Forget you?'

It was a desperate gamble, but from what I could glean of their relationship she would surely have told Zmyeevich the truth. She stood gazing at me, her body shaking, as if she were standing out in the snow. She took a step forward, then stopped, then took another.

'My God!' Her voice had become hushed. 'Is it really you?'

'It's me, Susanna.' I offered a sort of smile.

It seemed to work. She came across the room, holding her hands out in front of her. I took them in mine, genuinely

269

enjoying the touch of her cool flesh after so many years. It was only when she came close that I saw what I should have realized from the start – that she was pregnant, still pregnant, just as she had been at the moment of her death. The half-formed body of my child lived within her.

She snatched her hands away. 'How can I be sure?' she asked. 'Danilov isn't an idiot. He could have found out my name.'

'I could tell you other things about you; the name of the man who made you into a *voordalak*.'

'Which is?'

'Honoré.'

'He could have found that out too.'

I was on desperately thin ice. I was lucky that she had told Zmyeevich Honoré's name, but if I could only tell her things that I – Iuda – also knew, she might quickly cotton on. And if she were to ask me about anything that had occurred between her and Zmyeevich, I was lost. It was a track I should not have embarked upon. But there was a way out.

'What about a more practical test?' I asked.

'What do you mean?'

'Danilov could have learned as much about you as he likes, but he couldn't unlearn his pathetic morality.'

'Go on?'

'Do you think he could kill, just for the sake of killing? Do you think if I were Danilov I'd dare even suggest it?'

She grinned broadly. 'Oh, it's good to have you back.'

'Let's do it then.'

She shook her head. 'It's still light. Can't you tell?'

'Not any more.' It was a skill that had been genuinely lost to me in this human body.

She looked suddenly sad and put a hand to my cheek. 'It must be so terrible for you. But we'll go out as soon as it gets dark and find someone and you can prove yourself to me.'

'I can go out now,' I said.

She smiled. 'Don't be silly. We'll go together.' She went back to the door, then turned to the other vampire. 'Ilya, make sure he doesn't leave.' Then to me. 'I'll be back at sunset.' She tapped against her thighs excitedly with both hands. 'This is going to be so wonderful.'

She left. I sat down on one of the coffins. Ilya, as I now knew him to be, moved swiftly over to the door and closed it, then leaned against it, eyeing me. He said nothing. It was almost as though he were challenging me to try and get past him, but in this body I would not have stood a chance. And anyway, I had no desire to leave. My plan was working to perfection.

It was about three hours later when Susanna returned. She was not alone; accompanying her were two more vampires both displaying much the same surly mindlessness that I could see in Ilya. They reminded me of the creatures I had travelled to Russia with in 1812, and I suspected that the reason was the same – that they had repeatedly exchanged blood with Susanna and allowed her to rule them. It was a trick she had learned from Zmyeevich.

'It's time,' she said. Her eyes widened fractionally as she spoke.

I stood up and went over to her. She took my hand and led me along the passageway. We went through the low gap at the base of the stairs, and then turned along the corridor that led to the iron ladder. On the way we passed several small alcoves, in which were more coffins, along with a couple of large packing cases. At the ladder Ilya went first, then Susanna, then me, with the others following behind. Looking up I could see Susanna's petticoats and the occasional glimpse of her thigh as she climbed. My mind travelled back to the days when I had first known her and the faltering steps we had taken along the path to becoming lovers. Back then I'd felt embarrassed at even the slightest sexual arousal I'd experienced in reaction to such a sight. I'd long known what a fool I'd been as a child.

Soon we'd all climbed through the opening in the floor, high above ground level. Ilya lowered the flagstone back into place. We went down the stairs and came to the iron gate. It was not unlike the gate beneath Saint George's Church in Esher, which I'd once closed on Susanna, leaving her to her fate. She produced a key and began to unlock it.

'Shouldn't we tie his hands or something?' asked Ilya. 'In case he tries to escape.'

'Why would I have come here, just to escape?' I asked.

'Exactly,' said Susanna. 'Anyway, if he makes a run for it, we'll easily catch him. That body doesn't look like much.'

She opened the gate and we went through. Ilya locked it with his own key. We went down the stairs. At the bottom, Susanna stopped. 'Not all at once,' she said. 'We don't need to draw attention to ourselves. We'll meet by the Nikolai memorial.'

Ilya went first, then Susanna and I went together. She slipped her hand into mine as we crossed the floor of the nave. It was a little busier than it had been when I arrived. She looked up at me. Vivid as my memories of her were, I could not recall her in quite that pose before. Then I realized. All the time I'd known her back then, she'd been taller than me. She grinned. 'If anyone asks, I'm your granddaughter.'

We left the cathedral by the southern portal and walked across Saint Isaac's Square to the foot of the statue of Nikolai I. Ilya was already there. A few minutes later the other two arrived.

'Right then,' she said. 'Where do you want to go?'

'You know the city better than I,' I said. 'Somewhere there'll be enough for us all.'

She raised her hand to her face, tapping her fingers against her bottom lip. Then she came to a decision. 'This way,' she announced. We crossed the river and went down Demidovsky Lane, in the direction of the Haymarket. I was a little surprised by her lack of inventiveness. To me the obvious victim for this little experiment would be someone whom Danilov loved, for example the woman Nadya – his wife or mistress, I wasn't sure which. I could have volunteered the idea myself, but chose against it. I might find better uses for Nadya later. And besides, while I already knew that Danilov's resting soul did not have the power to prevent me from killing a stranger, it might balk at the act of killing someone so close to him, and reassert itself.

We went through the Haymarket without stopping, then crossed the Fontanka, finally to walk alongside a small waterway that I'd never visited before, but which I calculated to be the Vvedensky Canal. Ahead of us I could see the Tsarskoye Selo Railway Station. The closed carriage of a train, speeding through the countryside so that none could escape, would make a fine hunting ground for a group of vampires. But we didn't get that far.

She led us into a public bathhouse. There was a *babushka* at a desk by the door, collecting money, but we marched past her. She shouted after us and then went away into another room, warning that she would get help. There were a number of doors off the main hallway, behind any of which we might have found innumerable means of satisfying our passions, but Susanna chose the men's steam room. The five of us went inside.

It wasn't particularly steamy, but was stultifyingly hot. We were all dressed for outdoors, though for the vampires that was for show – neither the cold outside nor the heat within affected them. The same could not be said for me.

'Don't let anyone in,' said Susanna. One of her minions obeyed, going back to the door by which we had come. He took the leather belt from his trousers and wrapped it around the handles. It would keep us safe for long enough.

There were seven men in the room, the youngest in his twenties, the oldest probably over eighty. Some were fat, some thin. All were naked. Fourteen eyes stared at us in surprise – or more precisely stared at Susanna. One of them stood up. He showed no embarrassment at his nudity.

'Who the devil are you?'

She looked back at him. He was one of the older ones, and far taller than her. Her eyes scanned up and down his body, lingering for a moment on his genitals. Then she looked at me. 'Will this one do?'

I shrugged. 'He's as good as any.' I wondered if that was really how Zmyeevich would have put it.

She held her arm out towards him, offering him to me. I slipped my hand into my pocket. My fingers brushed against my double-bladed knife. I would have dearly loved to use it, but the risk was too great. It was too distinctive of me. I doubted if any of these five vampires had not heard the tales of horror that Richard Cain had inflicted on their brethren. At least one of them would know of his favourite weapon. But I still had the razor. I fished it out and opened it, then took a step forward.

The old man turned his head towards me as I approached and his expression changed from outrage to astonishment.

'Mihail! Mihail Konstantinovich! What the hell are you up to? Who are these people? Are they Bolsheviks or something?'

I smiled and exchanged a glance with Susanna, who seemed to share my enjoyment of the situation. It would not be as effective as killing Nadya might have been, but it would make the whole thing even more convincing if this was a friend of Danilov's. That was if Danilov didn't stop me. I took a step forward.

'For God's sake,' he bleated. 'Don't you recognize me? It's me – Roman Pyetrovich.'

I raised the blade high in the air.

'What on earth are you playing at, you fool? There are—'

I flicked the razor down towards his cheek, but he was quick for his age. His hand flashed upwards and grabbed me by the wrist, stopping the blow in mid-flight. He stared into my eyes, but now his face showed only terror. He was not strong, but then neither was I. We held the pose in a pathetic stalemate for several seconds.

Then, in just the same way that he was holding my wrist, Susanna reached up and took his. And that was just the beginning; she squeezed. The terror in his eyes turned to agony. He let out a feeble croak, as if suppressing the urge to scream for all he was worth, and at the same time let go of me. I raised my arm again, and chaos momentarily erupted. Three of the others – the younger ones – rushed towards us. The other vampires sprang into action. Ilya punched one of the men hard in the face, knocking him to the floor. The vampire who'd been at the door raised his hand and placed it against the chest of another, easily pushing him back against the wall.

The third man got close enough to me to be about to throw a punch, but Susanna's hand flashed downwards towards his groin. I didn't need to see to know what she had caught hold of. She applied the same pressure she had used on Roman Pyetrovich's wrist, and the scream that ensued was far louder. She threw the man across the room. Then she vanished behind Roman Pyetrovich, pinning his arms behind his back so that he could do nothing to defend himself. I put my left hand on his cheek, pushing his face to one side, then brought the razor ponderously across his throat.

It was not so deep a cut as those I'd used to deal with the old couple the previous night. It would bring about his death, but not quite so quickly. To convince Susanna I needed not only to kill, but to revel in the act. It was not something I shied away from. The blood shot from the wound, but soon eased to a gentle trickle over his collarbone and down his chest. Susanna's face peeped around from behind him.

'Now drink,' she said. 'Prove once and for all that you are who you say you are.'

I leaned forward, close to the gash in the man's neck. I could smell the cleanliness of his flesh, mingling with the slightest hint of the scent of his blood. I placed my mouth against his skin, not over the wound but a little below it, where the blood flowed. I pressed my tongue against it, tasting it, but that was enough. I flung my head away from his, forcing back the urge to vomit. I spat across the room, but still I could taste the blood in my mouth. I spat again.

'Funny kind of vampire,' said Ilya.

Susanna looked at me questioningly.

'I'm sorry,' I told her. 'But my body is still human. My mind may have the desires of a *voordalak*, but my body still has the tastes – and disgusts – of a human. I couldn't stomach it, no more than any of them could.'

I felt her hand on my arm. 'You poor creature. But you can still enjoy the kill?'

'Of course,' I smiled.

'Then do so.'

Roman Pyetrovich's body jerked as she tightened her grip on his arms, but still she managed to peer around his side so that she could see what I was doing. I lifted the blade again, this time with my thumb against the back of it so that I could press it deeper into the flesh. I put my other hand behind his neck to brace myself. He muttered a single word, 'No!' but offered little resistance. His eyes followed the edge of the blade until it disappeared from sight under his chin. It was only a moment later that it dug into him, slicing through every type of flesh that it encountered: skin, blood vessels, windpipe, cartilage and muscle. I didn't quite make it through to the bone. The blood flow was prodigious. My hand was covered in it, almost hidden inside the folds of flesh that hung from his neck. I knew I could have done better with my own knife, but this was good enough. I still felt some little nausea at it, but managed to control myself.

Susanna allowed the lifeless corpse to drop to the floor. I looked around. There were three distinct expressions on the faces in the room. On those of the three *voordalaki* there was a look of appreciation, respect even, and the grudging admission that I was who I claimed to be. On the men in the room there was only the appearance of unbelieving terror. But it was Susanna's reaction that was the most fascinating. In her face I saw something that I had never known in her in all the time we were together in our youth. It was an expression of supreme love. I envied Zmyeevich. She had never felt like that towards me. When we had been young, we had played together and as we had grown into adulthood, so the games we played had matured, but I had never meant anything more to her, nor she to me. We had been playmates to one another – playthings. For her Zmyeevich meant something far greater.

And she believed me to be him.

I knew that I must act my role convincingly. I raised myself upright and opened my arms wide, addressing them as though I were the host at a banquet. 'Well?' I said to them. 'I've taken my pleasure here. Isn't it time that you took yours?'

They required no second bidding. I leaned back against the

276

wall, folding my arms, and enjoyed the spectacle of seeing the four vampires – especially the one that appeared to be scarcely more than a little girl – feast upon the frightened, trapped, sweaty, naked men before them.

CHAPTER XVII

IT WASN'T SO VERY LATE WHEN WE GOT BACK TO SAINT ISAAC'S. Susanna and the others had gorged themselves, and I'd enjoyed being witness to it. Even so, I'd felt a little above it all, just as I had done in the old days, when I'd passed myself off as a vampire among so many of them. When we opened the doors the old woman who had seen us enter was there, with two heavyset men whom she'd evidently called on to eject us. We dealt with them easily enough – not that I was much help. Some of us were far too obviously covered in blood to walk back through the streets of Petrograd, but there were seven men's outfits available for us to choose from, for which the original wearers had no further use. Susanna had managed to indulge herself fully, but without a single drop of blood despoiling her dress.

She dismissed the others and we sat alone in the alcove where I assumed she slept. I waited until I heard their footsteps fade to nothing.

'Are you convinced?' I asked.

'Of course. I should have known from the moment you returned. I shouldn't have abandoned you after the ceremony.'

'You weren't to know. But there is much that *I* must know – so much that has happened since my death.' I knew I had still to tread carefully, that any mistake could destroy my hard work. I didn't even know when Zmyeevich had died, except that it occurred after my own death.

'I don't know exactly what happened to you after you left England. You said you were going home. I knew they'd pursue you, but I was sure you could defeat them. You don't know how much I dreamed of receiving some kind of message from you, summoning me to be with you at your castle. The years passed and the news that you were dead began to spread across the vampires of Europe, but I heard nothing.'

'So when did you find out?' It would give me some clue as to when it had happened.

She smiled. 'I remember it very clearly. It was the New Year – the new century. 1899 became 1900. I was in London, perched up on top of the Euston Arch with a couple of others, watching the drunks go by and waiting till their numbers thinned a little before we made our move. I mentioned you and how I hoped you'd come back one day and they both just looked at me, and then one of them told me. I killed perhaps forty people that night – scarcely drank a drop from any of them. That's how much you meant to me.'

'But you never gave up on me.'

She shook her head. 'You were the one who told me about the legends that a vampire could be brought back. And you'd told me where I could find your blood, and where I could find people whose blood you'd drunk. It was as though you'd worked it all out, and had just been laying the pieces out in front of me.'

'I'm not that clever.' I regretted it the instant I spoke. It was perfectly accurate – Zmyeevich was nowhere near intelligent enough to work out something like that for himself – but that didn't mean he had the humility to admit it. Fortunately she didn't remark upon it.

'You didn't have time,' she insisted. 'You knew about Purfleet and Piccadilly, but no more details. They hounded you out before you could get anywhere. The house in Purfleet was easy to find. I remember Richard talking about it.'

I felt the tiniest thrill at the sound of my name – and my Christian name at that – on her lips.

'It was his uncle's house,' she continued. 'He told me how he used to visit. He described it – it was the only place like it in the area. But Piccadilly is a long street. It took me years to find out which one was his. But finally I did and I broke in, and I found the vial of your blood.'

279

'And so you came to Russia?'

'Not straight away. First I had to find out about the ceremony. The Dutchman told me in the end – he told me a lot before I killed him. But he deserved it more than any of them after what he'd done to you. Then I had to find someone to be at the centre of the ceremony; a chosen one, that's how he described it. There was that bitch you'd shared your blood with – it's all right, I've forgiven you. I thought she'd be the easiest to get hold of. Of course, I didn't know then that you'd actually be occupying her body.' Susanna looked at me with a bawdy expression that I'd seen on her face before. 'Might have been interesting, though.'

I pretended to bridle at the notion, even though I had no idea who the people she spoke of were. She giggled.

'She was dead by then, though – consumption. She had a son, who'd have done as well, but the father had taken him to Canada and I didn't know where to start looking for them there. And I knew how you'd always hated the Romanovs, so I thought I'd come here and use one of them.'

'But you didn't, not one of the better-known ones anyway.'

'I knew I'd need help, so I started recruiting other vampires – sharing their blood. And then one of them – Sandor; you've met him – told me that a *voordalak* named Dmitry Alekseevich was looking for vampires for some kind of expedition into Russia – that he himself had been asked to join. Well, you'd talked to me about Dmitry Alekseevich Danilov, and I doubted it could be anyone else, so I kind of tagged along; not with them, always a safe distance away. Dmitry never knew I was there. But Sandor did, and he introduced me to others, and told them of the joy that could come from exchanging blood with another vampire. Soon I was in almost total control, and Dmitry didn't know a thing. There were only two of them that didn't succumb, and they never told him about me. They're both dead now.'

'But why did you decide to use Danilov instead of one of the more auspicious Romanovs? Why not the tsar himself?'

'Why take the risk? It was luck that I discovered Danilov was living here in the city, but after that he stood no chance.

I persuaded his mistress, Nadya Vadimovna, that I was living as a waif on the streets and got her to take me in. I hadn't really decided what to do with them, but then I was searching through their things and can you imagine what I found?'

'What?'

'Richard's notebooks. They confirmed that Danilov was who I'd thought, but it was better than that. I don't know if I'd have succeeded if it hadn't been for what I learned from those books.'

I managed to conceal a smile. 'So when was this?'

'In the spring. I would have acted sooner, but once Nikolai had abdicated, Dmitry moved out into the countryside, taking the others with him. I could have forced them to stay, but I didn't quite have a hold on all of them yet. And summer was on its way. But by autumn I was ready. We grabbed Danilov and . . . and you know the rest.'

I sat in silence for a moment, considering what she had said and pondering how Zmyeevich would have responded. In the end my words came from both of us. 'You are a truly remarkable creature, Susanna.'

She smiled. 'Anyone could have done it – with the right inspiration.'

I was filled by a thousand regrets. I had been a fool as a child. She had a mind so like my own, and I had not seen it. I had only seen her body, and felt a natural human reaction to that, and been ashamed of it. I thought I'd got rid of her but in truth I had transformed her into the wondrous monster who now sat before me, and whose affections, which should have been mine, were directed at the dead creature whom I pretended to be.

'You haven't asked,' she said.

'Asked what?'

'Don't tease. I know how much it means to you. It wasn't your blood that brought you to England, and I can't pretend it was me.'

I understood immediately what she meant. With Zmyeevich dead, it was of little interest, but I knew how obsessed he had been. 'Ascalon!' I said. 'You have it?'

She went over to one of the coffins and opened it. I stood to look, but could see nothing other than the silk lining. She reached inside and found some gap in the material, then she brought it out. She carried it over and showed it to me.

'I sleep with it every day to remind me of you.'

I took it from her hand, trying to express an awe which I did not feel, though in truth I was not unmoved by the presence of the relic. It was just as I remembered it. The bloodstains were still obvious around its tip. It had only briefly been in my possession. I had discovered it in the tunnels beneath the Armenian Church where it had been placed by the priests to whom Peter the Great had entrusted it. I had taken it to England – and now it was returned to me.

'I can't thank you enough. You've done more for me than anyone has ever achieved. You have recalled me to life. You have reunited me with Ascalon.'

'There's more I could still do for you.'

'You've done more than you need to.'

'You're still not . . . as you were.'

'Am I not?'

'You are a human.'

'Was I not once a human?'

'But you became more than human. You became a vampire.' She paused. 'Let me make you one again.' She blurted out the last sentence as though ashamed to ask it.

My mind raced. It had been my ultimate goal, but I wasn't sure I wanted it so quickly. Being human had its advantages and since I could not return to this state once I had abandoned it, I would have liked to savour them. On the other hand, as a human I was quite unable to protect myself. If Susanna were to discover that I was not Zmyeevich, I would be in mortal danger.

'Now?' I asked.

'Why delay?' She drew in a sharp breath. 'Unless . . .' Her gaze fell to the floor.

'Unless what?'

'You said at the bathhouse how your tastes have become once again human. Do you want to indulge them a little longer?'

She was not entirely wrong. I wondered if Zmyeevich would have felt the same as I did. 'I've enjoyed at least one good meal since my return.'

She still didn't lift her face to look at me. 'I didn't mean that. I meant . . . there are other bodily pleasures that humans enjoy.' Her eyes met mine. 'I don't mind – if you want to.'

I almost laughed, but then I considered the offer. Vampires are quite capable of the sexual act, but they take no pleasure from it. Sometimes it can be useful as an act of seduction, to persuade a human to do something more for them than merely being their dinner. That was true both of males and females. Now, though, I was human again and Susanna was right; I did experience human desires – even if they were the jaded desires of a sixty-year-old man. I licked my lips involuntarily – or had it been Danilov's will that caused it? It would be a delight, more than a century on, to feel once again the sweet sensation of her body as it engulfed me – to experience just once more what I'd thought I could never know again. That she offered it so willingly made the whole thing a little less appetizing. And there was the rub; however willing she was, she made the offer not to me but to Zmyeevich. At some inevitable point in the future, when she realized who I was, she would also remember this moment. How would she react to it? I realized that I did not care.

I put Ascalon on the floor beside me and then took her hands in mine and leaned towards her, preparing to kiss her. I remembered that day with her in my father's church, in the Chamber Pew, remembered it in every detail and relished the act, and the anticipation of its re-enactment. Then I had regarded the whole event as sordid, but given the life I had lived since it was one of the purest moments I had ever experienced. And now I had the opportunity to repeat it. I felt a stirring in my body that I had not known for decades and I knew that I would be able to deceive myself, to pretend for a few minutes that we were once again just Richard and Susanna.

But then the truth dawned on me. It was not in *my* body that I felt those yearnings; it was in *ours*. Whatever joy I was about to experience, Danilov would experience it too. How did I know it wasn't *his* desire that made my skin tingle and my mouth dry; *his* desire that pumped engorging blood into my loins? I would not share the moment – not with him nor with anyone. I had enough with my memories and if I were to share further pleasures with Susanna, they would be pleasures that only we could understand and that would turn Danilov's stomach. I would take my revenge on him now, immediately, for even daring to think such thoughts about Susanna.

I kissed her lightly on the lips, then pulled away. I saw the look of disappointment on her face, but smiled at her in return. 'There is only one thing I want from you, Susanna,' I said. 'I want to taste your blood and I want to feel the sensation as you drink mine. I want you to make me as you are – to make me once again a vampire.'

It was preposterous of me to feel such happiness at the look of joy that my words brought to her face. She flung her arms around me and hugged me tightly. I returned the embrace.

'Now?' she asked.

'Now.'

She quickly took off her coat and began to unbutton her blouse. 'You drink first,' she said, 'if that's all right. Take all you want. But not if you don't – I know it doesn't taste good to you yet. Then I'll drink every drop you have.' She was speaking rapidly, consumed by her excitement. 'You can lie here. I assume it'll take weeks as usual; maybe not, a second time. It doesn't matter. We'll protect you. Just think about it. In a moment you'll know my mind. You'll know how I feel about you.'

I was already beginning to doubt the wisdom of my actions. A new-born vampire and the one who makes him share to some extent their minds. In the moment of my death only I would know hers, but when I reawakened the interplay would be in both directions. She would know who I was and how I had lied to her. But by then I would again be a *voordalak* and strong enough to defend myself against her, if it came to it.

She was topless now. I remembered the first time she had allowed me to see her breasts – initially as a drawing she had made herself, and then in reality. They were as entrancing as my memories of them. But what she revealed also, more clearly than before, was the bulge of her pregnancy. My child lay within her. I knew that any affection I felt for it was spurious, that it hadn't even grown as far as being a sentient being, that it was merely an appendage to her body that had lain there for over a century. And yet its very existence gave me some slight hope that when I did reawaken and when she did learn who I really was, she might accept me and allow me to live, out of some affectionate memory of the time we had once spent together.

I knew in my head that the idea was madness, but I felt in my heart – in Danilov's damned heart – that there was some hope for me. There could only ever be hope for me as a vampire.

'Give me the razor,' she said.

I reached into my pocket and handed it to her. She opened it, then after a moment's consideration returned it to me.

'You do it,' she said.

She cupped her left hand under her right breast and pulled it upwards, looking down at her chest beneath. I reached out and drew the blade across at the point she was watching, along the line of her ribs. Blood slithered down from the gash like tears. She took in a sharp breath; it shouldn't have been very painful, not for a vampire. A look of concentration appeared on her face as she tried to defer the normal rapid process of healing so that I would be able to drink. I'd been unable to stomach the blood of the man at the baths, but I could feel this would be different – and I would only need a little. I knelt down beside her and tilted my head on one side, then I opened my lips and allowed them to descend on to the wound that would be for me a source of sustenance and eternal life.

'I'm afraid I haven't told you everything.'

My lips brushed against her pale skin as I spoke and became speckled with blood. I felt as though I had been swimming under water and had now surfaced and was finally able to breathe. It was the longest period I'd known for Iuda's mind to have sway. Did that indicate he was getting stronger, or was it just a random fluctuation? The only reason that it had ended was the path down which Iuda had been about to embark. Just as he had been able to prevent me from jumping from the roof and killing us both, so it seemed I had been given the chance to draw back from our being transformed into a vampire.

'You don't have to tell me anything more than you want to,' she said.

I moved away from her, sitting back where I had been on the closed coffin and wiping my mouth clean. She pouted exaggeratedly and let her breast fall from her hand. The wound to her chest sealed itself quickly, leaving only a smear of congealing blood.

'You'll want to know this. The spirit of Mihail Konstantinovich Danilov was not destroyed when his body was taken over. There are two of us now inside this brain. It alternates between one and the other who gets to speak, who gets to make the decisions. And that just changed. It's me, Mihail Konstantinovich, talking to you now.'

She looked at me. Twice she opened her mouth as if she were about to speak, then decided against it. A third time she was successful. 'Why . . . why are you saying that?'

'Because it's true.'

'You're teasing me.'

'Why would I?'

'How can anyone understand why you do what you do? Please, just forget about it.' She picked up the razor and offered it to me. 'Let's start again.'

'I first saw you in a courtyard near the Yekaterininsky Canal with Ilya. I thought you were a prostitute. You said that my mistress is called Nadya, but how could I know that our dog is called Polkan and our servant was called Syeva? You killed Syeva and hid his body in the dumb waiter. Need I go on?'

She shook her head meekly.

'Then get some clothes on, for God's sake.' I picked her blouse off the floor and handed it to her. She put it on.

'Can I speak to him – to Zmyeevich?'

286

'He can hear everything you say, but at the moment I'm the one who replies. But that's the other thing.'

'What?'

I swallowed hard. It was preposterous to feel pity for a vampire, but her circumstances were not of her making, and the joy she had displayed on being once again with Zmyeevich was all too close to human. Even so, I had to tell her.

'That other soul that's in here with me, that you were talking to. It's not Zmyeevich.'

'Really? Who, pray, is it then?'

'You know him as Richard Llywelyn Cain.'

She stood and walked across the alcove. 'That's not funny.'

'How do you think I feel?'

'And how's it supposed to have happened?'

'The blood you used; it wasn't Zmyeevich's – it was Cain's.'

'How convenient.'

'Think about it. Where did you find the blood? Cain's house. Who'd labelled it as Zmyeevich's? Cain. Who told you it was there in the first place? Ultimately, Cain.'

'That's not enough, though, is it? That's only half of it.'

'Cain bit me; just before he died.'

She stood in silence for a few moments, but I'd finally got through to her. She came and sat down again. 'I've been a fool,' she said morosely.

'Cain's fooled a lot of people in his time.'

She gave a hollow laugh. 'Give it up. There's no Cain. There's no Zmyeevich. There's just you. Just Mihail Konstantinovich Danilov, playing me for a *prostak*.'

'No.'

'I shouldn't be surprised how you found out so much about me. But I have to applaud your performance at the baths; the way you killed and then revelled in our killing.'

The memories came flooding back. I had experienced every moment; felt the blade dragging through the flesh, felt the warm blood flowing over my hand, seen the awful expression on his face. The worst of it was that he had been my old friend from the Japanese War, Colonel Isayev – the very man who'd first told me that Ilya was dead. He'd died thinking that it was I who had killed him. Others would think it too. If I had been seen there, or at the house on Vasilievskiy Island, or at the Hôtel d'Europe, then I was in trouble.

'Only a vampire could have done that. You just made the wrong assumption as to which one.'

'Richard could have done it even before he was a vampire.'

I nodded. 'I know. I know what he did to you, when you were both young.'

'How?'

'I can't search his memories, but if he recalls something I can perceive it.'

'So he was remembering me?'

'As soon as he saw you.'

'Prove it. Tell me something only he could know.'

'He fooled you over that before – told you things that both he and Zmyeevich knew.'

'And that Danilov could not,' she said contemplatively. 'You'll just have to be more precise, then, won't you?'

'Did you tell Zmyeevich that Cain was your baby's father?'

'Yes.'

'Did you tell him where it was conceived?'

She thought for a moment. 'I don't know; I might have done.'

'Did you describe the event to him in every detail?'

She fixed her eyes on mine. 'Go on.'

I had been exaggerating to say 'every detail'. All I knew were the images that had flashed through Iuda's mind minutes before when she had offered him her body. But it was a vivid memory. 'It was in a church,' I began. 'Not in the main nave, but in a sort of side chapel. The ceiling was painted white, as were the walls. We were in a cubicle with wooden seats on all sides, but room enough on the floor in the middle. There was a fireplace, but it wasn't lit. There was an opening looking out on to the main church, with columns, like in a Greek temple. I could see the pulpit beyond. You were on top of me – of him. That's the part he remembers most vividly. Afterwards you—'

'That's enough!' she shouted. Then quieter, 'That's enough.' There were no tears in her eyes, but beyond that she had every appearance of crying.

'You believe me?'

'The only unconvincing thing is that he remembers it at all.'

'I think he regrets it.'

'Regrets fucking me on the floor of his father's church?' She was shouting again.

'No. God no. Regrets what came after.' I had no idea why I was defending him, except that it was how I knew he felt.

'Is that why he came to find me today?'

'To be honest, no, not at all. He had no idea who you were until he saw you. We both came to see if you knew a way to get us out of this . . . predicament.'

'You thought I'd help you?'

'*He* thought you'd help Zmyeevich.'

'So why let me transform him into a vampire?'

'He thought that what's good for him must be bad for me.'

'He must have known I'd find out it was him when our minds joined.'

'He knew, but he wasn't concerned. He admires what you've become.' It was revolting for me to say, but it was true. 'I said he regretted what came after, but that's not quite correct. He doesn't regret that Honoré made you into a vampire, but that he didn't join you.'

She reached out and took my hand. 'Really? Truly?'

'Truly.' I squeezed her fingers in mine. 'You were the first woman I'd ever known. How was I supposed to understand how different you were from all the others that I'd not yet met?'

She looked up at me, recognition showing on her face. 'Richard?' she whispered.

'Yes, it's me now.' I wouldn't like to have to decide whether the words I'd said to her were true, but Danilov had spun her a pretty yarn and she seemed to be falling for it. It was our only chance of survival. I could never have said such things to her myself. He had played Cyrano to my Christian – though I doubted that he would be falling for our own Roxane. But he had pitied her.

'That wasn't very kind; pretending you were Zmyeevich.'

'No, it wasn't. But everything Danilov told you was correct.'
I bent forward and picked up the razor from where she had
dropped it, offering it to her. 'Do me the honour that you were
going to before. Make me a vampire again.'

'So that we can spend eternity together?'

When she put it like that it did not sound a tempting
prospect. She would not want it any more than I did. 'So that
we can make the world a more interesting place for having
us both in it.' An idea struck me. 'And who knows? Perhaps
together we will finally discover a way of bringing Zmyeevich
back from the dead.' Fat chance.

'I've already begun,' she said.

I tried not to react. Had she begun to bring him back, or
merely to look for a way? 'Really?' I asked.

She shook her head. 'Not now.' Then she took the razor
from me and began to walk around, not looking at me as she
spoke. 'You hurt me in many ways, Richard. You abandoned
me with our child. You offered me up as food to your pet
vampire. Even just now you chose to deceive me in the
cruellest of ways.'

'I've told you I'm sorry.'

'But we still haven't covered the foulest thing you've done to
me.'

I tried to think. 'Tell me then. Let me make amends.'

'Tell you the worst thing that you did? The worst thing that
can be done to *any* vampire?'

I began to understand. I said nothing.

'I only saw your face once more after you freed us. You
thought you were freeing just Honoré, but I was there too. I
saw you – I think you might have seen me. Then we went and
fulfilled Honoré's promise to you. We went to the rectory and
killed your father; ripped his throat out as he slept and fed
upon him. We stayed together, Honoré and I, for a little while.
I had much to learn. But finally we went our separate ways.
We were never far from each other's thoughts. The minds of
two vampires, one who created the other, are intertwined. He
was in Wallachia, enjoying a raid on a Russian encampment.
I enjoyed it too, seeing through his eyes. We shared the exact

same feeling of surprise when he opened that tent and found you in there.

'You'd grown, of course, grown into a man, but we both knew you instantly. I was tempted to let you live – you'd done me a favour after all – but he was hungry and it was no business of mine. And the prospect of seeing you die intrigued me. But it didn't turn out like that, did it? You were very resourceful. The sharpened point of a tent pole through his heart. And then . . . nothing more.'

'It was self-defence. You saw that.'

'Oh yes, absolutely true.' She was behind me now. I could hear the edge of suppressed anger in her voice and could imagine the expression on her face. 'But you and I both know how little that matters. You became famous over the years for your studies of our kind – or infamous perhaps. So you must understand that there can be no excuses such as self-defence when it comes to killing a vampire's parent. It's my duty. It's in my blood. I'm sorry, Richard – and sorry too, Mihail Konstantinovich, if you're listening – but this is simply how it has to be. I could do this in the usual way, but I'm not hungry, and I wouldn't want to sully my lips.'

Her dainty little hand grabbed me across the mouth and pulled my head back. Even then, I noticed the slight, sweet fragrance of it. She rested the blade of the razor against my skin, just above my Adam's apple. 'I won't make this quick,' she said.

I tried to struggle, but she had a *voordalak*'s strength and I was no match for her. All I managed to achieve was to press my throat harder against the razor and feel it cut into me. It was a minor wound and I knew there would be worse to come. Somewhere in my mind I could feel Danilov gloating, pleased that Susanna was about to achieve what he had been unable to and admiring the fact that she had chosen the weapon that I had been so happy to use in his hand. The pain would be nothing to him, knowing that I shared it.

She moved the blade over to the far left of my throat.

'Goodbye, Richard,' she whispered. Then she emitted a gasp. Her hand – and with it the razor – moved away from me. Her grip on my face relaxed and I managed to twist free. I turned and stood.

We were no longer alone. Opposite her was the tall figure of Dmitry, gripping her arm so that she could not wield the razor. She struggled against him but, just as a man like him would have been the stronger if they were humans, so too it was the case as vampires. I plucked the blade from her fingers.

'Who are you now?' Dmitry asked me.

'Danilov,' I replied. I didn't have time to think, so the best option seemed to be to lie. I realized as I spoke I should have said 'Mihail.'

'Rubbish!' hissed Susanna.

'What does it matter?' asked Dmitry.

With a sudden twist Susanna broke free from him and ran out into the corridor. 'Ilya! Sandor!' she shouted. 'Help me!' It was an impressive sound that she produced, echoing along the corridors.

'Where's Ascalon?' asked Dmitry.

'Who cares?' I replied. 'Let's just get out of here.'

'No! We must find it.'

I knew I wasn't going to get far without Dmitry, so it was better to do what he wanted. We both searched the floor. It was only moments before I saw it, nestling beside one of the coffins. I grabbed it and showed it to him.

'Here!'

We went out into the passage. Susanna stood blocking the way in one direction. Dmitry didn't hesitate, but went the other – towards the main chamber and the exit through the sewers. Susanna didn't move, but I heard her calling after us. 'You'll never make it.'

She was right. We didn't get as far as the stairs before the path was blocked by Ilya. I could see two more figures behind him. In the tight corridor Dmitry's physique seemed immense. Ilya looked puny beside him. Dmitry did not pause. He grabbed one side of Ilya's head and smashed it into the wall. I could see Ilya's face deform as his skull began to compress. But for a *voordalak* it would not be a fatal wound, and there were two more behind him.

292

'This way,' I said, turning back in the direction we had come.

'It's locked,' Dmitry shouted.

'I know a way.'

Soon we were back where we had started. Susanna was still standing there, blocking our path, a look of triumph on her face. I ducked into the alcove and allowed Dmitry to charge on past. He lowered his shoulder and hit her full in the belly. Any affection I had held minutes before for my unborn child was gone now, and I was pleased to see the pain on her face as she collapsed to the floor. Dmitry was already on his way and I leapt over her prone body before she could have a chance to recover.

Dmitry was halfway up the iron ladder by the time I reached it. I began to climb as quickly as I could. He'd now clambered through the opening and was peering back, holding the flagstone ready to be dropped into place. I felt a sharp pain in my calf, and I could not lift my leg from the rung. I looked down and saw Susanna's face staring up at me, her hand on my ankle. Her teeth were bared and her eyes were full of hatred. She continued to climb smoothly, sliding her body over mine, enveloping it, like a snake swallowing its enormous prey. Her intent was to pin me against the ladder and bring her mouth up to my neck so she could strike. Already her head was level with my knees, and that was just what I'd been waiting for. I raised my other foot and stamped down on her face for all I was worth. She fell back, releasing me and dangling from the ladder by only one hand. I carried on up and was soon through the opening. At the same moment Dmitry released the stone slab. I saw her dainty fingers scrabbling to get a grip on the edge. The stone fell into place and we heard a muffled scream. The mashed tips of two fingers remained caught in the narrow gap.

Dmitry nodded along the corridor to where the iron gate could just be seen. 'See? I told you; it's locked.'

'Then we go the other way,' I said.

Just as I remembered, the passageway soon led to another spiral staircase. We ascended. Behind us we could hear the footsteps of our pursuers. The stairs ended in a sturdy wooden door. That hadn't been there either, the last time I was here. I cursed my luck, but then smiled. There was a key in the lock. Dmitry had already seen it and a moment later we were through the door and locking it from the other side.

I breathed in the cool night air. We were outside. The whole of Petrograd lay as a panorama before us. As ever the streets were thronged with workers and soldiers. I could see as far as Palace Square, still densely packed. Behind us the red stone columns of the cathedral's central domed tower rose upwards. A smaller tower, topped with gold, was just in front of us. We were on a parapet that ran all along the building's roof. Fists began to bang from the other side of the door, but it looked strong enough to hold even vampires for a while.

'So what are we supposed to do now?' said Dmitry.

'We climb,' I replied. 'Or rather you climb and I hang on.'

We made our way over the shallow slope until we reached that smaller corner tower, then Dmitry descended until only his upper torso was visible. He clung on to the lead roof with his fingertips. I scrambled forwards and climbed on to him, wrapping my arms around his shoulders and gripping tightly on to his coat. He began to descend.

His instinct as a vampire was to go down head first, but I would have been quite unable to keep hold. For a while we could still hear them beating on the door, which gave us hope that they hadn't thought to come down and wait for us at the bottom, though they could have split up. Dmitry made easy work of the smooth walls, but there were two wide protruding ledges along the way that made things more difficult – particularly with me on his back. At each one I dismounted and let him get over the obstacle before pairing up once again. Soon we were on the ground.

There was a round of applause and a few cheers. Quite a crowd had gathered, but amongst them I saw none of the faces of the vampires who were pursuing us. I could only hope that the sound hadn't attracted their attention.

'This way,' said Dmitry, heading off at a run in the direction of the Admiralty.

I couldn't keep up for more than a few seconds. I slowed to a walk, but failed even to maintain that for long. Ahead I saw him turn and begin striding back. I ducked into a side street, so that we couldn't be seen from the cathedral, but I could do no more. I leaned against the wall and then gradually slid to the ground. My chest was on fire. I could scarcely breathe. Dmitry's dark figure loomed above me.

CHAPTER XVIII

'YOU FOOL, DMITRY. YOU BLUNDERING, HAM-FISTED IDIOT.' MY voice was a harsh whisper, emitted between tight painful breaths.

'You're welcome,' Dmitry replied.

It took me a moment to notice the sarcasm, but I was in no state to say anything further. I thrust my hand into my pocket, but found it empty. I tried the other side, but realized it was hopeless – this was not my coat.

'Shit!' I muttered. I lay back, panting, knowing that if I was calm there was a good chance the pain would recede on its own.

'What's wrong?' asked Dmitry.

'I need my pills. They're at home.'

'I'll go and get them.'

I shook my head. I didn't want Nadya to have to see him. 'Just let me rest.'

He said nothing more and for a few minutes we remained in silence, but for the rasping of my breath, which gradually began to return to normal.

'Who am I talking to?' he asked at length.

'Mihail, now. But it was Iuda until I sat down here.'

'I thought as much, though you might still be Iuda.'

I could only offer a grunt as a reply.

'Who's the Chinese Emperor?' Dmitry asked quickly.

'There isn't one. It's a republic now. I can't remember who the president is.'

'Good enough.'

'You should have let her kill me, Dmitry – kill us both. It's the only way.'

'I couldn't just leave you.'

'You could have been a few minutes later.'

He chuckled and then sat down next to me. 'I nearly was. You're lucky I got to you at all.'

'Not lucky,' I said, but he ignored me.

'You must have left by the time I got to the cathedral. I waited, and saw you all coming back; I followed you up the stairs, but the gate was already locked. I tried the hidden panel we used before, but it was bricked up behind. Then I remembered where Iuda had gone to recover, after Zmyeevich nearly killed him. I visited him there – in the sewers under Saint Isaac's Square. I knew there had to be a way through to the cathedral. It took a while, but eventually I found it, and found my way to you.'

'That's the way we got in,' I said. 'Iuda tried to convince Susanna that it was actually Zmyeevich who had been resurrected in me, not him.'

'Susanna?'

'Anastasia. It's her real name. Apparently she and Iuda know each other from long ago.' It felt intrusive to give Dmitry the full details.

'I overheard some of it. It makes more sense now. Did she have any ideas to get you out of this mess?'

'Aside from killing me, no.'

'You really think that would do the trick?' he asked.

'Of course. How couldn't it?'

He put his hands to his face and breathed out through his fingers. 'You remember when you drank Zmyeevich's blood? You'd hidden it in that nutshell like it was a poison pill.'

'Of course.'

'And after that, he daren't kill you, because you'd become a vampire and he didn't want that.'

'That was because of the Romanov blood he'd already drunk.'

'Exactly. And aren't you in the same situation here? Iuda drank your blood, you told me, just as he was dying. And a couple of nights ago Anastasia forced you to drink his. If you die while it's still in your body, you'll become a vampire – won't you?'

I let out a broad, mirthless laugh. 'Jesus Christ, Dmitry. You could be right. Cut it down to its basics and that's what we have. Iuda drank my blood; I've drunk his. If I die then . . . Forget all the hocus pocus and it's just the normal way.' I laughed again, this time at my concept of normality. 'And not even Iuda thought of it. Thank God you did. You're a good man, Dmitry.'

His eyes flashed at me and his nostrils flared. 'Don't presume to understand me, Mihail. I act for myself. It won't do me any good to have Iuda back.'

'You don't act just for yourself. You act for Russia too, some-times. You've convinced me of that.'

He seemed keen not to dwell on the subject. 'So what will you do now?'

'Survive,' I replied. 'For a few weeks anyway – or months, or however long it takes for Iuda's blood to leave me.'

'Will you be able to? What if Iuda just takes over and . . . walks you under a train or something?' It was an interesting method of death for him to pick. His own vampire parent, Raisa, had died that way.

'I don't think it's possible,' I said. 'I tried it – tried to jump off a rooftop – when I thought it might do some good. He managed to stop me. I'm sure I'll be able to do the same.'

'What if he just walks you right back in there with Anastasia and lets her do the dirty work?'

'I'll have to try and avoid it. Or hope I get the chance to explain to her. If you see her, do tell her what will happen if I die. Perhaps she'll become my protectress.'

'I'll be sure to mention it. But I have to go now.'

'It won't be dawn for hours.'

'No, but I have to . . . to feed.'

The images of those men in the bathhouse came back to me: their awful deaths, and the pleasure I had felt Iuda take at merely watching. Suddenly I guessed at Dmitry's predicament, and that of every one of his kind. Was he truly a vampire, or was he merely possessed by a vampire, which had taken him over many years before? I was possessed by a creature far worse. For him there was no return – and none for me either.

'Will you be leaving the city,' I asked, 'now that the Bolsheviks have won?'

'Maybe – maybe not. I'm on my own now. All the others are dead, or gone over to her, or just gone. But winter's coming, so the nights will be longer. Perhaps there's still something I can do for Russia.'

He stood up and offered me his hand. I let him pull me to my feet.

'What are you going to do afterwards?' he asked. 'Once Iuda's blood has left you.'

'If I can't think of anything by then,' I replied, 'then I'll die.'

'How? You said you can't kill yourself.'

I looked him straight in the eye. 'I'll find someone I trust to do it for me.'

It took him a moment to understand, and then he walked away without any hint that he would accept the undertaking. After a few paces he stopped and faced me.

'What about Ascalon?' he asked.

'What about it?'

'Do you think it's safe with you – with him?'

'It'll have to be.'

'Wouldn't it be better with me?'

'I don't think so,' I replied, not even pausing to consider it.

'I could easily take it from you.'

'Dmitry,' I asked, 'would you really want to? You went halfway around the world to get away from him. Do you really think a memento like that is going to do you any good?'

He stood and looked down at me, his eyes fixed on the pocket in which I'd put the relic. If he wanted it I would not be able to resist him. I could not imagine what thoughts – what memories – were going through his head. At last he took a deep breath and turned away. I watched him walk into the distance, then set off myself.

It was vile of me to go home, but there was nothing else to be done. And it would be just as vile of me to stay away. It was Wednesday evening when I had last seen Nadya, and now it was the early hours of Saturday. She had no idea what had happened to me, and in the meantime our nation's government had fallen once again. I had to let her know that I was alive, though I was not sure I could stomach telling her the truth of what had befallen me. I could have done that much by letter, or even asked Dmitry to convey a message for me. To go and see her face to face was far more for my benefit than hers. And beyond seeing her, I had more material needs. I required food, shelter, sleep – and above all my pills.

I didn't take the quickest route home, not because I had any desire to delay the moment, but out of the need to avoid the crowds I'd seen in Palace Square. I turned down Nevsky Prospekt and then went along the Yekaterininsky Canal. I passed the Church on Spilled Blood on the other side of the waterway, but I could see soldiers – regular soldiers, not Red Guards – on duty at each of the entrances. They must have discovered the corpses inside. If the police were in any functioning state they would be investigating. They'd have found the bodies at the bathhouse too by now, and probably those of the professor and his wife. What clues had I left at each of those sites, I wondered. Had I been seen – recognized even? If they had the slightest clue it was me, they could easily use my fingerprints to make a watertight case.

Could that be my salvation? Could it give me the weeks or months that I needed? A trial would take that long; certainly if I could find lawyers to spin it out. But even then I would not face the noose. After the revolution the death penalty had been abolished. I would rot in some gaol, but that would be enough. There would be nothing Iuda could do to stop it, unless he could convince them that we were insane. That wouldn't be so very far from the truth.

But there was still some hope that there might be a way to separate us that did not involve my death or incarceration. I'd failed to learn very much from Susanna, but there remained plenty she might know. She'd discovered a lot over the years. Like Iuda I had no idea who this Dutchman was, or the others she'd mentioned. Perhaps they were connected with those I'd witnessed finally putting an end to Zmyeevich's existence. His evil must have touched the lives of many across Europe and I'd be arrogant to think that my family's story was the only one in which he featured. But the Dutchman was dead according to Susanna, and so could be of no help. But the very fact that men like him existed gave me hope that the knowledge I required was out there.

At last I arrived at my front door. I'd had half a mind to sneak in, take what I needed and leave a note for Nadya, but I realized long before I got there that I had no keys and that the only way I would be able to get in would be to rouse her. If Syeva had still been alive a quiet tap on the door would have brought a quick response, but now I pounded loud enough to wake her, even at the top of the house. I realized as I began that I was doing her a disservice to suppose that she would be asleep.

The door was opened in seconds. She made no show of caution; she did not peek out through a crack to see who it was. She threw it wide open and stood for a moment, staring at me. She lifted her hands to her face and I embraced her, squeezing her arms against her chest, burying my face in her sweetly scented hair. Somewhere near by I could hear Polkan barking, welcoming me home. We held the pose for a few moments, then I felt her pushing at me, trying to break away. I took a step back, wondering what I had done wrong, but discovered that she merely wanted to free her arms. She put them around me, pulling me towards her, this time with her face upturned so that we could kiss.

I had never known a more joyous moment, and I wondered whether I ever should again. When in my youth I had killed Iuda – supposed I had killed him – I had felt it to be the culmination of my life's work, but there was no real happiness in it. This was quite different. This was a sensation of utter relief, of being found having been lost, of drinking a glass of cool water when dying of thirst. I was in the only place I should ever want to be.

Eventually, but still too soon, we had to separate. I closed the door behind me, then squatted down to stroke Polkan. He had stopped barking by now, but approached me tentatively. He didn't object to my fingers running through his fur, but neither did he roll on to his back to be tickled. He eyed me warily. He was a perceptive creature.

'Where the hell have you been?' Nadya tried to inject her voice with righteous anger, but it cracked as she spoke and the breath she drew afterwards sounded like a sob. She looked deathly. Her skin was pale and drawn in at her cheeks. I knew that I should tell her everything, and quickly – Iuda might return at any moment. But I was too much of a coward. I would tell her, I was certain of it, but not just now. For her a delay would make no difference. Whenever she learned the truth, she would be horrified – devastated. But for me the stay of execution would mean some little comfort, some pretence of normality – a chance to say goodbye to that very normality, for I knew it would soon be gone for ever. And yet every moment that I did not speak would make it harder in the end. Perhaps I'd already hesitated for too long in those few seconds I had stood in her embrace. But still I could not bring myself to tell her.

'Please,' I said, 'not now. Just let me sleep. Just let me be with you. I'll tell you everything in the morning.'

She gazed at me for a moment, then nodded and held out her hand. We went up the stairs together, with Polkan limping behind. Once in our room, my first action was to go to the drawer beside the bed. There were my pills, not in their silver box – that was lost – but in the paper wrapper in which the pharmacist provided them. I slipped one under my tongue. I probably didn't need it now, not like I had done outside the cathedral, but it calmed me simply to know I had taken it. I quickly changed into my night clothes and climbed into bed.

Nadya got in beside me. She kissed me without a word and then turned out the light. We lay in silence for a few minutes and then I heard her speak.

'Whatever it is, Misha, is it over?'

I couldn't lie to her. 'No,' I replied.

She said no more. Within minutes I was asleep.

When I awoke I was alone. It was light outside. From along the corridor I could hear the sound of Nadya gently singing to herself: *Tonkaya Ryabina*. I listened to her, enjoying the moment, knowing it wouldn't last.

> *Why do you stand swaying, slender rowan tree, your head*
> *bent over your roots?*
> *And across the way, over the broad river, just as alone,*
> *stands a tall oak tree.*

How could I, the rowan tree, go to the oak? Then I
  wouldn't stand bowing and swaying.
With my slender branches I'd press against him, and with
  his leaves, whisper day and night.
But it's impossible for a rowan tree to move to the oak.
  Such is its fate: forever alone, swaying.

She came to an end. I was glad that it was I who had awoken to hear it, and not Iuda. But I realized I could not be sure of that. Both of us could perceive; it was merely action that was limited to one or other of us. I had not moved since I woke – either of us could be in charge, perhaps whoever chose first to grab the reins.

I lifted my hand and touched my face. My arm moved in obedience to my will. I was still me, for the time being. I should also have known from the tears that I felt on my face, a result of hearing Nadya's sweet voice. But perhaps Iuda might have shed them. I had begun to learn something of how sentimental he could be.

I swung my legs out of the bed and stood up, then went on to the landing. Polkan was lying down at the top of the stairs. He raised his head, but did not come to me. Nadya had begun to sing again down below. I went in the direction of the sound. As soon as I began to move, Polkan was on his feet and making his way down the stairs in the sideways fashion he'd developed to avoid using his injured leg. He went straight to the bathroom on the second floor. I followed him and there I found Nadya. The dog lay down again, watching us intently.

'You slept well,' she said. It was mundane, considering the circumstances.

'I didn't wake at all?' There was always the possibility that Iuda had taken the opportunity to act while I was asleep.

'Not that I noticed. I've drawn you a bath.'

The tub of hot water looked inviting. I undid my buttons and began to undress, but my limbs were stiff and I let out a groan.

'Let me help you,' she said.

She stood behind me and held my nightshirt as I pulled my arms out of it. The ragged bandage that Susanna had applied was still there. Nadya reached out to it.

303

'May I?' she asked.

I nodded. She untied the knot in the linen. A straight, neat scab covered the line of the wound.

'There's a cut on your throat too,' she said. 'Neither of them looks like something a vampire would do.'

'Not exactly,' I replied.

'Careful you don't open that up when you're washing. I'll dress it properly afterwards. And then you can tell me all about it; especially what happened to your sideboards.'

She helped me out of my trousers and then went away. I heard Polkan's claws tapping unevenly against the wooden floor as he trotted alongside her. I climbed into the bath and lay still, my right arm hanging over the side so as not to soak the wound. I tried to think what I was going to tell her – how I was going to tell her. Any other problem would have been easy. I'd just speak the truth, and we'd swear to each other that we'd manage somehow, that even if the whole world was against us the two of us together would struggle through.

But it wasn't going to be two of us – there were three of us. Iuda would always be with me; I could see no way out of that. Whether I chose to live or die – if I had the choice – it would not be with Nadya by my side. How could it? What man could condemn the woman he loved to spend half her life with a creature such as Iuda? Or a tenth of it? Or a thousandth?

I washed myself and then shaved, still sitting in the bath. In the mirror I saw the little cut that Susanna had caused to my throat. At the time I had been praying that she would succeed and kill us both. Now I knew how awful the consequences of that might have been. But death was still my best hope – it just had to be delayed for a little while.

I picked up the towel that Nadya had left for me and went back up to the bedroom. I'd almost finished drying when she came in. She had two glasses of tea on a tray. She put them on the table. She seemed dreadfully sad, but doing everything she could to hide it. I went over to kiss her. Our lips touched lightly at first, but then we began to kiss more deeply, or at least I did. She hesitated for a moment and then yielded. Our tongues met. I ran my hand down her back and began to caress her buttock through her thin housecoat. She pushed me away and I looked to see her smiling, her eyebrow raised.

She stepped back and went to the door, where Polkan was lying quietly on the landing. She closed it. 'We don't want to be disturbed,' she said.

She came back and stood close to me again. I bent forwards to kiss her and felt her cool hands against me, her fingers running through the hairs on my chest and then downwards, across my belly and to my thighs. I undid the little bow at the collar of her coat, and then moved down to each button, one by one. I knew full well that I should stop and for just the same reason that Iuda had declined when Susanna had offered him the delights of her body. The other of us would always be there, and however blissful the act of love might be for both me and Nadya, it would become a monstrous perversion if it was an experience shared by any other. If shared by Iuda it would be the ultimate obscenity.

I raised my hands to push her away from me and tried to formulate the words of an explanation, knowing that only the truth would suffice. But my hands continued their task of undressing her.

It was too late – I wasn't sure by how long. I was no longer in control of my actions. If I had been, I would have stopped earlier. I had let my body control me, as was natural at a moment like this, and he had seized the vacancy created.

And now all I could be was a witness – a witness not merely by sight and hearing, but by every sensation – as the man I most despised in the whole world, Iuda, raped the woman I loved.

He wasn't cruel or brutal in any way. He contemplated it, and sometimes imagined it, but he came to the conclusion that he could do far more harm by being a considerate lover. He made sure that his every thought was clear to me, as if he was talking me through his plans. He even let me know that the very openness was part of the plan itself. He was a chess player, not a card player; there were no secrets to be revealed, no cards held close to his chest – everything that he did was in the open, accessible to any who had the wisdom to understand it. It was just the same, he informed me, as what he had done to Lyosha over Dominique. I didn't understand what he meant by it and he let the concept pass from his mind. He was saving it for later.

He had no desire to harm Nadya or cause her pain, not as a primary goal anyway. I was the chosen object of his disdain. It wasn't even an act of vengeance as such; I had simply raised my head above the parapet by killing him back in 1881. I had challenged him to a game – just as my grandfather had in 1812 – and he had accepted, and now neither of us could back out until the end. In other circumstances he might have delighted in making Nadya suffer, but that would make things too easy for me, made the path I chose too obvious. The simple question Iuda had posed for me was, what could I tell her?

I lay on my back thinking about it, her head resting on my chest, her eyes closed, a smile on her lips. What *could* I tell her? If I revealed the truth – that Iuda shared my mind – then the inevitable question would follow: who was that she'd made love to? If I said it was Iuda then she would feel tricked, abused, violated. She would feel no better for the fact that it was impossible for her to have known; any more than if he had physically forced himself upon her, she would have found refuge in the knowledge that she did not have the strength to resist him. In both circumstances there was a rational argument that she should feel no guilt, but this could never be a matter of rationality. If it had been Iuda then she had been raped, and that was the end of it.

But if I told her it was me, how much better was that? It would mean that I had made love to her in full knowledge that Iuda would draw from it every scintilla of physical pleasure that I did. No one sane would want to share such intimate moments with a third person even watching, so how much worse would this be? It would prove my selfishness, that my carnal desires were so overpowering that I had to exploit Nadya in order to satisfy them, and to hell with the fact that it would not only be me who got the pleasure of it.

And in truth I did not even know which of us it had been, not entirely. That was the genius of how Iuda had chosen to behave. If he had done something vile to her then it would have been easy; I would have been able to point at it and say, 'That was not me. That could never be me.' But there was no such moment. Everything he did I would have gladly done myself, and had done in the past. There were times when I felt that it was I who was kissing her, tasting her, caressing her; I who was in control. Was it simply because he was doing what I would have done, or was it that from time to time it was I who made the decisions, who told my body what it should do to hers? The reality was that it was not I or he who had taken Nadya that morning, but *we*.

And so the only option I had was to tell her nothing. Iuda had worked that out very early on. He knew that I would do anything to save her from the burden of not knowing which of us it was – of never being able to know for sure at any moment when we were together. And that meant I could not relieve my own burden by sharing with her that fact of my sorry state of being. I could never see her again, I knew that, not until I could find a way of freeing myself of Iuda. My task now, my additional task, was to invent a reason for my departure that would be convincing. But that would have to wait.

I held her tightly in my arms, then rolled across the bed so that she was lying on her back. I held her for a little longer, then stood up. I don't think she was asleep, but she was too contented to move. I dressed quickly, finding a new coat from my wardrobe. I transferred my possessions from the other one – I couldn't stand to wear it, knowing where it came from. There was the razor, Iuda's homemade knife and Ascalon. I wanted nothing to do with any of them, but I would not leave them here, not for Nadya to find. I also took my nitroglycerin pills. I allowed myself one last look at Nadya, then opened the door.

Polkan stood up as I left and began to growl softly. I tried to soothe him, partly out of affection, partly out of fear that he would rouse Nadya, but his unease about me of the night before seemed to have strengthened. I closed the bedroom door and hurried downstairs. I went into the kitchen and pulled out one of the drawers completely. Taped underneath it was an envelope, bulging with roubles. I took half of them and returned the remainder of our savings to their hiding place. It would be better to have my own money to spend than to give Iuda the need to steal from somebody else.

Then I went out to the street, and began to walk.

I'd given Danilov a lot to think about, but that was no excuse for him to completely abandon all awareness of the world around us. They must have picked us up as soon as we left his house. There were two of them; I could see that much. I couldn't make Danilov turn his oafish head to check for any more. One thing was plain; they weren't vampires. It was getting on for midday when we set off, thanks to the enduring needs of Nadya Vadimovna, and so the sun was high. Danilov had taken us along the Fontanka without showing any real intention of where he was heading. One of the men kept behind us. The other one was easier to spot, even though he remained the whole time on the far bank of the river. It seemed likely that there would be others.

I don't think it even occurred to Danilov that his route would take us close to the bathhouse that had been the scene of such merriment the previous night. He just needed to walk, to attempt to clear his mind. When we got close he realized and was about to turn away, but it was at that moment that I once more gained the opportunity to decide where our legs would take us. His idea that he might get arrested for murder was an interesting one, which might solve many of his problems. I knew he objected to having his name tarnished – much as I objected to someone else getting the credit for my good work – but if I pushed too hard it might prove to be for him the lesser of two evils.

I turned down the little canal again and stopped at the baths. There was a lot of activity. Two gendarmes stood at the door, preventing me from going in. I was pleased to note that they were regular police, not soldiers as we'd seen at the Church on Spilled Blood, so it seemed they hadn't connected the two incidents yet.

'Can't I come in for a bath?' I said.

'You a regular here?' one of them asked.

'No. Do I need to be?'

'It's just there's been a murder – several murders.'

'My goodness, how awful.' I tried to peer past them at what was going on inside, toying with the possibility that I would be recognized, not that I had any desire whatsoever to be arrested. No one that we had encountered face to face had survived, but we hadn't killed everyone in the building. Someone might have caught a glimpse of me. It was only a slight chance, but I enjoyed the thrill of the risk I was taking.

'I wouldn't, sir. It's not a pretty sight.'

I gave a slight grimace and then departed, heading back the way I'd come. One of my pursuers had followed me to the bathhouse and then walked innocently past when I stopped. By doubling back I might have lost him, but when I reached the Fontanka again I saw that the other one was still waiting for me, unmistakable in his leather coat. I crossed the river by the nearest bridge and made for the centre of town. The leather-coated man came with me. I was feeling hungry. Danilov had felt it too, but had done nothing about it. Perhaps he was trying to starve himself to death. It wouldn't work – he'd never keep control of himself for long enough.

I found a little place on the Haymarket for lunch, nothing like as grand as the Hôtel d'Europe, but it would suffice. Much as I would have enjoyed irritating Danilov by committing further burglaries, it was far easier to use the money he had provided, and I knew we ought to make it last. The man in the leather coat didn't come in. I looked out of the window, but couldn't see him. I was sure he was there. I ordered blini filled with mushrooms and fried onions. As soon as I bit into it a memory rushed back to me that at first I couldn't quite place. Somehow it was coupled with Danilov, but the precise connection was elusive.

Then it hit me. It was in another café, not unlike this, in Moscow this time, years before; it must have been soon after the end of the Crimean War. Similar blini with a similar filling had been on the table, but it had not been I who was eating – that was what had confused me. It was a young woman. I pictured her in my mind and smiled to myself. She was not unlike Nadya. They were about the same age, the same shapely build – not fat, but well rounded. For different reasons I knew that each of them was physically strong. Even the faces bore similarities. The hair, though, was different;

Nadya's was straight and dark, while that of the woman in my memories was a wavy auburn. It was not uncommon for a man to choose a partner who looked like his mother, even though he would rarely acknowledge it. But Danilov would not have known his mother, Tamara, until she was older. How that woman must have hated me, to make her son hate me so.

But not then. Then she had trusted me, like all of them do for a while. On that occasion, in Moscow, Tamara had not been alone. She had been dining with Dmitry, her half-brother. He'd been human then – in the last days of it. I'd rushed in and interrupted them in order to hand him a letter that would send him off across the country in chase of a wild goose that would ultimately end in his death – and rebirth. It had gone precisely as I'd planned it, and I'd spent a long time planning it. Only after that had things started going wrong. I had not been a vampire for so very long then. Had it already jaded me? Had I forgotten how to strategize, how to make the players dance around me with just a few softly spoken words which they didn't even have to believe, but would still be forced to act upon? I'd only been human again for a few days now and yet had already come close to convincing Susanna I was someone quite different, and put a barrier between Danilov and his lover that he would never find a way around. Perhaps I'd do better to remain human for a little while. It was a shame Danilov's body was so old, but it was good for another ten years or so. And now I knew the trick, I could take any body I chose, with a little work. Eternal life was no longer the preserve of the *voordalak*.

But I'd been fooled too in my life. I hadn't even known then that Tamara was Lyosha's daughter. I pictured her again and him, comparing their faces. It should have been obvious.

He's just as I imagined him.

I realized more quickly this time that the words were not spoken in the room. It was Danilov, his thoughts breaking through into mine. I sensed that he was happy, remarkably so. It took me a moment to understand why. These were my memories, but they meant more to him than they ever would to me. For him to see his mother again, from before he ever knew her, must have been a joy – like looking through an album of family photographs. And to see his grandfather – his hero, Lyosha – for the first time would be a greater delight still.

I decided to indulge him. What memory of his grandfather – of his grandparents – would I treat him to? There were so many moments of Lyosha's humiliation that I could allow him to visit, but not yet. Let him first witness a triumph – though not a complete triumph. Perhaps Lyosha at his most brutal, just so that Danilov would know how to really be a man.

It was back in 1812, again in Moscow, in a house that had long been abandoned as its owners fled Bonaparte's advance. We – a group of *voordalaki* and myself, the *oprichniki* – had made it our home. We'd boarded up the windows to keep the sunlight out, and even dug down to the sewers so that we could come and go without ever stepping outside. We'd led Lyosha to the place, to trap him, and now we had him. I was there, and two of the *oprichniki* – Pyetr and Andrei – and Lyosha's friend, Dmitry Fetyukovich. Lyosha was resourceful. He had an icon – an image of Christ – on a chain round his neck and he'd used it to try and scare us. Andrei ripped it from him and threw it across the room, but it had been distraction enough. Lyosha drew his sabre and swung it into Andrei's throat, cutting more than halfway through. It wasn't enough to kill him, but he could barely move.

Then Lyosha had leapt across the room and managed to climb up one of the boarded windows, bringing down the panel of wood, allowing a beam of sunlight to split the room in two: a barrier that no *voordalak* could cross, and with Lyosha on the other side of it. Of course, it made no difference to me; I was human then. I almost marched through to get at Lyosha, but thankfully the other two held me back and I remembered that I didn't want to give myself away. And then Lyosha had shown his true magnificence. He rammed the hilt of his sword into Andrei's stomach, causing the dazed *voordalak* to double up. Then he brought the blade down with all his might on the back of Andrei's neck. At first I thought it hadn't been enough, but then he gave his sword a savage twist and Andrei's head came free. It was dust before it even hit the floor.

I left the memory there. I could tell that Danilov was enjoying it, enjoying seeing his grandfather do what he himself so much enjoyed – killing vampires. Lyosha was luckier than his grandson; for him, once dead, vampires didn't come back.

I moved on to a different memory, just three weeks later. There were things that Danilov had to know. The remnants of Bonaparte's *Grande Armée* were fleeing Russia. They were crossing a frozen river – the Berezina – except that a late thaw had meant the ice of its surface wasn't quite so solid any more. Lyosha had caught up with me and chased me out on to the ice and knocked me into the freezing water. I clung on to his booted foot. He shouted down at me.

'So, was it Margarita or Domnikiia you were with?'

I'd fooled him so utterly. He'd seen me at a window with a woman, but he'd only seen her from behind. It could have been either of them: Margarita, the cheap whore, or Dominique, the . . . other cheap whore, but also the woman he happened to love, who was to become Tamara's mother. The woman and I had gone through the steps that would transform her into a vampire – if only *I* had then been a vampire. He had seen it all and been able to do nothing. Over the weeks I had manipulated his mind into thinking first one thing, then the other. That the woman he'd seen was Dominique, then Margarita, then Dominique again. Now he could never know, because he could never believe that what I told him was the truth, whichever side I settled upon. I had given him the punishment of eternal indecision.

As I stared up at him from the icy water I chose a name at random. 'It was Margarita,' I shouted.

I yanked his leg, knocking him over and sending us both into the foaming water. We surfaced close to each other. It was hard to believe how little I cared for my own life as long as I had the opportunity of tormenting him.

'I can't lie to you any more, Lyosha,' I said. 'It was Dominique.' I always preferred the French form of her name.

I dived down, deciding I'd done enough and now intent on escape, but the current took me.

I crashed into the makeshift wooden bridge that Bonaparte's sappers had so recently built. I managed to crawl out of the water and clambered through the open slats of wood. Lyosha was already on the bridge, edging towards me. He was almost upon me when I leapt out into the water again on the downstream side of the bridge. I thought I'd escaped him, but he managed to grab a handful of my hair. I could scarcely feel the pain of it tugging against my scalp, I was so cold. I dangled there, the water up to my neck, his fingers entwined in my hair the only thing holding me. I'd heard the whole story before, of course, from Mama, who'd heard it from Aleksei himself, but it was a joy to actually witness it as a memory, even if not my own memory. There were details here that Mama could not have known. And to actually be able to see my grandfather, to look up into his face and to feel his hand on me, was something I had never dreamed possible. There was a look of righteous anger in his eyes that I knew had been in mine when I thought I had killed Iuda. We even shared the same failure in that respect.

'Tell me the truth!' he screamed.

'I have told you the truth,' I laughed.

'When?' he demanded.

'Often,' I said, revelling in my own ingenuity.

He pushed me under the water for a few seconds. The cold was all-consuming, but I knew this was not the end, not quite. Seconds later he pulled me up.

'Tell me!' he shouted again.

'You can't torture me, Lyosha. I have the ultimate protection that you'll never believe me. I've told you everything – not just everything that's true, but everything else as well. All I can offer you is the ultimate enlightenment; not just what is, but what could be. To know everything is to know nothing. What's the point in asking any more? What's the point in forcing it out of me? You might as well torture a coin and expect it to turn up tails.'

He pushed my head back under the water. That, I thought, would be it. However brilliant my plan had been, it would result

313

in my own death, and yet I cared nothing for that. But then he pulled me out again.

'You're slow today, Lyosha. Do you still think you can get the truth out of me?'

He paused and shook his head, then thrust his hand down again and me with it. This time I was certain it would be the end.

I raised my head and looked around the café. I did not want to know the end of the story, of Iuda's lucky escape. But the rest of it had been a joy. It gave me no pleasure to feel a sense of gratitude towards Iuda, but feel it I did. In the depths of my misery he had shown me some slight benefit that could come from this wretched existence. He had shown me my mother, whom I had not seen in forty years, and my grandfather, and others whose names I had only heard mention of. I'd seen a glimpse of Dmitry Fetyukovich, the man whose ambiguous attitude towards the *voordalak* I was beginning to emulate. Would Iuda show me Vadim and Maks too? And what of the greater prize? I hadn't entirely understood the conversation, but both of them had mentioned her. Would Iuda at last allow me, in this strange way, to meet my grandmother, Domnikiia?

It would put me in his debt, and that was not a pleasant situation to be in. I would have to ensure that I was not too keen to see what he could show me, that I did not allow him to manipulate me. If I could manage it, it would be I who used him.

I looked down at my plate. I'd finished my blini without being aware of it. Outside the door I could see the man in the leather coat who had been following us. He'd been joined by another. That was a small but significant victory over Iuda too. He'd thought I hadn't seen them, but I had, and had ignored them and managed to keep that knowledge from Iuda. It was a skill I would have to hone. I didn't think Iuda understood the significance of the leather coat, but I did. And I'd been warned.

I stood up and put a few notes down on the table to pay for my meal. Then I went to the door and stepped outside. The two of them had watched me through the glass as I crossed the café. The one on the left put his hand on my chest to stop me. I pushed against him, not with any hope of getting past, but out of anger at his impertinence. He said nothing. The other one put two fingers in his mouth and whistled down the street. A car that had been parked on the corner began to move and pulled up opposite us. Another man got out – more a boy; he couldn't have been older than twenty. He too was wearing the ubiquitous leather coat. He stood in front of me and his comrade dropped his hand from my chest.

'Mihail Konstantinovich Danilov?' asked the youth.

It was a moot point, but I gave him the simple answer. 'Yes.'

He moved quickly. I caught the glint of metal across his knuckles just before his fist buried itself in my stomach. I doubled up, pain and nausea filling my body, but he pulled me up by the hair so that he could speak to me.

'Welcome to the new Russia.'

CHAPTER XIX

THEY BUNDLED ME INTO THE CAR AND WE DROVE OFF. I WASN'T too badly hurt. The idea had been to shock me enough so that I wouldn't offer any resistance. They weren't to know I was intending to hand myself in. We went a little way down Sadovaya Street then turned left on to Gorohovaya. I was sitting in the back between two of them, but through the windscreen I could see the spire of the Admiralty building, marking the conceptual centre of the city. The three main arteries – Gorohovaya Street and Nevsky and Voznesensky Prospekts – all converged upon the Admiralty, and the Great Neva flowed past it. It was a reflection of how deeply Pyotr had valued the navy. Both Saint Isaac's, Petrograd's spiritual hub, and the Winter Palace, its seat of royal power, were near by, but it was to the military and specifically naval heart that all travellers were drawn.

We turned on to Admiralty Square and then immediately stopped. I recognized the building. It was on the corner of the block and so although the entrance we were using was on Admiralty Square, it was officially situated on the street we had just turned off: Gorohovaya Street 2 – not as infamous an address as Fontanka 16, but that was only because it had not had so long to establish itself. And yet this building shouldn't have been in use at all. It was only after the failed revolution of 1905 that the Ohrana – the tsar's secret police – had moved here from Fontanka 16. But the Ohrana had not lasted very long in its new home. After the revolution in February the Soviet had insisted on the organization's dissolution. Now, though, it seemed the Bolsheviks had chosen to resurrect it.

I was taken inside and up two flights of stairs to a windowless room. It was no different from any other government office. There was a desk with a leather chair on one side of it and a wooden one on the other. There were two telephones, an ashtray and some piles of paperwork. On the wall behind was a map of Petrograd. There was a pair of filing cabinets in the corner and beside them another door, which was closed. Everything but the desk and chairs had a thin layer of dust on it. The new regime had only just moved in.

They searched my pockets and put what they found on the desk. One of them listed the items on a piece of paper. Then they pushed me on to the wooden chair and cuffed my hands behind my back. They left me. It was ten minutes before anyone came in. He was in his thirties and dressed, as they all were, in the brown leather coat; his just a little longer than a jacket, but not long enough to be called an overcoat. He clearly styled himself on Trotsky: the same spectacles, the same carefully sculpted beard and moustache. His hair was slicked back with pomade, which somewhat tainted the image. A lit cigarette protruded from his lips. He sat down in the leather chair and studied the document he had come in with, then read through the list of my possessions that they had left for him. Finally he looked up at me.

'You are Mihail Konstantinovich Danilov?'

I said nothing.

'You will answer, please.'

I wondered why Danilov was reluctant to respond to so straightforward a question, particularly since he had already confirmed his identity outside the café. Then I realized; he did not because he could not. It was up to me.

'That's right, yes.'

'You live at Panteleimonovskaya Street 2 with Nadya Vadimovna Primakova and a servant Syevastyan Pyetrovich Obnizov?'

'Syevastyan Pyetrovich doesn't live with us any more.' I remembered Danilov telling Susanna about it. 'He's dead.'

The man opened a drawer in his desk and tutted. He

tried another and found a pencil with which he made the appropriate correction to the paper in front of him.

'And you were a member of the Fourth State Duma, until its dissolution?'

'I was.'

'A member of the Kadet party?'

I nodded, though the term meant nothing to me.

'When were you first elected to the institution?'

That I couldn't answer. 'I can't remember,' I said lamely.

He looked up, narrowing his grey eyes. 'I'd advise you to take this interview seriously. Your prospects for the future will not be promising if we determine you to be a counter-revolutionary.'

I almost chuckled, but managed to contain myself. I'd presumed that we were here because of the murders. I'd been surprised at how quickly the wheels of justice had moved. But this was nothing more than a general act of score-settling by the new regime. I was mildly impressed that Danilov had done anything in his life to merit such attention.

'About five years ago,' I said. It was a pure guess, but he seemed satisfied by it.

'And before that you were in the army?'

'That's right. I fought at Geok Tepe.' That was where I had first encountered Danilov. 'And against the Japanese.' That was where Danilov had known the colonel that I'd killed.

The man nodded. 'And after that you were one of the founders of the Military Air Fleet?'

'That's right.' I could only assume he wasn't trying to trick me.

He put down one sheet of paper and picked up another: the inventory of my possessions. He tapped the ash from his cigarette as he read, then began poking through the items where they'd been laid on the desk. He pushed the paper envelope of tablets towards me.

'What are these for?'

'I get chest pains.' I knew that well enough.

He wrote something down on the paper. 'You'd better keep them then,' he said.

'Aren't you worried I might kill myself – take them all at once?' Even as I spoke I realized it might be a good idea, if I could achieve it while my blood was still in Danilov's body.

'I couldn't give a shit.' He picked up the folded wad of bank-notes. 'Your money will be kept, of course.'

I said nothing.

'What about these three?' He indicated the razor, my double-bladed knife and Ascalon. 'Why are you carrying concealed weapons?'

'The streets are dangerous out there.' It was interesting that he had immediately identified Ascalon as a weapon.

He picked up the lance and examined it, rolling it between his fingers. 'This is an odd thing to have on you.'

I knew that I mustn't make too much of it. 'I got into a fight,' I explained. 'Just grabbed what came to hand.'

He continued to peer at it, then finally put it down and wrote again on the papers in front of him. Then he looked up at me.

'You'll be taken from here to a place of internment until such time as your fate can be determined. Your possessions will be kept, pending your possible release. Your relatives will be informed – I imagine that will be Nadya Vadimovna.'

I nodded. I could see no reason not to let her know of Danilov's humiliation.

'You're not going to string me up then?'

'The death penalty no longer exists in Russia. However, you can make things easier for yourself if you tell us the names of anyone else who has the same sympathies as you.'

I could offer nothing. 'Don't you know who the other members of the Duma were?' I asked.

'There's nothing wrong in itself with having been a member of the Duma. It's your support of the Provisional Government that raises problems – and your speech last summer denouncing Comrade Lenin.'

'I'm no Kornilovite.' I'd picked up the term from one of the leaflets I'd read and concluded it was a good thing not to be.

'That will be determined. But you must know those who are.'

319

Ordinarily I'd have thrown him a few names, just to stir up the waters, but I knew so little it was better to say nothing.

'No?' He stubbed out his cigarette in the ashtray. 'Very well.' He stood up and went to the door. As soon as he'd opened it the two thugs who'd brought me into the room came through. I noticed now that both of them had holsters on their belts. 'Take him,' said the man who had interviewed me, then returned to his chair.

They unlocked my handcuffs and stood me up, then fastened my hands behind my back once again. I went with them to the door.

'Comrade Danilov.' I turned. He was still in his chair, holding out his hand towards me. 'Don't forget your pills.'

I couldn't take them because of the cuffs. He stood and came over to me, then put the envelope into my pocket. The other two marched me out of the office and back the way we had come. Although the building was new to me, it seemed familiar. I had worked for the Third Section, based at Fontanka 16, during Nikolai I's reign, before setting up my own offices in Moscow. The passing of seventy years and the transfer of power from the old order to the new had made little difference to the way they worked. They took me down the stairs and then outside by a different door, at the side of the building. We emerged on to Gorohovaya Street and came to a halt.

'The car will be here in a moment,' one of them said. He was evidently new to the job, or he would not have been so polite.

'Where are we going?' I asked.

He seemed about to answer, but his comrade merely growled, 'You'll find out soon enough.'

A car rolled up. It might have been the same one we came in, but I couldn't tell. For the most part they looked identical to me. On the journey here I'd been thrilled at the new experience of riding in one of these vehicles. If I had been in a position to express myself I would have seemed in a merry mood for one who had just been arrested. To Danilov though it was a mundane activity.

But much as I might have enjoyed it, I didn't plan to partake

320

of the next leg of the journey. It seemed we were in for a long incarceration, by the end of which Danilov would be free of my blood. I doubted he would allow me to take all his pills at once. The more polite of my two escorts went to the car and opened the door, then began to climb inside in front of me. Now was my chance.

I pretended to stumble, but as I did so, pushed myself forward on to the car door, slamming it against my captor. His calf was caught between the door and the body of the vehicle and he let out a cry. Meanwhile the other one had let go of my arm and I began to run, heading as fast as I could down Gorohovaya Street. With my hands still restrained behind my back I had little prospect of getting very far. But that wasn't my plan.

'Stop, or I'll fire!'

The shout came from behind me. It was precisely what I'd hoped for. Ever since Dmitry had so cleverly pointed out what neither I, nor Danilov, nor Susanna had realized – that if I were to die now I would rise again as a vampire – the tables had been reversed. Now it was I who should seek death, and Danilov who should avoid it. I was sure he would be able to stop me in something so blatant as a leap from a high building, just as I had stopped him, but this might prove more fruitful.

On either side of me, pedestrians separated, not to allow me to pass, but to get themselves out of the line of fire. Ordinarily I'd have weaved from side to side, to make myself a more difficult target, but today I kept in a dead straight line. And I didn't run so very fast either, though Danilov's body could achieve no great speed even if pushed.

A shot rang out. I flinched, anticipating the feeling of the bullet entering me, but instead heard the ping of it hitting the brickwork of the building beside me. He'd got his eye in now. The fatal shot was only moments away.

I tried to stop and turn at the same time. My instinct was to raise my hands, but I knew that I couldn't. In the end, with the speed I was running at, none of it worked and I fell forward on to the pavement. My cheekbone banged heavily against the stone and at the same moment the sound of a second shot reached me. I sensed the bullet whistle overhead, but I was in no danger from it. I heard the sound of booted feet running towards me. I made no attempt to move. There was still the risk that Iuda's pretence of trying to escape had given them excuse enough to finish me there and then, with a shot to the back of the head, but I doubted they would risk it – not on a busy street like this, with so many witnesses.

Two pairs of feet came to a halt beside me. One of them kicked me in the ribs and I rolled over on to my back.

'Moron,' said a voice.

A hand grabbed the collar of my coat and began to drag me along the pavement. It had been a good idea of Iuda's; he'd been unlucky that the man was such a bad shot. I would bear it in mind. Iuda and I desired precisely the same thing – to die. I just wanted to delay it a little while. Being shot in the back while trying to escape wouldn't be such a bad way to go, when the time came.

We reached the car and I was hauled up to my feet. This time I climbed in obediently. Again I was squashed between the two figures. We drove along Admiralty Square, then turned left between the Admiralty and the Winter Palace to get on to the Palace Quay. I'd already guessed where we were going; now I could see it. The Peter and Paul Fortress sat there across the Neva, like a long shallow boat floating low in the water, the spire of the Peter and Paul Cathedral stretching up into the sky as its mast. Back in February the crowds had forced its gates to open and liberated the few prisoners inside. That had been a turning point in the revolution; our Bastille Day. Only three days ago it had turned its guns on the Provisional Government, and now it was being used to house the enemies of the new regime. Not just tsarists – though there would be a good many of those – but anyone who supported a form of government other than the one dictated to us by Lenin and Trotsky. They were right to arrest me; I *was* their enemy.

We crossed the Neva by the Troitsky Bridge. The fortress loomed ever larger. Before long we were on Petrogradsky Island.

Moments later we were on the much smaller Ioannovksy Bridge, which took us to the Ivan Gate of the fortress. I felt a certain irrational pride at being here. My grandfather, Aleksei, had been imprisoned within these walls after the Decembrist Uprising, as he waited to be sent into exile. On the other hand, Iuda had been held captive here for a while too. I'd been here myself, but only on business for the Duma and to visit the cathedral. I would have to get him to show me the ropes.

The driver got out and spoke to the sentry at the gate and soon we were let through. My cuffs were removed and I was handed over to the fortress guards. They might have been Bolsheviks too, but they wore the uniforms of regular soldiers. There was little doubt as to the side with which their sympathies would lie. I was taken to the Trubetskoy Bastion and walked along a grim corridor with windows on one side looking out on to a courtyard and solid wooden doors on the other. The walls were a dull grey for the most part, with a broad layer of maroon pretending to be a wainscoting. The ceiling was white. It was all carefully calculated to demoralize. About halfway along a guard sat at a table between two of the windows. He looked up as we approached.

'Danilov,' said one of my escorts.

The guard consulted his list and then searched through a ring of keys. I felt a disproportionate degree of outrage to know that my name was written down there. It proved that my fate had been discussed – had been determined – in my absence, hours, perhaps days in advance. I had walked through the streets of Petrograd a free man while they had known that I was no such thing. It was nothing new in Russia – the fate of the individual was not a matter for him to decide, but for the state. It was only chance that meant on this occasion I was happy with the decision.

The guard stood up and led us to a door. He unlocked it and I walked inside. The door slammed shut and I heard the key turn. It wasn't too awful; about twice the length of the camp bed that stood against one wall, and maybe four times as wide. There was a large, high, rectangular window that currently managed to fill the chamber with the light of the setting sun. As well as a bed there was a table, but no chair. The whole place smelled of bleach.

I lay down on the bed. I doubted I could have managed a better outcome if I'd planned it. What harm could Iuda do me now? What harm could he do Nadya? Locked up in this cell, we were both powerless. It wasn't inconceivable that I might remain here forever. Over the centuries there'd been enough men whom tsars had sent here who had never come out again. It wasn't the end that I would have chosen for my life, but of all the prospects I'd considered over the last few days, it seemed the most amiable. But I might not be here for ever. Exile was another ancient Russian tradition, though perhaps the Bolsheviks would shy away from it. Would Nadya want to follow me to Siberia – or wherever – as my grandmother, Domnikiia, had Aleksei? I couldn't allow it. Even far out there in the east I would still be sharing my existence with Iuda.

But death was a more likely outcome. I couldn't imagine that the repeal of the death penalty would last long under the Bolsheviks. There might be a trial, but I would stand by my beliefs – although that might not be so simple. Iuda would be speaking some of the time and would do whatever he could to keep us alive. Such ever-changing swings of opinion might lead them to think me mad, but even life in an asylum would be an acceptable outcome.

And whatever happened I would preserve my honour, at least in the eyes of those I cared about. Exiled or executed or left to rot here, it would be for standing up for what I thought was right. Even to be condemned as a madman wouldn't be too bad. The only risk was that some clue would connect me to the murders. Even so, we would hang – and I would know, as would the Lord, that my honour remained intact. Above all, Nadya would never learn my true fate, or discover who it was who had made love to her that night.

And if we were to be executed, for whatever crime, it would not be soon – Iuda's blood would have left me. If we died, we would die; both of us; I a little before my time, he long after his. I'd beaten him; just as my mother did; just as my grandfather did.

Danilov seemed quite confident of what he'd achieved. He had good reason to be. He'd considered all the obvious possibilities for our fate and found a way to see in each of them an outcome that favoured him more than me. That didn't leave me without hope. I no longer had the physical strength of a vampire, but I still had my wits. I'd been incarcerated in this gaol once before, and had left it a free man, without any resort to force, or threat, or violence.

But it seemed the gaolers had learned from their mistakes. This was not the cell I had been in before, by chance the same cell that Lyosha had occupied even longer ago. This was built much more recently. I looked around, but saw no pipes upon which I could tap messages to the outside world. And anyway, I had no friends out there that I might turn to. In all the world only Dmitry and Susanna even knew of my existence, and neither was likely to help me, not knowingly. On the other hand Danilov did have friends. He would not call on them for aid, but if the chance arose – if one visited while I possessed our body, or if I could write – I might petition them.

But Danilov would try to thwart me in whatever I attempted and had as good a chance of getting his way as I did. He had overlooked one thing, however. Whatever our fate, we would be together for some time – for the rest of his aging body's life as far as either of us could guess, however long that might be. We would share each other's thoughts. Did he really believe that that could ever be as unpleasant an experience for me as it was for him? So far he'd seemed to enjoy it – my recollections of members of his family that he had never known. And who was it that he still yearned to meet? His grandmother, Dominique. I would oblige him.

I would begin with our first encounter. I cast my mind back. We met, unsurprisingly given her profession, in a brothel, in Moscow, on Degtyarny Lane, delightfully named after the tar factory that once stood near by. I'd been inside, chatting to her colleague, Margarita. She'd been looking out of the window and saw the two of them arrive. She pulled back the bolts and opened the door. Standing outside were Lyosha and a pretty young thing I soon learned to be Dominique.

'Good evening, Aleksei Ivanovich,' I said.

He blanched, as well he might. He'd already become mistrustful of me. It must have horrified him to find me here, where he came to hide from the world.

'Aren't you going to introduce me to this delightful young lady?' I continued.

Lyosha said nothing, but she was not so reticent. 'I'm Dominique,' she said, holding out her hand. I bent forward to kiss it and noticed how Lyosha bristled as I did so. My plans against him weren't well formed at the time. I'd been intending to get at him through his wife in Petersburg – which I did too, eventually – but it was then that I realized how useful this woman might also be against him.

I saw her on a few other occasions and noted how, from behind, it was very difficult to tell her and Margarita apart. Then my mind turned to Shakespeare and I realized how the comedy of *Much Ado about Nothing* could so easily be transformed into the tragedy of *Othello*.

Even so, it took weeks before I had the chance to spring my trap. There were so many things that could have gone wrong, but I knew Lyosha well enough to understand how jealousy would consume him. It was easy to bribe Pyetr Pyetrovich – the brothel-keeper – to tell Lyosha that Dominique was not at home, and to inform me when he had seen Lyosha creep into the house opposite, where, as I had predicted, he would find himself a good viewpoint to peer across the street and into Dominique's room. Now the show could begin. It didn't matter which of the girls – Dominique or Margarita – participated, as long as he only saw her from behind. But that was easy enough to orchestrate. In the end I was happy to discover how willing each of them was, each for her own reasons. Had the evening been for my benefit I might have taken them both. But Lyosha could only be allowed to see one, and then not clearly.

By the time he arrived at his hiding place, both of us were in Dominique's room. The girl was naked, I stripped to the waist. We were standing close to the door, away from the window. I turned up the lamp so that he would be sure to see us, then kissed her lips before stepping back to take in the shapely naked curves of her enchanting body. Her long dark hair hung over her left shoulder, concealing one of her breasts. I let my eyes linger over her body, then returned my

326

gaze to her beautiful face. I'd had to make a choice between Margarita and Dominique and in the end I had chosen.

It was . . .

Dominique.

Suddenly Iuda's words made sense to me: his last words and his first words. The last words that I had perceived rather than heard, back in 1881, as he drank my blood in the tunnels beneath Malaya Sadovaya while the light of the Yablochkov Candle burned him to nothing. It was a desperate message that he had not quite been able to complete.

'Tell Lyosha. It was . . .'

And then the first word he had spoken as he awoke in my body in the Church on Spilled Blood. I'd almost forgotten, but he was merely finishing the sentence he had begun thirty-six years before.

'Tell Lyosha. It was Dominique.'

And even if he had completed it, I wouldn't have believed him. He couldn't be trusted on the matter, he'd made sure of that. The events he'd recalled at the Berezina proved it. He could have screamed 'Margarita' nine hundred and ninety-nine times and I would still not have believed him, for fear that on the thousandth he would mutter 'Dominique'.

But now I had stronger evidence – the evidence of Iuda's own memories, and he could not lie about those. Nor had he finished with his recollections.

He reached out and took Domnikiia's hands in his own. She was as beautiful as I had imagined her to be. Mama had always told me that she resembled the empress Marie-Louise. I'd looked at pictures, just so that I might know her better, and now that I saw her the resemblance was obvious, though Domnikiia was far more beautiful. Her face was a delight, her body perfection. She could barely have been nineteen at the time.

I put my hands to her waist and lifted her off the floor, feeling a twinge from my wounded arm, but she wasn't heavy. I pulled her towards me and she realized what I was trying to do. She put her arms round my neck to take some of her weight and wrapped her slender legs around me. I felt her breasts pressing against me and her silken hair between us caressing my skin. I felt the urge to run, tried to think of other things, but it was Iuda who controlled this memory, not I.

I carried her over towards the window. It was a cold night, but the curtains were open. I made sure that her back was all that could be seen, and tried to hide my face too as we kissed, knowing that a sudden revelation would be more shocking. I put my hands underneath her buttocks to take a little of her weight, but also to caress her. I pushed her up against the window and she flinched a little at the cold touch of the glass. I stepped away again, running my fingers along her spine. Then our lips separated.

'Stand up,' I whispered.

She unwrapped her legs and dropped to the floor, her hands still clasped around my neck, her eyes looking up into mine. I took a step back, knowing now that my face could be seen. I didn't hesitate. I gazed down at the curve of her neck and parted my lips. Her hair still hung over her shoulder, so I brushed it behind her. Then I descended upon her throat. I was long practised in imitating the actions of a vampire, and it was simple to make something that she perceived as merely a kiss seem to an observer – to Lyosha – to be the unmistakable bite of the *voordalak*. I pinched her flesh a little between my teeth, and ran my tongue against it, but I made sure I didn't break the skin. I looked out through the window into the night, knowing that Lyosha could see me, making sure he was aware that this was for his benefit – that he had caused this.

I did not remain very long like that, bent over her. I raised my head and she sat back on the windowsill, her arms stretched out on either side of her, her fingers curled around the lip of the wood. I reached into my pocket and took out my knife – my double-bladed knife. I closed my eyes and drew its twin points horizontally across my chest. The pain was minimal, but enough to excite me further. I felt the blood running down over my stomach.

'Go on,' I whispered. 'You promised.'

She looked unsure, but slid down from the windowsill and walked towards me. She bent her knees slightly to be at the right level. She placed one hand against my chest and another on my shoulder and pulled herself towards me. Still she kept her lips a few inches away from me. I put my hand on the back of her head and pulled her close. I felt her lips touch me, but they did not part. She had no taste for my blood, but it did not matter. I threw my head back and closed my eyes, mimicking ecstasy, then stared directly at where I knew Lyosha to be.

Domnikiia pulled away. I didn't resist. Our scene was finished. She took my hand and led me away from the window. I could have ended it then – what was the point now that we were unseen? But I had paid for more, and back then I was still human. She sat down at the foot of the bed and then began to crawl back up to the head. She lay there, one hand behind her head, one knee bent, the other straight.

I quickly removed my breeches and stood before her, now completely naked. I climbed on to the bed and crawled towards her. Soon I was above her, our faces close to one another. I kissed her and ran my hand across her body; down her side, across her belly and finally between her legs. She shivered as I touched her and a thrill ran through my body. We lay like that for several minutes until finally I moved my hand away and crawled on top of her.

She made no sound as I entered her. I tried to fight against the recollection, to focus on sight or sound, or on any sensation other than touch, but Iuda's memory was complete and detailed, as if he remembered every stroke of his body, every squeeze of her thighs, every scratch of her fingernails. And sight and sound were just as bad; he never took his eyes from her face, as if even then he had known how this memory might one day serve him, that one day he could use it to destroy Domnikiia's own grandson. I heard her moans and whether they were real or pretended made no difference to me. Finally I felt Iuda's ultimate pleasure, both physically, and in the knowledge that he was taking what belonged to Lyosha – and in the knowledge that he was showing it to me.

And at that moment, as had probably been the case back in 1812, he lost interest. His memory faded in an instant. I sat up. Iuda was gone from my mind, though I could sense that his presence still lurked. But for now I was once again in charge of my body and the memories that ran through my head were my own.

But the memory that came back to me was the most recent one.

It may have been second-hand, but it had become part of my past too. However I tried to expel such thoughts, all I could perceive was my grandmother's eyes looking up into mine, the taste of her skin, and the sensation of my body inside hers.

I stood up and staggered across the cell, then collapsed on to my knees. Tightness gripped my every muscle and my body began to convulse. For a moment I thought it was the same sensation I had just experienced in Iuda's mind, but this was different – a reaction to it. I vomited into the corner of the cell. There wasn't much, only the blini I'd had for lunch, but I continued to retch, with nothing more to bring up.

It wasn't simply the physical act that revolted me, nor the way that Iuda had managed to take the same trick he'd performed with Nadya and repeat it, a thousand times worse. The ultimate horror was the realization of the truth about Domnikiia. However loyal she might have been to him in later years, she had deceived Aleksei. She had played Iuda's game, and demonstrated what a *prostak* Aleksei was. At the moment of his darkest need, she had sided with his enemy. Everything that my grandfather had ever believed about her – everything my mother and I had ever believed – was destroyed.

MARCH

CHAPTER XX

IT MUST HAVE BEEN AN ENORMOUS EXPLOSION. FROM THE DIRECTION the sound came it was on the other side of the Neva, but it was still deafening, and enough to make the walls of the cell shake. Seconds later came another blast, and then a third and a fourth. Beforehand we'd heard the sound of biplanes, and could still hear them, between the explosions. It was difficult to make out what direction they were going, but the sound of the bombs moved progressively eastwards, and became quieter, muffled by the fortress itself.

The Germans had tried raiding Petrograd from the air before – from aeroplanes and Zeppelins – but they had never been able to get close enough. We'd heard from the guards that day by day the Front was approaching the city. Now it seemed they were near enough to strike. The guards saw it as typical of German treachery to advance even as Trotsky negotiated a peace, but to us it seemed like good politics – forcing the best terms out of the enemy. Neither of us was happy at how often we found ourselves in agreement over such matters.

I got up off the bed and went to stand beneath the small window, listening to the biplanes' engines. The sound began to get louder again and it became obvious that the aircraft were coming about. They might be simply returning to their airfield, but they could just as well be taking the opportunity to make a second pass. Petrograd had little hope of defending itself against a strike from the air. There was no sound of gunfire. The city had had artillery to protect it against this sort of attack since the early days of the war, but it had proved ineffective even on those rare occasions it was called upon. Major-General Boorman had been responsible for it, but he wasn't given enough resources to do the job properly. I'd worked alongside him in the early months; it made sense, given my expertise.

It was mid-February now, as far as we could reckon. I'd begun by scratching figures on the wall to mark the passing days, but Iuda deemed it a waste of time. He was, he felt, quite capable of remembering what day it was. What he wasn't capable of, despite his confidence when we arrived, was escape. He hadn't even managed to formulate a plan. He thought about it almost constantly, but without coming to any conclusion. Sometimes I managed to fall asleep while he would remain alert, considering the possibilities, but when I awoke I would discover that nothing had changed and that he had devised no ingenious mechanism whereby we might gain our liberty.

I was content with it. If we were to rot here, then that was a better outcome than I had at times feared. I knew that I could never be with Nadya again, but her letters were some consolation. I was allowed to write to her within a few days of my incarceration and explain my predicament. I begged her not to visit me and she complied. She wrote a letter to me every day, though I did not receive them every day. I would get them in batches, once or twice a week. They were opened, of course, but Nadya and I had both lived long enough under the tsar to know that letters to and from prisoners would be read, and there was no reason to suppose things would be any different under Lenin.

Try as I might, I could find no way of conveying to her the real fate that had befallen me – worse than imprisonment; my conjoining with Iuda. It would have been a challenge to formulate that news in a way that would have made it past the censors, but I never even got as far as that hurdle. I simply did not have the guts to tell her.

And yet constantly I feared that someone else might tell her instead, that Iuda's consciousness might grasp my hand as it moved across the page and direct it to write vile lies to my beloved – or worse to write the truth. But my fear went unrealized. Iuda never tried to influence what I wrote. It wasn't out of kindness, he made that perfectly clear. He was just keeping his powder dry, knowing that one day a few false words from him could utterly destroy her – and me. There was another factor, though; we didn't even know what his handwriting would be like. Was it bound to the body or to the mind? He was itching to find out, not least from the point of view of scientific curiosity, but he never did, aware that such information would either put my mind at ease or make me more wary of him.

The worst of it was, I could not even picture Nadya now in her daily routine. I could not imagine where she was and what she was doing as I lay inactive upon the bed. The problem lay not in the strange, shared world of my mind. It was simply down to the fact that I had no idea where she lived. Susanna knew our old address, and that was dangerous. I couldn't imagine what kind of vengeance she might seek, or even if she would bother, but she knew of our house on Panteleimonovskaya Street – she had lived there – and so Nadya was in danger. I'd told her to find somewhere else to live and then, realizing that it was better to keep everything from Iuda that I possibly could, I'd instructed her not to tell me her new address. I sent my letters to our former neighbour, Vera Glebovna, to forward to Nadya. So far she had not failed in her duty.

Of late I'd had some slight consolation. Nadya had told me in one of her letters how on every Friday evening she came and stood on the Palace Bridge, a little after sunset, and looked out towards the Trubetskoy Bastion, where she knew my cell to be. Today was Saturday – if Iuda's reckoning was right – and so as usual the previous evening I had sat and faced south and even though all that had confronted me was a stone wall I had been able to see Nadya there, with Polkan sitting obediently beside her.

And there had been other ways to occupy my mind. Iuda delighted in remembering events from his long, vile life – events that would be of particular interest to me. He did not always dwell on his victories, but sometimes instead revealed memories that were pleasant to me. It was a delicate balance that he struck. He worked out that I could ignore him if I really tried, so he had to tempt me in. And I was willingly tempted. Anything was worth it to see, almost as if real, my mother and my grandfather. I had no further interest in Domnikiia. He had more memories of Mama, and few that were unpleasant to me. They had worked alongside each other for the Third Section in Moscow for over a year, for most of which Mama had harboured no suspicions of him, and therefore he had found no reason to harm her. He didn't shy from reminding me that during that time she had been working in a brothel, but I knew it already. Neither did he ever fail to note, for my benefit, that it was the same building – the same brothel – in which he and Domnikiia had tricked Aleksei another forty years before. In his recollections, every time he passed by, he looked up at that window.

Of Aleksei he had fewer memories. For such enemies it was surprising how little time they had spent together – how rarely their paths had crossed. They had only met on a few occasions in Moscow, and the strange thing was that my interest lay almost as much in how the city had changed as it did in seeing my grandfather. Iuda particularly liked to recall an occasion when he tricked Aleksei into meeting him at a lonely, snow-covered crossroads somewhere south of the city, where the dead body of a soldier hung from a gibbet. I was as surprised as Aleksei must have been when the body sprang to life and grabbed him, revealing itself to be one of the *oprichniki*. But even on that occasion Aleksei had triumphed – if escape can be counted as victory. Iuda liked to replay the time when he had been making love to Aleksei's wife, Dmitry's mother, Marfa, and Aleksei had walked in on them, but he enjoyed it less than the memories of his time with Domnikiia – both because Marfa was not such an attractive woman, and because the fact of her infidelity hurt Aleksei less.

His favourite was to think of the weak, pathetic, aged Aleksei, seated in a bath of freezing water as Iuda dunked his head beneath the surface. But he always cut that memory short. It didn't matter – I knew what happened next: how Iuda had been defeated by my mother, how, with Dmitry's help, she had locked him in a cell beneath the Kremlin, and stolen a few precious hours with her father before his death.

But that was not a memory; the events had merely been recounted to me by Mama. I had few memories of my own that would be of any appeal to Iuda. He had no interest in anyone other than himself and for all I had dedicated my life to his destruction, we had only met twice – though I had observed him secretly on other occasions. I was happy to remind him of his incarceration beneath Geok Tepe, strapped to a wooden chair that was all he had known for three years; of his being captured and bound by Dmitry, his head locked in a scold's bridle, and then of his being bundled into a crate. I loved to recollect the fight between him and Zmyeevich in Saint Isaac's, when his body had been burned until almost nothing of it remained. Most of all I liked to relive the moment when I finally defeated him, as every molecule of his body had been reduced to ash by the light of the Yablochkov Candle. But even then, the memory could hurt me almost as much as it did him. I could not recall it without also hearing his words: 'Tell Lyosha, it was . . .'

The sound of the biplanes became louder once again. They had begun dropping bombs on their return sweep; closer now – almost overhead. I stood close to the wall and inclined my ear towards the window above. They sounded like Friedrichshafens, although I couldn't be sure. They'd brought out a new model, the G.III, at the beginning of 1917, but I'd never observed one. Then I heard the strangest sound: an explosion, close by, but not like any of the others. There was cracking and splintering, followed by an enormous roar. It took me a moment to realize that one of the bombs had landed on the frozen river, shattering the ice. I could only pray that no one had been trying to cross. Even if they weren't caught by the blast, they wouldn't last long in the freezing water. I was reminded of Iuda and Aleksei on the Berezina.

And then it was as if the cell wall had hit me in the face. I bounced off it and fell back on to the cold stone floor. That blast had come from very near by – the bomb must have detonated somewhere in the fortress. I'd been thrown forwards and then back. I put my hand to my face and felt blood on it, but it wasn't serious. There was still hope, though. The fortress made a clear target for any crew with the last of their payload to dispose of. Perhaps in a few seconds there would be a direct hit. The roof would cave in and my . . . *our* miserable existence would be ended once and for all. And there was nothing Iuda could do about it.

*

I leapt to my feet and strode to the door. It took no more than a moment to cross the cell. Whatever Danilov might think, there was *something* I could do about it. I banged on the door with the flat of my hand and shouted.

'Guard! Guard!'

I pressed my face close to the grille and looked up and down the corridor, but could see no one. What would they care anyway? They didn't have the brains to make a decision for themselves. They'd been told to keep us here and even if the place were in flames that was what they would do until they were instructed otherwise. Even so, I was surprised to get no response, not even a cheery, 'Shut your fucking mouth, you filthy *burzhooi*.'

I went back to sit on the bed. I was hungry. It was then that I realized we'd not been given any breakfast. We'd not seen hide nor hair of a guard since the previous night. Even before the bombs had started dropping the whole place had been unnervingly quiet. I heard one more explosion in the distance, and listened as the sound of the machine – Danilov had called it a biplane – faded. Then all was silence. I went over and banged on the door again, but didn't shout this time. Still there was no response. I stood with my ear at the grille for five minutes, but didn't hear so much as a footstep.

It seemed that Danilov's wish had been fulfilled. They'd left us here to rot.

It was the evening of the following day before we heard any other sound. No guards had looked in on us; we still hadn't been fed, though we'd had the jug of water that they'd left us two nights back. It was already dark, but that did not mean it was late – we were still a few weeks short of the equinox. Brisk footsteps sounded in the corridor outside. I fancied I caught the light tapping of a shorter pair of legs trying to keep up. They stopped outside our cell and I heard keys jangle and then turn in the lock. The door opened.

The figure in the doorway – filling the doorway – was sporting the familiar leather coat that marked him out as a Bolshevik.

I didn't bother to take more than a glance at him. A few of them had visited over the months, asking the usual questions about who else I knew to be plotting counter-revolution. When Iuda had been asked those same questions, he refused to answer because he knew nothing. I had a few ideas, but I wasn't going to help them – not least because I had no desire to be released for good behaviour.

'Mihail?'

I turned. It was Dmitry. My legs weakened at the shock of seeing him – of seeing any familiar face. Somewhere inside me I felt a twinge of revulsion at being so happy at the sight of a creature such as him. Revulsion too to realize that he had proved one of my few true friends in the entire world. I rushed over to him, stumbling as I did, and found my arms cradled in his as he helped me to stay upright. I could find no words with which to greet him.

'Mihail?' he asked again, emphasizing the question.

I nodded. 'For now,' I said.

'Who's the president of the United States?'

'Woodrow Wilson,' I replied.

He eyed me suspiciously. 'You might have picked that up from somewhere. You've been in here a long time.'

'Does it matter?'

He shook his head.

'What *is* the date, anyway?'

'The third of March,' he said. 'Sunday.'

I let out a brief laugh. For all his genius, Iuda had been way off.

'What?'

'I'd thought it was still February.'

Now Dmitry laughed. 'It is, in a way. Everything's changing. They've switched to Western dates. No silly debates; they just decreed it. January the thirty-first was followed by February the fourteenth. It makes so much more sense. It'll be the metric system next, mark my words.'

Dmitry should have possessed a better sense of history than I did, but to me his enthusiastic words smacked of the more lunatic extremes of the French Revolution. 'You sure today's not the tenth of Brumaire?' I asked sourly. Somewhere at the back of my mind Iuda corrected my random guess at a Revolutionary date; today, apparently, would have been the twelfth of Ventôse.

'It's nothing like that. This is just sensible; doing the same as everyone else.'

'You're evidently working for them now.' I indicated his coat.

'I work for no one,' he snapped. It reminded me – or perhaps Iuda – of years earlier, when Dmitry had denied working for Zmyeevich. 'It's convenient. And you were right. These aren't the offspring of the Decembrists, but they could turn that way, with a little guidance.'

'Is there a date for the elections yet?'

'Elections?'

'To the Constituent Assembly?' It had been promised and then postponed and then promised again half a dozen times since the revolution. When it happened it would be the first truly democratic institution ever to govern Russia.

'The elections have already taken place.' Dmitry avoided my gaze as he spoke.

'And?'

'The assembly convened on January the fifth. It sat for thirteen hours. Then the Bolsheviks dissolved it.' He couldn't conceal his embarrassment at the announcement, but forced himself to be positive. 'The Soviets are democratic bodies too. They'll do just as well.'

He was whistling in the dark, but I had no desire to argue with him.

'I hope you've not come here to set me free,' I said. 'Let me assure you now, while I can, that this is by far the best place for me to be. Iuda may tell you differently, if he gets the chance, but don't believe him.'

'I brought you these,' he said, holding out his hand. He didn't deny his reason for being here.

I instantly recognized what he was offering me. I snatched it off him with unnecessary haste. The silver box itself was of little interest. I opened it to examine the tablets within. I counted; there were seventeen of them. Despite the undemanding regimen of the gaol we'd had a number of attacks; sometimes when I was at the helm, sometimes Iuda. It had become almost as instinctive for him as it was for me to reach into our right pocket when the constriction came. We'd both tried not to use up the limited supply we'd been able to bring here, but there hadn't been many to start with and the guards ignored our pleas for more when they'd finally run out.

'Where did you get these?' I asked. It had been so long that I couldn't remember when I had last held the silver box.

'They were at the Church on Spilled Blood, along with your coat and papers. I went back there to tidy up after you; to make sure there were no clues leading to you. And . . .' He paused.

'And what?'

'To see if there was anything left of what they needed for the ceremony.'

'Was there?'

He shook his head. 'Nothing. I take it you've hidden Ascalon somewhere safe.'

'Who's to say I haven't destroyed it?'

'Have you?' He moved his head slightly, his stare becoming a little more confrontational.

'No. It's safe.' In truth I had no idea. I'd not seen it since they took it from me at Gorohovaya Street, but there was no reason to suppose it wasn't still there. 'You've been holding on to these for a long time,' I said, showing him the pillbox before slipping it into my pocket.

'For a long time I thought it better not to come and see you at all.'

'What changed your mind?'

'The city's being evacuated,' he announced. There was no inflection to what he said. It was simply a statement of fact.

'What?'

'The Germans are getting too close – there's nothing we can do to defend it. Better to leave them with just empty buildings.'

'Or burn the city down – like Rostopchin did.' I understood what I was talking about, but the thought was not mine. Iuda had been there, had seen it, though in a different century and a different city, when Moscow had been abandoned and then put to the flame, just to prove to Bonaparte that he had won nothing. Since then no enemy army had come close to the Russian heartland – until now.

Dmitry didn't notice the sarcasm in my voice. 'It's been suggested, but it shouldn't be necessary. The Germans will make peace – Trotsky's sure of it – but they could get better terms if they held the capital. They won't bother marching as far as Moscow, even if that's where the government's based.'

'So Moscow's going to be the capital again, after all these years?' That dated back to long before even Iuda was born.

'Only temporarily.'

'Even so, Nikolai gets what he always wanted.'

'How do you mean?'

'He hated having Petrograd as the capital.' He wasn't the only tsar to feel that way. For some it was too Western-looking, and deliberately so. Pyotr had wanted a European capital for a European nation. Every reactionary tsar preferred Moscow – every progressive one Petersburg. The move was suggestive of where the new regime stood.

'They'll come back here once there's peace. The Germans will be straight off to fight in the west.'

'In that case, I think I'll take my chances here, thanks all the same.' I went and sat resolutely down on the bed, making it clear I had no plans to go anywhere.

'And what about Nadya?'

I turned away from him. I could hardly be surprised that he had worked out where my true concerns would lie, but it was still disconcerting to discover that he cared what became of either of us. I could only thank the Lord that he did. By hiding away here I'd put myself in a position where I could do nothing to help Nadya. I couldn't even judge how serious things really were.

'I can't be with her,' I insisted. 'You know that.'

'You think she'll leave without you?'

He was right, but still I looked for another way out. 'Are things really as bad as all that?' I asked lamely.

'The Germans are less than a hundred and thirty versts away. With the city abandoned they could be here in hours. You've heard what they do to civilian prisoners – especially the women.'

I turned to face him. 'That's just propaganda.'

342

'Well, that's all right then, isn't it?'

I was a fool even to try to argue. At any moment things might change and it would be Iuda making the decisions. He was certain to choose to leave, but after that it was unlikely he'd offer any support to Nadya. But there was still one problem to be overcome.

'I don't even know where she's living now.'

'I do,' Dmitry replied.

We had barely stepped through the door of the cell when I discovered that I was once again in command of our actions. I said nothing to Dmitry. He led us out of the fortress to the west. It seemed he had the authority to do it; no one even bothered to challenge him. There can't have been more than a dozen guards left in the place. We stepped down on to the frozen Kronversky Channel for the short walk over to Petrogradsky Island.

'Where are we going then?' I asked, hoping the question sounded as if it came from Danilov.

'She's got an apartment on Fonarniy Lane. It's not much, but it does for them.'

'Them?'

'Her and the dog,' said Dmitry. 'You're Iuda now, aren't you?'

I smiled to myself. He was very astute. 'For the time being,' I said. 'Why don't we just cut across the ice?' We were heading west along the bank of the Kronversky Channel; it wasn't the fastest route.

'You'll see.'

A few moments later I understood. We cleared the fortress and the view across to the far bank of the Neva opened up. Where I had expected to see a smooth, snow-covered expanse instead lay a rugged landscape of scattered boulders – boulders made not of rock but of ice, like icebergs breaking off from a glacier, except they were not free to float away. They would have been difficult enough to scramble over, but I knew that that was not the real danger.

'It's from the air raid yesterday,' said Dmitry. 'Even if we could get past, the ice still won't have frozen properly. We could easily fall through. And there's always the chance of another raid.'

'It'll be a long way round if we stick to the bridges.'

He gave me a look of confusion, but said nothing. I soon understood why. After only a few more minutes of walking I saw stretching ahead of us a wooden bridge that I'd never seen before, spanning the Lesser Neva just at the point where it split from its broader sister. We crossed it and arrived on Vasilievskiy Island, close to the stock exchange. There had always been a need for a bridge at that point, but it was another sign of how much had changed in the years I had been . . . absent.

The streets were busy, and we seemed to be going against the flow. Every form of transport that could be drummed into service had been. The modern motor cars were few and far between; I could only guess that that was because they were the most desirable and so had been taken first, as well as moving fastest. Around us even horse-drawn carts were a rarity. Those that there were had been piled high with crates and cases, so that the horses strained and had to be pulled or beaten by their owners to get them to move. People tried to clamber on to some of the emptier wagons, but soon gave up, realizing they could travel faster under their own steam, on foot. It was their property that needed transporting. Mostly, though, the streets were clogged with small handcarts, pulled by one or two people – generally the men of the family, dragging their few possessions behind them as their wives and daughters walked alongside.

I'd seen it all before – a century before, and then not in Petrograd but in Moscow. Then it had been the threat of a French invasion that had set the people to flight; this time it was the Germans they feared. Then what had seemed like a humiliating retreat had in fact been a stroke of tactical genius. I doubted that the same applied here. For a start, Russia was failing to make use of her greatest ally – winter. In Moscow it had been winter that had closed the trap which the Russians had set. Now winter was almost over. If the Germans arrived, it would be to witness the first green shoots of spring. And I wasn't too sure just how empty they'd find the city. I couldn't really judge from the hordes that we passed, but my guess was that there would be many in Petrograd who would welcome the arrival of a foreign occupier. For anyone with a little money it would mean a much better life than they had under the Bolsheviks. The Germans might even restore the tsar.

But there was one other difference from Moscow in 1812. Not a single wounded soldier was part of the retreat – at least not that I saw. There had been no Borodino, no heroic last stand. This was not a military retreat, it was a political one; a government fleeing because it could not muster its own defence, and a population scurrying after them for fear of being left behind.

We walked along the embankment, close to the university, close to the house where I had killed the professor and his wife. I glanced at Dmitry, but he gave no sign of associating the crime with me, if he'd even heard of it. I didn't need to mention it. I recalled standing at that high window and trying to step forwards at Danilov's volition, only to thrust myself back moments later under my own will. Neither of us had realized it then, but if we *had* died then thanks to the blood of my erstwhile body that ran in our veins we would have risen again as a *voordalak*. Now that was no longer the case. I could only guess at how long it took for the alien blood to disperse, but our time in the fortress had been more than enough. Now I had to be wary of death; and that meant that Danilov would welcome it, though not just yet – not while his beloved Nadya was in danger. And she was in danger – more so than he realized.

'Come on!' I said to Dmitry, quickening my pace. He glanced at me and began to walk with long strides, so fast that I could barely keep up. There was nothing to be gained by telling him that I was now myself again. Iuda's thoughts had not been clear, but they frightened me. I knew that Nadya was at risk from the advancing Germans. That was reason enough for me to fear for her, but Iuda seemed to understand that there was some other,

345

even greater threat to her. And yet how could he know anything that I did not?

We crossed the Moika and then walked along its bank, before turning inland again. Soon we were on Maksimilianovsky Lane. 'You remember this place?' I asked.

Dmitry nodded, then looked up at one of the houses. 'It's where Luka used to live.' There was a weariness to his voice. I knew how he felt, though it must have been worse for him. Between us – Dmitry, Iuda and myself – we had lived for over three hundred years, and all spent much of our time in Petrograd. I was the youngest, and even for me the memories weighed heavily; memories like those of Luka, my half-brother, who had been a member of the People's Will – and murdered by them. How much more profound must the sensation have been for Dmitry and Iuda? It was a banal question: 'You remember this place?' I could have asked it on almost any street in the city and for at least one of us – often for all three – it would have meant something: a petty victory or a minor defeat. In the end all that those years amounted to were the three of us here together; Iuda and I inescapably bound, Dmitry through some sense of guilt or familial loyalty that I would never fathom.

We turned the corner into Fonarniy Lane and walked south past a couple of houses. Dmitry led us through an archway and into a courtyard. The *dvornik* was not at his post, and the main door stood open.

'Where?' I asked.

'Top floor,' said Dmitry.

We went through the door and he bounded up the steps two at a time, but with surprisingly little noise. He was by his nature a hunter. I followed more slowly, eager as I was to see Nadya; I hoped desperately to still be myself when I finally set eyes upon her. Dmitry was waiting for me on the top landing. He indicated a door. I reached out to turn the handle, but then hesitated. It felt like an intrusion. This might have been Nadya's home, but it was not mine. Instead I raised my hand and rapped on the wooden door.

There was no response. I tried again, but still there was nothing.

'You're sure this is the right place?' I asked.

346

Dmitry nodded. He leaned forwards and listened intently, looking puzzled. Seconds later I could hear what he did, and could make more sense of it. It was the sound of claws scampering across the wooden floor.

'It's Polkan,' I said.

Now he was scratching on the other side of the door. I banged harder and shouted, 'Nadya?' Polkan's claws scrabbled more frantically, but there was no human response. I tried the handle, but the door was locked.

'Step back,' said Dmitry.

I did as I was told. 'Careful of the dog,' I said. Polkan wasn't so well trained that I could tell him to stay back.

Dmitry took hold of the knob, then swung his shoulder against the door. It seemed so slight a movement, but it carried an enormous strength. With a sound almost like the report of a bullet the frame splintered and broke away. The door only moved a couple of inches before Dmitry's hand restrained it. It was an impressive exhibition of controlled power. Polkan began to bark in short, aggressive yaps. Dmitry opened the door fully, as if it had never been locked, and stepped inside. I followed.

As soon as he saw me, Polkan fell silent. He studied me for a moment, then trotted towards me, his tail wagging. I knelt down and stroked his snout, letting him lick my hand. It was a more friendly greeting than last time we'd met. Perhaps in the intervening months his memory of me had faded so that he could no longer perceive the subtle distinction between what I had been and what I had become. Perhaps I'd simply learned to become more at ease with my condition, and so he was more at ease with it too.

'Where's Mama?' I asked him. 'Where's Nadya?'

He turned and ran down the hallway. I followed him. There was a strange, unpleasant smell about the place that took me a moment to recognize: dogshit. Polkan was normally well-behaved in that respect, so he must have been left alone for some time for this to happen. I couldn't see anything, but he would have gone to some dark corner to do it. He turned left through a doorway. By the time I entered he was already sitting on the bed, looking pleased with himself. There was every indication that it was

Nadya's room – I recognized so many of the things she liked to keep closest to her. How could I miss them? They were scattered across the floor. Every drawer had been pulled open and turned out. The place had been ransacked.

'Mihail! Come here!'

I followed the sound of Dmitry's voice, out across the hall and into another room – evidently the living room. I looked around; it was in the same state as the bedroom. Dmitry stood in the middle of it, ignoring the detritus around him. He raised his hand and pointed ahead of him. 'Look.'

I turned. His finger was stretched out in the direction of the wall above the mantelpiece. One might have expected to find a picture or a mirror hanging there, but there was nothing. The wall was blank but for three words scrawled on it in black, probably using coal from the fire. It was a short message, but there was absolutely no question as to who it was from, or who it was to:

Bring Me Ascalon

CHAPTER XXI

'IS SHE STILL AT SAINT ISAAC'S?' I ASKED. 'SUSANNA, I MEAN.'
'How should I know?'
I turned to look at him. It didn't matter whether he knew or not. She'd hardly have gone into hiding, not while I had what she wanted. 'She *must* be there,' I said.

'She could have written that weeks ago.'

I shook my head. 'It can't be more than a few days. Polkan's not starving.'

'You're going to take it to her then?'

I remained silent, thinking.

'Let me do it,' he said. 'It'll be safer. Just tell me where you've hidden it. I'll go and get it.'

'No. It's all we've got to bargain with. I'll go and see her, tell her where to find it – once Nadya's safe.'

'Ascalon may not be the only thing she's interested in. It could be a trap.'

'She doesn't give a damn about me.'

'Not you – Iuda. She wants revenge. And she won't care that you'll suffer as much as he does.'

'She can't do a thing until she's got Ascalon,' I said. 'God knows why it matters so much to her.'

'Iuda might have some idea.'

'If he does, he's not telling me.'

'We'll just have to wait then, won't we? Till he comes back.'

'I'm not waiting.' I made for the door.

349

The dog insisted on walking beside me all the way, quite oblivious to the change in my nature that had occurred soon after we left the apartment. It still limped with its front right paw, just as when I'd first encountered it. It wasn't a long walk to Saint Isaac's, but it gave me time enough to think. I had some guesses as to what Susanna might want with Ascalon, but I couldn't be sure. The only simple fact was that it was stained with blood. If legend was true then that was the blood of the dragon that Saint George had slain. It was equally possible that it was Zmyeevich's own blood, or that of one of his victims. If it did belong to Zmyeevich then it gave another chance for his resurrection. If that of the dragon, then who could guess what might be achieved? Clearly Susanna knew better than I did – she had heard the truth directly from Zmyeevich's lips.

None of it mattered. My main aim had been to get out of the Peter and Paul Fortress, and that had been achieved. Susanna could have Ascalon for all I cared and could use it to resurrect Zmyeevich if she wanted – or even the dragon itself. I wasn't going to put my life at risk either to help her or to hinder her. Dmitry was right – I'd be a fool to just walk in there. Susanna wanted revenge upon me almost as much as she wanted Ascalon. All she had now was Nadya, and what did I care for her? It wasn't as though our one night together left me with any burgeoning affection. If I could simply get away then Susanna would have nothing. I might even be able to break into the building on Gorohovaya Street and get Ascalon myself, not that I had any use for it with Zmyeevich dead. But did I need a use for it? As I'd explained to Dmitry, I didn't make plans, I made moves, and taking Ascalon seemed like a better move than leaving it.

But Dmitry was still my immediate problem. He was stronger than me and faster than me, and he was intent on fulfilling Danilov's wish of confronting Susanna. I fancied I understood his motivation a little better than Danilov did. I knew what it was like to be a vampire, and I knew that while much of the former human was stripped away, there was a core that remained. Whatever drove the man – obsessed him – might also, with some dark twist to it, drive the *voordalak*.

With me it had been my scientific curiosity, with him his bizarre sense of honour. I should have guessed it from the moment he kicked me into that dungeon beneath the Kremlin. There weren't many honourable vampires out there, but not many had been tricked into the choice of becoming one in the way Dmitry had. And there were other currents that ran within him, not least his ties to Zmyeevich and how he had fought to sever them.

There was one obvious way I could be free of him, by changing my mind – or changing Danilov's mind – and accepting his offer to fetch Ascalon himself. There would be the bonus of knowing how he would suffer to be in contact with an item so redolent of his former master. But if I did, I couldn't be sure I'd ever see him or it again. A better plan would be to send him on a wild goose chase, allowing me to avoid a meeting with Susanna and giving me ample time to rescue Ascalon myself. I'd be out of the city – out of the country – before either of them knew they had been cheated.

We were just crossing Saint Isaac's Square. It was more crowded here than it had been elsewhere. People were heading for the railway stations, all of which were to the south and east of the city. Again we were going against the flow. I looked across at Dmitry.

'I think we can do better than this,' I said.

'What do you mean?'

'I mean we can have it all. We can save Nadya and keep Ascalon out of Susanna's hands.'

'How?'

'You go and get Ascalon. It's at our old house. I'll go to Susanna and tell her where to find it. I'll make something up, obviously, but I'll walk free with Nadya and by the time Susanna realizes what's wrong, we'll all be long gone.'

Dmitry stopped and nodded thoughtfully. 'Sounds like a good idea. I've only one question.'

'What's that?'

'Who wrote *The Cherry Orchard*?'

I made a run for it, but he was too quick. His hand grabbed my wrist tighter than a vice. He walked briskly across the

351

square, pulling me along like a reluctant child. There was nothing I could do to resist him.

'I think we'll stick with the original plan, shall we? And if I were you I wouldn't do too much to remind Susanna of just who you are.'

We were at the manhole now, close to the southwest corner of the cathedral. Dmitry pulled the cover up without relaxing his grip on my wrist. The dog peered into the darkness and began to bark. It walked gingerly down the iron steps. If this was the route by which its mistress had been brought here then perhaps it could smell her.

Dmitry pushed me down after it. He was forced to let go of me and I knew that I might have a chance. The sewers below led in every direction, and I could easily elude him. But the moment passed in an instant and I felt his hand gripping me by the back of my collar. There was no chance that I could struggle free. Danilov's physical frailty was proving to be to his advantage.

Through the open hatchway a little light shone down from the streetlamps above. It was not enough to see very far, and I knew that the path would soon lose all illumination. As a *voordalak* Dmitry would be better used to the darkness, but even he could not manage without any light whatsoever. He reached into his pocket and took out an electric torch much like the one Danilov had used. He handed it to me.

'Turn it on,' he said.

I did as I was told and shone the beam towards the gap at the top of the wall. The dog began to bark loudly. I kicked at it but its reactions were too fast. It stood a few feet away, continuing its noise.

'Shut it up,' I hissed to Dmitry.

'Why?'

'It'll give us away.'

'So what? We're coming to talk to them.'

He squatted down and hugged his arms around my knees before bringing himself upright and raising me to the level of the dark gap that led to the passages beneath the cathedral.

'Climb through,' he said.

352

I had no option but to obey. I crawled along and dropped down into the corridor beyond. It would take Dmitry a few seconds to catch up with me, but I wasn't going to try to escape him now. I knew what lay ahead, perhaps just after the next bend in the tunnel, and so for the moment Dmitry might be my only hope of protection. He landed softly beside me. Behind us I could still hear the muffled sound of the dog's barking, but mercifully the creature was unable to climb the wall and follow us.

The doorway formed by the bottom of the spiral staircase was open. We went through and along to the chamber beneath Senate Square that I had unearthed so many years before. The door was open. I went in first, followed by Dmitry.

Susanna turned as we entered, smiling broadly. It was not an expression that I had ever seen her use when I had known her in life. She had smiled, to be sure, out of amusement or happiness, but this was the forced, affected smile of victory. I had used it myself often enough. It did not suit her. She leaned back against the well in the centre of the room, her hands resting against it on either side of her. I noticed that on her finger she wore a familiar ring – a golden dragon with emerald eyes and a red, forked tongue. It had once belonged to Zmyeevich, but I had stolen it from him. How it had got to her I didn't know. Against the far wall Nadya sat on a closed coffin. She didn't appear to be constrained in any way. Standing close to her was one of the vampires I'd seen here before – Ilya, if I recalled the name correctly.

Susanna took a breath to speak, but Nadya interrupted her. 'Is it you, Misha?'

There was only one explanation for it – she knew it might not be Danilov, that it might be me. For all his attempts to keep it from her, somehow she had found out. I tried to decide which of us it would be wiser to claim to be.

Susanna answered for me. 'Of course it's Mihail. Do you think Richard would have come here to save you?' She turned to me. 'I should explain, I rather let slip your predicament to her. I presumed you'd already have told her – one or other of you – one out of love, the other out of a sense of . . . mischief.'

She glanced over her shoulder to Nadya. 'Mind you, if it *is* Mihail, he doesn't seem very pleased to see you.'

Dmitry spoke from behind me. 'He didn't have much choice whether he came or not. I made sure he got here.'

Susanna stood upright. As she did so her brow wrinkled and a look of pain ran across her face. She put a hand to her stomach. The moment passed quickly. When she spoke, her voice was calm. 'It doesn't really matter which of you it is, does it? You both know where Ascalon is. If one of you refuses to tell me, I'll wait for the other.'

'Aren't you going to thank me first?' I asked.

Nadya turned her head away. She knew Danilov well enough to tell that it was not him speaking.

'Thank you?' said Susanna. 'For what?'

'For delivering Danilov's woman to you.' It was evident that ambiguity was not going to help me.

She smiled again. This time it was more recognizably her. 'As I recall I collected her myself – with Ilya's assistance.'

'And how did you know where she lived?' I was taking a gamble. There were a dozen ways they could have found her, but one seemed most likely.

'Ilya saw her, and followed her home.'

'Saw her standing on the Palace Bridge, I imagine. Looking out across the Neva.'

Susanna looked surprised, as well she might. 'How did you know that?'

'Because I suggested she do it.' I looked over to Nadya. There were tears forming in her eyes. 'Didn't I?'

'It sounded so like you,' Nadya whispered. 'Like him.'

'It was, for the most part. But occasionally Danilov drops his guard, even in the middle of writing a letter. I only needed to add one sentence, asking you to be there, so that I – he – could look out towards you.'

'So you deliberately suggested she go somewhere where one of us would see her?' said Susanna. 'How would that help you?'

'Because I knew you'd try to use her to get at Danilov. That would mean he'd have a reason to escape – and if we both wanted to escape it seemed more likely that we would. It didn't go quite as I'd planned, but I'm a free man.'

'Hardly free,' she said. I raised a questioning eyebrow and she nodded her head, indicating that I should look behind me. I turned round. In the corridor, beyond Dmitry, one of her other henchmen had arrived. That meant three of them against Dmitry – Nadya and I would be of no value in a fight. And that assumed Dmitry would be inclined to side with me. But I didn't plan to fight.

'I will be, once you agree to my terms.'

'Your terms?'

'We'll step outside, just you and I. Then I'll tell you where Ascalon is. You can run along and get it, and I'll be on my way.'

'What about the woman?' She inclined her head towards Nadya.

'She's of no interest to me . . . any more. You'd be doing me a favour to keep hold of Dmitry too. He's rather more on his nephew's side than he is on mine.'

I felt Dmitry stiffen behind me. I expected some sort of blow from him, but nothing came. I turned. The other *voordalak* had moved closer and was holding him fast, his arms twisted behind his back. Dmitry was strong enough to break free, but for now he bided his time.

'If we leave here, what guarantee do I have that you'll tell me anything?'

'You're far stronger than me. I wouldn't be able to get away.'

'So why should I let you go afterwards?'

'When I tell you, you'll be in quite a hurry to get to Ascalon.' I wasn't going to use the same lie I had on Dmitry – there were good reasons to suppose it wouldn't work on Susanna. My plan was to tell her that Ascalon was packed away and loaded on to a train that was due to leave the city in less than an hour.

She pursed her lips and blew out through them, thinking intently.

'I'd hurry, if I were you,' I said. 'I could change my mind at any moment.' I smiled. 'I mean that quite literally.'

She straightened up. 'Very well.' She flicked her fingers and pointed. 'Ilya! Help Sandor with the big one.'

Ilya looked at her sullenly. 'It's a trick,' he muttered.

'Just do it,' snapped Susanna.

Ilya obeyed. I stepped aside to allow them to drag Dmitry into the chamber. Against two of them, there was not much he could do to resist. They took him to the other end of the cell, close to where Nadya was sitting. The way out was clear. Now could be my chance to run, but I doubted I would get far. Much better to allow Susanna to escort me to the surface. But then my mind was made up for me.

'Don't waste your time.' I turned, as did Susanna. It was Dmitry who had spoken. 'I doubt you'd get the truth from him anyway.' I realized what he was going to say next at the same moment he uttered the words. 'It's at his old house, on Panteleimonovskaya Street.'

Susanna's brow wrinkled. 'No it isn't,' she said dismissively. 'We already—'

I didn't wait to hear the rest. I ran. The corridor was long, straight and dark, but I had a good idea of how far it was to the steps. Behind me I could hear feet pounding almost from the moment I began to move. I slowed to a walk and put my hands out in front of me. I'd judged it well. After only another foot I felt the rough stone of the spiral staircase against my fingertips. I moved my hands down and was relieved to discover that the doorway at the bottom was still open. The footsteps behind me were closer now. I didn't hold out much hope, but still I bent forward to crawl through.

A hand grasped my ankle, gripping as tightly as Dmitry had held my wrist. It pulled and my body lurched backwards. I couldn't move my hands fast enough and I fell forward on to my chest. My face banged on to the stone slab and I tasted blood. I began to slide across the floor, back in the direction I'd come. I tried to tilt my head up to keep it from scraping against the stone, but I knew I wouldn't manage it for long. I kicked out with my free leg and twisted at the same time. The grip on my ankle became momentarily loose, but it hadn't been my intention to escape. In a fraction of a second the hand gripped me again, but now I was on my back. It was still an uncomfortable way to travel, but at least I would be done no permanent harm.

'Put him with the others,' said Susanna.

Ilya reached down to me and I took his hand to haul myself up. I walked over and sat beside Nadya on the coffin. It took all my willpower not to embrace her. The urge had been just as strong ever since I had set eyes on her, but I'd had no power to act on my desires. Now it took all my will to suppress them.

Susanna faced Dmitry. 'Did he tell you that? That it was at their house?'

'One of them did,' Dmitry replied. 'I think it was Iuda.'

'It hardly matters which. We've already torn the place apart – it's not there.'

'It's at Gorohovaya Street 2,' I said. They both turned and looked at me. There was no option but to tell her. Perhaps it was a stupid thing to do, but it was what Iuda was trying to prevent, so it seemed like a good idea. 'The old Ohrana building,' I continued. 'They took it from me when I was arrested. It's probably still there.'

'Is that possible?' She asked Dmitry rather than me.

'Why should I tell you?' he replied.

'We'll know soon enough.' She turned to the vampire she'd addressed as Sandor. 'Come with me. Ilya, you stay and make sure they're here when I get back.'

'All of us?' asked Dmitry.

'I've told you the truth,' I said.

'You very probably have, but I'll be back within the hour, and if I have Ascalon then this will all be over.'

'And you'll let us go?' said Dmitry.

'That was the deal, wasn't it?'

There was ambiguity in her voice, but she said nothing more. A moment later she and Sandor were gone. Ilya went over to the door and then looked towards us. 'Don't try anything. I'll be just outside.' He closed the door behind him and we heard the key in the lock.

I turned to Nadya and grasped both her hands in mine. I looked into her eyes. 'It's me now – honestly it is.'

She looked back at me, but only for a second, as if to confirm who I truly was, then she flung her arms around me. I wondered if she was really capable of telling the difference – even now that she knew there was a difference – but it would be better to let her believe that she could. We held each other for a few moments. I sensed Dmitry stand and pace across the room towards the door. I would have liked to stay like that for ever, but we didn't have time to waste.

'Did they hurt you?' I asked.

She shook her head, but I could see that there were tears in her eyes. 'I was fine. They even brought me food. But the worst of it was they left Ilya to guard me – my own brother. I couldn't stop myself from talking to him. I'd convinced myself that it wasn't him; that it was just his body that some monster had taken over. But it *is* him. It *is*.' She was crying now. 'I recognize him. The way he talks. The things he remembers. It's not Ilya gone bad. It's Ilya doing what he really wants. What he's always wanted. He told me. And you've told me a dozen times; they have to be willing.'

'I'm sorry I got you involved with this.'

'It's not your fault.'

'I should have spotted what Iuda was doing.' Looking back, I could almost remember writing the suggestion that Nadya stood there on the bridge myself. I wasn't quite sure how Iuda had influenced me. Had he been in control of my hand as I wrote? That was how it generally worked. But was it possible that he could act in other ways? Could he simply plant a thought in my brain for me to act upon? If that was the case, then I had the slight consolation of knowing I might be able to do the same to him.

'It doesn't matter. Did you see Polkan?'

'He's fine,' I said. God knew what might happen if Susanna encountered him on her way out.

Dmitry had been silent since Susanna's departure, but now he spoke. 'We need to get out of here,' he said. He seemed to be in a state of shock.

'I told her the truth,' I said. 'We can just wait till she comes back.'

Nadya gave a hollow laugh. 'Why should she let us go once she has what she wants?'

'It's like I told you,' said Dmitry. 'However little Susanna cares for you, she loathes Iuda. She'd never let *him* go. As for Nadya – well, Susanna will be hungry when she gets back.'

He was right. It wouldn't take them long to get to Gorohovaya Street from here. 'Can you break down the door?' I asked.

He shook his head. 'Not with Ilya waiting on the other side.'

'If we can get him in here, we can deal with him easily enough,' said Nadya.

'How?' I asked.

She rapped on the coffin beneath us with her knuckles. 'It's made of wood, isn't it?'

I understood what she was planning, but it was hard to believe she'd go through with it. 'He's your brother,' I said, unable to express more than that simple fact. She stiffened and breathed in deeply through her nose, not daring to look into my eyes. Then a new resolution possessed her and she knelt down to prise open the lid.

Moments later we had it free. We rested one end of it against the side of the coffin, so that it sloped up like a ramp. It wasn't anything fancy – just stained pine – so it wouldn't be too difficult to break. I jumped up and landed with both feet square in the middle of the coffin lid. It bent and squealed, but did not break. As it flexed back to its natural shape I was catapulted into the air like a Chinese acrobat. I managed to land safely.

'Let's try together,' said Nadya. She reached out across the lid and we braced ourselves against one another, hands gripping forearms. There was no need for a countdown. We looked at each other and then jumped together, landing on the thin sheet of wood at precisely the same moment. This time it offered little resistance and we found ourselves standing on the stone floor amongst its shattered remains.

'What was that?' shouted Ilya through the door.

'Why don't you come and see?' I called back.

If he did, we would have to hurry. It took us only a few more seconds' effort to smash the remains of the wood into smaller pieces. I kicked them around with the toe of my boot until I found one that looked suitable. It was sharp and strong. I'd probably get splinters in my hands from using it, but that didn't matter. I picked it up and looked at the door, but there was no sign of Ilya coming in.

I turned to Dmitry, eager to show off my new weapon, but he wasn't interested in the slightest. Instead he was leaning over the filled-in well at the centre of the chamber, picking up bits of the rubble and broken bricks and casting them on the floor behind him. He was looking for something.

'If you're trying to find a weapon,' I said, 'I've already got one.'

'We don't need that kind of weapon,' he said. Then he froze. He took two paces backwards, away from the well, his eyes fixed on it but to one side, as though he were trying to avoid looking at it directly. 'Did Iuda ever tell you about the mirror he invented? The mirror that can allow a vampire to see its true image.'

'He said something of it.' In truth, it wasn't very much. Iuda's memories about it were guarded. He was proud of his invention, but terrified of it too. He'd never dared look into it himself for fear of what he might see. Dmitry was displaying a similar terror now.

'There used to be one along that wall.' He gestured behind him. 'I was wondering if they might have dumped some of it here when they broke it all up.'

'And did they?'

'I think so, yes.' He raised his arm and pointed, still making sure that he could only see it out of the very corner of his eye. 'Get it for me.'

I shone the torch where he was pointing. Something glinted. I reached forward to take it, and then hesitated, drawing my hand back.

'It's no danger to you,' said Dmitry.

I knew as much, but the fear I felt seemed primeval. It came from Iuda, who was fully aware of what was going on, even though he could not influence matters other than to make me afraid. The thought spurred me on. I grasped the fragment of glass between my fingers and pulled it out of the debris that encased it, wiggling it a little to set it free. At last it came loose. It was about the size of my hand; the sort of thing that a lady might carry to help her with her make-up, except for its sharp, jagged edges. Still Iuda's fear influenced me, and I held it at such an angle that I would not see my own reflection.

In doing so, I inadvertently pointed it in Dmitry's direction. He threw himself back against the wall and flung his arms up to cover his face.

'Careful, you fool,' he hissed. 'Point it at yourself. It'll do you no harm.'

I wasn't so sure. I was possessed by Iuda's spirit, and Iuda had been a *voordalak*. Who knew what we might see in there. I for one was curious, and Iuda's trepidation piqued my interest still further. I turned the glass towards me. At first all I could see was the reflection of the room. I made sure I didn't catch even a glimpse of Dmitry. It was as I'd expected from Iuda's explanation. I could see two reflections of everything, separated by a fraction of an inch. The crystal from which the mirror was made bent the two polarizations of light along slightly different paths. I probably understood the science better than Iuda. In our solitary hours in the fortress I'd told him what I had read of the new quantum theories of light. He'd immediately begun to consider the ramifications of the theory. It was strange – I could almost look back on those unspoken conversations as happy memories.

I turned the mirror closer towards me. I could see the double reflection of my upper arm, and then of my shoulder, and finally of my face – two faces. I only saw it for a moment, but I would swear that the two images were different. One was familiar; I'd seen it almost every day: curled grey hair, a square face with a wide jaw, dark eyes, a nose that was slightly too large for the rest of the face. The only thing that surprised me was the beard that I'd grown while imprisoned. But the second face was familiar too. It was lean, with long, straight blond hair and pale, narrow eyes. I hadn't seen it for many years, but now it was just what I should expect to see when looking at myself.

I pressed the glass up against my chest so that it could reflect nothing more. I could imagine no scientific reason why I should have seen Iuda's face in it. The image was as likely to be a hallucination born out of my own anxiety as a genuine reflection, made up of rays of light.

'See something?' asked Dmitry.

I shook my head. 'What did you want it for?'

Dmitry was over by the door now. He beckoned me to join him. 'When I say, slip it under.' Then he knocked sharply against the wood. 'Ilya? Are you still there?'

The response was muffled, but clear enough to comprehend. 'I'm not going anywhere.'

Dmitry sat down with his back to the door and began to speak. 'I know what it's like, Ilya.'

'Know what what's like?' came the response.

'I've done it too – shared my blood with another *voordalak*. It seems wrong at first, but then, after a while, you have to keep going back. And then it doesn't feel so bad. It starts to seem like the right thing to do. But it's not. What did she tell you, Ilya? How did she persuade you to start?'

He waited for an answer but none came. There was little doubt that Ilya was hearing every word.

'It doesn't matter, I suppose. What matters is how much you've changed. You won't notice it – I didn't – because it's all such small steps. But look back. Once you were proud – had a will of your own. And now you can barely tell your thoughts from hers.'

It can't have made pleasant listening for Ilya. It didn't for me either. I could recognize too many parallels with my own state. Could I really tell which of the thoughts that passed through my head were mine and which were Iuda's?

'I got out, though – out in time,' Dmitry continued, his voice quavering. 'And you can too.'

'I know what you're trying to do.' Ilya's voice was unsteady now.

'I'm trying to help you. I always have. When you returned to life, undead, I was the first other vampire you met, remember? I helped you then and I want to help you now.'

'I don't need your help. I have Anastasia.'

'And she's changed you, Ilya. You can't see it, but I can. And I can prove it. I've got a mirror here, a special one, that'll show you how you've changed. Do you want to see?'

There was no answer. Dmitry nodded to me and I put the mirror face up alongside the crack under the door, then gave it a little shove. It disappeared into the darkness, though I could still

362

hear the sound of it scraping against the stonework until it came to a halt. Dmitry put his finger to his lips, though I'd not been planning on saying anything. Beyond the door there was only silence.

Then we heard the slightest cry. An intake of breath that just caught the vocal cords and made a sound like the grunt of an animal. In a human it would be the expression of the most profound misery – in a vampire too.

Dmitry was on his feet in a moment. He signalled to me to step back and then charged the door. On the first attempt a large crack appeared straight down its centre, but it did not yield. He ran at it again and this time the two halves separated – one remaining supported by the hinges and the other falling to the ground with a clatter.

Ilya sat slumped across the corridor. He held the mirror in one hand, resting it on his belly. He stroked its surface with a finger of the other, as if trying to touch whatever it was he saw in it. In an instant Dmitry was at his side, as though at a relative's sickbed. He snatched the glass from him and threw it back into the room. I kicked it away into a corner. Dmitry dragged Ilya's unresisting body into the chamber and leaned him against the wall. I stepped forward, raising the wooden stake we had created from the coffin lid and preparing to strike. Dmitry took a step back, still gazing down at his former comrade. Then he turned towards me, and saw what I was about to do.

His fist flashed out, catching the back of my hand and knocking the weapon from it. 'What the hell are you doing?' The expression on his face was of genuine horror. It did not suit the creature he had become. 'There's no need for that. He's no danger any more.'

'All right,' I said. Even so I reached down and picked up the stake. My eyes never left Ilya, but his face was vacant and empty. He showed no sign even of being aware of our presence. 'We might still need this later,' I explained.

Dmitry thought about it for a moment, then nodded. 'We need to get going,' he said. 'Fast.'

He went out into the corridor. I turned back to Nadya. She was standing among the splintered remains of the coffin lid. Her eyes too were fixed on Ilya. It can't have been a pleasant scene for her to witness. After everything, he was still her brother.

'Come on,' I said. 'Stay close.'

Her eyes flicked away from him and on to me. She nodded. I turned to follow Dmitry. He was already at the spiral staircase when I reached him, waiting for us to catch up.

'Where's Nadya?' he asked.

I looked back, expecting to find her close behind me, but the corridor was empty. In the distance I could see the dim glow of the doorway. I ran back, terrified as to what might have happened. I'd left her in there, alone, with a vampire. He'd seemed entirely subdued, but how quickly might he recover? I silently cursed Dmitry for not letting me finish him. I was at the door in seconds. I need not have worried.

Nadya was in no danger. She stood facing the wall, with a shard of pinewood held limply in her hand. Her palms were bloody from where its splinters had dug into them. Where Ilya had been sitting there was now a desiccated corpse, still dressed in Ilya's clothes. In places the bone showed clearly, in others his darkened skin clung to it. He was young as a vampire – his true death had occurred less than two years before. Even now his body could only decay as far as nature would have allowed it in the time. Nadya turned her head to look at me. I reached out to take her hand and to lead her to safety. For a moment she resisted, but then came with me.

'I know,' I said. 'It wasn't him. It wasn't Ilya any more.'

But she understood the situation perfectly. 'It was,' she murmured.

CHAPTER XXII

IMANAGED TO DRAW SOME AMUSEMENT FROM THE FACT THAT Nadya appeared to greet her dog with as much affection as she had her lover. But I suppose in the dog's case there was no doubt as to what actually lurked behind those dark, moronic eyes. The creature was waiting for us just where we had left it, indicating that this was not the route Susanna had taken. We all quickly climbed the steps back out to Saint Isaac's Square. The place was quiet now. Those who were fleeing the city had already left; those who were staying had shut themselves up in their homes. Later on it would become livelier as Petrograd's more resourceful citizens came out to see what they could loot from their neighbours' abandoned shops and homes.

'So what now?' It was Nadya who asked the obvious question.

From the way both of them stared at me it seemed that I was expected to answer it. Now that we were free and the immediate threat of Susanna taking her revenge on me was lifted, my priorities had changed. Dmitry was a useful ally. Even though he had no reason to do anything to help me, he would protect Danilov, seemingly to the point of risking his own life. I had no need of Nadya's company. I toyed with the idea of telling Dmitry just what she had done to his comrade down there beneath the cathedral, but such a revelation might do me better if left to a more appropriate moment. The very fact that Danilov knew it was a possibility gave me just a little more leverage to use against him. But still I had to answer her question.

'I'm not sure,' I said. It seemed like the sort of response Danilov might come up with.

'You two have to get out of the city,' said Dmitry. 'Go to Moscow – or even further. There should still be trains running.'

'You're not coming with us?' asked Nadya.

He shook his head. 'I'm going to follow Susanna to Cheka headquarters.'

'To where?' I spoke before realizing that my ignorance might reveal who I was.

Dmitry looked at me sternly, then his face softened. 'It happened since you were arrested, but it was already starting, even then. We don't have the Ohrana any more. Gorohovaya Street 2 is the headquarters of a new organization now – though it's not all that different. It's called the Chrezvychaynaya Komissiya, but people just refer to it by the initials – Che Ka – the Cheka. They keep confiscated items in the evidence room, on the third floor. Susanna won't know that, so I may have a chance to get there before her.'

'How come you know so much about it?' I asked.

'Because that's where I work,' he snapped. 'I'm what they call a Chekist. At least that's what I'm pretending for now.'

If he knew the building as well as he claimed then there might be a chance – I hadn't given up on Ascalon altogether.

'I'm coming with you,' I said resolutely. 'I might be able to help.'

'Misha, no. Leave it to Dmitry,' pleaded Nadya.

'For God's sake, you stupid woman, I'm not "Misha"; I'm Iuda.'

It was a joy to watch as her face collapsed into tears – certainly worth any slight advantage that their knowing my current identity might give them. I felt a sudden pain in my jaw and I staggered to one side. Dmitry had cuffed me. It was painful, almost as though he'd dislocated it, even though it was only a casual blow on his part. I rubbed it and grinned at him.

'Danilov feels it just as much as I do.'

'I think we're all in agreement, though,' said Dmitry. 'With you like this, it would be better all round if you stay with me and not with Nadya.' He turned to her. 'You go to the Nikolaievsky Station and get three tickets to Moscow. We'll meet you there.'

'Three?' I asked. 'You're coming with us?'

'I'm going to make sure you both get there.'

'And how's she going to pay for them?'

Nadya seemed about to say something, but Dmitry interrupted her. 'That shouldn't be a problem.' He reached into his pocket and took out a roll of banknotes. He handed it to Nadya. 'I doubt these are worth half what they were a few days ago, but it should be enough. Don't be afraid to use them all if that's how much it costs. Now let's go.'

We walked together along Gogolya Street until we reached Gorohovaya.

'This is where we part company,' said Dmitry. 'If we're not there by midnight, go alone. We'll find you in Moscow.'

She nodded. I took a step towards her as if to kiss her good-bye. She almost fell for it, but she overcame her instinctive response in time. She scowled at me. I chuckled. She stepped towards Dmitry. He seemed a little taken aback, but even so he leaned down to allow her to kiss him on the cheek. She scarcely managed to hide her revulsion at so intimate a contact with a vampire, but it was all clearly for my benefit. I wondered what Danilov would be making of it.

She strode off in the direction of Nevsky Prospekt, the dog at her heel. I stared after her, with no interest on my own part, but aware that this might be the last time Danilov ever saw her, and knowing that it would hurt him to dwell on the moment. Dmitry grabbed me by the sleeve. 'Come on!'

We walked up the street until we were opposite the door by which we'd been taken out on our way to the Peter and Paul Fortress. It stood ajar. We crossed the road. Even before we were back on the pavement I could see the arm and hand of a man protruding from behind the door.

'Shit!' muttered Dmitry.

Inside it was clear that the doorkeeper was dead. His throat was bloody. It was a strange reflection of Dmitry's loyalties that he should be disturbed by it. He bounded up the stairs two at a time. I tried to stay close, but Danilov's body was pathetic. He had disappeared by the time I'd climbed the three flights, but I was shown the path by a streak of blood smeared across the wooden floor. As I walked past it I saw another body, killed in the same way, lying face down beside a desk. I turned his head to one side with the tip of my toe and was pleased to see a face I recognized: it was the Trotsky-impersonating thug who had sent us to the fortress in the first place. I was surprised that there weren't more bodies – I didn't imagine Susanna would be merciful – but I supposed that most of them had already evacuated to Moscow.

I heard a sound from further ahead and went to investigate. The whole floor was open, without walls dividing up the rooms, although bookshelves and filing cabinets formed alcoves for the individual desks. Further along, though, there was something different. A large metal cage stood in the middle of the room itself, quite tall enough for a man to stand up in. It reminded me of the cage that Aleksandr II had had set up at Fontanka 16 to allow him to talk to me in safety. Perhaps it was the same one – this place was where the Ohrana had moved to. Here, though, the purpose was different; this was to keep thieves out, not to keep vampires in.

The gate was open and Dmitry was inside, searching through boxes and cabinets. The whole place was stained with blood. I could see a human foot sticking out from behind one of the boxes, but as I moved I discovered that it was not attached to any body. I looked around and saw that it wasn't just blood that was spattered in all directions: it was the remains of one body – perhaps more than one – ripped to shreds and thrown about the place. Perhaps I'd been wrong. Perhaps this cage had been used to keep someone in; used by Susanna so that her victim could not escape as she vented her wrath on him. I should have been delighted; proud at the part I'd played in fashioning such a creature of malevolence, but instead I could only feel disgust. I had been in Danilov's body too long and it was beginning to have an effect on me.

'All the months I've worked here, and I never thought to look,' said Dmitry, half to himself.

'Look where?'

'In here. I should have known – should have felt it as I walked past.'

'You're sure she's taken it?'

He pushed a cardboard box across the desk towards me. 'This has your name on it – Mihail's name.'

I looked down at it. Inside sat my double-bladed knife and the razor I'd used. There was certainly no sign of Ascalon – nor of the money we'd had, but that was to be expected.

'There's a chance they put it somewhere else,' I said. 'Help me look.'

'No,' he replied. 'She has it. If she didn't she'd still be here, still searching. She wouldn't give up.'

'She'll be back at Saint Isaac's by now.'

'I doubt it. I don't think she's going there.'

'Why do you say that?'

'You used to be a vampire, didn't you? Look at the blood – it's drying. The cathedral's only ten minutes from here. She'd have been back before we left, if that was where she was going.'

'So where is she?'

Dmitry thought for a moment, then shook his head. 'I don't know. We should get to the station.' He walked out of the cage and headed towards the stairs. He seemed to have overlooked the fact that his plans and mine might be anything other than convergent. But I didn't have to think about it for long. It was still better for me to stick with him for now – and Moscow would be a safer place than Petrograd. I was about to follow, but I didn't want to leave empty-handed. I reached into the box and picked up my double-bladed knife. Moments later I was following him down the stairs.

For all that Petrograd had fallen quiet, the Nikolaievsky Station was busier than I had ever seen it. The clock in the tower told me that it was almost a quarter to eleven. The statue of Aleksandr III – the hippopotamus – still stood in the square opposite. Today the hordes that seethed around it had no yearning for revolution on their minds. They sought freedom, to be sure, but freedom from

369

the oppression of a foreign invader. We pushed our way into the station. Dmitry was a useful man to have around if you wanted to elbow your way through a throng like this one.

Inside it was even more tightly packed. There were trains in at half the platforms. We pushed our way through, trying to find a vantage point where we might be able to see Nadya, but it was impossible. With a whoosh of steam one of the trains began to roll out. Railway guards held back the crowd that surged forward in disappointment to see it go. I could only wonder that any form of organization remained, but the rail workers were an institution unto themselves. Their union – the Vikzhel – was one of the few that had been strong enough to stand up against the Bolsheviks during the coup. Now they seemed intent on staying at their posts to the last, and on getting as many out of Petrograd as they could.

'We should split up and look for her,' I suggested.

'You'd like that, wouldn't you?'

I felt momentarily affronted to be mistrusted, but the words were addressed to Iuda, not me. I could have corrected his mis-apprehension, but it would have taken precious seconds for me to prove who I was, and I couldn't really see how his knowing would change things.

'Anyway,' he continued, 'I've got a better idea.'

With that he grabbed me by the waist and hoisted me into the air before lowering me on to his shoulders. If I'd been a five-year-old boy it would not have looked unnatural, but even though I was not as tall as Dmitry I was still a full-grown man. Aside from the ridiculous nature of the image we must have presented, anyone thinking about what Dmitry had achieved would wonder at his immense strength. And yet not a soul remarked upon it. Dmitry slowly turned in a circle, like the engine for some great lighthouse of which I was the lantern. Even at that deliberate pace there were hundreds of passengers for me to examine each second. I felt sure it would be impossible for me to miss the face of the woman I loved, and yet I feared that I would.

We had turned through almost 360 degrees when I finally saw someone I did recognize, though it was not Nadya, nor was it anyone I had been hoping to encounter. It was the vampire Sandor. He, like me, was staring intently, his eyes fixed on something ahead of him. I followed his gaze and at last I saw her – Nadya. She was pushing through the crowd away from him. It might have been coincidence, but then she glanced behind her and I saw the fear in her eyes and I knew she was fully aware that she was being hunted.

I bent forward and spoke to Dmitry, shouting to be heard over the noise of the crowd. 'She's over there. Sandor's there too. He's after her. Susanna can't be far away.'

I jumped down from his back, using his shoulders to soften my descent, then pushed him in the direction we needed to go. Again we made easy progress, as he comfortably thrust aside any who did not see his approach and choose to move away voluntarily. Although he didn't have as good a view as I'd had, his height was still enough for him to see them, now he knew where they were.

We moved towards the side of the station, away from the tracks, and the crowd began to thin. I was able to walk alongside Dmitry. He pointed ahead of us to a tall brick archway in the western wall of the building.

'They went through there.'

I broke into a run, but stopped as I reached the arch so that I could look through. Dmitry was seconds behind me. It opened on to a walled yard. There were packing cases stacked so high that even Dmitry would not be able to see over them. Some were broken open, with their contents spilling out. There was nothing of much value. Anything that might be sold or eaten had been taken. There was no sign of Nadya or Sandor, but the piled crates made the yard into something like a maze. The narrow alleyways between them would conceal anyone who was in here.

'Nadya!' I shouted.

The response came quickly, 'Mi—' but was cut short. Dmitry indicated that we should split up. Soon he had disappeared from view. I shouted Nadya's name again and this time the response came in the form of a bark which I recognized to be Polkan's. Then came a continuous low snarling. It gave me some sense of which direction to take, but the twists and turns between the crates meant I could not follow the sound directly.

Finally I saw them. Sandor had Nadya pressed up against a wall,

371

his hand over her mouth so that she couldn't shout out. Polkan had his teeth sunk deep into Sandor's leg, trying pathetically to drag him away. I could see bloodstains around his muzzle, but it didn't seem to bother Sandor. Clearly, though, he had something to fear, otherwise why did he need to keep Nadya quiet? But it wasn't me that concerned him. He saw me moments after I saw him. He pulled a foul expression that was something like a grin and then stepped back. He kicked hard at Polkan, sending him sliding across the ground. The dog was on his feet again in seconds, emitting a throaty growl and keeping his eyes fixed on Sandor. But he didn't approach.

Then behind Sandor appeared the man he was really afraid of – Dmitry. He'd found a different way through the labyrinth and now he and I were at opposite ends of the alley, blocking Sandor in – though I didn't represent much of a barricade. I looked past Sandor towards Dmitry. Sandor immediately understood. He shot a glance over his shoulder to confirm what he suspected. It took him no time to realize he wasn't going to escape that way. He launched himself in my direction. I braced myself. My only hope was that I could hold him off until Dmitry reached us.

I didn't need to worry. Before he'd even moved two paces Sandor found himself sprawling on the floor. I saw a smirk on Nadya's face and looked down to see the raised foot with which she had tripped him. He had no chance to recover. In seconds Dmitry was on him. He flipped him on to his back and then hauled him up by the lapels, lifting him up off the ground with his feet kicking, trying to find support. Sandor could have made more effort to resist than he did, but he clearly recognized he was beaten. He'd fought alongside Dmitry for long enough to know what a formidable opponent he was. Perhaps he hoped that if he gave in without resistance Dmitry might show him mercy. He might well have been right, given what I'd seen of Dmitry's attitude to Ilya, but I wasn't going to allow it. Nadya had had the right idea with her brother, and I was going to follow her example.

I still had the makeshift stake that I'd made in the cellar beneath Saint Isaac's. I marched forward and lunged. It was an easy strike, the sort of thing that a cadet would learn in his first day at fencing school – if they'd still bothered to teach them how to fence. My only concern was that the wooden blade might go through Sandor and into Dmitry, but even if it did, it would be on the wrong side for his heart.

I felt a satisfying resistance as the blade penetrated Sandor's body, and then a sudden relaxation of it as his heart was pierced. His life departed and the integrity of his body vanished. His boots slipped out of his trousers, followed by a tumbling cascade of dust. His coat gradually collapsed, as though air were being sucked out of it. Soon it had no more bulk than it would have done if hanging from a coatrack. His head fell to one side, tearing away from his neck as though it were made of tissue paper. It brushed against the shoulder of his coat and disintegrated. This one had been a *voordalak* far longer than Ilya.

Behind it Dmitry's face was revealed. At first his expression was one of puzzlement, but as he saw me it changed to anger. He was still holding Sandor's empty coat by its lapels, but he threw it aside. He grabbed the stake and twisted, wrenching it from my grip and jarring my wrist. He snapped it in two and let the pieces fall to the ground. He raised his hand to strike me, but contained himself.

'There was no need for that,' he said. 'Not with Ilya; not with him. Don't you think you owe me that much?'

There was a sense of disappointment in his voice that brought his words home to me. I still could not fathom what drove him, but he had gone against his nature to help me. I should have been able to suppress my hatred of vampires enough to reciprocate. But I couldn't face admitting it to him.

'Don't blame Danilov,' I said.

It was a remarkably easy way to deceive him – to pretend it was Iuda's will that moved my hand as I thrust the stake into Sandor's back. There was no question that I had intended to destroy the vampire, but as to lying about it – was that really the sort of thing I would have done before? Perhaps in that Iuda *was* influencing me. Or perhaps I was merely learning from him.

Dmitry scowled. I wondered if he would hit me again. But his hand fell to his side. He turned and went over to Nadya. She was leaning against the crates, gasping for breath.

'Are you all right?' he asked.

I put my hand on her arm to try to help her upright, but she shook it off. There was a downside to my pretending to be Iuda.

'I'm fine.' She addressed her words to Dmitry. It was absurd for me to feel jealous of him, but that didn't lessen the emotion. I felt the urge to tell him she had just as much vampire blood on her hands as I did.

'How did Sandor find you?' I asked.

'He didn't.' She still looked at Dmitry as she spoke. 'I found him. He was at the parcel office giving instructions for a crate to be loaded on to a train.'

'A crate?' I asked. 'How big?'

'Big enough.' Now she looked at me, then back to Dmitry. It was clear that we all understood what she meant. Dmitry himself had travelled that way in the past.

As had I. And yet neither Dmitry nor Danilov thought to ask the obvious question. On Dmitry's part it might have been down to stupidity, but the reason that Danilov remained silent became suddenly clear to me. However much he wanted to speak he did not have the power to part his own lips. I, on the other hand, did.

'Did you see where the train was going?' I asked.

She nodded. 'Tyumen.'

'Tyumen?' I knew of it, though I'd never been there. It was a large enough city – for Siberia – lying far to the east, hundreds of versts beyond even the Urals. 'What can she want there?'

'Isn't it obvious?' snarled Dmitry. 'It's not Tyumen she's interested in. It just happens to be the nearest railway station to the place she really wants to go.'

'And where, pray, would that be?'

'Tobolsk.' Dmitry spoke the word as if it carried great portent. Nadya seemed to pale a little. To me it meant nothing – just another provincial town, no more interesting than Tyumen.

Dmitry spoke clearly and deliberately. 'Nikolai Romanov and his family are currently under house arrest in Tobolsk.'

'The tsar?' It must have seemed a stupid question to ask,

but I had not come into this world until months after His Majesty's downfall.

'The former tsar,' Dmitry corrected me, alert to the politics of the day.

'What does she want with him?' asked Nadya.

'Can't you guess?' said Dmitry.

She looked at me expectantly. For all that she despised me, it was still me she turned to on a question like this. It was a matter of pride that I should give an answer. I rubbed my hand across my face. There was nothing clear to it. Even Susanna must have been guessing. 'Zmyeevich always believed that Ascalon was precious to him, yes? When Pyotr stole it from him, that was half the reason that Zmyeevich wanted vengeance on the Romanovs. There were always rumours about its power.'

'What rumours?'

'A lot of it was about what would happen if Ascalon was destroyed. There were those who said that it would bring about Zmyeevich's death, others that it would make him more powerful than ever. That's why no one ever dared – not Zmyeevich's friends nor his enemies – in case they got the result they didn't want.'

'But Susanna wouldn't take it to Tobolsk just to destroy it,' said Nadya.

'Obviously not. She must know something more. It must be to do with Romanov blood. That's why she needs Nikolai.'

'You have Romanov blood. Why not try with you, like she did before?'

'I don't know,' I snapped. 'Perhaps *because* she'd tried it on me – on Danilov – before. And look what she ended up with. She wouldn't want *three* of us in here.'

'Three of you? You, Danilov and Zmyeevich?'

'That must be what she's planning to do – to resurrect Zmyeevich in some way.'

'Like you?' said Nadya. 'In His Majesty's body?'

'I'm guessing. Perhaps it won't work like that at all. Perhaps it will just transform Nikolai into a vampire. I doubt Susanna knows for sure.'

'Does it matter?' asked Nadya. It was a strangely cold-hearted thing for a human to say.

'*Does it matter?*' Dmitry had seemed uninterested in our discussion, as if none of it were new to him. Now he was as appalled at Nadya's indifference as I was amused by it. 'You may think we're at threat from the Germans, but the real terror that faces Russia is civil war. It's already started in the east. They don't all want to bring back the tsar, but they hate the Bolsheviks enough to unite under his banner. Of course, Nikolai's too weak for that, too weak to even lead his own people. That's why he lost Russia in the first place. But Zmyeevich in Nikolai's body? That's better than he ever dreamed of. And he'd be the leader to defeat Lenin and Trotsky and all of them.'

'For once, Dmitry, I agree with you.'

'Really?' Understandably Dmitry was less than convinced.

'Not about Lenin or the Bolsheviks or any of that. They won't be around for long, anyway. But Zmyeevich was danger-ous enough before. If he had a following – a real, human following – he could take over the world, and that wouldn't be good for anyone. I know I tried to help him before, to put Aleksandr I under his power, but that was a different era; a different world. Russia was weak then and he could have her. Not now.'

'So you want to stop Susanna?'

'I'll do anything I can.'

'Bullshit!'

'What?' asked Dmitry.

'He's lying to you,' I replied.

'He?'

'Iuda. He knows more than he's telling you.'

'About Ascalon?'

I nodded. Dmitry appeared to have immediately accepted who was now speaking, but I could see that Nadya was more wary. 'I don't know what he's planning – he's hiding that from me – but he understands more about Ascalon than he's letting on. He just wants to get his hands on it *and* Nikolai before Susanna does.'

There was more to it than that, but it was a sensation rather than a palpable thought. I was unable to express it in words; I needed more time to understand.

'That doesn't make him wrong,' said Nadya.

I thought for a moment. 'No. No, it doesn't.'

'We *must* go after Susanna,' insisted Dmitry.

I turned to Nadya. 'When did the train to Tyumen leave?'

'About half an hour ago.'

'There won't be another till tomorrow,' said Dmitry.

'We may be able to beat her,' said Nadya. 'I've already got tickets to Moscow. From there we can take the Great Siberian Way straight to Tyumen.'

'If it's running.'

'It's still better than waiting here,' I said. Getting to Moscow certainly seemed like a good idea, but not for quite the reason Nadya suggested. For one thing I could think of a faster way to get from there to Tobolsk. For another, I didn't like the way Nadya had said 'we' when describing the pursuit of Susanna.

'Will the train get to Moscow before dawn?' Dmitry asked.

'It's scheduled to,' said Nadya, 'but who can tell these days?'

'I'll have to risk it. Let's go.'

We went back to the station concourse. It was heaving even more than when we left. There were crowds around the ticket offices and at the entrances to the platforms. Railway officials shouted at the people to calm them, telling them that there would be room for them all, if not on these trains then on the next, that the trains would keep running until everyone who wanted to leave Petrograd had done so. I didn't see how they could be so confident – the Germans might well have different plans. The people were smart enough to understand that, and pushed all the harder to get through. Even though we already had tickets, I didn't see how we had any chance of getting on a train.

I felt a tap on my shoulder. It was Nadya. She pointed towards the station exit, where I could see Dmitry striding away from us. 'What's he up to?' I asked.

'He said he was going to get help.'

'Help? From who?'

She shrugged. We could do nothing but stand and wait. I

slipped my hand into Nadya's and squeezed it through her glove. She reciprocated. I looked down at her. 'It's still me,' I said. 'When it *is* me.'

'We'll get you back,' she replied. 'Just you. We'll find a way.'

Dmitry returned quickly, and he was not alone. The two men beside him could almost have been his twins – both were dressed in dark leather coats identical to the one he was wearing. But neither of them had the same stature, or presence. They were clearly Bolsheviks, possibly even Chekists. As they passed us I noticed that one of them had a pistol in his hand. Dmitry led them directly to the crowd that thronged against the gate to the platforms. He shouted a few orders, which were met with little response, then repeated them more loudly. This time his two lieutenants began shoving people aside. The crowd soon got the message and began to part.

When there was a gap wide enough to walk through, Dmitry beckoned to us. I let Nadya go ahead, but kept close behind her, my eyes fixed ahead of me, not daring to look at the people on either side whose places on the train we were usurping.

All around there were mutterings – no one had the guts to shout – of dissent. I managed to make out one of them. 'Even a fucking dog gets treated better than us these days.' I heard Polkan yelp as one of them kicked at him, but he managed to scamper off ahead to safety. Soon we were on the platform. One of the Bolsheviks called over the train guard and spoke to him. There was a debate between them, with which Dmitry joined in. Then he beckoned us over.

'He wants to see the tickets.'

Nadya showed him. The guard inspected them in detail, then shrugged. 'This way.' We followed him to a first-class carriage in the middle of the train. He opened a door to reveal a crammed compartment. There were a few seated, but most of them were standing to make more room. There must have been twenty in a compartment designed for six.

'Come on,' said the guard. 'Get out. These seats have been requisitioned.' There were moans from within, but they soon quietened at the sight of the three leather-clad figures outside. 'There's still room towards the front,' the guard explained. The passengers began to spill out on to the platform, carrying their meagre possessions with them. The guard pointed up towards the locomotive. A few of those inside left by the far door, into the corridor that ran the length of the carriage.

Soon we were inside – Nadya, Polkan, Dmitry and myself. I was glad to see that Dmitry's new friends would not be coming with us. The guard closed the door. Dmitry opened the window and leaned out, addressing the two Bolsheviks. 'Many thanks, comrades. You have done great work for the party. I'll see that you're rewarded.' He closed the window and sat down. The two of them remained standing outside.

'You have some useful friends,' I said.

He scowled at me. 'I'm sorry, I should have let you stab them in the back, now they've served their purpose.' I wasn't sure whether he'd forgotten who he was speaking to, or had realized who it was killed Sandor. Either way it was a telling point. However much I despised Bolsheviks, they were human, and I would do all that I could to save their lives. I made a distinction between them and vampires, not on the basis of their character or behaviour, but simply upon their nature. Most vampires would make a similar distinction, differing only in the fact that they favoured the other side. But it was a difference that Dmitry could not see.

The other passengers of the packed train pressed against the windows that divided our compartment from the corridor. Mostly they were turned away, but a child's face peered in, his nose pressed against the glass, bearing a look of fascination as though he were staring into a sweetshop. Nadya stood and opened the door. The two people closest – an elderly man and woman – turned to face her.

'Please,' she said, 'there's plenty of room. Come and join us.'

The man looked around the compartment for a moment and then took half a step forward, but his wife put her hand on his arm to hold him back. She tilted her head towards Dmitry and muttered the word 'oprichnik'; the term had survived since the time of Ivan the Terrible as an expression of contempt for agents of state oppression. The man stepped back and slid the door closed.

'More fool them,' said Dmitry. He stood and went over to the door. The old couple saw him and tried to retreat, but had nowhere to go. Dmitry raised his hands above his head and posed there dramatically for a few moments. Then he simply pulled the curtains across the windows, so that we could no longer see the other passengers and they could not see us. I had no objections; it would make the journey less uncomfortable for everyone concerned.

I sat next to the outside window. A stream of evacuees processed along the platform, eager to find the last few places on the train. Occasionally one would come to the door of our compartment, but the two Chekists saw them off. After about twenty minutes I heard the brakes release beneath us. The couplings tightened and the train began to roll slowly out of the station. A few of those still on the platform made a dash for the nearest door, but I didn't see if any of them made it. None came to ours.

Moments later we emerged from under the station roof and began to gather speed. Outside I saw Petrograd at its least inspiring – tracts of warehouses, located close to the railway for easy loading and unloading. We passed over the Obvodny Canal and soon we were out in the countryside. This was the same route by which I had first come to what was then Saint Petersburg, aged just twenty-three. I leaned out of the window to look back at the city, but there was nothing to be seen. I'd hoped I might catch a glimpse of the spire of Saint Peter and Saint Paul's, or the dome of Saint Isaac's, but the darkness was impenetrable and, anyway, they were both too far away. I recalled what Mama had told me about Aleksei Ivanovich's final departure from the capital, taken from the Peter and Paul Fortress in a boat that would begin his journey to a Siberian exile.

I was leaving with greater dignity than he had, but I too was travelling to Siberia. I wasn't going into exile, but I was on a journey to face my destiny just the same. And although I could not predict the future, I felt certain, just as certain as Aleksei must have felt all those years before, that I would not be coming back.

CHAPTER XXIII

DANILOV WAS QUITE CORRECT. I HAD MY EYE ON ANY possibility for drawing advantage out of the situation with Nikolai, Susanna and Ascalon. But to a great extent, our interests in that regard coincided. What both Danilov and I yearned for most was to be separated from one another. True we'd each be satisfied simply to see the death of the other, allowing the survivor to take full control of our mutual body, but we'd both be happy to find a solution whereby each could take a body of his own – and I had a most illustrious body in mind for myself. Or was I being too logical? An amicable separation might be the most rational outcome for us both, but Danilov had a pathological loathing for me, born out of a hatred passed through his family from generation to generation. I could feel it seething within him whenever his mind came to the fore. He had dedicated his youth to killing me once; I could see no reason for doubting that he would happily set himself to the same task again, in whatever form I found new life. And therefore, for my own protection, I would be forced to kill him at the earliest opportunity.

And therein lay one great difference between us. For him that earliest opportunity might present itself a good deal earlier than it did for me. Danilov would be happy to lay down his own life if it entailed me losing mine. He had tried once, but I had managed to prevent it. I couldn't be sure that would always be the case. Since that time he'd never had the chance. For a few weeks my blood had run in our veins and so our death would have meant rebirth as a vampire. By then we had been in a gaol cell and he'd thought I was no danger to anyone. And besides, what means of suicide had there been? Now he had more important matters to attend to: saving the former tsar from Susanna – and from me.

There was no point in trying to hide anything from him. I could mutter the words, 'Dive thoughts, down to my soul: here Danilov comes,' but if my deliberations were concealed from him they would be concealed from me, and I knew that careful preparation would be required. And thus any plans I laid would have to be quite out in the open, their consequences inevitable, however broadly they were known. It was Danilov himself who had pointed it out: there could be no secrets between us – ours was a game of chess, not of whist. I smiled to myself as I recalled the occasion on which that comparison had first crossed our mind.

I looked at Nadya, reflected in the carriage window that was acting as an almost perfect mirror thanks to the darkness outside. She caught my gaze and smiled at me. I returned the expression, but evidently I got it wrong in some way, for she scowled and turned away. She was getting better at telling us apart, even by the slightest nuance of our face. Did she look back, I wondered, to that last time that we had made love, and try to decide just who it was had kissed her, caressed her and entered her? Just which of us had made her gasp with pleasure? Whether she had chosen the correct name to shout out loud at the moment of her ecstasy? Had she compared us in her memory as she now compared our smiles and was able to differentiate one from the other?

But perhaps it was unfair to ask her to decide between us on the basis of so little information. She and Danilov would soon be taking leave of one another – for ever as far as either of them knew. That, surely, would be the occasion when they would each desire one final taste of the other's flesh. Danilov would resist, but I, if I got the chance, would not. Was that even necessary? It seemed like a lot of effort for so little gain. Why not just tell her about that first time, just before we were arrested, tell her that it had been me and not her beloved? But no, that would be too much. Better to let her be unsure, to know it could have been me, but never to be certain that it was, just as I'd made Lyosha unsure about his whore Dominique, though his grandson now knew better. I had no idea precisely what Susanna had told Nadya. Most importantly, had she revealed the exact date on which I had taken up residence in Danilov's body? And if so had Nadya considered what that implied for the last night they had spent together? If not I would happily clarify the matter – when the time was right.

For now I could only take pleasure in my memories. I turned away from the reflection in the glass and stared directly at Nadya. She closed her eyes and pretended to sleep, but that didn't matter. My recollections were not for her benefit. They were not even for mine, though as the body I occupied took pleasure from them, inevitably I did too. But primarily I did it for Danilov. He had been separated from his lover for several months. How he must have missed her. I knew from his dreams that he did. I would help him to remember every inch of her.

I stood up abruptly and paced across the compartment, trying to dismiss Iuda's thoughts from my mind. They were a little less sullied if they came from my memory rather than his, but it was still the case that he would be able to enjoy my recollections to just the same extent that I was revolted by his. Two heads turned towards me in reaction to my movement – Dmitry's and Polkan's. Perhaps Nadya genuinely had fallen asleep, or perhaps she was determined not to react to me – to Iuda – in any way. Dmitry raised an eyebrow to enquire as to what was the matter, but I shook my head briefly to say it was nothing. He returned his gaze to the window, his eyes seemingly able to penetrate the gloom which mine could not.

I sat back down again. I knew that I had to occupy my mind, and I had plenty to occupy it with. Despite Iuda's claim to openness, he was still hiding things from me – things that he didn't fully understand himself. But I could discern from him the overarching belief that if he could just make a slight change to Susanna's plans, if he could just ensure that it was he who revealed

Ascalon's unknown power to Nikolai, then somehow he would be free of me – and I of him. As he'd acknowledged, my next desire would be his immediate death and he would guard against it, but it would be a chance – the only possible pathway I could discern to regaining all that I had lost. But despite that I could not ignore the fact that if he was to leave me he would require a body of his own. There was only one candidate that I could envisage: the former tsar, Nikolai himself. It was a gargantuan price to ask anyone to pay for my freedom, least of all a cousin, however unacquainted we might be. But how much more had I – my family – done over the decades to protect his? And I would be free of Iuda.

That was the best outcome I could envisage. It was an improbable one, and though I might strive to achieve it, I knew I must also prepare for more likely eventualities. I stood up again and leaned across Nadya, hoping not to wake her. Despite the revolution and the coup, this was still a first-class carriage and it was still maintained as such. In a pigeonhole fixed to the internal wall there was writing paper, envelopes, pens and ink. I took what I needed and sat back down, pulling the collapsible table out from the arm of the chair so that I could use it to write on. At times the train ran over rough sections of track, and I'd keep my pen away from the paper. At others we would glide smoothly, and I would write as quickly as possible in the time I had. Throughout I kept a fierce concentration, on the lookout for Iuda's influence, remembering how he had previously managed to inveigle his way into my consciousness and slip those few treacherous words into one of my letters to Nadya – words that had been her undoing.

Once I'd written the letter, and signed it, I read it back through, trying to analyse every sentence, every word, to verify that it truly expressed what I had intended to say; that it had not been adulterated by some twisted lie that issued from Iuda's imagination. As I read, I noticed I was dropping off. It was the small hours of the morning now. I hadn't risen early, but since dusk – since Dmitry had walked into our prison cell and set us free – I hadn't had a moment's pause. I forced myself to focus, to read the words in front of me, but I began to doubt my own judgement. Could it be Iuda who was making me drowsy? If he'd

384

managed to commandeer my thoughts for long enough to make me write something that went against my heart, might he not also be able to distract me at just the moment I read it? And yet I could see nothing untoward.

I tapped Dmitry's ankle with my foot. He wasn't asleep, and turned to see what I wanted. I handed him the letter. I leaned forward so that I could speak softly, all the time looking over at Nadya to see if she was awake – if she reacted.

'Read this,' I said. 'Tell me I wrote it.'

His only response was a frown of incomprehension.

'Read it. You know Iuda. Tell me if there's anything you think *he* might have written rather than me.'

He raised an eyebrow. 'You being?'

I tutted. 'Just tell me who you think wrote it, and if there's anything in there that's . . . amiss.'

It didn't take him long, and he read it again to be sure. 'There's nothing here that sounds like Iuda. But it doesn't sound all that much like you either.'

'You don't know me.'

'You mean what you say in this?'

'If it comes to it.'

'And how are you going to do it?'

I paused. 'I was thinking of asking you to.'

He leaned forward further so that our faces were scarcely an inch apart. He glanced over at Nadya. 'That's a lot to ask,' he hissed.

'You've done it a thousand times, and not given a shit about it.'

'I've only once killed a friend – killed someone who put his trust in me. His name was Milan Romanovich. My second ever meal. It seemed like such fun at the time, but his face haunts me, even now.'

'I need to put my trust in you. And I don't want you to drink my blood – I just want you to kill me.' I thought of telling him he could drink my blood too, if it would sweeten the deal, but I knew the suggestion would insult him.

'You want me to?'

'I *may* want you to. I don't know how things will turn out. But I want you to be ready, to be prepared if I do ask.'

He turned back to the window. I could only feel pity for him.

How could he ever have guessed that his life would come to this, that he would be begged by his own nephew to end his life? I was luckier. Mama had raised me from the cradle to be ready to face my dark fate. I'd had a respite of forty years, but I'd never been truly convinced. That it should end like this came as no surprise.

'How will I know it's you who asks?' he said, still gazing out into the black emptiness of the Russian night.

'Would Iuda ask it?'

'Who knows? In the right circumstances. He'd want to die if it meant he became a vampire.'

'You'll just have to make a decision.'

'You're happy for me to pass judgement on your life? And on his?'

'I've done as much in the past.'

'I could ask you one of those questions – about history.'

'It might help, but Iuda's had time to learn. And how could you know he hadn't taken charge the moment after I'd answered? Whatever happens, *dyadya*, it'll come down to you.' The use of the word *dyadya* – uncle – fell somewhere between sentimental and manipulative, but it didn't seem to bother him. He thought for a moment longer, then turned to face me.

'I can't promise what I'll do,' he said, 'but I'll try to do what's right.'

He handed the letter back to me. I folded it and put it in the envelope. I wrote the name of the addressee and a few specific instructions. But I did not seal it, not yet. Dmitry might do his best, but I couldn't rely on him. There were other ways. I leaned back in my seat and began to search my memories. I wasn't sure what I was looking for, but I knew the effect I was after. Most of my recollections of Iuda I'd already revealed to him – his imprisonment in Geok Tepe, his battle with Zmyeevich, his death at my hands. I knew that they might bear fruit, but I'd used them all before, perhaps too often. I needed something new – something that had only occurred to me recently.

I'd first seen it a long time ago, but had looked at it with idle curiosity many times since. It was a single sheet of paper that I'd found hidden between the pages of one of Iuda's notebooks. It was a charcoal drawing, initialled and dated:

Iuda would have been in his teens then, Susanna – and I was now sure that she was S.M.F. – much the same age she appeared to be now. The picture must have meant something to Iuda for him to have kept it so long. It had all made sense to me down beneath Saint Isaac's, when Susanna had thought us to be Zmyeevich and had offered us her blood. When she began to undress and our eyes fell upon her breasts I'd felt from Iuda a rush of emotion such as I had never guessed could exist within him. It was more than simple lust, it was . . . nostalgia – the aching desire to change wrong decisions made long ago. That was when I had begun to understand the drawing – the image of one of those breasts, created by Susanna's own hand. I examined it in my memory, admiring the way it blurred to nothing where it would have joined the body, the way the slightest strokes of charcoal gave it the appearance of illumination, the way that such imprecise draughtsmanship gave so precise an impression of reality. I enjoyed the image, sexually as well as aesthetically, imitating Iuda in his emotions when he looked at Nadya, partly to goad him, but more to remind him of how he had once surely felt.

And then I sensed his momentary absence. It was like the sudden, fleeting loss of gravity when the wheel of a car drops into a depression in the road. Iuda had withdrawn into himself, either to hide from the memory, or to relish it alone. It was the same way he had managed to insert that one sentence in my letter to Nadya, but now I had learned from him. I slipped my hand into my pocket and found what I wanted. It was small enough to fit next to the letter, but it made the envelope bulge. I was still able to seal it. I put the whole thing into my pocket. I couldn't tell whether Iuda had yet returned, but it would not be long. My safest course of action would be to sleep. I didn't find it difficult.

I was awakened by Dmitry shaking me. I opened my eyes. Nadya was asleep, as was Polkan, curled up beside her, his head resting in her lap. I looked up at Dmitry.

'It'll be dawn soon,' he said.

Out of the window it was still black as pitch.

'You sure?'

'Less than an hour, but we won't be in Moscow by then, and I have things to do.'

'Things?'

'To get ready for the rest of the journey. I can't travel like this during the day. But who knows, we may even end up on the same train.'

'I'm not going by train,' I said.

'A car won't be any faster.'

'I have a better way, if it works.'

He didn't ask for further explanation. Instead he handed me an envelope. I tried to push the thought of the letter in my own pocket from my mind. 'When you get to Moscow,' he said, 'I want you to make arrangements for a package to be transported – a large crate. It's to be picked up from the address in there and delivered to the post office in Tobolsk.'

'I don't imagine they'll treat you as a high priority.'

He reached into his pocket and took out another roll of banknotes. 'Use as much of this as necessary. You'll probably need the rest yourself.'

'They'll just keep the money.'

'I think not. Read it if you like.'

The envelope wasn't sealed. The letter, signed by Dmitry, said the same as he'd told me. The address was in the town of Khimki – it was on the railway line, twenty versts or so from Moscow. But it was the notepaper on which it was written that would persuade whoever I handed it to. Unlike my letter, the heading was not that of the railway company. It was of an organization with a typically longwinded title:

Всероссийская Чрезвычайная Комиссия по
Борьбе с Контрреволюцией и Саботажем
The All-Russian Emergency Commission for
Combating Counter-Revolution and Sabotage

The initial letters of those two words – Ч and К – formed the much simpler title of 'Cheka'.

'You'll probably get there before I do,' I said.

388

'I doubt it. The journey will be reasonable to Tyumen. They should be able to load me on a truck from there, but if not I'll have to wait until dark and make my own way to Tobolsk. Nikolai's under house arrest at the Governor's Mansion. I'll try to meet you there.'

'Why Khimki?'

'I know some people,' said Dmitry.

'What do you mean, "people"?'

'I think of them as people.'

'How far is it?'

'We've just crossed the Skhodnya. It won't be long.'

'We must be close to where she died,' I said.

'She?'

There were two women who had died here, minutes apart. Mama had witnessed both events. But only one of them would matter to Dmitry. 'Raisa Styepanovna,' I told him.

'I never really knew,' he said mournfully. He had reason to be sad – Raisa was the one who had transformed him into a vampire. He had loved her in life and in undeath he had been as close to her as any *voordalak* is to its 'parent'. 'Iuda drove her half mad with his magic mirror. That's why I understood what an awful thing it was to do to Ilya. After that it was difficult to perceive her thoughts.'

'She was pushed under a train – beheaded. It must have been very quick.'

'I assume it was Tamara who did it.' He followed up quickly, as if apologizing. 'Don't worry – I'm sure she had her reasons.'

'Actually it wasn't Mama, though she was there. It was my grandmother, Domnikiia.'

Dmitry snorted. 'I never liked that woman.' As he spoke I thought I saw half a smile on his lips. In the past I would have defended her, but not now I knew the truth, not now that I'd seen her with Iuda. And yet she'd sacrificed her own life that day in order to save her only daughter – my mother. She spent the best years of her life in exile with Aleksei. Could she really be condemned for one act, however cruel?

'Can I ask you a favour?' Dmitry's words interrupted my thoughts.

'What?'

'That icon you wear, the one of Jesus. Can I have it?'

I felt myself pale at the very thought of giving it away. My hand instinctively went to my chest to touch it, and I noticed that it was hanging in front of my shirt, not hidden inside it as usual.

'What would a vampire want with the image of Christ?' I asked.

'You know as well as I do that it's just a myth about crosses and things. And I don't want it to bring me closer to God, either.'

'My mother gave it to me,' I said. My voice sounded pathetic, like a child's. I knew I would have to give it to him if he insisted – it was so little to ask for what he had done.

'And her father – *my* father – gave it to her. And his wife, Marfa, my mother, gave it to him. I think it really belongs to my side of the family.'

I could hardly argue with him. I reached up and pulled the chain over my head. I looked at the image one last time. Mama had always said that she pictured Aleksei as looking like that during the years they were apart – she could hardly remember his real appearance. Now I'd seen Aleksei face to face, thanks to Iuda's memories. There wasn't much direct resemblance, but there was an air to Aleksei, a sense of reassurance that he exuded, that explained why Tamara's earliest memories of him had become confused with the image in the icon.

I held it out and he took it from me. I curled my fingers a little as the silver chain slipped through them, as if trying to keep hold of it. I felt the little knot where it had once been hastily repaired. Neither Mama nor I had ever known what had broken it, but now Iuda had shown me. It had happened long ago in 1812, when the vampire Andrei ripped the icon from where it hung around my grandfather's neck.

Dmitry put the chain over his own head and tucked the icon into his shirt. 'Thank you,' he said.

'I don't suppose your comrades in the Cheka will be happy to see you wearing that.'

'I don't suppose they will.' He pulled down the window, causing light flakes of snow to billow into the carriage. 'We're not scheduled to stop at Khimki, so I'll be disembarking the hard

390

way.' He looked over at Nadya, who was still asleep. 'Best not to wake her. Just say goodbye for me.'

He raised his hands and held on to the baggage rack above the door, hanging from it for a moment as he pulled his legs up and swung them out through the window. He sat there, looking out. Now that the window was open I could just make out flickering hints of the countryside rushing past. He'd been right about dawn being close – it was starting to get lighter.

'I'll see you in Tobolsk,' he said. He pushed off with his hands and was flung sideways as the air caught him. I thought I heard the thud of his landing, but it was difficult to tell over the sound of the train. There was little chance of his being hurt, as long as he hadn't fallen back under the wheels. A few seconds later it got suddenly lighter as we raced through Khimki station. I didn't really know the place, but it wasn't a big town. He should easily make it to his 'people' before dawn.

I closed the window and sat back down again. Nadya was moving; the sound must have woken her. Her eyes were still closed, but she was stretching and yawning. When she finally did open them, she looked around blinking.

'Where's Dmitry?' she asked. She narrowed her eyes and looked at me. 'Did you do something to him?'

I laughed. There were two misapprehensions there: that I would and that I could. 'You think I threw him out of the window? You think I've got the strength? Anyway, for the moment I'm me, not Iuda.' I wondered why I'd not made that clear from the first. Perhaps I was just irked by her assumption as to who I was, or who I might be, however rational it happened to be.

'So where is he?' She still didn't sound convinced.

'He threw himself out. He couldn't stay on the train; it'll be light soon.' I tried to expel any trace of annoyance from my voice; what I was going to say next mattered. 'He asked me to say goodbye.'

'Isn't he coming to Tobolsk?'

It wasn't an argument I wanted to have – not yet. 'I'll explain when we get to Moscow.'

*

The sun was just peeking over the buildings as we stepped out on to Kalanchyovskaya Square from the Nikolaievsky Station. It had the same name as the station in Petrograd and if I'd cared to look behind me I'd have seen that it was a very similar building too. The terminus was a little narrower, but the central section of the façade with the distinctive clock tower was almost indistinguishable. And why not? They were built to mark the ends of Russia's first major railway – it would be wasteful to create two designs where one would do. As to the economy of names, they had once been distinct, but with Tsar Nikolai I dying within five years of the line's completion, it was inevitable that one or other station would be named after him. Neither city would relinquish that honour, and so they shared the name.

We'd already made arrangements for Dmitry's package – for Dmitry – to be collected and delivered. The Cheka letterhead and the cash made it all very simple. If everything went according to plan, it should be an easy journey. He would come in, as we had, to the Nikolaievsky Station and then it would take just the short haul of a porter's trolley to carry him across the square to the Yaroslavsky Station, the terminus for the Great Siberian Way. I could see it from here: a bizarre building designed, like the Church on Spilled Blood, to emulate the architecture of a bygone age. It fitted in better here than it would have done in Petrograd, but it still appeared preposterously contrived, certainly for something as modern and functional as a railway station. Just opposite us they were rebuilding Kazansky Station – people sometimes just called this 'Three Station Square' – and had chosen to do it along similar lines to the Yaroslavsky. It was as yet unclear how the final building would turn out; it could hardly be worse than its prototype.

I headed across the square to the tram stops, looking at the signs for the one I wanted – a number four, if things hadn't changed too much since I was last here.

'Why don't we go straight to the station?' asked Nadya, pointing at the monstrous building. 'We can't let her get too far ahead of us.'

'I'm not going by train,' I said. 'And anyway, we've got to find somewhere for you to stay, first.'

'What?'

We joined the queue for the tram. It wasn't so very long, but I doubted we'd make it into the first car that came along.

'It's too dangerous,' I whispered to her, not wanting those around us to hear.

'I'm staying with you,' she replied in a similar tone. I was lucky there were so many people near by. Nadya wanted to argue, but would be loath to cause a scene.

'Either way, we'll need a place to stay when we come back here. And someone has to look after Polkan.' The dog looked up at the sound of his name, then returned to taking in his surroundings. He'd never been to Moscow before.

'You seem to have this all very well planned.'

This part of it, I did.

We stood in silence as one tram came, filled up and left without us. Five minutes later another arrived and we managed to get on, though we couldn't find a seat. I was older than most of them and Nadya was a woman, but still no one offered. The tram rumbled down Myasnitskaya Street and towards the centre of the city. Soon we were in Lubyanka Square, nowadays dominated by the grand, monolithic edifice of the All-Russia Insurance Company. I wondered how long it would be before it was seized by the Bolsheviks to turn into some state building with a preposterously long name. I couldn't see them being happy with so capitalist an institution as an insurance company for very long. We circled round Red Square and the Kremlin to the north. It was only when we crossed Tverskaya Street that we got a decent view – the Resurrection Gate leading into the square and the tower at the northern corner of the Arsenal. Already within the ancient walls the Bolshevik government that had fled Petrograd would be establishing itself in the old – and now new – capital.

We turned south and passed the Manège. It would have brought back memories for Dmitry if he'd been here; it was where he had trained when he first came from his home in Petersburg to join the cavalry. Then we reached the Aleksandr Garden, built on top of the Neglinnaya River. Somewhere beyond that, in a secret dungeon beneath the State Armoury, was where Aleksei had finally met his end, cradled in my mother's arms. Almost immediately the tram turned west down Vozdvizhenka Street. We got off at Arbat Square and headed into the maze of little streets and alleyways to the southeast.

'I know where we're going,' said Nadya.

'Happy to be home?' I asked.

'Papa told me never to come back here; that he never wanted to see me again.'

'I think it was me he never wanted to see again, actually.'

'I don't think he's got anything against Polkan. We'll send him in first.'

I managed a laugh and felt her squeeze my hand. We soon arrived at the foot of the set of five stone steps that led up to the front door. It was familiar, though it had been years since I'd been here. It was still a grand home, even though the paint was peeling around the door and window frames. The steps had been swept clear of snow, unlike those of the houses on either side. I began to climb, but Nadya held back. I turned to her.

'Do you think it's a good idea?' she asked. 'To invite Iuda into our house?'

'He won't be here for long.'

'He doesn't need long.'

I had no argument for her. All I could do was hold out my hand. She took it and we approached the door together. Polkan clambered shakily up the steps and sat at her side, away from me. I banged the heavy iron knocker. There was silence for almost half a minute, and then finally I heard soft, slow footsteps from within. Bolts and chains behind the door were drawn back and the handle began to turn. I remembered Mama's descriptions of this house – the house where she had grown up – and half expected to see the face of Dubois, the butler, revealed as the door was pulled open.

Instead we saw the aged but unmistakable figure of Vadim Rodionovich Lavrov, Nadya's father. He was thirteen years older than me, which put him in his mid-seventies. He looked us up and down, first Nadya, then me.

'I thought you might come here,' he said.

I was about to speak, but Nadya got there first. 'We've nowhere else to go.'

He turned away from us and walked back into the house. For one dreadful moment I thought he was going to close the door on us, but he spoke as he shuffled away. 'You'd better come in.'

Nadya and Polkan went first and I closed the door behind us. Vadim led us to a familiar drawing room. 'It always comes to this,' he said, offering us a seat. 'The Lavrovs taking in the Danilovs.'

It was a fair enough comment, and also the reason I had felt confident that he would do the same as his grandparents had done in adopting Tamara, then aged just five, when Aleksei and Domnikiia went into exile. Nadya and I both smiled weakly, but said nothing.

'Are things in Petersburg as bad as they say?'

I doubted that it was senility that made him forget the new name of the city. There were many of his generation that didn't accept the change.

'It's not that things are bad,' said Nadya. 'It's that they *might* be. The Germans are close. No one wants to risk being there when they arrive.'

'Your bags are coming along later, I presume.'

'We have nothing.'

He shook his head. 'It's a terrible thing, this war.'

'You heard about Ilya, I take it.' Nadya shot me a glance as I spoke, but I knew what I was doing.

The old man nodded. 'His CO sent a letter. He died bravely, so it said. Somewhere in Romania.'

'The First Battle of Cobadin,' I added.

'That's right.'

'I was always surprised he didn't join the navy, like you and your father.'

'And become one of those bastard traitors on the *Avrora*? Better for him to die in battle. He always wanted to be in the army – took after his great-great-grandfather.'

'Vadim Fyodorovich?'

'The man who brought the Danilovs and the Lavrovs together – for better or worse.' He looked at us, one and then the other, smiling. 'I was just about to eat. Come on.' He stood up and made his way out of the room. I didn't know when Nadya had last eaten, but for me it had been over a day. We didn't decline the offer.

'What does the dog have?' he asked.

'Whatever we leave,' said Nadya.

Vadim chuckled. 'There won't be much for him today then. Don't worry – we'll find something.'

We entered the dining room. It was a huge, formal place, an inheritance from a different age. I had eaten here many times before, in happier days. Now there was just one plate, one knife and one fork laid out at the far end of the table.

'The food's in the kitchen,' he said.

'I'll get it,' volunteered Nadya.

'We'd better lay a couple more places,' said Vadim, but as soon as Nadya had disappeared through the door, I took him by the arm and pulled him to one side.

'I won't be staying long,' I said.

He looked puzzled. 'Why did you come, then?'

'To bring Nadya.'

'You're *leaving* her?' For a man who had so objected to our relationship, his horror at the prospect of my ending it was a surprise.

'Not like that. There's something I have to do. It's too dangerous for her.'

'Something to do with the war?'

I shook my head.

'And not to do with the revolution either, I suspect.'

'No, something else.'

He nodded, and looked into my eyes. 'I understand.'

I couldn't doubt that he did – really did. Neither Mama nor I had ever told any of the Lavrovs about the curse that plagued our family, but who could imagine what they had worked out over the years, what stories had been passed from father to son? They would never have guessed the entire truth, but they must have known it was something beyond the everyday disputes of mortal men.

'When I come back we'll find somewhere of our own, but at the moment we have nowhere.'

'Don't worry,' he said. 'I'll look after her.'

*

It was a remarkably good lunch, or breakfast, or whatever the appropriate name for the meal was. There was even wine – a red Burgundy. Vadim explained that food was not quite so scarce here in Moscow as in Petrograd, simply because of the city's location at the centre of so much farmland. But I suspected there was more to it than that. He had clearly been assiduous in making sure he knew where food could be purchased, and how much to pay for it. He was a man who knew how to look after himself.

From the moment I first saw him I was surprised how much he looked like his namesake, Vadim Fyodorovich. He was thinner, and frailer, and had no beard, but there was something in his voice and especially his eyes – I would never forget Vadim Fyodorovich's eyes – that was unmistakable. It brought back memories; memories that I found strangely pleasing; memories that I knew Danilov would be enjoying too. I suspected that even Nadya might draw comfort from tales of the exploits of her heroic forebear.

After lunch we returned to the drawing room. Vadim almost immediately began to doze off. I looked directly at Nadya. 'Of course, you know I met your great-great-grandfather, don't you?'

Vadim turned his head towards me and half opened his eyes, but even if he heard it he didn't seem to balk at the apparent absurdity of my claim. As Danilov had suspected, he surely knew more than he was letting on.

'I suppose you did,' said Nadya. It was enough to make it clear that she was aware of who I now was.

'If you're not interested, I'll quite understand.'

She thought about it for a moment. 'No,' she said cautiously, 'go on.'

I knew where my story would end, but I had to choose where to begin. It was obvious enough. 'I first met Vadim Fyodorovich on the same occasion that I met Lyosha, in a room above an inn not far from here, just off Tverskaya Street. This was in August of 1812. It's long gone now – half burned down in the Moscow Fire, the rest demolished not long after the war. To be honest, I can't say I really noticed Lyosha on that occasion. Vadim was obviously their leader. Lyosha and Maksim Sergeivich were whispering to each other, giggling like schoolboys. But Vadim seemed to understand from the start how much we might be able to achieve.'

'Tell me what he looked like,' said Nadya.

'He was a big man – no taller than average, but solidly built. He must have been in his . . .'

I think I enjoyed listening almost as much as Nadya did. And I couldn't help but believe that Vadim Rodionovich was listening too, although he pretended to be asleep. Quite what he made of it, I didn't begin to guess. Inevitably Iuda spoke of his encounters with Aleksei, which I enjoyed, but we were treading old ground. In the months together at the Peter and Paul he had conveyed everything he had to tell on that matter. But it was pleasant to hear a little more of Vadim and the others. I had the added privilege of being able to experience Iuda's memories directly, as well as hear the descriptions of them that he gave to Nadya and her father. Inevitably, he lied, but it was only the necessary deceit of the raconteur – to make a story run more smoothly, to make a character more convincing. He made his relationship with Aleksei seem more one of good-natured rivalry than bitter confrontation. In truth, in those early weeks of their acquaintance, perhaps it was. And, of course, he never made any mention of Zmyeevich or of a *voordalak*.

Domnikiia cropped up frequently in both his mind and his words. That was to be expected. It was she who had come to live in this house with the unborn Tamara still growing in her belly. Iuda spoke of her with utmost politeness, but whenever he mentioned her name he ensured that an image of her naked, glowing flesh, passionately entwined with his, flashed across his mind. I don't know whether he did it specifically to hurt me or simply because he could not block out what was evidently such a precious memory to him. But his words did not venture into that aspect of their relationship.

He told of their first sally out to meet the advancing French, and of the retreat back to Moscow, and of the evacuation of

Moscow. I couldn't help but feel that his descriptions of that were a little tinted by our recent experiences in Petrograd. But despite how much I was enjoying his stories, I had to ask myself what *he* was gaining from it. Was he trying to ingratiate himself with Nadya? Was he trying to delay our departure? Was he simply – and this was the least persuasive of them all – being nice? It did not matter. With him in charge there was nothing I could do, even if I'd wanted to. And I didn't. I couldn't ever imagine wanting to stop listening to the stories he told. And although I knew Vadim had died in the Patriotic War, I'd never discovered quite how. Perhaps I'd learn something.

'. . . each of them in turn, but they had nothing more to say. Ioann and I turned away. We crossed Red Square, and passed Saint Vasiliy's, following the slope down to the river. Ioann went his own way and I continued over the river by the old wooden bridge. I realized I was being followed before I was halfway across, but it was a long time before I had the chance to take a good enough look behind me to see who it was. The obvious candidate was Lyosha.'

I looked over at the old man. I was sure he was awake now, listening. Nadya stared at me with an intense interest. I could sense Danilov lurking somewhere. I hoped I'd have the chance to finish my story.

'I headed west along the embankment and then crossed back over by the Stone Bridge. As soon as I'd gone around the Kremlin wall and got out of his view I ran as fast as I could. The Neglinnaya was still an open ditch back then, so there were plenty of places to hide. I saw my pursuer pass and was a little surprised to find that it was not Lyosha, but Vadim. I should have guessed. I'm sure you don't want to hear unkind things about him, my dear, but he really wasn't the stealthy hunter that Lyosha was. Lyosha managed to follow a number of us without being detected.'

Nadya gave a slight smile, as if it was nothing. She was right, it was only the slightest speck of dust on her ancestor's reputation. But my story was not yet told.

'He looked around, trying to find me, and then took a guess

and set off into the Arbat. Perhaps he even came this way, though I don't think your family lived in Moscow then, did they?'

'They were in Petersburg,' muttered Vadim Rodionovich, without opening his eyes. 'My father had just been born.'

I nodded. 'That sounds about right. Well, I hadn't meant for Vadim to lose track of me completely, so I ran after him into the Arbat and eventually managed to work my way through the side streets to end up in front of him. It's really just as hard to get someone to pick up your trail as it is to lose them, I can tell you, but in the end he saw me, and believed I hadn't seen him.

'So then I headed home, or rather to one of the abandoned houses we'd been making use of. It was near Kuznetskiy Bridge. That was the quarter where all the French used to live, so nice houses – as you'd imagine – and they'd made a run for it earlier than most. I got a good way ahead of Vadim, but made sure that even through the darkness he would be able to see me as I entered. I wanted a little time to prepare. I left the door unlocked, so that he'd have no trouble getting in.'

Still they showed no sign of suspecting what was to come. Perhaps Danilov did, but for now he was unable to do anything about it. Soon it would be too late.

'I went straight upstairs – we weren't using the ground floor at all. I looked into one of the rooms, but closed and locked the door – I didn't want Vadim going in there.' I didn't tell them why – the bodies of four French soldiers lay on the carpeted floor, their throats ripped out and their blood drained. Later on in the occupation, the room would become full, and then, once the French had departed, we – they – would begin to feed on Moscow's native population.

'I went into the next room off the landing. We'd removed all the paintings and boarded up the windows. There'd been a large mirror in a gilded frame hanging on one wall. We'd taken it down, but not removed it; it was leaning beside the window. The nail that had supported it still jutted out several inches from the wall. Next to that was a folding silk screen, with an oriental motif. There was a single wingback chair, facing away from the door. I could just see someone's arm. I walked around and discovered it was who I had expected: my comrade Andrei. I'd told him to be here.

'"You got one?" Andrei asked.

'I nodded. "He's right behind me."

'Andrei moved quickly and stood against the wall, his head hiding the long nail from view. I took his place in the chair. In the mirror I could see the doorway, and anyone coming in would see me.

'The door opened and in the reflection Vadim locked eyes with me. He stood still for a moment, one hand on the doorknob, a look of surprise on his face – as well there might be. His other hand clutched his sabre. After a moment he spoke.

'"So Aleksei was wrong then. You're not *voordalaki*."

'"Does that make you feel safe – to know that you are facing mere humans, no different from yourself?"

'"It makes me concerned that one of my best officers has gone mad."

'I gave a slight chuckle, but I don't think he had meant it as a joke. "I'm sure Lyosha had the best of reasons."

'Vadim walked further into the room, his sword still raised. He glanced over at Andrei. "Just the two of you here?"

'"It will be enough," I said. Andrei stepped away from the wall and walked towards the mirror, before turning again to face Vadim. Instinctively Vadim adjusted his stance so that his back was to the wall, protected by it.

'"Enough for what?" he asked.

'I glanced over at Andrei and noticed that he was licking his lips. I would have liked to prolong the moment, but I knew I must cater to the whims of Andrei and his kind if I was to keep a hold over them. "Enough to show you the error of your logic."

'Vadim glanced over at Andrei and realized his mistake. It was the same failure of reasoning that Lyosha had committed, but in reverse. Lyosha had seen that the others were vampires and assumed I was. Vadim had seen that I was not

401

and assumed that Andrei was not. But now that Andrei stood in front of the mirror, it was clear that there was no reflection of him. Vadim made the wise move and headed for the door, but I was closer and went to intercept him.

'It was unnecessary. Andrei crossed the room swiftly and already had Vadim in his hands. He held him up by his lapels. Vadim kicked in the air and against Andrei's shins, but to no avail. I'd like to be able to tell you that he screamed, but in truth he remained quite silent. Andrei shifted his grip, now holding Vadim under his chin. He walked forward briskly towards the wall, as if taking a run-up to hurl Vadim some great distance. And hurl him he did, but there was no distance to travel. Vadim slammed into the wall. His head banged against it, his arms splayed out sideways. Andrei stepped back, letting his hand drop to his side. But Vadim was motionless. He did not walk away, but neither did he collapse to the floor. He remained there against the wall, his body hanging limply, his feet not quite touching the ground.

'I went over. Andrei's aim had been perfect – we'd discussed it in advance, of course. The head of the nail protruded just a little, to one side of Vadim's Adam's apple. It was enough to take his weight. What was down to pure luck was that the injury to his neck had paralysed him, but not killed him. I lifted his arm and it fell back lifelessly. But when I looked into his face his eyes flickered desperately across me and across the room behind, as if simply by seeing something he might discover a way to save himself. He tried to speak, but it must have been agony even to move his jaw. I hoped that the rest of his body had been merely immobilized and not deprived of its senses, but it didn't really matter – his imagination remained intact, and that would be enough.

'I stepped back and allowed Andrei to come closer. He looked at me in just the way a dog seeks permission from its master before eating, but I did not delay the moment. I was as eager to watch as he was to feed. I nodded my acquiescence. Andrei stepped forward, his teeth bared, and crooked his neck to the best angle on Vadim's throat, but I didn't need to see what he was doing. Instead I kept my eyes fixed on Vadim's face.

He could make no noise as Andrei's fangs sank into his flesh, could utter no shout. And yet the human soul must find some means to express its agony. Vadim had only one way to do so, and it meant that I could watch in pleasure and fascination as his eyes began to scream.'

CHAPTER XXIV

I RAN TO THE DOOR, ALONG THE PASSAGEWAY AND OUT OF THE house. I lost my footing on the steps and found myself splayed on my back in the snow. I breathed rapidly, staring up at the cloudy sky. The worst of it was that I had been too late. I had guessed what Iuda was planning from the moment he mentioned Vadim following him. From then on I'd been trying to do something, to say something, or to flee the room. That I had finally been able to do so only in the instant at which it became too late indicated a strengthening of Iuda's power. The timing could not be coincidence; Iuda had gained some control over it, however slight. He had been able to resist me. Perhaps he was now in complete control, and had merely chosen that moment to yield, having determined it was the best way to cause me suffering.

A hand reached down to help me to my feet. It was Nadya.

'You see now why I can't be with you,' I screamed at her. 'He can't be trusted. *I* can't be trusted.'

She said nothing.

'How's your father?' I asked more calmly.

'I didn't stop to find out. He's just sitting there, gazing into nothing. I'm sure he took it all in.'

'Why didn't you stop me – stop Iuda?'

'How did I know what he was going to say?' Her voice betrayed her anger.

'Couldn't you have guessed?'

'And then done what?'

I hugged her. I feared for a moment that she might resist it, but she did not. 'Forget about it,' I said. 'I'm going to go now.'

'To Tobolsk? To save the tsar?'

'And to find a way out.'

'A way out?'

'A way to be rid of Iuda.'

'You think it's possible?'

'It must be. And the good thing is that Iuda wants it as much as I do. Ascalon is the key.' I was guessing. Somewhere in my head I could hear Iuda laughing.

She pulled away and looked up at me. I expected her to suggest something that would mean I should stay for just a few more minutes. I would gladly have accepted, even if it meant facing her father after what I'd said. But Nadya was more practical than I could be.

'I'll get your things.'

She went back inside. I looked up at the house, up at the window of what I knew had been my mother's room, from where she had stood as a child to watch her father leave, not knowing then that he would never return. Domnikiia had been standing beside her, apparently as concerned as Tamara. What had really been in her mind? Had she been thinking of Iuda – of the evening they spent together? Mama never suspected a thing; it was no small blessing.

Nadya came back out with my coat and hat and scarf. Polkan was at her side. I put the clothes on and squatted down beside him. He seemed entirely to have forgotten his misgivings about me. I stroked his muzzle and whispered a goodbye. Then I stood again. I held Nadya's hands and we kissed. It was a long, deep, passionate kiss. We had exchanged nothing like it since . . . since it had been Iuda who kissed her. I successfully fought the urge to pull away. I would not allow Iuda to spoil this moment – this memory – for either of us. At last we stepped apart. Nadya glanced downwards and broke into a smile. I followed her gaze to see Polkan staring up at us adoringly, his tongue hanging from one side of his mouth.

I let go of Nadya's hands and reached under my coat, into my jacket pocket. I took out the letter I had written, feeling the firm lump within. I gave it to her. She read the words on the envelope silently, but I knew them well enough.

To Nadya.
To be opened only if I do not return within a month.
With all my love,
Misha.

She looked up at me, her eyebrows raised in concern.

'You won't have to open it,' I said. Again I heard laughter.

She nodded contemplatively. 'Go now,' she said.

I tried to turn away, but found myself unable. For a moment I thought that Iuda was in control once more, but it was something simpler, more natural than that.

'I can't,' I said. I felt a quaver in my voice. My eyes were wet. 'Not while you're here.'

She smiled at me, but soon turned away. Polkan gave me a confused glance, but followed her. They climbed the stone steps and she closed the door behind them without turning her head in my direction again. I walked away. At the end of the street I took one last look behind me. She was standing there, at the window of what had once been my mother's room, watching me go. She did not wave.

At Arbat Square I boarded another tram – a number 13 this time, though I found it difficult to see how the bad luck associated with the number could make my life any worse. We set off north along the Boulevard Ring. The journey would take about half an hour, and after that it would only be a short walk to—

I pulled myself up, realizing the mistake I was making. It was I who had boarded the tram, but it might be Iuda who had to disembark. He needed to know what my plan was – certainly this first part of it.

'Iuda,' I thought, almost as if speaking. 'Iuda, I need to explain where we're going.'

I paused instinctively, waiting for a response, but I knew he was incapable of giving one. It was unnerving, but I had little doubt he was paying attention.

'You need to know where we're going,' I continued. 'It's the Khodynka Field. You must know where that is – it was around in your day, though it's changed a bit since. Get off the tram at Petrovsky Park and then go left, to the southwest. It's only a verst or so – you can't miss it. Once you get there, just wait until I come back. Trust me – it's the quickest way we'll get to Tobolsk.'

That was enough to tell him for now. He wouldn't even be able to guess at what that vast open space was currently used for. He would have known it as the location of the hippodrome. A lot had happened there since then – awful things. In a sense Khodynka was where the whole revolution began. It was 18 May 1896, just four days after Tsar Nikolai's coronation. The field was to be a place of public celebration. Around half a million people turned up – stayed up celebrating through the night. Nikolai had promised gifts for all: bread, sausage, pretzels, beer – and a cup decorated with the monogram of Their Imperial Majesties. But in the early morning gossip started spreading through the crowd. It was nothing terrible – just the rumour that there wouldn't be enough free pretzels to go round. But it was enough.

They pushed forwards towards the wooden stalls, each person trying to get his share before supplies ran out. The police tried to keep order, but they were ridiculously outnumbered. People fell into the ditches that had been dug for army training and were crushed under the others who landed on top. Some were just trampled by the surging crowd.

In the end there were about 1400 dead. You could hardly blame Nikolai for that. He'd just said the people should have a party, and he expected his underlings to organize it properly. But you *could* blame him for what happened next. After he heard about the tragedy, he went to a ball held by the French ambassador. They say he was influenced by his uncles, and that may be true, but it set the trend. Throughout his reign he never killed his subjects, he just did nothing about it when they died.

It was the same on Bloody Sunday – he didn't order the troops to fire, but he never did enough to make up for it afterwards. And in February he just did nothing. That's what lost him his throne.

If Danilov was continuing to ramble on, I could no longer hear him. It was a shame. The forty-year gap in my knowledge of history made me uncomfortable. It was amusing as well as fascinating to learn that it was the bumbling incompetence of Tsar Nikolai which had brought about the downfall of the Romanovs. I'd met a few of them in my time, and it sounded as though Nikolai had the worst combination of the characteristics that they all shared in some measure. Some were strong, others weak. Some were conservative, others progressive. Some were autocratic, others took advice. But to be conservative took strength. Nikolai, from what I had learned, believed in the God-given authority of the tsar, but did not have the personal conviction to carry it through. He took the wrong advice, and then stuck to it with a degree of arrogance found only in a genius or a fool.

But Danilov had also managed to intrigue me. How could a journey to this wide, flat, empty space on the outskirts of the city help to speed our passage to Tobolsk? I might have imagined it to be the site of a new railway station, but that did not seem likely – especially since I'd already learned that the Yaroslavsky Terminus was the best starting point. I could not imagine how the distance could be covered any more quickly than by train. Even these new motor cars seemed slow and unreliable in comparison, although I'd only seen them operate in the restrictive environment of the city.

I felt confident, though, that this was no trap. I could sense in Danilov's mind no hint that he had discovered a means to rid himself of me, however much he lied to his mistress about it. Even if he had found a way, I was sure that saving the tsar from whatever Susanna had planned was a higher priority. But I knew I must be wary.

Ahead I saw the golden dome of the Petrovsky Palace, surrounded by parkland. I stood to get off, but hesitated for a moment. It would be an elegant plan on Danilov's part if he had persuaded me to walk willingly to my own execution. That, though, was to project my own emotions on to him. Where I would always want to exhibit my genius to the world, he would be happy merely to achieve his goal. But in the time we had been together, how much of my personality had infiltrated his? How much of his mine?

I really had no option. I stepped down from the tram. I knew the way to the Khodynka Field well enough, though I'd never been closer than I was now. It didn't take me long to get there, but it was a vast expanse and Danilov had given no indication as to which part of it he wanted to visit. After a quarter of an hour I'd come to a point where I could survey the whole area. What I saw made little sense to me, but had clearly been designed with a purpose. The area was wide and flat, and largely barren but for a few large huts, big enough to be warehouses, and one squat brick building. Most of the field was made over to short grass, but cutting through that were two straight roadways. I was standing at the eastern extreme of one of them; it must have been over a verst to the other end. From above the two would have formed the shape of a cross. They were of a dark grey, verging on black, and seemed to have been macadamized in some way, though by a process more advanced than any I'd seen.

The strangest thing about the place was the vehicles – I could only presume that was what they were – which were stationed near the huts. My instinct was that there would be more of them inside. From a distance it was difficult to make them out, but they were not like the motor cars I had seen on the roads. They sat higher on their wheels, more like traditional horse-drawn carriages, except that they had only one axle, not two – more like a Stanhope. On each of them one end, the thinner end, drooped and rested against the ground, as if waiting for a team of horses to be put into harness and raise it up. But that was only the view I had from the side.

From the front – or the rear – I could see that these machines were preposterously wide. Sticking out from either side of them were long, flat planes of, presumably, wood, though possibly some other material. Each had two of these, one above the other. Clearly they had a purpose, and my mind began to formulate what it might be.

My thoughts were shattered by a horrendous noise coming from behind me. It was the same as the sound made by the engine of a motor car, but far louder. I turned, afraid that it would knock me down, but for a moment could see nothing. Then my eyes fixed more accurately on the source of the sound. It was in the air. My embryonic theories as to

409

the nature of these vehicles was confirmed. It was a flying machine – not some kind of navigable balloon, but a vehicle that actually supported itself on the air, as a bird does. When the German bombs had fallen on Petrograd I'd been unable to see where they came from. Danilov had used the word 'biplane', but it had made little sense to me. Now I realized what these machines were, and how they had managed to travel so far and drop their explosives so precisely.

I didn't have much time to consider this wondrous feat of engineering. It passed just a few feet over my head, the wind of it throwing me on to my back. I quickly rolled on to my stomach and watched its descent. The wheels touched down on the straight roadway in front of me, and it gradually slowed from the speed it had required to maintain its suspension in the air to one more suited to travelling over the surface of the Earth. Soon it turned and headed slowly towards one of the huts.

From somewhere near there two men emerged, running. It took only a moment to realize that they were coming in my direction. I managed to get to my feet, but I knew I wouldn't be able to outrun them – nor was I certain that I wanted to. Was this what Danilov had been planning? Now they were close enough for one of them to shout to me.

'What the hell are you doing? You'll get yourself killed.'

I said nothing, but waited for them to approach. I slipped my hand into my pocket and fingered my double-bladed knife. That would not have been part of Danilov's plan, but it might prove useful. The younger man of the two continued to speak.

'And what about the damage you could have done to the aeroplane? Who the devil are you, anyway?'

The older man had stopped in his tracks. He was saluting with a mechanical rigidity. It took me a moment to understand that the object of the gesture was myself.

'Lieutenant,' he said sternly. 'This man is Colonel Mihail Konstantinovich Danilov.'

'Who?'

'Colonel Danilov. One of the founders of the Service.' The

older man, a captain, relaxed his salute and came forward to offer me his hand. I shook it. 'It's good to see you again, sir.'

'You too, captain,' I said, hoping that I wouldn't be pressed any further in regard to how well I remembered him, or what his name was.

'You'll be wanting to see Major Tsigler, I expect.'

'That's right. Is he here?' I could only assume that this was what Danilov had intended.

The captain and the lieutenant led me across the field towards the low square building from which, I guessed, the whole place was commanded. As we walked I saw another of the vehicles coming in to land. It bounced off the roadway a couple of times, then slewed to the right, on to the grass. Clearly this was a technology that was in its infancy. Even so the vehicle and its operator were unharmed. We soon reached the building and I was shown into a small office with a desk and two chairs. On a side table sat a samovar. A window overlooked the field. The walls were covered with maps, with annotations that were unfamiliar to me – evidently specific to aviation. I was left alone for a moment and then the door opened. A major walked in – I could only guess it was Tsigler.

He grabbed my hand and kissed me on each cheek. 'Mihail Konstantinovich. How wonderful to see you.'

'You too,' I replied.

'Sit! Sit!'

I took the chair he'd indicated.

'Tea?'

'Yes please.'

He went to the samovar and drew two glasses, giving one to me. He sat on the corner of his desk, close to me.

'I heard rumours about your problems with the Bolsheviks. All over now, I take it?'

'I hope so,' I said.

'I thought that might be why you've come to see me.'

I could tell from the tone of his voice that he was fishing. I'd gladly have told him why I was here, but I still wasn't entirely sure. It seemed that Danilov intended for us to fly to Tobolsk. I had no reason to doubt it was possible, but I knew that if I raised the point there would be a dozen follow-up questions that would reveal me quite ignorant of what Danilov should readily know. At best they would think he had grown senile, and that would not help our cause. All I could do was procrastinate and await his return.

'All in good time. But first tell me how you've been faring since the revolution.'

He chuckled and moved behind the desk to his chair. 'No worse than most, I suspect. We are, of course, no longer the Imperial Russian Air Service. We are in fact a department of the All-Russia Collegium for the Direction of the Air Forces of the Former Army. Our commander is Konstantin Vasilievich Akashev – you remember him, of course.'

'Vaguely,' I said.

He looked puzzled; evidently I should have had a clearer recollection. 'Well, after he was exiled for that plot against Stolypin he went to Europe – learned to fly there, first in Italy then France. When the war started he flew for the French, but then came back here in '15. Wasn't allowed in the air, of course, not with his past, but we let him work in the factories. Didn't hear of him much, and then after October he popped up as a leading Bolshevik and since he's the only one with any flying experience they put him in charge.'

'He any good?'

'Hard to tell. His main worry at the moment is not to lose too many pilots to the other side.'

'To the Germans?'

This time his frown showed deeper concern. 'No, to the Whites. This whole thing is turning into a civil war. The Reds would rather destroy planes than lose them – same goes for pilots. Now there's peace with Germany, we can all move on to the next war.'

'Peace?'

'Hadn't you heard? Trotsky finally signed the treaty yesterday – at Brest-Litovsk.'

'So the whole evacuation to Moscow was a waste of time.'

He shrugged. 'As I said, it's not just the Germans they're afraid of. To be honest, Mihail, I'm worried. We're not like the other forces – you know that. I don't think there's ever been more than a handful of Bolsheviks in the whole service – none amongst the flyers. That's why they're scared of us. They haven't infiltrated us, so they're going to have to break us. Just yesterday I received—'

'Look, Sergei, I won't beat about the bush. I need a plane.'

Simply to be able to speak again was like breathing after being submerged under water. I couldn't blame Iuda; rather I had to admire him. He'd done a good job of hiding his ignorance. But time was pressing.

'A plane? What for?'

'I can't tell you, but it needs to be long-range; the longest you've got.'

'How far are you planning to travel?'

I hesitated. It was a preposterous journey. 'Around two and a half thousand versts.'

He raised an eyebrow, but didn't laugh out loud. 'A trip to Europe? No, you'd never get through with the rest of them still at it. East then – to Siberia?' He stood and looked at the chart on the wall behind him. 'That would take you to somewhere around—'

'Tobolsk,' I said, saving us both some time.

He leaned forward, grinning, his hands on the desk to take his weight. 'I knew it!' he said. 'I knew it wasn't over.'

Tsigler had always been a staunch royalist and I'd been counting on the fact. Even the hint that I might be doing something to rescue the tsar was enough to bring him to my side. I didn't need to tell him just what I was saving Nikolai from.

'Do you have anything like that?' I asked.

He smiled and nodded. 'You ever flown a Lebed XII?'

I smiled back. 'I took one up when they were first being tested, back in '16. Just for a spin around the airfield. But that would be perfect.'

'I can go one better. We've got a Lebed XIII.'

'I thought they never made it off the drawing board.'

'A few did. And we have one here. Mind you, it still won't take you much over four hundred versts in a single hop. You'll have to

413

keep stopping to refuel, but we should be able to load you up with enough. When do you need to go?'

'As soon as possible.'

He put his hands together, pressing his lips against his fore-fingers. I was asking a lot of him, but I knew where his loyalties had always lain. After a few seconds he snapped to a decision. He stood and went outside. Five minutes later he was back.

'She'll be ready in half an hour, with more than enough fuel to get you there. I don't imagine you'll be bringing him back here, but you'll need to get more juice if you want to do anything like that. They're putting in some provisions too. Have you worked out your route?'

'I thought I'd stick to the railway line out to Tyumen, then follow the Tura until it joins the Tobol.'

He nodded. 'That's your best bet. I've told them to fit you up with a searchlight, but you'll have to keep low during the night.' He went to a chest of map drawers and opened one. He pulled out a chart and rolled it up. 'This should help you, but it's pretty much as you said.'

'I don't suppose you've got a map of Tobolsk itself?' I asked.

He went to another drawer and searched through it. Eventually he found something. He showed it to me. 'His Majesty's staying here, at the Governor's Mansion.'

He circled it with his pencil. It was odd to hear the phrase 'His Majesty', even though it had been only a year since it had been commonplace. I did not relish its return; neither did I like to deceive Tsigler by pretending that I did.

'The best place to land would be on the river – the Tobol merges with the Irtysh just south of the town. The ice should still be solid enough. If not, one of the fields to the west.'

He opened a drawer in his desk. 'You'll need these too.' He handed me a flying helmet, gloves and goggles. 'They're mine, but I can easily find some more. They should fit you.'

'Thanks,' I said.

We sat in silence, sipping our tea. I had the urge to engage him in idle conversation; he might be the last friend I ever spoke to. But I could think of little to say. In truth, we weren't very close. We'd been thrown together, along with many others, out of our

414

mutual fascination with aviation and out of the army's desire to put this new technology to some military use. As I recalled he'd accused me of being a revolutionary when I'd taken my seat in the Duma, but he seemed to have got over it.

The time passed slowly, but eventually the lieutenant I'd met earlier returned. 'All ready, sir,' he said.

We got up and went outside. The sun was low in the sky, but it wasn't yet dusk. I wondered where Susanna and Dmitry had got to. She wouldn't be at Tyumen yet and even then she'd have to get to Tobolsk by road. If she managed it before dawn we'd have no chance. Dmitry would be a long way behind her, assuming his package had even been collected.

My heart beat a little faster as I saw the biplane parked on the runway. It looked almost new, painted in the gold and orange of the Second Petrograd Air Group, with the white, blue and red flash of the Russian flag on its tail. God knew what it was doing down here. I wouldn't have been able to tell it from a Lebed XII, but supposedly the XIII could go faster and further. It was meant for a crew of two, but I'd be able to handle it alone. The machine gun was still mounted behind the observer's seat, well out of my reach.

I looked inside. The observer's seat itself had been removed and the space filled with metal fuel cans. I would have to remember that we would be back-heavy, though the centre of gravity would shift as one by one they were used up. The lieutenant opened up a set of portable steps and placed it beside the trailing edge of the lower wing. I climbed up then carefully placed a foot on the wing itself, making sure to put my weight on the wooden frame and not the unsupported canvas. I licked a finger and held it in the air, but it was unnecessary.

'The wind's just north of easterly, sir,' said the lieutenant.

I thanked him, then looked down at the pilot's seat. As promised there was a tin ration box, and beside it a thermos. I stowed them underneath, then slipped into the seat. To be honest, that time I'd tried out the Lebed XII in Petrograd had been the last time I'd flown, but I knew it would come back to me. Tsigler stood at the propeller, ready to start the engine. I opened the choke and turned on the ignition, then gave him the thumbs up.

He put both hands on the edge of one of the twin blades, then pulled down rapidly, expertly stepping away as he did. He might have been a senior officer, but he knew how to perform every task that was required on an airfield. In the early days we'd all had to. The engine fired twice, but didn't spring to life. I pulled the throttle out a little. Tsigler tried again. This time the propeller began to turn. After two painfully slow rotations it almost halted, but I adjusted the fuel again and the engine began to purr. I slowed it to a comfortable idle. Tsigler walked away and the lieutenant pulled the chocks clear of the wheels. I increased the revs and we began to move.

We were just about at the cross where the two landing strips met. One ran roughly north–south, the other east–west, though they didn't align precisely with the compass. I needed to take off into the wind, so I taxied to the western end. Once we were clear of the officers, I spoke out loud, quietly and precisely.

'Iuda, you need to pay attention to everything I do. I'll get her airborne, but if you have to fly her, just keep her steady and follow the railway. Stay low. I'll take you through a landing as soon as we get the chance, so make sure you pay attention. You may have to do it yourself if we get low on fuel.'

Even as I spoke, I realized the madness of what I was describing. It was as though I were a pilot in the grip of some sleeping disease. If Iuda were to take over, it would be as if I wasn't there at all. But I was confident he would prove to be a quick learner. He wanted to live – more than I did. That would inspire him.

I turned the plane around and let her build to full revs. I couldn't remember the XII well enough to be able to say that this was more powerful, but it was certainly an impressive machine. We were just passing the buildings when I felt the wheels lift off the ground. I gave a wave to the three officers, and we were away.

CHAPTER XXV

IWAS PREPOSTEROUSLY EXCITED. THE ADVANCE OF SCIENCE – OF technology – had always been a steady, piecemeal thing. That had its appeal, but left room for little that was an utter surprise, that was totally new. In the four decades I had slumbered, this novel means of transportation had arisen from nothing. If I had been alive then this would be but the last of a sequence of small steps. I would feel as much exhilaration as did Danilov on comparing the Lebed XIII with the XII – and that gave him exhilaration enough. But for me this was like being a child again, entering into a world that adults had grown to find mundane and taking joy from each new discovery.

Danilov was enjoying it too. He repeatedly looked over the side to gaze down on Moscow, thus giving me the pleasure of seeing the city as I had never seen it before. But he had a serious intent too. He was teaching me what I needed to know when the moment came that I would have to fly this aeroplane myself. Much as he and Tsigler had discussed, he was following the roads, even here in the city. For all that the streets looked like a map, there were no names on them. It would be easy to get lost.

We tracked the Petrograd Highway back towards the centre of the city, then turned along the garden ring. We can't have been more than a thousand feet up, below the clouds, so it was all easy to see. To the south I could make out the Kremlin, Red Square and Saint Vasiliy's, and even the Moskva beyond. Every gleaming dome and spire looked different from up here, almost as if they had been designed to be viewed from this angle, rather than from the ground. Perhaps they had been – they had been built to please an absent God. Now, finally, man could take his place.

The wings dipped to the left as we turned. I had already worked out that this was how we could manoeuvre. But it gave us the added advantage of having a better view on that side. There was a mess of railway tracks beneath us, and I caught a glimpse of the Yaroslavsky Terminus. I could only agree with Danilov as to its hideousness. We straightened up along the line of the tracks, heading north. I was glad it was Danilov who was guiding us. I wouldn't have been able to pick the correct line, and we might well have ended up back in Petrograd. But he was quite confident.

The tracks split and curved to the east, then split again. Before very long we were well out of the city, with only a single railway line stretching ahead. I wanted to turn and look behind us, but I had no control over our movements. Thankfully Danilov was possessed of the same desire. He twisted his head back, keeping just one hand on the controls. The city looked exquisite, lit by the rays of the setting sun. I sensed that Danilov was saying farewell to it. And that would mean that I was too.

We turned forwards again. We had drifted a little off course, but Danilov soon corrected us. Ahead we saw a train, travelling at full steam away from Moscow and into the east. We overtook it easily, going at comfortably twice its speed. Danilov began to talk me through the controls, showing me how to use the joystick and the pedals at my feet, explaining what the dials and gauges in front of me meant. It seemed clear enough, but I knew that I was someone better capable of understanding on an intellectual level than a practical one. I could comprehend more readily than most the mechanisms that conspired to make a rifle so effective a weapon, but I had never been a very good shot. Worse still, in most flying lessons the student would have the chance to take the controls for a few moments and then hand them back to the teacher. For us this would not happen. At some random moment I would be given command and Danilov would not have the opportunity to correct my mistakes for several hours.

As it grew darker Danilov took the aeroplane low. There was no moon to act as a guide, but the electric lamp slung beneath us could just about pick out the railway line, though only from a distance of a hundred feet or so. What had begun as exciting now became tedious. There was nothing to see but the dim spot of light on the tracks below. Occasionally we lost it, but Danilov soon had us back on course. It was a frightening idea, though; we could so easily break the link with our only reference and be adrift above the vast Russian steppe. There was a compass in the cockpit, but it could only tell us in what direction we were going, not where we were.

Suddenly I felt as though I was falling backwards. I could see nothing but the stars. The engine began to strain. I turned my head and caught a glimpse of what might be the ground, far behind me. At the same moment I realized that I was able to turn my head – that I was once again in charge of our body. I was flying the plane – and flying it badly. I pushed forward on the stick and we began to flatten out, but also to slow down. Then we were falling, as if the magic that had been holding us aloft had suddenly been taken away – as if, like Peter walking on the Sea of Galilee, I had failed to show the faith that had been so strong in Danilov, and was now sinking to my death.

But I knew it was no magic that kept this machine in the air. Even if I didn't understand the engineering, I understood the basic science. It was some application of Bernoulli's principle. The airflow over the wings caused a loss of pressure that lifted them up – and that lift increased with the speed of the airflow. I pulled out the throttle and we began to speed up, but still the aircraft jerked and twitched like a leaf caught in the breeze. At last I managed to coax it back to steady, controlled flight, keeping the wings level on either side of me, and holding the tail just high enough. I felt a momentary pride at my skill, but it soon dissipated. I was completely lost. I didn't even know our altitude. Below, the light disappeared into darkness before it reached the ground. I descended cautiously and soon I could see woodland rushing past below us. I went a little further, until we were again at around 100 feet.

There was no sign of the railway. I looked at the compass. We were heading almost due south. Previously our path had been northeast. I turned left until we were back on the right bearing. Now we were travelling parallel to the railway, assuming it hadn't changed direction, but I still did not know where it was. Given that we had been heading south, it was probably to the north, but we could have gone in any direction while the plane was out of control. I turned north, looking out of the cockpit for any sign of the track, but also counting seconds. I saw nothing. After a minute I turned back south and stuck to the course for 90 seconds. Still there was no sign of the railway. I continued the process, increasing the duration and therefore the distance of the journey each time. It was on the ninth pass, almost half an hour later, that I finally saw the tracks – *some* tracks at any rate, and I doubted there would be more than one line out here.

I turned back on to them, heading once again northeast, and feeling quite proud of myself for the way I'd handled things. But I still didn't feel confident to land the thing. I looked at the fuel gauge; we had half a tank left. I could only hope that Danilov would return in time. He was an idiot. We had no control over when the change between us took place – we couldn't even predict it. It would get us both killed. And that meant he wasn't an idiot. That was what he wanted. He didn't care about the tsar, or Ascalon. His one goal was just the same as it always had been – my destruction. But I wasn't going to make it easy for him. I gripped the joystick with new resolution. I would fly this thing, and if need be I would land it.

I watched as the fuel gauge gradually moved closer to empty.

We still had a few minutes left when I brought the plane in to land. I hadn't rushed. I'd been back in control for some time, but there was no point in landing before we needed to. I could only say that I was impressed by Iuda's handling of the aeroplane, not so much in his regaining control, but in the methodical way he had got us back on course. During the war we'd lost as many planes to bad navigation as we had to German guns.

I talked Iuda through what I was doing. We would have to break the journey up into five or six legs, and that meant five or six landings. The chances were he would be in command for at least one of those. There were plenty of fields long enough for us to land and take off. I chose one right beside the railway. It took me only minutes to refill the fuel tank from one of the cans we had brought. I left the engine running. Then we were away again. As we flew, I remembered Nikolai Ivanovich Kibalchich. He had been a brilliant engineer and had told me his dreams of building a machine that would take men to the moon. His idea had been nothing like this – it was based on rockets – but he would still have been overjoyed to see how much had been achieved by others with the same boundless imagination that he possessed. I remembered us discussing the fact that though it would be men like him who designed such a vehicle, it would be a man like me who piloted it. That had been proved correct. It was my conversations with him that had sparked my curiosity and made me so keen to be one of the pioneers when the military finally realized the power of what Kibalchich had envisaged.

I wondered which he would have been happier to witness coming to fruition: his dreams of powered flight or his dreams of a Russia free from the tyranny of any tsar. He had not come close to seeing either. He'd been hanged in 1881 for his part in murdering the only decent tsar I'd ever known – Aleksandr II.

As we flew on into the night it began to grow bitterly cold. The fact we were so low meant the temperature was better than it might have been, but I doubted we would survive until morning. And there was always a risk the ailerons would freeze up. When the fuel again began to run low, I looked for a place to spend the night. I wanted to avoid civilization. Any town out here would be under the control of either the Reds or the Whites. I could prove my loyalty to neither, and each would want to requisition a weapon as valuable as a Lebed XIII. Eventually I saw a field with a barn in it. By my reckoning we were still some way short of Vyatka. Once we'd landed it was no problem to find wood for a fire, and we could spare a little fuel to get one started. The barn was big enough for it to be safe to have the fire inside. I had to stop the aircraft's engine, which would mean starting it again in the morning. That would be easy enough with two of us.

I laughed out loud. It was a good thing, I suppose, to regard Iuda as a separate being from myself, so separate that he had his own physical presence. Better that than admit that with every day our minds were bound more tightly one to the other. And for now it didn't matter. Even on my own I'd be able to start the engine – it would just take a bit of running back and forth from the cockpit to the propeller as I adjusted the controls. I opened the tin box and found some sandwiches in there, filled with sausage. The tea in the flask was almost cold, but it was delightfully sweet. I lay back against the barn wall and fell asleep, warmed by the fire.

I awoke to find that we were flying. Ahead of us the sun was just beginning to creep over the horizon. Evidently Iuda had awoken before me and managed to move our body without disturbing my slumbering mind. He'd even managed to get the plane started and to take off. I was impressed by his skill, and by his determination to get to Tobolsk as quickly as possible.

Beneath us the railway tracks rolled unceasingly by. All morning we saw only two trains, one in each direction. The roads were busier. On one an armoured car stopped and took some shots at us, but Iuda smoothly dipped away and returned to our planned route a few versts later, when we were out of sight. He didn't bother to consult the chart, but I noted the towns and cities as we passed over them, first Vyatka and then Perm. After that we crossed the Urals and we were truly in Siberia.

Iuda landed us for that stint, refuelled, and took off again. After about an hour I discovered that I was again in command. Just like Iuda I momentarily lost control as our hands went limp for a period during which he was not able to use them and I was not aware that I was supposed to. I regained control more quickly than he had, but I realized he couldn't really be blamed for what had happened; it would be the same for even the finest of pilots under these circumstances.

As we passed over the city of Yekaterinburg I looked at the fuel gauge. We were doing well. With luck we'd be able to make it all the way with just one more refuelling. We made the stop about a hundred versts before Tyumen, after which we still had spare in the cans. At Tyumen we left the railway and followed the river northeast. It meandered wildly, and it was easier to climb to a higher altitude and get a view of its general direction than to stay close and follow its every twist and turn. The road to Tobolsk followed the valley. I wondered if Susanna or even Dmitry was somewhere down there, in a lorry, safely shielded from the sun. It would be dusk soon. We weren't going to make it to Tobolsk by then, not by several hours. It might be that we were already too late. It was Tuesday evening now – almost two days since Susanna had left Petrograd. If she'd been lucky with her journey she might already have arrived. On the other hand, she might not get here until tomorrow. We would soon know.

As chance would have it, it was I who was granted the honour of bringing us in for our final descent. Just as Major Tsigler had suggested, the broad, white river made an obvious landing strip. I could only hope that the ice was still thick, but I was in little doubt. It was colder here than it had been in Petrograd.

I took a long approach. For most of the trip the wind had been from the east, but now it was northerly, which aligned roughly with the river. That would make it easier. I turned into the wind and pushed in the throttle, pulling back on the stick as Danilov had shown me. I was only a few feet from the ice now. I'd already done this, on snow, so I felt confident. Even so, I was cautious; we had distance enough for a gentle touchdown. Then, without warning, we dropped like a stone. I tried to understand what was happening, but my only guess was that close to the ground the wind was coming from a different direction. I revved the engine up to full power, hoping to gain enough lift to give us some kind of soft landing.

To that extent it worked, but in achieving it I was distracted from the dozen other factors that required attention. The wing dipped to the left and brushed against the ice. That wouldn't have been so bad, but just ahead was a bank of blown snow. The wingtip sliced into it and came almost to a halt; the rest of the plane did not. We pivoted round the point where it was stuck until the wing became free. Our momentum carried us on in the direction we had been travelling, but now our motion was sideways. We were still in the air, but no longer flying. Now the leading wing hit the ice and dug into it. We flipped right over. The wing collapsed and the fuselage began to fall, still spinning.

I found myself out of the plane, sliding across the ice on my back. I heard a regular thumping sound, accompanied by the noise of the engine, struggling to stay alive. As soon as I came to a halt I rolled on to my stomach and looked. It was an awful mess. The right wing had been torn away completely. The left was twisted under the fuselage, tipping the plane forward. The sound I'd heard was the one remaining blade of the propeller thwacking against the ice. Soon the engine could do no more and stuttered to a halt.

I stood up and mentally checked my body, but found nothing that felt worse than a bruise. I wondered if I should go and rescue what few possessions we had in there, but something – Danilov's years of experience – held me back. Seconds later I saw flames begin to flicker around the engine. It was nothing much at first, but soon the canvas that formed the skin of the plane began to burn too. There would still be a little petrol in the tank and more in the refuelling cans. Whether it would burn or explode I did not know – and I wasn't going to stay to find out.

Fortunately the map that Tsigler had given us was in my pocket. There was a single wooden bridge over the river, shown on the map, which acted as a reference point. The Governor's Mansion – indeed the whole town – was situated on the right bank. It was impossible that the burning aeroplane would not attract attention, but that might be to our advantage. There would still be guards at the mansion; the spectacle might draw some of them away. I climbed off the ice near the foot of the bridge. It didn't take long to find the place. It was an uninspiring building: square and squat – two storeys high.

I guessed it was about a hundred years old. Looking back towards the river I could see the glow of flames, and a column of smoke rising high into the air. No one could miss it, and therefore no one would be paying much attention to guarding the prisoner. It couldn't have worked better if I had planned it.

I skirted warily around the building, considering the best way to break in.

Iuda would have done better to have invested his caution in flying the plane than in getting into the house. But I couldn't blame him. I'd had hours of training before ever taking an aeroplane in to land; and I'd never had to put one down on ice like that. There was a wooden fence between us and the mansion, but it was little problem to climb over. The entrance to the building was an excessively grand portico whose roof formed a balcony accessible from the rooms on the first floor. At the window that looked out on to the balcony I saw the silhouette of a girl, staring into the night. I don't think she saw me. I knew that all four of the tsar's daughters lived here with him. That could well be one of them, perhaps his youngest, Anastasia. Or it could be a different Anastasia.

I looked around but saw no one on guard. As I got closer, I could see why. From a distance the untidy heap near the door had looked like a pile of earth. That should have raised my suspicions. The ground was iron-hard here and there would be no cultivation possible until spring. If the mound had been paler I might have taken it for shovelled snow, but as I got closer I could make out that its dark brown was the familiar colour of a Bolshevik's leather overcoat.

There were two of them, one heaped on top of the other. I pulled the first one away by his shoulder. He rolled over and then slid down his comrade's back on to the snowy ground, their leather coats offering little friction to one another. It was a familiar wound – his throat had been ripped open. It had been done quickly – to kill rather than to feed – and recently. I doubted he'd been dead even half an hour. I turned the other one over to see much the same injuries. They wouldn't have stood a chance;

even for hardened thugs such as these, the sight of a young girl trudging through the snow would have aroused more sympathy than suspicion. That was presuming that Susanna had come alone, but I could not see who might have helped her. She had run out of allies.

I realized I'd come without a weapon, but I was in a garden and it didn't take long to find something appropriate. Along the fence that I'd climbed over there were a number of saplings planted. It was easy enough to use Iuda's knife to cut one free of the post that supported its flimsy trunk, but more of a struggle to pull out the post itself. It was a little long, perhaps, but had already been sharpened to a point at the base, as if made for the purpose.

I balanced its weight in my hand, judging where I should hold it so that I could thrust it forward with the greatest force. I went back to the portico. The door stood open. I went inside.

I found myself at the end of a corridor that ran the full length of the building to another door. There were further doors on either side. The décor was uninspiring, as was to be expected; the ground floor was for the servants. The only break in the corridor was a little way down, on the left, where it opened on to a staircase. By my reckoning this would lead up to the room where I'd seen the girl. I began to ascend, taking cautious steps, the stake held out in front of me. There was a half-landing with a window as the stairs turned through 180 degrees. I carried on up. At the top was a pair of double doors, closed. I reached out and pressed the handle. The door opened smoothly. I stepped through.

It was a huge room, laid out almost like a ballroom, with all the furniture set against the walls rather than in the centre. I didn't suppose that the former tsar had held many balls there, but clearly he liked to mimic the grandeur of his previous life – or more likely his wife did. Between the tall windows the walls were decorated with paintings of a former time – ancient princes and generals who reflected Russia's lost glory. One of them I recognized, Pyotr Mihailovich Volkonsky. He'd been a friend of Aleksei's. In one wall there was a fireplace, piled high with glowing logs. Above it hung a pair of crossed sabres.

At the window, looking out, just where I had seen her, stood the figure of a girl. I could not see her face, but the slight protrusion of her belly told me who she was. She turned. If she was surprised to see me, she didn't show it, though she had no reason to suspect anyone had been aware of her departure from Petrograd, let alone her destination. She gave the slightest hint of a smile.

'Ever the resourceful one, Richard.'

I felt a little affronted. As far as I could recall it was *my* resource that had brought us here so swiftly, not Iuda's. 'Where is he?' I asked.

'Romanov?' She nodded her head towards one of the doors, immediately beside where she was standing. 'He's through there. You're just in time.'

I eyed her warily, raising the stake in both hands. I'd have to walk close by her to get to him. She lifted her arms in a gesture of openness and took a few paces away from the door. I walked over to it, still keeping the sharpened tip pointing towards her. I reached behind me and turned the handle, then backed into the room, never taking my eyes off her, but aware that at some point I would have to turn and face what was inside.

It was a strange way to take in a room, the reverse of what one would normally experience. The first thing I noticed were the curtains, opened, that hung over the door I'd come through. There was another door to my left, similarly adorned, but this time obscured by the heavy velvet. To my right was a desk facing out towards the window. I could sense that there was a man sitting at it, but without turning – and I dared not take my eyes off Susanna – I couldn't make him out. There was a dog at his feet, a King Charles spaniel, who looked up at me. With two steps further back I could see who the man was, not that I had expected anyone else: Nikolai Aleksandrovich Romanov, my first cousin once removed. Many Russians, even now, would have been in awe of him, but in my time I had known many better men, a few better Romanovs and one better tsar. I owed him nothing as my emperor.

'Who the devil are you?' he asked.

I broke my gaze on Susanna and looked him in the face. We had never met, but I had seen countless pictures of him. He looked older than in any of them, older than his forty-nine years. He was leaning forward, his elbows on the desk in front of him so that his

427

hands were raised to the level of his eyes. Between them he held a short length of wood, stained with dark blemishes and sharpened to a point at one end: Ascalon. He had been examining it closely when I distracted him.

'My name's Danilov,' I said. 'Mihail Konstantinovich Danilov.'

I'd expected him to know the name, but his reaction was one of more than mere recognition. He let Ascalon drop to his desk with a clatter. He rubbed his hands through his beard and across his cheeks. 'God be praised,' he muttered. Then he shouted it. 'God be praised!'

He stood up and came round his desk to approach me. 'My great-uncle told me all about you. Always in our hour of need you have been here, you and your ancestors. I should have expected it as soon as she came; as soon as she gave me that.' He cast his hand behind him in the direction of Ascalon. 'I should have had faith.'

He reached out to shake me by the hand, but both of mine were fully occupied holding the stake. I let go with my right and he grabbed it in both of his.

Instantly I was in a different place. A narrow stairway leading down to a cellar. It was night – the early hours. In my arms I was carrying a boy. He was thirteen years old, but small for his age, weak, ill. There was a queue of us on the stairs, but soon we were in the cellar. There wasn't much room, not for eleven of us. I looked at the faces around me. My wife was there, and my four daughters. The four others were the only ones who had remained loyal to us: my physician, a footman, a maid and a cook. Around my ankles scampered my little spaniel, Joy. She had remained loyal too. I turned round, back towards the stairs. They'd said we were being evacuated. Evidently we would have to wait here some time.

'Could you bring some chairs?' I asked.

The man standing at the bottom of the stairs, our gaoler, shouted up. Moments later three hard wooden chairs were brought down. I placed my fragile son in one and offered the second to my wife. I took the third. Then the room began to fill, with more men coming down the stairs. Soon the little cellar was preposterously crowded. I had to stand up again, just to see what was going on. There were eleven of them, not counting our gaoler, the same number as there were of us. That in itself was suspicious. They tried to spread themselves through the room, each pairing off with a single member of my family or our entourage, as if fulfilling the promise made on some fantastical dance card. But in the cramped space it was impossible to move anywhere.

The gaoler cleared his throat. He had a piece of paper in his hand which he read from.

'In view of the fact that your relatives are continuing their attack on Soviet Russia, the Ural Executive Committee has decided to execute you.'

I turned quickly to look at my family. 'What?' I whispered. 'What?'

The gaoler repeated the sentence, reading it again, though it was short enough for him to remember by heart. I wondered where they would take us to perform the act, how much time we had, whether they would separate us – the men from the women, the adults from the children. I began to pray that in the coming hours we would have time properly to say goodbye.

But the gaoler had scarcely finished speaking when his hand emerged from his pocket holding a revolver. He was standing just two feet away from me. He fired and I felt a thump against my chest. My legs grew weak and I began to fall. The gaoler fired again, but not at me. I heard my little boy scream and then fall silent. Until then I had felt no pain, but now every agony shot through me. I could not move, I could not speak, I could only perceive, and I knew that that would not last more than a few moments.

The other assassins had rifles rather than pistols and they began to fire. Bullets ricocheted across the cellar. Bodies fell – I could not see who – and the monsters finished them off with bayonets. I tried to breathe, but could not. Nor did I want to. My heart had been still for seconds now, blown apart by the bullet. My eyes gazed out across the cellar floor, across the pools of blood to where the spaniel pawed at the dead face of my beloved son. I tried to reach out to him but I knew there was no point. My only consolation was that we had died in the same moment.

And then . . .

CHAPTER XXVI

I HAD NO DOUBT AS TO WHAT IT HAD BEEN: A VISION OF THE future – of Nikolai's future, of his death. Whether it would be soon or distant I did not know. The children looked young, but I was too out of touch to know just how old they were now. Danilov would understand it better. I could not explain precisely why we had been privileged to behold such a foretelling. It must have been down to the common blood that ran in our two bodies and the proximity of Ascalon. Perhaps even my presence had played a part, putting our mind into a more fluid state, in which it was open to such prophecies. I could not even be sure if I had witnessed the scene myself, or whether Danilov had and I was merely privy to his thoughts. But the body in which the Romanov blood flowed was ours now, not his. I was as much Nikolai's cousin as Danilov was.

But one thing that I *could* deduce was that Nikolai was not to die tonight, here in this room. Whatever plans Susanna might have for him, they did not involve his immediate death. Or if she did plan for him to die, then her plan would fail. But even of that I could not be sure. I did not know whether our vision was of what might be or what must be.

Nikolai was still clasping my hand. His eyes gazed straight into ours, wide with fear. Perhaps he had seen what we had seen. Beyond him Susanna still stood in the larger room. The whole experience had taken only seconds to pass through my mind. Nikolai let go of me and stepped back. Susanna came forward and stopped in the doorway, leaning against the frame. She watched us silently.

'What's she told you?' I asked.

Nikolai turned away. He picked Ascalon up off the desk and clutched it to his chest. 'She says this is the lance that Saint George used to slay the dragon. Is it true?'

'It's the lance that Peter the Great gave to the Armenians for safety; that much I know. The rest is legend.'

'The legends are true,' insisted Nikolai. 'Pyotr ripped Ascalon from where it hung around Zmyeevich's neck, after Zmyeevich had drunk his blood. He knew the power that it held.'

So many of them spoke of Ascalon's power, but I could hear in their words only exaggeration. I had studied it when it was in my possession and found little of interest. And yet it was stained with blood and I knew the influence that blood could exert on men's lives. I only existed because of the few drops of Danilov's blood that I had once managed to sip. If Ascalon held any potency at all I was determined to discover how I could be its master and how I could use it to put me in sole charge of the body I now occupied – or allow me to take possession of another.

'What power is that?' I asked, trying not to appear too eager.

Nikolai turned to face me. His complexion was ashen. 'It made Zmyeevich the monster that he was.'

'You know that he's dead then?'

'I saw it with my own eyes.'

Just as Danilov had done – it made sense. 'And how did Ascalon turn Zmyeevich into a *voordalak*?'

'He . . . he found it. He saw the dragon's blood on it and knew what it could do for him.'

'Tell him the truth!' Susanna snapped.

'That is the truth,' Nikolai insisted.

'The truth – or your children die.'

Nikolai swallowed. He sat down at his desk and gestured that I should sit too. Susanna remained where she was. I clutched the stake that I had grabbed outside in both hands, pointing its tip towards her. It was my only weapon and I wanted her to see that I had not let down my guard.

431

'Zmyeevich didn't find it. It was given to him while he was imprisoned in Budapest, in the castle of Visegrád.'

'When was this?' I asked.

'During the reign of my predecessor Ivan III. Zmyeevich – Vlad as he then called himself – was given it by Ivan's ambassador, Fyodor Vasilievich Kuritsyn. Kuritsyn got it from Ivan himself, and Ivan got it from his wife, Sophia Palaiologina, who was the niece of—'

'Of Constantine XI,' I interrupted. 'The last Byzantine Emperor.'

Nikolai nodded. 'The last Roman Emperor. Constantinople had fallen to the Muslims in 1453. The heart of Christendom was destroyed. Ivan saw the chance of fulfilling Moscow's destiny – of making it into a third Rome. He started calling himself tsar. He married Sophia. And he adopted the symbol of Byzantium – the double-headed eagle.

'But as heir to the Byzantine throne – albeit self-appointed – Ivan knew that he must seek vengeance on those who had pillaged the city. He was fighting the Mohammedans on two fronts. In the east he was on the verge of defeating the Golden Horde, but he needed a way to hold back the Ottomans. And he found one.

'Wallachia was ruled by Radu cel Frumos – Radu the Beautiful – though after his conversion to Islam he was called Radu Bey. He was born a Christian, but chose a different path. He even fought alongside Sultan Mehmet II at Constantinople, helped him as he dragged his ships across the land and into the Golden Horn so that he could devastate that once beautiful city.'

Even now, Nikolai could not admit the truth of what had happened five centuries before. Constantinople had been on the brink of collapse. It was saved by the Turks, not destroyed. That, though, was not the point of his story.

'But Radu was not the rightful Voivode of Wallachia. That honour fell to his older brother Vlad, whom Radu had usurped. If Vlad could be made strong again he could throw out his brother, and begin to take back the lands that belonged to Christendom. And Tsar Ivan had a way to make him strong

– Ascalon. He had seers who understood the blood magic, and heralds who had unearthed a fascinating lineage. Vlad was descended from Saint George himself. In their battle, the dragon had bitten George – drunk his blood. If a descendant of George could consume the dragon's blood then he might become . . . Well, no one knew. But he would be able to defeat his brother.

'And so Ivan sent Kuritsyn with Ascalon to visit Vlad in his prison in Budapest and to present Ivan's offer to him. If he would take the lance and plunge it into his heart and let the blood that stained its wood mingle with his own, even as he died, then he would become powerful – as powerful as the dragon itself, and he would have Russia's eternal gratitude.'

'And did Vlad do it?'

Nikolai shrugged. 'Presumably. But it didn't have the effect Ivan was expecting, not immediately. Radu died soon after. Vlad was freed, and he marched back to Wallachia, only to be killed on the way. His body was buried in the monastery of Comona. For a while anyway.'

It was all news to me. My mind raced to make sense of it – to exploit it.

'And what happened to Ascalon?' asked Susanna.

'Kuritsyn brought it back to Moscow. It remained in the Kremlin. Its story was passed down, even when the Romanov dynasty replaced the Rurik dynasty of Ivan. It was only when Pyotr needed help to defeat the Swedes and to build his new capital that he thought he could make use of Ascalon. Pyotr had his own seers, who knew magic, and together they used Ascalon to summon Vlad, or Ţepeş, or Dracula, or Zmyeevich as he came to be known in Russia. Some say Zmyeevich was already reborn when it happened and had been for centuries, others that Pyotr's magic dragged him from his grave. Either way he came, and brought an army with him, and helped Pyotr to build his city. Pyotr gave him Ascalon, and he wore it around his neck, close to his heart – the heart which it had pierced to make him what he was.'

'And then?' I asked.

Nikolai lowered his head and said nothing. It was Susanna

who answered my question. 'After that, you know the story. Pyotr betrayed Zmyeevich. He let Zmyeevich drink his blood, but did not drink in return. He took back Ascalon. And he tried to have Zmyeevich killed. But Zmyeevich escaped, and swore one day to return to Russia and take vengeance on the dynasty – on the nation – that had so cruelly betrayed him. You can understand his feelings.'

'The gods visit the sins of the fathers upon the children,' Nikolai murmured.

'So what are you going to do about it now?' I asked Susanna.

She smiled, but it turned into a wince. She moved her hand as if to clutch her stomach, but then the pain abated. 'I'm going to try again.'

'Try what?' I asked.

'Try what we attempted with you in the Church on Spilled Blood. Try to bring him back.'

'Zmyeevich? You need his blood for that, don't you? Where are you going to get that from?'

She walked over to the desk and picked up Ascalon, caressing it in a way that was unpleasantly sexual. Zmyeevich's dragon ring was still on her finger, making a scraping sound as it ran over the wood. 'His blood . . . or that of the one who created him.'

'The dragon's blood? On there? Will that work?'

'Who knows? It'll be fun to find out, won't it?'

'But it won't bring back Zmyeevich. It'll just turn Nikolai into a *voordalak* – make him another offspring of the dragon.'

'Don't you understand? Zmyeevich *was* the dragon. When Vlad Țepeș stabbed himself in that gaol in Hungary it entered him. It threw out his soul and replaced it with its own. The same will happen with Nikolai.'

'So why didn't you try that in the first place, on me?' I asked.

'Because I didn't know, not then. We've uncovered a lot since. Even so, I can't be certain what will happen. It would be much safer to use his blood, if I had any.'

'But if it works,' said the former tsar, 'I'll live for ever?'

We both looked at him. I was appalled. Susanna merely laughed. 'After a fashion, yes,' she said.

'Zmyeevich died,' I said. 'You would too, one day.'

'But not for a very long time.'

A look of joy began to spread across his face. I'd never held him in any great esteem, but now any vestige of admiration I'd had for him was lost.

'It would disgrace your family,' I said. 'Aleksandr Pavlovich gave up his throne rather than accept that fate.'

'You forget,' replied Nikolai, 'I no longer have a throne to give up.'

Suddenly he was moving towards the door, but Susanna was quicker. She grabbed his arm. He looked at her. 'I'm coming back,' he said. 'I've nowhere to run.'

She considered for a moment, then let him go. He disappeared out of the room, the little spaniel at his heel. Susanna looked at me. After a few seconds' silence she spoke.

'What happened to Dmitry?'

'He'll be here soon.'

'I imagined he'd be coming with you.'

'We'll manage without him if we have to.'

'"We"? Oh, you mean you and Richard. Two heads are better than one, I suppose?'

I hadn't meant anything – it had been a slip of the tongue, of the sort I'd been making too frequently of late. But I played along. 'Cain's outwitted you and Zmyeevich more than once.'

'It must be you that's letting the side down then.'

Something in the room beyond disturbed her. She turned to look. For a moment I was filled with the hope that it might be Dmitry arriving at last, but it was only Nikolai returning. Susanna stepped away from the door to let him through. He was not alone. In front of him stood a young boy. I recognized him as the child I'd carried down to the cellar in my vision. It was the tsarevich, Aleksei Nikolayevich Romanov. It was said he was named after his ancestor, Tsar Aleksei, but I'd always wondered whether there was also some acknowledgement of the debt the Romanovs owed my grandfather. The boy stopped and looked nervously around his father's study, standing almost beside Susanna. They could have been brother and sister.

'My son is ill,' Nikolai announced. 'Gravely ill.'

435

That much was rumoured across Russia, but I did not know the details. Susanna's face indicated that she was a little surprised.

'He has a disease of the blood: haemophilia. If he cuts himself, he does not form a scab. If he bruises himself, he can bleed internally for hours. It's an inherited disease.'

'Inherited from Zmyeevich?' I asked. It was more than a casual interest. If the disorder were connected with the blood curse of the Romanovs, then I too might be affected.

But Nikolai shook his head. 'It comes from his mother's side of the family. My wife received it from her grandmother, Queen Victoria of England. She spread a scourge through the royal households of Europe worse than anything Zmyeevich ever managed. Her own son Leopold was the first to die of it. It only ever seems to afflict men.'

'Delightful story,' said Susanna. 'But what of it?'

'He is a Romanov,' said Nikolai, as if that explained everything. He laid his hands on his son's shoulders, with a gentleness that reflected his fear for the boy's fragility. 'He carries Romanov blood in his veins.'

'So?'

'Use Ascalon on him. Make him immortal. Let him live.' Nikolai was pleading now. This was the man who had passed his son over as tsar because he could not bear to be parted from him.

Susanna looked from father to son and back again. Then she snorted. 'I don't think Ţepeş would be happy to be confined by a body like that. And besides, yours is the body the people will follow – the Whites, that is.'

'Sir, what are you talking about?' the boy asked his father.

'We're discussing how to make you better.'

'How?'

'With this.' He leaned across his son to where Susanna still held Ascalon and took it from her. It seemed such an innocent action that she let him take it. I myself didn't notice anything untoward. But as soon as he had the lance in his hand, Nikolai ran out of the room, dragging the boy by the collar behind him. Susanna reacted faster than I, but in seconds we'd both followed them out into the larger room.

436

The tsarevich was on his back in the centre of the floor. He was trembling. I could see tears in his eyes. But he did nothing to resist his father's will. Nikolai had one hand resting on the boy's chest, but had no need to hold him down, such was his son's deference to him. In his other hand Nikolai held Ascalon high in the air, ready to plunge it into Aleksei's heart. It was a recreation of Abraham binding Isaac to the altar.

The pointed blade remained where it was in the air. Nikolai looked at me, then at Susanna, then back to me. 'I'll do it,' he said. 'I swear.' He seemed to be trying to threaten us with the prospect, though it was an act he wanted to perform for its own sake.

'You'd better get on with it, then, hadn't you?' I told him.

He stared at me, scarcely able to believe that a Danilov, one of the guardians of his family, could be so callous. But it was what he wanted – I was only offering encouragement.

It had the desired effect. Nikolai looked back down at his son and raised the lance a little higher. The tsarevich uttered a single word: 'Papa?' Ascalon had begun to move, but at the sound of his son's voice Nikolai hesitated. It was enough for Susanna.

She flung herself across the room, her hands stretched out in front of her. They clamped on to Nikolai's wrist and her momentum twisted him over on to his back. The two of them struggled, but it took Susanna little time to rip Ascalon from his fingers. Meanwhile Aleksei had rolled away and was sitting up. His hands were touching his body, checking whether he'd been injured. Susanna shouted across the room at him.

'Get out of here, you little shit. Go!'

Nikolai's voice quavered. 'Do as she says, Lyoshka. Go back to your room. I'll come and find you later. And not a word to Mama, or your sisters. Promise now.'

The tsarevich stood up and went to the door, saying nothing.

'Promise me!' His father's voice was raised, but still full of endearment.

The boy turned. 'I promise.' Then he was gone. Neither

Susanna nor Nikolai moved from where they were, sitting beside one another against the wall.

'There's a simple way out of it, you know,' I said.

'And what's that?' asked Susanna.

'Once you've stabbed His Majesty with that thing, once he's become a vampire, then he can turn his son into one by the usual process.'

Nikolai looked up and into my face. A new sense of hope spread across him.

'Would that be possible?'

'You know it would. The boy would have to be willing, of course, but he seems like the sort who'd obey his father's wishes – however unholy they might be.'

Nikolai turned his head away. His eyes fell on the spot where moments earlier his son had been lying defenceless. He shook his head and began speaking softly and rapidly. It was too quiet for me to make out the words, but it had the mood of a prayer.

Susanna got to her feet. As she did so, she drew breath sharply through her teeth and both hands went to the bulge in her stomach. She shuffled painfully across the room to a chair and sat down, breathing heavily. She still held Ascalon in her hand.

'Are you all right?' I asked.

'It comes and goes.'

'The baby?'

'*Your* baby.'

I shrugged. I couldn't deny it, but neither could I see any relevance in the fact. It might have been my child, but it was her problem. That didn't mean I wasn't curious about the scientific processes involved. 'It's been there, just the same? Since the day you died?'

'It's always there. Never growing, never changing.'

'I'm surprised you haven't got rid of it.'

She let out a short, angry laugh. 'You think I didn't try? In 1809 I'd had enough. Oh, it didn't hurt then, but it showed, and that was causing me problems. I'm sure you can guess the easiest way for a girl like me to lure humans to a quiet place where she can feed. But men prefer a virgin, and being pregnant is about the best proof you could have that I'm not.

'I was in London, and I wasn't the only girl in town in the same predicament. I went to see a woman. Everyone told me that I was as likely to die as the child, but I knew that wasn't going to be a problem – she wasn't going to use a wooden stake to get rid of it.' She paused, lost in the memory. 'It was metal: a long, thin blade – flexible. She poked it around inside me, and she seemed pretty confident that she'd killed it. She said it would come out in a day or so.'

There was passion in Susanna's voice, but it was the wrong kind of passion. She spoke as though complaining, as though describing bad service she had received in a shop. There was no hint of pity, not for the child. What did I expect? She was a *voordalak*. What was more concerning was my own sense that she should display some more womanly reaction. Was I deceiving myself to pretend I cared so little about my offspring?

'Of course, it didn't come out,' she continued. 'Why should it? It's a vampire, like me. I was in no danger and neither was it. Whatever damage she did to it, it healed as quickly as I would have. I knew I'd just have to live with it. I should have lived with it – should have left it at that.

'But a few years later I was in Paris – this was just before Waterloo. I heard of a doctor there with a different, more specialized technique. He didn't try to kill the foetus, but he had the skill to cut the birth cord, to starve the unborn child of blood and to let it die in the womb.

'That sounded as though it might work. You can't kill a vampire by starving it, but you can weaken it, send it into a state of dormancy which is as good as death. And once it was like that, perhaps my body would reject it – perhaps I'd be able to do something to drag it out.'

'You could have had it cut out,' I suggested. 'A caesarean section.'

'"From his mother's womb untimely ripped"? Don't think I didn't try that, but there's this thing about vampires – we heal. I tried to hold it off, but it wasn't possible, not with a cut like that. And the surgeon didn't stick around long once he saw his work being so neatly stitched up by an invisible hand. I asked other vampires to try, but they wouldn't lay a finger on me, not once they knew what it was for.'

'So you went to this doctor in Paris?'

She nodded. 'He used a similar blade to the one the woman had in London – just as long, but with an edge rather than a point. He was very quick and dextrous, told me it was all done in seconds. He enjoyed his work, I could tell – not the fact that he was helping girls who were desperate, nor even because of the money. He just liked having the chance to look, to touch, to— I was his last patient, and his was the first blood to flow into my body without my having to share it with that thing inside me. I knew it had worked almost straight away. I felt stronger, no longer having to provide support for the leech that nestled in my belly.

'But he – I imagine it as he, if I think of it as a creature at all – he's a resourceful child. I don't know if he gets it from his mother or his father. Probably a bit of both. We're both survivors, aren't we, Richard?'

She looked at me as if expecting an answer, but I gave none.

'It was two days later I first felt the pain – the same pain I felt just now, that I've felt at least once or twice every day since. The thing needed blood, and it wasn't getting it through the birth cord, so it decided to get it the way a vampire normally does: with its teeth. It bit me; bit the inside of my womb and drank the blood from me. You wouldn't think it even had teeth at that age, but with a *voordalak*, who knows? It can't drink for long because I heal, so it just moves to a new place and tries again. He doesn't need much – he's not big, is he? He only wants what's rightfully his, what we used to share when my blood flowed into him. I should have left it at that.'

I glanced over at Nikolai. He was hanging on her every word. His face was sallow – sickened – but his lips had a curl of triumph to them. 'It's taking revenge for what you tried to do to it,' he said.

'No. It has no mind; no desires. It just reacts like an animal. It senses blood. It needs blood. It takes blood. And we're the same, except for the thin cloak of intelligence we wrap around ourselves to hide our embarrassment.'

She stood up, moving cautiously at first, testing to see whether the pain had gone, but with greater determination when she discovered it had. She held Ascalon in her open right hand, hefting it. 'I'm not going to wait any longer. Let's get this over with.' She crossed the room in a few brisk paces and leaned forward to grab Nikolai by the front of his shirt. She lifted him up off his feet and slammed him against the wall. It was just the action that Iuda had recalled Andrei performing on Vadim, except that here there was no nail. Nikolai was shaken, but uninjured. Susanna let him drop on to his feet. She ran her thumb swiftly down the middle of his chest and the buttons of his shirt sprang away, revealing the curly greying hairs of his chest. She put her hand against it, feeling for his heart, and smiled when she found it.

She kept one finger against his skin, marking the point she had selected, then used the other hand to place Ascalon's tip at precisely that location. She held it in place with her left hand, and pulled back her right arm, preparing to slam against the blunt end of it with the heel of her hand and drive it home.

'No!'

It wasn't as if she were going to heed my shout, but it was sufficient to distract her for a moment, and that was time enough for me to run the width of the room and get beside them. She was standing too close to Nikolai for me to make any use of the stake in the way I'd intended. Instead I employed it simply as a bludgeon. I swung out and the weight of its shaft connected with the side of her head, producing a heavy, satisfying crack. It would undoubtedly have knocked a man unconscious, if not killed him. Even on Susanna it had some effect. She staggered across the room and slumped against the far wall. She stood with her back to it, her fingertips pressed against the wallpaper as though she needed it for support. She scanned the room blearily, unable to focus. I could see a smear of blood close to her temple, but whatever damage I had done would quickly be repaired.

Ascalon had fallen from her hand and rolled into the corner, equidistant from the two of us. I ran to get it. Still she didn't seem alert enough to react. I reached down and picked it up. If I could just get away now and find a place of safety, then that would be enough for the moment. I turned and headed back for the double doors. From the corner of my eye I could see that Susanna was already regaining her senses. I broke into a run. I stopped for only a moment to open the door, but it was long enough.

I felt her leap on to my back; her forearm was across my neck and her legs were around my waist. With her free hand she tugged at my hair, pulling my head to one side and exposing my neck. I could not see her face, but I could well imagine what she planned next. I could only run backwards, hoping to slam her against the wall behind me and shake her off. But I'd miscalculated. Instead of hitting the wall we smashed into the window. The wide ledge caught me at the back of the knees just before we hit the glass and I fell, whipping her body against the window panes. I heard the glass shatter and felt her grip loosen. I'd managed to keep hold of both my possessions: Ascalon and the stake. I rammed the blunt end of the stake into where I guessed her stomach to be and heard a grunt of pain. Her arms fell away and I was able to take a step forward.

I twisted to look back at her. Her head was out on the balcony. Her torso was pierced by shards of the broken window, but none of it would do her any harm. Her head was lower than her legs and she was squirming to get up, like an upturned woodlouse. I swung round to leave again, as fast as I could run.

'Look out!' The cry could only have come from Nikolai.

I turned to see what was happening. Perhaps that was a mistake. This time the force of her charge was enough to knock me on to my back. Ascalon flew from my hand and landed somewhere I could not see. Susanna crawled up my body, her mouth wide open, her fangs gleaming. I took the stake in both hands and raised it above my head, then brought it down hard on her face. I'd thought I had the blunt end aiming down, but I was mistaken.

The sharp point met her face on the bridge of her nose and was deflected to one side, so that it finally penetrated her skin just below her left eye. Her entire skull collapsed, splitting open on either side of the wound. I felt her blood – and more – splatter across my face, and tasted it in my mouth. The spike came to a halt somewhere in her neck. I knew it was not enough to kill her, but it would take her some seconds to recover, if not longer. I kicked out and her body rolled off me on to its back. Her hands went up to her face, searching for the weapon that she could not see. I wondered if I should pull it out and finish the job, but it seemed like too much of a risk. Already I could see that her face was healing. One eye blazed at me with wrathful indignation. If I removed the stake she would recover still more rapidly. And I knew that my main concern should be to get Ascalon as far away from her as possible.

I looked around the room, but could not see it. In my mind I tried to recreate the moment I had dropped it. I realized that it could only have gone out through the door. I followed and saw it there on the landing. I didn't know how much time I had, so I merely kicked it down the staircase. It bounced off the carpeted steps and came to rest on the half-landing. I ran down after it, holding the banister for support, planning what I'd do next. I'd carry on down, beyond the half-landing, leaving Ascalon where it was. When I was a little way down the next flight, when it was at my level, I would reach out behind me and take it. That would be the quickest way.

I was beaten to it. Before I even reached the turning point in the stairs I saw a hand emerge from around the corner. Someone was climbing up the lower flight. The hand stretched forward and its long fingers curled around Ascalon, picking it up. The figure continued to ascend. I backed up the stairs, but I didn't want to have to return to face Susanna. Finally the man turned the corner on to the half-landing and I could see his face.

It was Dmitry.

A wave of relief struck me. I ran down to him, but already I could feel the shortness of breath that was an inevitable result of such efforts. 'Let's go,' I said.

He stood for a moment, oblivious to me, staring down at the shaft of wood that he held in his hand, as if unable to believe in its existence.

'Dmitry!' I hissed.

He looked at me. 'Is she up there?'

'Yes, and Nikolai, but, Dmitry, it's too much of a risk. We have to get Ascalon away from her.'

443

'Why?'

'She thinks she can use it to bring back Zmyeevich.'

'No,' he said resolutely. 'Let's get this over and done with, once and for all.'

He strode past me and up the stairs. I still felt the urge to run, but he was right. They were both vampires, but pitted against each other it was unthinkable that Dmitry would not be able to defeat Susanna. And for what little it was worth, he had me on his side. And Nikolai, though I could not be sure he wouldn't choose the gift of eternal life if it was offered again.

Dmitry was already several paces ahead of me when I followed him back into the room. Nikolai had scarcely moved, except that he had slumped to the floor and was sitting with his back against the wall. Susanna had recovered remarkably. The bloodstained stake had been thrown into a corner. The wound to her face was no longer open, though a livid scar ran down it, centred on the point that my blow had struck. Even as I looked, it was beginning to fade, but despite that, there was an unevenness to her face, an asymmetry, as though one side were a little lower than the other. It was like looking at a reflection in a cracked mirror. Perhaps that would heal too – or perhaps she would be like it always.

Dmitry surveyed the room, taking in Susanna, Nikolai and then me. Then he turned back to her. He raised his hand towards her then paused, as if reluctant to let go. But the hesitation didn't last long. He gently tossed Ascalon across to her.

'Get on with it,' he said.

CHAPTER XXVII

I LAUGHED OUT LOUD. DMITRY'S APPARENT CHANGE OF HEART wasn't in any way amusing, but Danilov's sense of utter deflation as he realized that the creature in which he had placed such unquestioning trust was just as treacherous as every other *voordalak* he'd ever encountered was a delight to experience. Even so, I'd been just as taken in by Dmitry, and of the two of us I was the greater fool – I really should have known better. Dmitry, Susanna and Nikolai all looked at me. None of them seemed to share my amusement.

'Oh, don't be so bloody po-faced!' I snapped, speaking chiefly to Dmitry. 'You've been a master of deception. Take some pride in your genius.'

He managed a smile. 'You're Iuda now. That's good.'

'Good?'

'That's why you're here. We're not interested in Danilov.'

'But you're interested in me?'

'There are two people in this room who despise you, Cain. Soon there'll be three.'

I could count more than two already. I was sure Nikolai had no affection for me, and technically Danilov was in the room as well. But I understood what he meant. 'The third being Zmyeevich,' I said. 'Supposing your little trick with Ascalon comes off.'

Dmitry's chest seemed to swell a little as I uttered the great vampire's name. 'That's right,' he said.

'But why, Dmitry? You were in his thrall. You wanted to get away – to be free of him. And with his death, you are.'

He shook his head. 'I was never free. All those years ago, you explained it to me. You said that if two *voordalaki* exchange blood with one another there comes a point where one of them – the weaker one – loses himself completely to the stronger. You thought I hadn't yet reached that point, but you were wrong. I sailed to America, I lasted there for a decade, but eventually I had to return, had to find Zmyeevich and taste his blood once again. But by the time I got back to Europe, he was already dead. And you're right, I was free of him, but it wasn't a pleasant freedom. I went back to America bereaved. I'd lost all hope.'

'And what about your love for Russia?' I asked. 'That epiphany you experienced as you watched *The Rite of Spring*?'

'That was true enough. But once I'd come home, I soon realized that Russia could not rule itself. It needs a strong leader. Stronger by far than him.' He nodded in Nikolai's direction.

'Someone like Zmyeevich?' I said.

'It never occurred to me until I met Susanna. I should thank you for introducing us.'

'You've been working with her – from the start?'

He shook his head. 'For me it began that night in the Church on Spilled Blood. I was as much a prisoner as you, but once I'd heard what she planned to do – once I'd heard that she believed she actually could – then I knew there was nothing I would do to stop her, even if I'd been free.'

'He was as disappointed as I was when the ceremony failed,' said Susanna, teasingly.

'I was relieved!' snapped Dmitry. 'I knew that I couldn't defy him, but fate had intervened on my side, so that I would not have to.' He looked at me. 'When you had Ascalon in your hands, I could have ripped it from them, but I managed to resist – and you were wise enough not to give it to me.'

'You didn't resist for long,' I said.

'Once you were in prison my need for him – for Zmyeevich – became stronger than ever. I knew there must still be hope, so I sought out Susanna in the tunnels beneath the cathedral. She didn't trust me at first, but it was easy to convince her of my love

446

for him. We spent those months looking through all the works she'd gathered on the subject, until finally we knew there was a way – but we needed Ascalon.'

'And you were the last person to have it,' Susanna explained.

'If I'd guessed it was with the Cheka, this would all have been a lot easier.'

'Once we knew where Nadya lived we had you. We made sure she never saw Dmitry. And then we sent him to get you so that you could discover she'd gone. How do you think he knew where she lived?'

'How did you think I knew you were lying about Ascalon being at Panteleimonovskaya Street?' he added. 'I'd already ripped the place apart.'

'And you did exactly what we expected and told us where it was,' said Susanna.

'And then things went wrong, didn't they?' I said. 'I don't imagine that it was part of the plan that she should keep you down there with us while she rushed off to Tobolsk.'

Dmitry gave her a sideways look. She smirked.

'I just didn't want to share the moment,' she said. 'No hard feelings?'

'I can't say I wouldn't have done the same. But we're both here now. We'll greet him together.'

'And discover which of you he remembers more fondly?' I asked.

'We know which of the three of us he regards with *least* affection, though, don't we?' said Susanna. 'He'll be de-lighted you made it here, so that he can take his share of our revenge.'

'Revenge? Revenge for what?'

'For what you did to us,' said Susanna.

'For turning you into vampires?'

'Don't pretend you did that,' she hissed.

I could not say I had done so directly, but in both cases it was ultimately down to me. I had thrust Susanna into that crypt with Honoré. I had tricked Dmitry into falling in love with Raisa.

'Your crime is that you killed those who did,' said Dmitry, with similar venom.

'I didn't kill Raisa,' I said.

'So you admit you killed Honoré.'

'You know I did.'

'And you drove Raisa mad,' said Dmitry. 'That was the reason for her death.'

'So what have you got planned for me?'

'We have no plans,' explained Susanna. 'We'll leave that to Zmyeevich. He has such an imagination. But I'm sure it will be very, very slow.'

'And what about Danilov? Anything you do to me, he'll feel too.'

'So?' replied Susanna. I noticed Dmitry glancing uneasily at her as she spoke. He was the weaker of the two and I would have to find a way to exploit it. She waited a moment, but I had nothing more to say. She turned her attention back to Nikolai.

'No,' said Dmitry. 'Let me speak to him first.'

Susanna let her hand fall to her side as Ascalon grasped at it. She took a step back. Dmitry moved forward, standing squarely in front of the man, who looked up at him wearily.

'Do you know what I am?' Dmitry asked.

'I take it you're a vampire, just like her.'

'And do you know *who* I am?'

The former tsar shook his head.

'My name is Dmitry Alekseevich Danilov.'

Nikolai snorted. 'Another Danilov – though in this case, not one that I've ever heard of.'

'You should have heard of me, Romanov, not because of my family, nor because I'm a *voordalak*. You should have heard of me because I am a Russian. One of your people. And yet you know none of us. And because you didn't know us, we destroyed you; me and thousands like me – millions. I was there in February, we stood against your troops, when we took Petrograd, when we finally caused your downfall. But I've always been there. The people have always been there.

'In 1881, I was there. I was one of those who carried out

the people's will in executing your grandfather, Aleksandr II, blowing his weak body apart and letting his little grandson watch as he bled to death. And I was there even before that. I was there on the fourteenth of December 1825, when we stood and faced the cannons of your namesake, Nikolai I. We failed then, but it was then, as my comrades fell beside me, that I knew one day your family would fall. Even then, a century ago, I was there.'

The room was silent, but for the sound of Dmitry's breathing. He stood, bending forward towards the former tsar, waiting for some reaction. But it was not Nikolai who replied.

'No you weren't!' All eyes turned to me the instant I spoke. 'You weren't there, and you know you weren't. And I know it too, because I *was* there.'

Dmitry looked at me bewildered. 'What do you mean?'

It was as though he genuinely believed it. Perhaps he did, after so many years; so many years of repeating the story, telling people how he wished it had been instead of how it was. Each time he would have filled in a little more detail, and begun to remember the story better than he remembered the event, until the truth was lost amongst his own make-believe.

'I mean I remember. I remember the truth. You were there with your father. The Governor General had just been shot, and I came and joined you. I begged you to leave. Told you that your mama was afraid for you. Told you that if you stayed you'd die alongside your comrades. Told you it would be safer to run away. Even your papa joined in. And you did run away, across Senate Square and to safety.'

'No!'

'Try to remember, Dmitry. It's what happened.'

'I stood there, beside you both, and faced the guns.'

'Then why weren't you arrested? Why weren't you sent into exile with your papa?'

'I ... I ...'

'Give it up, Dmitry. Who are you trying to impress? Her? She doesn't care. Nikolai? He knows already – knows you're a coward just by looking at you.'

Dmitry spun round to face the wall, his fists clenched tightly in front of his eyes. He bent forward slightly, as if in pain. 'Just do it, Susanna!' he shouted. 'Do it now!'

Susanna began to approach Nikolai. She raised Ascalon above her head, ready to bring it down upon his breast. And for the first time since we'd arrived, Nikolai seemed to show some interest in his own existence. He leapt to his feet and grappled her, grasping her wrists one in either hand. He'd already had a taste of how strong she was, but with luck he might hold her off for a few seconds.

I turned round. Behind me was the blazing fireplace and above it the two crossed sabres. I ran forwards, launching myself off a footstool beside the hearth and then grabbing the mantelpiece with my hand. I reached up and just managed to grasp the foible of one of the blades. As I fell back down it came with me, as did the other sword and no small amount of the plaster to which they'd been fixed. I let everything drop to the floor, except for the sword I'd been after, which I now held properly by the grip.

I ran across the room to where Susanna and Nikolai were still locked in combat. Their arms were down now, close to their chests, with Ascalon pressed between them. To my left I could see that Dmitry had begun to recover his composure. Within seconds he would be able to help. I didn't have much time. I swung the sabre back over my shoulder, then brought it down hard. I didn't have a clear shot at her neck, which would have been the only possible fatal blow. Instead the blade connected with the small of her back. It must have shattered a couple of vertebrae. The pain would have been all-consuming.

She arched her spine backwards and put her hands behind her, letting out a shriek of agony. Her head was flung back, exposing the whiteness of her neck. With luck I would be able to do it in a single stroke, and her head would be off.

And yet I hesitated. The sight of her like that, her face, her pale skin, her vulnerability, brought back to me memories of the girl I had once known. The girl I had loved. The girl I had betrayed. I knew she had to die, and yet I could not bring myself to do it. I cursed the body that contained me, cursed the sentimentality that had seeped out of Danilov and into me. It was he that was preventing her death. And time was precious.

Every fibre of my will was intent on bringing that blade down on to Susanna's sweet, delicate neck, but it was Iuda, not I, who had command of our muscles. However much he might try to convince himself otherwise, he was as deluded as he had revealed Dmitry to be. It was he who was being sentimental. It was he who could not kill the girl he had once loved. His hesitation might have cost us dear, but instead it gave Nikolai the moment he needed.

Susanna was still bent back, vulnerable and in agony. Nikolai reached out to her with his left hand and placed it on her shoulder, pulling her towards him. His right hand thrust forward and in it I could see that he held Ascalon. I felt my lips beginning to form a shout of 'No!' but there was not enough time for it to become a word. I perceived Iuda's horror at the same moment that I worked out the danger for myself. Whatever effect the dragon's blood that stained Ascalon would have had on the former tsar, might it not have the same effect on Susanna? I could only guess that, when they knew one another, she and Zmyeevich had exchanged blood.

But it was too late. Ascalon's tip pressed against her belly, just below her navel, causing it to dent inwards. The cotton of her dress yielded, as did her flesh, and the short length of wood slid smoothly into her. A croaking noise emanated from her throat. Dark blood began to seep from the wound, increasing to a waterfall as Nikolai mercilessly pushed the blade further into her. There was a look of twisted hatred on his face as he swivelled the shaft around inside her, forcing it deeper, until finally there was no further he could go.

At the same moment, I felt suddenly cold. A ripple seemed to run through the atmosphere, like the blast of a high explosive, but with no sound to accompany it. I couldn't see him, but I heard Dmitry gasp, as though it had affected him too. Nikolai snatched his hand, stained with Susanna's blood, away from the lance and cradled it against his chest.

Only Susanna remained unmoved. The three of us stared at her, each frozen in action: Nikolai caressing his own hand; Dmitry taking a pace towards us; I with my sword held high. She looked down at where the wooden spike protruded from her stomach, and then began to giggle.

'Well, that's not going to do anything, is it?' she said.

She reached down with one hand and tried to pull the shaft out of her, but it was stuck fast. She used both hands, and gave it a little twist as she did to loosen it. There was a squelching sound and it began to move, causing more blood to issue forth as it did. Eventually it was out of her. She held it upright in her hand, as though it were a candle, lighting her to bed. Her own blood now hid the ancient stains. The hole in her belly was already shrinking, healing. In less than a minute it was gone, but the rent in her dress remained, revealing no scar – only smooth, white skin, smeared with crimson.

She smiled. 'Well then – where were we?'

As she spoke, I noticed that her face was still not symmetrical after the injury I'd inflicted earlier. The right-hand side was perhaps a quarter of an inch lower than the left. There was no noticeable seam between the two halves. The effect was disconcerting, but it was not enough to put me off. I'd realized some seconds before that I was once again in control of my body. I would not waste the opportunity.

I swung the sabre, at the same moment taking a step to the left; Nikolai was a little too close to us and I did not want to catch him. It missed him by only inches. As I began to move, so did both Dmitry and Susanna. He charged towards me, but I knew he would not make it in time. She began deliberately to fall to her right, to escape the attack, but I was already going too fast. She had scarcely moved when the blade hit her on the left side of her neck. It was a stroke I'd practised again and again as a child, on a straw dummy, while Mama urged me on, and corrected me, and told me to repeat it until I'd perfected it. That had been a long time ago, but I hadn't lost the knack.

The blow lost most of its momentum as it hit her spine, but it got through, severing it, if I'd done what I intended, between the fourth and fifth cervical vertebrae. That would not be enough, though. I knew that her head must be completely detached from her body. Now I applied my full weight to the sword, relying on force rather than momentum; at the same time I pulled the sabre back towards me, so that the motion became a slicing action rather than a simple direct cut. It meant that I got through the flesh quicker, but also that I was running out of blade. If the tip came free before I'd got through the last inch of skin that connected her body to her skull then I would have to try again – and I didn't think I'd get the opportunity.

I felt the pressure resisting the sword suddenly vanish and the tip of the blade flicked upwards as I briefly lost control of it. Susanna's head was in the air, but still close to the bloody stump of her neck. A few tendrils of flesh stretched from one to the other, but as her head began to fall, they snapped. It was as though that were the signal for the rest of her body to collapse. The head fell to the floor, but was dust long before it hit. A tail of grey powder hung in the air behind it, like a comet's, marking its path of descent. The blonde hair lasted longer, indeed its transformation was scarcely perceptible, except for the slightest change in its colour. She would have been lucky had she lived to old age – a few greys amongst the gold would not have been easily noticed. But when they reached the ground, the strands that had once been soft, supple and yielding proved themselves brittle. They shattered silently to nothing, as though they were strands of glass.

I heard two sounds, a fraction of a second apart: one a heavy thud and the other a lighter click. I looked. The cause of the deeper sound was obvious. Ascalon had fallen from Susanna's crumbling hand and bounced on the floor. It lay there, not quite still, rocking from side to side. I had to scan the parquet floor to see what had caused the other sound. It was Zmyeevich's ring – the golden dragon with emerald eyes and a forked red tongue. It had fallen from Susanna's finger; fallen *through* her finger.

The desiccation of her body was mostly hidden from view. Her dress crumpled, slowed by the necessity for the air to escape through the narrow egresses of her collar and sleeves. The atmosphere around it became hazy with the particles that were expelled, but finally the material lay in a pile on the wooden floor, not quite flat, thanks to her boots and whatever other fragments of undecayed matter lay beneath it.

I took a step back and to one side, twisting to face Dmitry, my sword at the ready, though I doubted he would make so easy a target. Moreover, I still wasn't convinced that he was my enemy.

He sighed. His eyes gazed down at Susanna's dress. Then he looked at me. 'She always wondered if there might still be some vestige of affection for her lingering in you. Seems she was wrong.'

'It's me. Mihail.'

He nodded. 'That explains it.'

'Your Majesty,' I said, without turning to look at him, 'could you pick up Ascalon and give it to me.'

I held out my hand behind me and moments later felt the solid shaft of the ancient lance placed there. It was sticky with Susanna's blood; blood that had left her body before her death, and which therefore survived her. Perhaps one day it might be used to resurrect her, just as Iuda had been resurrected. It was not a fate I would wish upon anybody, and it would not come to pass.

I glanced briefly at the fireplace on the far side of the room, not wanting to take my eyes off Dmitry for a moment more than was necessary. In it logs glowed hot and red; I could see occasional flames flickering between them. It wasn't a difficult throw, but Ascalon was in my left hand. I carefully swapped it with my sword, always with my eyes on Dmitry, not giving him a chance to attack. I had to look away from him in order to throw it, but even then he did not move. My aim was true. The lance bounced a little from one side of the grate to the other, then settled down. It would take a minute or two to catch. Dmitry could easily have plucked it out; any burns he received would heal in moments. But he would have had to turn his back on me.

'Aren't you going to rescue it?' I asked, tempting him.

'I think not.'

'You'd let your last hope of raising Zmyeevich burn to ashes while you stand and do nothing?'

'I need no hope. I have certainty.'

'What?'

'Zmyeevich lives. You felt it; so did he.' He nodded towards Nikolai, behind me. 'We all share his blood. We sense him. Tell me you don't.'

I said nothing. He was right; there was something, something

454

that I couldn't quite place. Something that had left me as I sat in that tea shop on Tverskaya Street and experienced Zmyeevich's death. It had been there since the moment Nikolai had stabbed Susanna with Ascalon.

'What about you, Romanov?' Dmitry continued. 'You know he's alive, don't you?'

'Something's alive.'

There was a cold terror in Nikolai's voice that made me turn as soon as he spoke, forgetting the need to keep my guard up against Dmitry. The former tsar's eyes bulged wide, staring down at the floor, down at the pile of clothes that were all that remained of Susanna. I followed his gaze.

Beneath the crumpled dress something was moving.

It was a twitching motion, a rising and falling, but with each undulation causing a little forward progress of just a few inches. I could only see the movement of the cloth of her white dress, not the creature that pulsated beneath it. A rat would not have moved like that, and anyway it was too big for a rat. I pictured a severed hand, pulling itself along by its fingers, rising up as its nails gripped the floor beneath, and then falling as they stretched out to find new purchase. But I knew it was not a hand. I knew exactly what it was – I simply could not bring myself to believe it.

The motion was slow, but determined, heading for the hem of the dress at a point somewhere between me and Nikolai. In seconds it would emerge, and its form would be revealed. I felt the urge to anticipate the moment, to reach forward and flick the cloth aside with the tip of my sword, but I could not move. For a moment I wondered whether the decision was now Iuda's and not mine to take, but I realized that my immobility was down to simple terror.

Now the thing had almost completed its journey. The bulge in the material was only an inch from its hem. Now when it rose the edge itself lifted, revealing a dark black archway from which something currently hidden would soon emerge.

It was a hand that came first, but not the crawling hand of my imagination. This hand was tiny – malformed, with fingers that could scarcely move independently. It was no bigger than the tip of my thumb. A second hand appeared alongside it, and both pulled against the smooth parquet, the minuscule fingers spread wide to get the best grip, like the feet of a frog climbing across a rock.

With one more heave the head appeared. It was bald and wrinkled. The colour of the whole thing was a deep pink – like scalded skin. The head rose up. Its eyelids were closed, but then they opened wide to reveal its eyes – black, as though consisting only of a pupil. Immediately it recoiled, agonized, and lowered its head to stare at the floor, its only motion the regular pulse of its shallow breathing. It was still only half out of the white cloth, and so we could not see its legs.

It looked up again, scanning the room, curving its head in a single slow arc. Then it opened its mouth.

The teeth were monstrous. There were only two of them, long, white and sharp, aligned side by side at the centre of the upper jaw, still stained red with the last drink it had taken of its mother's blood. It inhaled deeply. I could see a tongue flicker behind those two awful fangs, as if it were smelling the air like a snake does. Like a serpent does.

It lowered its head and began to move again, now at a slightly different angle, and with more purpose. The rest of its body and then its legs were revealed, all of that same tender pinkness. The legs were even less well formed than the hands; they pushed along behind the creature, but the vast majority of its strength and movement came from its arms.

Even so, it was moving quicker now. I looked along the line that it was travelling, and saw its goal: the ring – Zmyeevich's golden dragon ring. The glittering emerald eyes were not the same as the black of the creature that crawled towards it; the creature's tongue was not forked and red like that of the dragon, but in some disconnected way the one was a representation of the other. Zmyeevich had had the ring made as an image of the monster whose blood had made him what he was. And now this awful, half-formed being was once again carrying the life force of what should have been long dead. Whether it was the reincarnation of Zmyeevich or of the dragon, or some chimera formed of the two, I did not know. I did not know if there was even a distinction between those entities. The dragon had lived again in Zmyeevich; the dragon lived again in this . . . this tiny, vulnerable, unborn child.

It was close now, close to the object of its desire. It stopped, exhausted, and hung its head, breathing deeply. Then it looked up, and reached out with one hand, desperate to touch the golden serpent, not a ring from its perspective, but something large – large enough to be a crown.

I brought my sword down swiftly. It was an easier kill than Susanna had been. There was little sinew to get through, little bone. I crushed its neck rather than severing it, but the action was just as effective. The head rolled to one side, the body to the other, proving that they were no longer connected. A little blood began to seep from the broken neck. I regarded it as a merciful killing – too good for the soulless monster that occupied that little body, a blessing for the human being, however incomplete, that it had once been.

'No!'

There were two voices, shouting the same word at the same time. One was Dmitry, the other myself. But I had more to say.

'My son!' This time I could barely manage a whisper.

It had been more than a century since his conception, and in all that time I had never regarded him beyond the nuisance that he caused me by his very existence. I had not even bothered to consider whether the child was a boy or a girl, but now as he lay dead in front of me, the nascent evidence was plain to see. I had certainly never thought of him as alive – not when I'd suspected that Susanna had survived her encounter with Honoré, not even when I'd seen her face to face once again in Petrograd. It was only when she had begun to describe how he was no longer a part of her, how he fed from her, that I began to have any sense of him as a being.

I could only thank the fates for Danilov's cold-hearted hatred. He had managed to throw off all sentimentality, first in killing the mother and then the child. He was right. It was a blessing, but it was a sacrifice too – a worthwhile sacrifice to

457

make the world safe from Zmyeevich, and more importantly to make me safe.

But as I looked down I could only wonder what real harm even Zmyeevich's formidable mind could have done in so puny a body. I doubted whether he was yet developed enough to command the power of speech. But I was a scientist, and my mind teemed with possibilities. Even so feeble a creature had blood – blood that could be extracted and stored. And then the whole thing could begin again, just as it had done in the Church on Spilled Blood, with the body of a chosen one, a Romanov, who was better formed to carry Zmyeevich's soul.

It was an ingenious idea, but I was not going to suggest it to Dmitry. I doubted he had the imagination to arrive at it for himself.

The worst of it was that the body was still there, still in its two separated parts. Its mother had decayed instantly, but the child's remnants lay there, just like any other lifeless human flesh. I tried to make sense of it. When a *voordalak* dies, the forces that hold off death evaporate. If the creature was decades old, then it would decay in seconds to the state of a decades-old corpse – to dust. This then was newly born as a vampire, or to be precise newly born as Zmyeevich, created only in the instant that Ascalon had entered its heart.

'You'll pay for this.'

I looked up. Dmitry's face was ablaze with anger. His fangs were bared. I raised my sword a little, shaking it, reminding him of what I could do with it, but he was beyond fear. And I knew that in a face-to-face fight I'd be able to do him little damage. I'd do better to flee.

I turned and ran across the room to the broken window. I took one last glance at Nikolai. He stood bewildered, unable to comprehend the events that had taken place around him, unable to control them. It was an apt summary of his reign.

I jumped through and landed on top of the portico. It was still dark outside, though dawn could not be far away. It seemed no one had discovered the two dead guards, nor been awakened by the commotion. I threw the sword down on to the snow below, then lowered myself over the edge. It was easy enough to shin down one of the pillars that supported the overblown structure. It took me only two steps to reach my sword, but as I grasped it I heard a noise. I looked behind me. Dmitry was at the door. He had chosen not to follow me directly, but had taken the stairs in the hope of overtaking me. It had almost worked.

I ran blindly. After only a few paces I slipped and found myself sprawling in the snow, but still moving, sliding across it. I was on my feet in an instant. Coming in we had climbed over the fence, but I had no time for that. The gate at the end of the path was open and I made for it. At random I turned left on to the road. I looked around me, trying to work out where I was, and took the only street that seemed familiar. I was scarcely more than walking now. My legs were weak. Dmitry would easily catch me. I risked a look over my shoulder. He wasn't running at all, just striding boldly. Even so, he'd soon be on me. He had a sword in his hand – the twin of the one I carried.

I pressed on down the snowy street.

CHAPTER XXVIII

I WAS AGAIN IN COMMAND OF MY BODY, BUT I CONTINUED TO RUN. I knew I'd have to stop soon. The frozen river stretched out in front of us. Iuda had looked for landmarks that he recognized and we'd found ourselves back where we'd started. A little way upstream was the wreckage of the plane. The fire had burned itself out, but I could still see what was left of the fuselage, floating now in the water rather than sitting on the ice. The fire had easily melted the frozen river in a wide circle, centred on where we had crashed. A small crowd had gathered round it, but even as I watched, two or three of them turned and left.

I stopped. I knew that I could make this easy for myself. I turned round. Dmitry was only a few feet away from me. He came to a halt. He was scarcely short of breath. I was almost at the point of collapse. I held my arms open at my sides, my sword hanging limply in my hand.

'I don't know why I'm running, Dmitry. I've nothing more to run from. I don't pretend to understand you, but I asked you a favour, only a couple of days ago, on the train. I'm going to ask you again. Kill me and kill Iuda too. I can't escape him, and if he lives he'll find a way to make us into a vampire, and that would be worse than death for me. Whatever feeling you have, Dmitry, whether you do it out of love for your family, or hatred of me, just end it for me, now.'

'How do I know who I'm talking to? Is it Mihail or is it Iuda?'

'It's Mihail, believe me.'

'Prove it,' he shouted. 'Tell me this. What happened in Khodynka Field in 1896? Come on, tell me.'

I hid my laughter. He'd been right that the system would fail eventually, that before long Iuda would have learned too much. It was pure coincidence that Dmitry had hit upon that one event – he couldn't know how we'd got here. But there was no point in confusing the issue.

'There was a stampede at the celebrations of Nikolai's accession. Thousands died.'

'So you *are* Mihail. And tell me, Mihail, who was it that killed Zmyeevich? Who slaughtered that innocent child?'

I could have lied, but again I thought my purpose was better served by telling the truth. If he would not kill me out of pity, then perhaps he would do it out of hatred.

'I killed him, Dmitry. I deprived him of his last chance of life. I denied you the resurrection of the one you love. Isn't that reason enough to kill me? And you'll be killing Iuda too.'

Dmitry approached. I let my arms hang a little limper, and pushed my chest out towards him. He raised his sword, ready to strike. I hoped he might grant me a quick death, but if his desire was for revenge, then something slow and painful might be more to his liking. A wound to the gut. It would take me hours to die. But I was prepared. He pressed the point of his sabre against my belly and pushed. I felt the sharpness of its point against me, but I knew it was nothing compared with the pain I would endure once my flesh was pierced. He pushed harder, causing my stomach to dent inwards. It reminded me of Ascalon pressing against Susanna. Perhaps Dmitry was reminded of it too.

'No,' he said.

'What?'

'If you want to die, Mihail Konstantinovich, then I want you to live. I want you to live with Iuda inside your skull, with you every day of your life. I want you to know that you can never go back to Nadya, never again touch her, for fear of what Iuda might make you do. You will be like King Midas. Unable to touch anything that you love. Unable to be with anything you love. Not Nadya, not even that stupid dog. You'll never be able to have anything to love. And maybe one day Iuda will persuade someone to make you into a vampire, and then perhaps we'll meet again. And you'll tell me what you are, and I'll be able to tell you why you're like that, and remind you of what you did to deserve it. I'll look forward to it.'

He turned and walked away. I had no time to waste. I raised my sword and brought it down hard on his shoulder. Perhaps if I'd wanted to I could have killed him, but that wasn't the plan. The blade bit deep through his overcoat and drew blood. He turned back to me.

'If you won't kill me out of choice,' I said, 'I'll make you do it. I'll make you fight.'

I slashed at him, catching his cheek and drawing blood. He did nothing. Next I went for a more direct attack: a classic lunge. My sword went straight through his heart. Still he did nothing to defend himself. I had to be more of a threat. I raised the sword high. It was a terrible ploy, leaving my entire torso open to attack, but I was not fighting to win. I brought the blade down, this time genuinely aiming for his neck. He sensed I was in earnest and parried. Now the fight began for real.

I continued my assault, each strike now aiming to decapitate him, and always leaving myself open to a riposte that never came. He parried every blow, but never counter-attacked. Even so, with his greater strength and height he began to push me back. Soon we were out on the ice. I had winter boots on, so could gain some purchase, but it was difficult to manoeuvre. I made a lunge for his stomach, but he twisted to one side and caught my blade with his, almost knocking it from my hand. But in the process he lost his balance. He slipped on the ice and fell to one side, rolling right over to end up on his back. His sword was still grasped firmly in his hand, pointing upwards.

I took the opportunity. I ran forward and threw myself into the air; threw myself on to the tip of his sabre, praying that he would not have time to move it.

I had only a fraction of a second as our feet left the ground to alter our trajectory, but it was enough. Dmitry had no time to lower the sword, but it didn't matter. The tip sliced through the side of my coat, but missed me by almost an inch. It had been worth a try, but Danilov should have known it would fail. Long ago in our relationship we'd established that he

462

could take no step so monumental as suicide. We both knew that at the very moment of the act, my mind would win out and I would be able to step back from the brink.

I landed on my back and we lay side by side for a few moments, both breathing deeply, but whereas his breaths sounded slow and strong, mine were quick, harsh and rasping.

'Dmitry,' I panted. 'It's me now, Iuda. Listen to me. If you really want to have your revenge on Danilov, then you can. Do what you said, but do it *yourself*. Make me into a vampire. You know better than any that the victim has to be willing. Well I am willing. *I* am at least, but there may not be much time. Drink my blood. Let me drink yours. Then kill me and send Danilov into everlasting torment.'

'And what torment would you suffer, Iuda?'

'I wouldn't. But who do you hate more right now: the man who sent Raisa mad or the man who killed Zmyeevich?'

It was a desperate chance; my best – my only hope of being free of Danilov, and it was out of my hands. Dmitry would decide. He thought about it, but not for long. I'd judged him well. Soon he was up on his knees. He unbuttoned his leather coat, and the jacket underneath, and finally his shirt. He pulled them all open. 'Cut me then,' he said. 'Cut me and drink. I'll do the rest.'

I lifted up the sword, holding it by the grip, but also by the blade so that I could guide the tip precisely. I pressed it against his skin and then drew it sideways.

A line of blood followed as I cut.

I rammed the sabre forwards with all my strength. It twisted and slipped between his ribs; I felt it emerge from his back. He screamed and brought the pommel of his own sword down on the side of my head. That might have been a fatal blow in itself, but he'd pulled it, realizing that he still did not want me dead. Seconds later we were both on our feet. I rained a hail of blows down on him, each of which he deflected with instinctive parries of his sword. Now, though, it seemed that he was on the back foot; it was he who retreated with every stroke of my blade and I who advanced.

Behind him the burned-out wreckage of the Lebed loomed larger. The crowd who had been looking out at it had seen us now. I could hear them shouting, but could not make out their words. It sounded like some kind of warning, but what they might be warning us about, given that we were so obviously fighting to the death, I could not guess.

I was feeling weak now. I paused, still holding my sword out in front of me, but not using it. I watched its tip swaying from side to side.

'What's the point, Mihail?' Dmitry asked. 'I'm not going to kill you, and you don't have a chance of killing me. Just accept it. You're going to live. And every day that you live, you'll have Iuda beside you.'

I began my attack again, and he continued to defend, but with utmost self-control. His blade never once so much as scratched me.

'Oh, Dmitry,' I said, 'you *are* going to kill me. And it was you that told me how you were going to do it.'

'You're bluffing, Mihail. I won't kill you. And I've told you nothing that's going to help you.'

'Haven't you? What about that ballet you love so much – *The Rite of Spring*? What about the Chosen One?'

We fought on for a few seconds more, but I could see in his eyes that he was thinking about it. Then realization hit him. He lowered his sword, then threw it aside, watching it as it skidded across the ice.

'I won't help you,' he said.

He turned around and walked away from me. I started to run after him, but moments later he vanished.

It took me a second to understand what had happened. We were close to the aeroplane now, and to the gap in the ice that the fire had caused. The water was beginning to refreeze and there were chunks of ice bobbing about, but it wasn't stable. Dmitry had fallen through. Already I could see his head as he floated up to the surface again. I threw myself on to my back, but continued to slide along. I dug my sword into the ice, sending a flurry of white powder into the air. Eventually I came to a stop. Perhaps I should have let myself plunge into the freezing water to drown, but I knew now that I did not need to. The pain in my chest and lungs told me that.

I felt arms around me, pulling me back. The men on the bank had seen what had happened and had come over to rescue us. Two of them dragged me a little further away, to where the ice was solid. I had no strength to move. One man propped me up and I lay back against him. Ahead I could see the attempts to rescue Dmitry. Three of them were lying flat out, face down on the ice, each clutching the ankles of the man in front of him. The one closest to Dmitry had a rope with a loop tied in it. He threw it out to Dmitry, who grabbed it. He put it over his head and under his arms. He could have dived down and swum away, but it would be many versts before the next hole in the ice appeared. Freezing could not kill a vampire, but he would fall into a slumber, trapped until spring. He could have climbed out on to the ice by himself, but there was no sense in rejecting help if it was offered.

The tightness of my chest had lessened now, or perhaps I was just numb. Instead the pain was in my left arm – in the forearm, close to the wrist. It really had all been Dmitry's idea, just as I'd told him. In *The Rite of Spring*, in the final part, the Chosen One danced and danced and danced until, exhausted, she collapsed and died. For an old soldier such as me it would be ungainly to dance myself to death, but a soldier can fight, and if he faces an enemy that he cannot defeat, then he must go on until he has no strength to continue. My heart was failing now. Soon it would be over. I only hoped they could drag Dmitry out in time for him to see it.

I reached to my pocket, knowing that it was where Danilov kept his pills, but my hand was cold and shaking and I could not make it do what I wanted. Danilov had kept his plan well hidden, and I'd walked right into it. I only hoped there would be time for me to walk out again before it closed.

'What do you want, comrade?' said one of the voices near me. 'You need something?'

'My pills,' I said. My voice sounded weak and hoarse. 'In a silver box.'

465

I felt a hand reach into my coat pocket and search, then in my jacket pocket.

'Nothing there, comrade.'

'Other side,' I said, but I knew it was hopeless. Danilov always kept his pills on the right. They looked but found nothing.

'Don't worry. You'll be all right.'

'I'm dying,' I said.

'We've sent for a doctor.'

It was too late. Danilov understood his body better than I did; I could tell from his sense of elation that he was confident of death's imminent arrival. Already I'd begun to lose sensation in my body, replaced simply by a dull ache that ran through every bone and muscle in me. I noticed that it was getting lighter. I wondered if that might be a part of the process of dying, though I had died before – twice before – and not experienced it. Then I realized; it was almost dawn. The sun's rays were just hitting the buildings of Tobolsk over to the east. Soon they would be upon us.

I looked over at Dmitry. They had just about hauled him out now. I'd been here before: on the Berezina, when Lyosha had dunked my head beneath the water and tried to drown me; on the Neva, when he had shot me, and killed me, and I'd slipped through a hole in the ice much like the one Dmitry was now being pulled from. Lyosha had failed, both times, but his grandson had got me. The first time I'd managed to come back, but it wouldn't happen again. It had turned out that the only way a Danilov could finally get me was by dying himself. I'd never played chess with either of them, neither Lyosha nor Mihail, but if I had, I was pretty sure this was how it would have ended. I was happy to call it a draw.

Dmitry was on his feet now, though I couldn't really focus on him. The men were trying to help him but he was pushing them aside. Then he realized: it was seconds from dawn. He looked around, but there was nowhere for him to hide. He had only one option. He turned and dived neatly back through the hole in the ice from which he'd just been pulled. The end of the rope slithered after him, but one of the men got his hands on it, then a second. They began to haul him up once again. I couldn't fathom why they were so keen to come to the aid of a man who so clearly did not want to be rescued. But human nature is a strange thing – I'd never understood it. And yet I'd always known perfectly how to exploit it.

I closed my eyes, hoping that death would come quickly. The aching of my limbs was agonizing now, but I could suffer it. I knew it would be over soon. I did not welcome my death, but I welcomed my freedom. And I welcomed Iuda's death, just as I had welcomed it so long ago.

Perhaps Iuda was right to call it a draw, but I saw it as a victory; it was what I wanted and not what he wanted – that was enough. And he'd forgotten something about chess; it wasn't always about winning the game, you also had to win the tournament. And to do that, sometimes a draw was enough.

I discovered that it was true what they said, that your life flashes before you. For me there were two lives, mine and Iuda's. My own memories were to be expected: images of Mama and Nadya were the most prominent in my mind, but I recalled my father too, and my uncle, Aleksandr II – the only decent one among them.

Iuda had lived far longer. His memories flew past. England, Susanna, Oxford, the Crimea, Wallachia, Moscow – and then there was a familiar face, a memory that I grabbed on to. Iuda tried to pull it away from me, but he could not. He was too weak. I forced him to recall.

Dominique was sitting on her bed. She was dressed for her trade, but not yet undressed for it. She looked up as I opened the door and recognized me instantly.

'Get out,' she spat.

'Is that any way to speak to a paying customer?' I asked.

'I get to choose my customers.'

'That's a privilege not afforded to many whores. Most only get to choose their lovers. Though in your case they're one and the same.'

'What do you want?'

I sat down in the chair opposite her, putting my hat on the

dressing table. 'I want to offer you another choice, concerning your lover, Lyosha. The choice of whether he lives or dies.'

'What do you mean?'

I allowed myself a slight smile. 'You know what I am, I take it? What my friends are?'

She nodded.

'Then you will understand what they can do to Lyosha, now that he's their prisoner.'

'You're lying.'

'Lying? You read the letter I sent, didn't you? The one that had him galloping off to meet me in Kurilovo?'

'Of course.'

'And yet, as you can see, I am not in Kurilovo. I am here. And your beloved Lyosha is being held captive by my friends.'

It was a straightforward lie. Danilov had outwitted us at Kurilovo and if I knew him at all would already have killed those of them that were left and would be racing back here to save the lovely Dominique from me. But she did not need to know any of that.

'At my word he can either be killed or set free. And my word depends on yours.'

'What do you mean?'

'All I desire, my dear Dominique, is a single night spent enjoying the indubitable pleasures of your body. You've done it a hundred times before for money; how much nobler do you think you'll feel about doing it to save your lover's life?'

'Is that all?'

'That's all. You may find some of my tastes a little unusual, but you'll come to no harm if you play along.'

'And afterwards I suppose you'll go and brag about it to Lyosha.'

'He will never hear of it from my lips, I give you my word. And I think we can be confident that you will never tell.'

'You're a bastard, you know that, Iuda?'

'Why do you say that?'

'Because you work out exactly where a person's weakness lies, and then you twist the knife in it to get what you want.'

'And your weakness is?'

'You know what it is. I'd do anything for Lyosha. Anything.'

'Then I take it we're agreed.'

Perhaps there was a God. Of all my memories, that was the one that I'd tried hardest to keep hidden from Danilov. I'd shown him what came after, shown him time and time again until he was sick to the stomach, and yet he'd never questioned how Dominique and I ended up in that situation. There was a delightful elegance to it, that an evening I had used to destroy Lyosha's faith in Dominique had been of use to the same effect with her grandson a century later. But now, sadly, he knew the truth. Even though it was knowledge that – like all his knowledge – he would only possess for a few moments more, it would make him happy.

I opened my eyes. The sun was clear in the sky now, above the rooftops of Tobolsk. I couldn't tell how much time had passed. The three men were still playing tug-of-war with Dmitry, trying to bring him back to the surface. From the effort they were putting into it, he clearly hadn't broken free of the rope. Even with his enormous strength there would be little he could do to resist them, nowhere that he could find purchase. He was a strong swimmer, but not stronger than three men standing on solid, if slippery ground.

A fourth man was peering into the gap in the ice. He held up his hand and gave a shout. The others started to pull harder, while he knelt down to look more closely. He was a big man, and reached into the water, grabbing Dmitry as he came close to the surface. With one final heave he dragged Dmitry clean out of the river and left him lying on his side on the ice. Those around them began to applaud.

Dmitry's eyes met mine. I doubt he could tell that I was dying. He pushed himself up, trying to stand, trying to get back into the water and below the ice, but it was too late. The sun was already on him. His face vanished into a halo of gleaming light. His wet clothes began to steam. The three men who had been on the rope ran, but the fourth stayed where he was. He was caught by the explosion as Dmitry's body burst into flames and his heavy garments were ripped apart, knocking the man on to his back. More ice melted, and he was in the water. I fell back as the two men beside me rushed to help. I lay there, gazing up at the blue of the morning sky.

Iuda was mistaken. It brought me little happiness to know that Domnikiia had acted only out of love for my grandfather; not because it wasn't a good thing, but because I should have known it from the start. Aleksei had not been fooled by Iuda's trickery. He had ignored it and trusted his heart. He was a better man than I.

I could see nothing now, not even the blue above me. I felt no pain, because in truth I could not feel my limbs or my body. I felt the cold, hard ice where my head rested against it, but nothing more. I had only my thoughts, and with them, Iuda's thoughts. Many fear the idea of dying alone, but for me it sounded blissful; better that than to have to breathe one's last in the company of a creature that had done so much to destroy everyone I loved, and everyone who loved me. I prayed that, if there was a God and He could find in His heart any reason to be merciful to a sinner like me, then He would bless me with just a moment's solitude at the end.

I breathed out, and knew that I would never breathe in again. My body grew suddenly cold and I prepared for the end. But even in that moment, an overwhelming sense of joy overcame me. It was too wonderful to believe. I searched every crevice of my mind, but it was true. He was gone. Iuda was gone. He had died before me, if only by an instant. I was free.

It would only be for a moment, but I knew I must relish it. I tried to cling on to the seconds I had, tried to recall every happy memory, every true friend I had ever known, but I had no time. I filled my mind with the things that I loved. I saw Nadya, and Mama, both of them smiling at me, both of them proud of me. I pictured my father, my grandfather, even Polkan.

And then . . .

EPILOGUE

My Darling Beloved Nadya,

As I write these words I am sitting on the train from Petrograd to Moscow. When I look up from the paper I see you. I look up often. I have never hidden my family's history from you, and that makes it easier now for you to understand what I must do.

I face two dreadful dangers. One is a threat to the whole of Russia, to the whole of the world. The other is more personal. In the case of the first, you will know by now, I think, how matters have been resolved. If the Whites have marched into Moscow and Petrograd, led by a strong and invigorated Tsar Nikolai, then you alone will understand the truth. Zmyeevich will have achieved his wish and our country will at last be his. If that is so, then I beg you to flee. Leave Russia, leave Europe, get as far away as possible. Nowhere will be safe for ever, but Europe will be in danger sooner. Zmyeevich will not stop at Russia. Nation by nation he will take the world. Nation by nation he will subject his people to misery.

On the other hand, if Nikolai remains imprisoned in Tobolsk, remains the proud, pathetic fool who lost his country to its people, then all will be well. If he is dead, then all will be well too, for I cannot escape the fact that I may have to carry out such a dreadful act, if there is no other way.

As to that second threat, if I have not returned now then I never shall. There may be some mechanism whereby I can break free of Iuda, or he of me, but I have no inkling of what it might be. Even if I could discover it, I would be afraid that Iuda would find a way to exploit it more to his benefit than mine. In a sense I am lucky that I have some control over him. It is better that he is bound to me, constrained by me, than free to wreak his vile havoc. But if I find that it is in my power to destroy him completely, then I will do so, whatever the cost to me.

I have considered every other option, but none of them is good enough. I have tried prison, but he found a way to set us free. I could mimic Aleksandr I and force exile upon myself under a new name, but he would find a way to return. I still hold out some little hope, but it seems that death may be my only escape. Iuda has experienced death and I know that he fears it, but I know too that there is nothing in it for me to be afraid of.

And so farewell, my dearest Nadya, and farewell world. Be happy, my darling. I would not ask you to forget me, but when you remember me, try to remember me in more pleasant times. When Polkan hears a sound and looks up expectantly at the door, pretend for a moment that it is I who is about to come through, and that all will be as it once was.

And if I have done what I set out to do, if I have stopped Susanna and destroyed Ascalon, then go out into the world with some hope. Russia has many dangers to face, but she has faced them before and thrived. There will be a civil war, I am sure, but can one really believe that the nation which routed Bonaparte might destroy itself? Can one believe that a people who have had the sense to overthrow tyranny will be unable to govern themselves in a way that benefits everyone? From all the great minds that have led this revolution, can we not find a few who will be wise enough and beneficent enough to guide us to a better future?

I know that such men exist and that they will take the reins of power and that you, and all the people of Russia, will enjoy the happiness and prosperity you deserve.

I am only sorry that I will not be with you.
Goodbye, my darling.
Yours for eternity,
Misha.

Nadya had read the letter a hundred times. By now she could remember it by heart. But she had known its contents from the very beginning, when she had held it, and felt the hard, rectangular shape within the envelope, and understood that it was the silver box in which Mihail kept his pills. Even so she had not opened it. She had obeyed Mihail's instructions and waited a month for him to return, and then another, and another.

She told her father, Vadim Rodionovich, nothing of what Mihail had written, but he seemed to understand. He asked no questions. In July the news had come of the former tsar's execution. There was no real pleasure to be taken from that, but it proved one thing – that he could die. And that meant Mihail had succeeded. Even though Nikolai had not transformed himself into the leader of the Whites, Nadya had never been sure. But now she was. Just as sure as she was that Mihail was dead.

Nadya Vadimovna walked down the stone steps from her father's house and on to the pavement. Polkan followed more slowly. He was getting older, and steps were an increasing problem for him. But he'd still rather walk by her side than stay at home when she went to the shops.

It was the height of summer now and Moscow was warm, too warm to tell the truth. Nadya preferred the cold. But she liked the sunlight, and today the sun shone brightly across Moscow. She walked down to the river and looked up to see it gleaming on the domes of the Kremlin. She went over Mihail's letter again in her mind. There was little in it to give her solace, but there was something – his sense of optimism. He had lived his whole life with that optimism. That was why he had joined the army. That was why he had been a member of the Duma. That was why he had fought Iuda, and defeated him. And if Mihail's final thoughts had been that Russia could be a country that bestowed happiness on all who lived in her, then who was Nadya to disagree?

There would be peace. There would be prosperity. There would be freedom. If not, then what had Mihail's death been for? She gazed upwards and felt the sun on her face, then quickened her step and walked across the bridge towards the market, towards the future, and towards the worst horror of all.

CHARACTERS OF THE DANILOV QUINTET

Aleksei Ivanovich Danilov	Russian soldier and spy who defeated the *oprichniki* in 1812 and saved Tsar Aleksandr I from Zmyeevich in 1825 by helping to fake his death. Sent into exile after the Decembrist Uprising.
Dmitry Alekseevich Danilov	Only son of Aleksei Ivanovich Danilov, by Marfa Mihailovna. Became a vampire in 1856.
Marfa Mihailovna Danilova	Wife of Aleksei and mother of Dmitry.
Domnikiia Semyonovna Beketova	Aleksei's mistress who accompanied him into exile in Siberia in 1826.
Margarita Kirillovna	Colleague of Domnikiia Semyonovna who worked with her in a brothel in Moscow in 1812.
Tamara Alekseevna Danilova also known as *Tamara Valentinovna Komarova*	Illegitimate daughter of Aleksei and Domnikiia. Mother of Mihail Konstantinovich
Mihail Konstantinovich Danilov	Illegitimate child of Tamara Alekseevna and Grand Duke Konstantin Nikolayevich, Tsar Aleksandr II's brother.

Iuda also known as *Vasiliy Denisovich Makarov, Vasiliy Innokyentievich Yudin, Vasiliy Grigoryevich Chernetskiy* and *Richard Llywelyn Cain*	The only human among the twelve *oprichniki* who came to Russia in 1812. Under his true name of Cain, experimented on vampires. Became a vampire himself in 1825. Subsequently an officer of the Third Section and later the Ohrana. Killed by Mihail Konstantinovich in 1881.
Susanna Fowler	Richard Cain's childhood sweetheart. Left by him to the mercy of the vampire Honoré d'Évreux.
Honoré Philippe Louis d'Évreux, Vicomte de Nemours	Vampire who fled to England after the French Revolution. Captured and imprisoned by the young Richard Cain.
Zmyeevich also known as *Dracula, Ţepeş* and *Vlad III, Prince of Wallachia*	The arch vampire who brought the *oprichniki* to Russia in 1812 and who sought revenge for the trickery played upon him by Tsar Pyotr the Great in 1712. He visited Russia again in 1825 and 1881.
Vadim Fyodorovich Savin	Aleksei's commander, who died during the campaign of 1812. Great-great-grandfather of Nadya Vadimovna.
Maksim Sergeivich Lukin	Comrade of Aleksei, who died during the campaign of 1812.
Dmitry Fetyukovich Petrenko	Comrade of Aleksei, who died during the campaign of 1812.
The oprichniki	The nickname for a band of vampires defeated by Aleksei in 1812. Individually they took the names of the twelve apostles.

Prince Pyotr Mihailovich Volkonsky	Adjutant general to Tsar Aleksandr I, who conspired with Aleksei to fake the tsar's death.
Raisa Styepanovna Tokoryeva	Vampire who helped Iuda to escape Chufut Kalye in 1825 and who turned Dmitry Alekseevich into a vampire.
Vitaliy Igorevich Komarov	Tamara's husband. Murdered during the cholera epidemic of 1848.
Luka Miroslavich Novikov	Tamara's son by Vitaliy. Murdered by the People's Will in 1881.
Sofia Petrovna Lvovna	Leader of the revolutionary group the People's Will, which assassinated Tsar Aleksandr II in 1881.
Nikolai Ivanovich Kibalchich	Member of the People's Will. He designed the bombs that killed Aleksandr II. Also developed early concepts of rocket travel.
Nadya Vadimovna Primakova	Great-great granddaughter of Vadim Fyodorovich Savin. Mihail Konstantinovich's mistress.
Ilya Vadimovich Lavrov	Nadya's brother.
Vadim Rodionovich Lavrov	Vadim Fyodorovich's great-grandson, father of Nadya and Ilya.

ABOUT THE AUTHOR

Jasper Kent was born in Worcestershire in 1968, studied natural sciences at Trinity Hall, Cambridge, and now lives in Hove. As well as writing the *Danilov Quintet* – of which *The Last Rite* is the concluding volume – Jasper works as a freelance software consultant. He has also written several musicals. To find out more, visit www.jasperkent.com